A Valley to Harness

A Novel for the World's Revolution

Jason A. Bartles

Published by Two Doctors Media Collaborative, LLC as part of The World's Revolution. Learn more at https://www.theworldsrevolution.com.

Map Design by Fernando Salvaterra

Learn more at https://www.patreon.com/tomeofsalvaterra

Cover Design by Sarah MacCready

Learn more at https://semaccready.com/for-authors/

ISBN (E-Book): 978-1-952706-42-4

ISBN (Paperback): 978-1-952706-43-1

TABLE OF CONTENTS

SEDIMENT VALLEY
THE LAKE
THE GROTTO
THE SQUARE
THE TUNNEL
LADY DUGGERY'S MANSION

For Matthew, who always lifts me up.

PROLOGUE
EMBER AND MIST

A SOLITARY EMBER FLICKERED in the cavern beneath Sediment Valley. Like this land and the people who inhabited it, the ember belonged to a man. He embodied it. He wore it on his face. The shifting line where ash met glowing coal cut across his cheeks, creating the illusion of a sharp, square jaw.

As the man with a scar crossed the damp chamber, his tactical boots left a desiccated trail, like footprints in the sand. But his embers flickered on the edge of extinction. Without words, they told of a battle to harness the forces of nature once and for all. He had taken a few blows, but the wind was at his back.

Ember plodded along.

Behind him, he dragged the battered body of another man who became the mist. He had been a worthy adversary. Mist had lashed Ember's face with a ferocious, stinging rain. He had almost snuffed him out. As Ember trembled on the floor of Mist's laboratory, his contempt stoked a new fire, and the resulting heat wave consumed his unsuspecting rival.

Where Ember's hand now clutched Mist's forearm, wisps of steam rose and dissipated within the chamber. The humidity was almost unbearable, but it would not disturb him for long. Ember would warp the climate to his liking.

Across the cavern's vaulted ceiling, mineral-rich water seeped through the rock and hung from stalactites. The irregular drip, drip . . . drip echoed in the distance. With time he would plug every crevice. No leaks or cracks would mar the foundations of the new world he set out to make in his own image.

Ember stopped when his boot clanged against metal. He released Mist, and the man's body puddled on the cavern floor. Ember leaned down to check the rise and fall of his prisoner's chest. He needed him alive.

A small, green jewel wrapped in golden tendrils dangled from a chain around Ember's neck. A feeble light pulsed from within, threatening to go dark. Its cadence matched the smoldering scar across his cheek. He showed no concern for the ticking clock.

Ember yanked a matching chain from around Mist's neck and attached it to his own. The man gasped for air. Ember placed this man's body within a large golden ring that rested on the ground. He bound his hands and his feet to the inside wall of the ring with rubber straps. Without flinching, he plunged a gastric tube into his prisoner's stomach and a waste tube into his abdomen.

Ember kneeled in reverence before the golden ring that imprisoned the man formerly known as Mist. He dug his smoldering fingertips into the clay to siphon the Earth's forces. The growing light from his scar and amulets refracted off the ring as it levitated.

Tendril-like green lights pushed through nodes attached to the clay below and the rock above. As Ember channeled the planet's energy, the tendrils unfurled like fiddleheads rising from the moss, seeking connection with each other and the levitating ring.

The ring began to spin, and its prisoner stirred. Energy from the Earth coursed through his body. He let out a roar, guttural and tectonic, to loosen his bonds. His body became slick with sweat and dew, trying one last time to slip free.

The tendrils of light recoiled.

Ember was not dismayed. He dug deeper into the clay, flexing his physical form. His scar, deprived of oxygen, faded into the darkness of the cavern.

The tendrils receded toward the nodes.

Before they buried their heads, Ember found a source of unlimited energy. He grabbed hold of the Earth from deep within the bedrock. He clutched it, stood tall and outstretched his limbs to withdraw it from the cavern's floor. He lifted his chin, exposing the coals that burst through his skin to the air. Flames licked his cheeks and spread across his taut core. Ember concentrated the heat and blasted his prisoner's body to purge him of any lingering liquid power.

The man who had once become the mist dried and shrunk inside his chains. The golden ring gained speed as the tendrils of light resumed their agonizing crawl toward one another, writhing until they became entangled in a thick vine that stretched from floor to ceiling.

Mist would rise no more.

In the cavern beneath Sediment Valley, Ember's amulets shone at full brightness. As his flames roared, he let out a triumphant laugh that echoed throughout the muggy chamber. Ember's work had only just begun.

PART ONE

TO HARNESS

Chapter I

Henry

THE LOG CABIN BALANCED on Henry's fingers as he lifted it from the turntable. Three days of work had come to fruition on his replica of the founder's mansion atop the southeastern ridge. It had taken him one day to bake and cool all nine layers of lemon poppyseed sponge, which he soaked with a zingy syrup. On the second day, he plunged dowels deep into the cake's crust as if tunneling through metamorphic rock. Then he carved the mountain's slopes and frosted its ridges.

When he rose before dawn today, he still had to construct the mansion for the top tier. He poured molten isomalt sugar into triangular windowpanes that rose behind a pretzel-lined deck. He made solar panels from black-dyed fruit leather and a stone fence from malted chocolates and birdseed. He piped tiny clumps of moss and grass, planters overflowing with tulips, and squirrels frolicking in the yard. His deft hands had crafted a stunning little world, cozy and evergreen, that was meant to withstand the ages.

Henry steadied the back side of the mini mansion on one of the dowels, slipped his fingers from the bottom, and delicately removed the offset spatula without nicking a single blade of grass. His creation wobbled under its own weight. He held his breath and readied his hands to catch any of the thirty inches of cake standing before him. He hoped he had locked the bakery's front door to prevent anyone from barging in at this crucial moment. He was indeed tucked safely inside and returned his attention to the showstopper. The bottom tier, bound in crisscrossing straps of tempered chocolate, finally absorbed the shock. He let out a deep sigh as the entire structure settled into place.

With one hour to spare, Henry fashioned a miniature Lady Duggery from modeling chocolate, sculpting the glamorous proprietor of Sediment Valley with utmost reverence. He replicated her slender body, dressed her in a fondant-tweed Chanel suit, and added a candy pearl necklace and earrings. The design was based off a full-page spread from the company magazine, *SustainAble Times*. He would never forget sitting in the break room and seeing her profile on the cover. The article promoted her newest project—an eco-friendly community nestled alongside a tributary of the Lehigh River. If successful, it could become a model for mid-twenty-first-century Appalachian living.

While Henry had appreciated her lofty goals, it was Lady Duggery's ability to revive century-old fashion that had truly stolen his breath. As he read the piece, she drew him under her spell with the promise of a stable place to call home and an offer to work his dream job, in which he had trained even as the world fell apart around him. Before his unpaid lunch break ended, Henry safeguarded her portrait inside a plastic baggie and tore the perforated lottery application page from the magazine. They hired him two days later and arranged for his immediate transfer from the SustainAble "plant-based proteins" factory in Pittsburgh to his very own bakery in Sediment Valley.

Every luxury ingredient and specialty tool reminded him of his debt to Lady Duggery.

As he color-matched her hazel eyes to the glossy photograph, he realized he had made a rookie mistake. He had miscalculated the proportions. When stood beside the mansion, the figurine of Lady Duggery towered over the valley. There was too much ambiguity in her monumental height. She was at once supremely regal and terribly monstrous, the crown jewel and the all-seeing hegemon. Sculpting your patrons was a risky gambit—and one she had not requested of him.

Henry loved his new life, cradled in this valley like a chickadee in Lady Duggery's soft hands. If it weren't for her, he would still be elbow deep in processed food slime or locked up for lascivious behavior. He did not want her first impression of his work to be misinterpreted, so he appreciated the realism he had achieved and made a mental note of his mistake.

Underneath the counter where no one would see, he smushed her into an unrecognizable ball, crammed it into a dirty peanut butter jar, and chucked the whole thing in the trash. He missed, and the jar bounced off the side of the bin. He gasped when it hit the floor. It spun wildly until he picked it up and dropped it in the trash.

He admired the photograph of Lady Duggery one last time before returning it to the wall above the bakery's main door.

The clock struck noon, and Henry shook off the nerves. His first major commission was complete. He had just enough time to box up the cake and deliver it to the actual mansion on top of a very real mountain. He taped together a few cake boxes to make one large enough to surround his masterpiece and lifted the hefty package onto a utility cart. He probably should have assembled it upon delivery, but it was too late now.

He untied his apron. The yellowing fabric against the pink undertones of his hands reminded him to get some sun this summer. Before, he had never considered sunning himself under smog-free skies, having to peel skin that burned from UV rays instead of chemical irritants in the air. *This is the life,* he thought. He threw on the oversized delivery coat, a repurposed letterman jacket from the previous century in hunter green with off-white leather trim. He buttoned the snaps to keep it from slipping off his bony shoulders.

On his way out, the light switch sparked. He felt electric, energized, and for the first time like his life might actually have meaning beyond mere survival. *Lady Duggery will not regret hiring me,* he said to himself. A little bell chimed as Henry wheeled his precious bundle outside.

The bakery sat on the town square in the wooded valley, though square was a bit of a misnomer. One long stretch of local businesses—a grocery, an exchange, a clinic, and others—lined the base of the southern ridge. Across the street, an oblong park, filled with dogwoods and phlox on the cusp of blooming, spread before the stores. At the far end, a grassy knoll, ideal for lunchtime picnics under dappled sunlight, attracted friend and family groups to share a bite at the river's edge.

The square was busier than usual. Long, sapphire-blue banners with a black X on them draped from every storefront and streetlamp. Little girls wore white bows in their hair, and the boys fastened azure bands around their forearms. Today was

Founder's Day, and Lady Duggery had invited the bigwigs from the Pennsylvanian Militia to a dinner party at her mansion. They protected Sediment Valley from the world that burned just beyond the surrounding peaks. They would be treated to a feast in her honor capped by champagne and a slice of Henry's cake. The honor was all Henry's.

Once a cluster of cyclists whooshed past him, Henry hopped into the eastbound lane and powerwalked with his cart. The road veered toward the river's edge, the valley widening just east of the Square, and Henry gripped the cart to keep it from running away as the elevation dropped. A handful of renovated campers dotted the lower parts of the ridges. A young man, affixing a Militia armband to a scarecrow, waved at Henry as he passed. A communal garden would soon sprout with corn, green beans, soy, cabbage, and tomatoes in the terraced fields. They grew most of what they needed within the valley, but weekly shipments from SustainAble's greenhouses bolstered their stocks with plant-based proteins and specialty products.

Behind him, Henry heard egregious honking from a cyclist. He was already as far to the right as he could be. He had no patience, especially not today, for rule-breakers and delinquents. He prepared to let this hooligan know their behavior was unbecoming of a resident of the Valley when he heard a familiar voice.

"Wait up!" A golden helmet screeched to a halt beside him. It was Brisa. Out of breath, she must have been pedaling hard. Her bronzed skin glistened in the afternoon sun.

"I'm a bit busy right now." Henry kept walking. He did not dislike Brisa so much as he preferred his own company. Her cheerfulness, burning hotter than even his commercial oven, sapped his energy. She needed to befriend everyone in the valley. She tried relentlessly to get him to join her bike club or take a hike with a big group of people. He could probably use some fresh air, but he just wanted to keep his head down and focus on his bakes. He had never known the world to be so quiet that birdsong could wake you before dawn, and he wanted to absorb as much of that peace as he could. Not to mention the patron he intended to impress.

"I won't slow you down," she said. She hopped off the bike and walked alongside him. "Is that for the Founder's Day party?"

Henry nodded. In her presence, he confronted the idea that others would see his creation. He worried the replica would be too chintzy for such a prestigious event. Maybe he should have chosen a more elegant design, something more conservative. All white with fresh flowers. Or a more patriotic tribute to the flag of the Midwestern Federation. As Henry and Brisa approached the gated entrance to the mansion, he considered dumping the entire cake into the river, never to be seen again.

"Well?" asked Brisa.

Henry snapped out of his spiral of self-doubt and gave her a confused look. Brisa stopped dead in her tracks, balancing her bike against her hip.

"Do you want some help or not?"

Henry opened his mouth to say no. Refusing assistance was a knee-jerk reaction. He had grown accustomed to relying only on himself. But the shale path that wound its way into the woods and up the side of the mountain opened his mind. "You must have better things to do," he offered.

"It's no problem," she insisted.

"I guess," he said. It sounded rude, but he was already fixating on the weight of the cake he so stupidly stacked into one massive package. There was no way around it. He would have to rely on Brisa or beg one of the guards to help him, and everyone knew it was best to be under as little surveillance from the Militia as possible. All things considered, it was a lucky coincidence that Brisa showed up right when she did.

Brisa leaned her bike against the fence. The bikes belonged to everyone, so there was no concern over theft. Still, Henry had to stop himself from reminding her to lock it up.

Behind the arched gate stood a security booth wrapped in windows and aluminum siding. Flapping black and blue banners draped from every possible ledge. *Why did I not cover the cake in the Militia's signature colors?* he thought. He heard his older brother's voice, a distant echo from childhood, chiding him as he had always done: *Henrietta screwed it up again, folks.* He felt so small.

Brisa nudged Henry to pay attention. Two guards, jacketed in bullet-proof armor, approached Henry, Brisa, and the cake.

"ID," said one of the guards through speakers built into the side of his midnight blue helmet. In the visor, Henry's face reflected back at him. No marking or detail distinguished one guard from another. They may as well have been produced in a factory. They practically had been, steeped as they were in the Militia's curriculum and media over the previous decade.

Henry tapped his wristwatch to the guard's tablet to confirm his identity. "I have the cake Lady Duggery ordered." His voice shook.

The other guard shot a picture of Henry's right eye, verified his identity, and then aimed it at Brisa.

"This is Brisa . . . um?"

"Brisa Arroyo," she said, tapping her wristwatch as well.

"My assistant." Henry nodded toward the steep ridge.

The guards tapped their tablets, and the one in the booth gave the thumbs up.

Henry considered the massive box before him, the steep hill, and his skinny arms. He had half a mind to abandon the cake and run away. Before he could, Brisa pulled at his sleeve.

"Let's do this," she said, and together they took their first, cautious steps toward the rocky path.

Chapter 2

Colson

Colson knocked outside Lady Duggery's chamber. He held a serving platter with savory bites for her to sample before the Founder's Day party. He resisted the urge to loosen the cheap polyester bowtie that scratched at his throat. This old-timey butler outfit was beyond indignity, but she expected him to play the role for their guests. And he would play it well.

After a moment, the door unlocked and swung open. Lady Duggery stared at herself in a tri-partite mirror that housed a series of virtual displays. Some of them were connected to the surveillance feeds around the valley, allowing Colson to catch a glimpse of his kitchen staff, a scene from the lake's edge where a mother and son fished, and what looked like an overwrought metal door in a dimly lit hallway. Or maybe it was a tunnel. He couldn't tell. Then he noticed himself framed in the doorway from the front and behind. The bags under his eyes were visible even from across the room.

"Full mirror," Lady Duggery ordered with an accent that Colson still struggled to identify. Her intonation aspired toward the transatlantic. There was a softness to the letter A, but her Os still maintained some of that Philadelphia sound. Colson had once tried to catch her pronunciation of the word "water." Would she flatten out the A into an "ah" or say it like "wooder?" He had concocted a theory that she simply avoided the word altogether to maintain her affected accentuation. The displays faded, leaving only the ticker for cryptocurrency markets and her daily meditation reminder: *Nuture yourself and the rest will follow.*

The image of Lady Duggery in triplicate now stared back at him. She sat on a chartreuse velvet stool with her hair wrapped in a plump towel. An eggshell silk robe lightly grazed her taught frame. She faced her mid-century modern vanity and vigorously rubbed a skin-lightening cream into her naturally porcelain face. She was not content to be white; she aspired to the ethereal transparency of a jellyfish, allowing her to float up behind her enemies, launch a many-tentacled assault, and disappear before they even knew she was there.

The smooth edges of her walnut-stained vanity provided a veneer of simplicity. Clean lines carried across the entire room to the low-lying bed, the simple sheer window dressings, and the minimalist dresser. She had extended the aesthetic even to her break-in-case-of-emergency satphone which rested neatly inside a wooden box.

Colson had earned enough trust to see her in this state, half-dressed beside open drawers crammed with tiny palettes, crumpled squeeze tubes, dirty brushes, and stained sponges. He only wished she would allow him to fill the space with some greenery—an orchid or two, at the very least. But right now, he had more important matters on his mind.

Normally, he had no problem speaking directly to her face, but today he was at his wit's end managing the final preparations for Founder's Day. The staff never met his expectations. He simply could not absorb a triple dose of Lady Duggery's intensity reflected back at him, so he shifted his attention toward the assortment of powders and floral perfumes.

"Did you bring me something delicious?" she asked.

"Ma'am, these will take your breath away," said Colson in his best imitation of a 1950s butler. He lifted the cloche to reveal a spread of canapés and amuses-bouches alongside a lowball glass of whiskey, neat. He kicked open a folding tray and rested the platter beside her.

"What's with all the seeds?"

He hoped she would notice them. She reached for the lowball, gave it a swirl, and threw it back in one swallow. If she got the shakes from it, she did not let it show.

"The seeds represent tonight's theme: regeneration, new growth, potential for expansion," said Colson. He underscored the words with a swish of his free hand. He had rehearsed this speech in his head many times. "They seemed like a fitting symbol to celebrate the start of this new era in Sediment Valley. The massive construction projects are finished. There is a waiting list a mile long to even get in the lottery for the few remaining positions. The renewable power grid is purring like a kitten. The public is on your side, both here and across Pennsylvania. The future is full of unlimited potential for growth and endless possibilities, especially for you."

"Hmm," was all she uttered. She waved her French-manicured pointer finger over each of the samples as if completing a mental checklist in her head.

It was vital he convince her of his theme of the seeds, or his true plans would fall apart. Colson had considered seeking her approval in advance, but that ran the risk of her shooting it down. Lady Duggery held strong opinions and was not afraid to voice them. But he had also cultivated a solid connection with her. Not quite friendly. No, Lady Duggery did not have friends. But a close working acquaintanceship, which seemed as intimate as anyone could be with her. He was attentive to what she said between the lines and anticipated her desires, like the lunchtime whiskey. He wagered she would not force him to redo the entire menu mere hours before the highest-ranking military officers of the Militia and the bigwigs at SustainAble feted her successes.

She turned back to the mirror without tasting anything. "Nix the part about regeneration."

"Excuse me?"

"You said the theme was *regeneration*, new growth, and potential for expansion. Nix the regeneration part. It implies we have allowed something to lapse that must be repaired."

"Of course, ma'am. I should have caught that myself." Colson, relieved at her minor criticism, lifted a flask from his apron.

Lady Duggery waved him away from her lowball and pointed to her bronzed bar cart by the window. "You look like you could use something to take the edge off," she said.

"That's your special collection," he said, shaking his head.

"Come now, you deserve it."

"Maybe one."

"Moderation is only key for those who have to conserve their resources." She gestured again for him to pour two glasses from the crystal whiskey decanter.

They clinked a cheer and drank to her health. Colson let out a little yip of excitement. "That'll wake you up!"

"Now about your clothes."

Colson looked down at the formal uniform, which he only wore on special occasions, worrying he had placed the cummerbund too high. It never felt right. He could not find any stains or wrinkles. Nothing out of place. But Lady Duggery always caught the smallest inconsistencies.

"You look like you're wearing a costume. I had something more fashionable made for you. Over there." She gestured to a gift-wrapped box with an oversized bow laying on her bed. "It's one thing to revive a timeless fashion, but it's another entirely to look like you're desperate to get back to a world that no longer exists. I cannot have the head of my staff sending the wrong impression."

He held up the cream and navy outfit. It wasn't his style, if he even knew what that would be anymore, but it was an improvement over the itchy tuxedo jacket.

"Try it on."

He stepped behind her dressing screen while she continued her beauty regimen.

"What do you think?"

At first glance, the navy turtleneck complemented the cool undertones of his deep black skin. The cream jacket and slacks were made of the softest, most luxurious cotton he had ever worn, used to synthetics as he was. Still, the new outfit constricted his neck. He tugged to stretch it out, but it retained its grip. He cleared his throat. Then he double-checked the fly and stepped out from the screen.

"Give me a little twirl," her three reflected faces said.

He spun in place, pausing at different angles to allow for her appraisal.

"Yes, I think that will work very well. I've already had one of the servants hang the other outfits in your room."

"You're too kind, ma'am." He gave a little bow, but that word, "servant," prickled at the back of his neck.

"I've been quite pleased with your work so far, Colson. Continue on this path, and there will be a place for you by my side as we expand our empire beyond the walls of this little valley. I think you know we're only at the beginning. It's not impossible that you could be sitting in your own mountaintop mansion one day."

"My focus is on the Founder's Day party, right now, ma'am." He bowed his head once more. "But I thank you for your confidence in me." He was not sure if it was the whiskey, the new clothes, or the unexpected pep talk—and from Lady Duggery of all people—but his confidence improved. He was energized to meet the rest of the day, despite his exhaustion, and blow this place up from the inside.

They won't see me coming, he thought. *Not even her.*

A buzzer sounded from Lady Duggery's display, and the security feed from the main gate replaced the center screen. Two unknown figures stood beside an enormous box resting on a utility cart. The Militia guards working the booth asked if Lady Duggery expected a delivery.

"Do you know about this?"

"That must be the cake," said Colson. He checked his wristwatch. "They're almost late."

"A cake?" Lady Duggery approved the delivery and turned on her stool. "Let me guess." She tapped the back of her powder brush on her knee. "Lemon poppyseed, right?"

A vibrating panic coursed down his spine. "Um, yes, ma'am." Colson swallowed hard. She had eyes and ears all over town. He feared this meant his cover had been blown, his plans for the party discovered. The major power players would arrive in only a few hours, and so many higher-ups in the Militia were never in the same place at the same time. He was too close now to be found out. "How did you know?"

"It was rather obvious, wasn't it? Given the theme. What better than lemon poppyseed in the springtime? You've gotten to know my tastes too well, I fear." She let out a rare, little lighthearted laugh that Colson thought must have been what she sounded like as a young girl, back before the United States had fractured into five nations, when the coasts stretched for miles beyond their current shores, when the citizens of that long-gone country still had at least some semblance of bodily autonomy. He almost let his fear flip over into nostalgia for a world riddled with man-made crises created by the same people who now profited from the self-sown chaos and destruction.

Lady Duggery licked her lips seductively. "I can't wait to taste it," she said. "That baker came with the highest recommendation from the Militia."

"Right," he said with a bit of relief. He was pretty sure it was just an educated guess on her part, and a lucky shot on his part, to have chosen one of her favorites. For a fleeting moment, he wondered why the Militia would have a preferred baker, but that was neither here nor there. "Do you require anything else?"

She turned back to her vanity and waved him away.

"And Colson," she said as he crossed the threshold. "Chin up."

Colson nodded and the door closed firmly in his face.

CHAPTER 3

HENRY

"It's heavier than it looks," said Brisa.

Henry wanted to say he had warned her, but he thought better of it. He nodded instead.

Henry and Brisa's first few steps were out of sync, and the cake box slanted more than he considered safe, but they slowly moved their feet in tandem.

Lady Duggery rarely descended from her compound, so the steep trail could not have been too inconvenient for her. What's more, her friends, her deliveries, even her enemies came to her. Henry preferred being neither friend nor foe. He thought of himself as a shadow jester, providing whimsy not through acrobatics on full display in the throne room, but through edible delights dropped at the entrance and assessed by discerning palettes long after his retreat. He could never handle the pressure of watching his patron sink her teeth in his confections while awaiting her judgment in person. He would simply die if he had to sustain a bad review.

The path jutted from the valley floor before swerving between tall pines. Daylight fell into shadow beneath the trees. A cold breeze whistled through the branches, and the path leveled out, widening into an overlook.

"It got chilly," said Brisa.

"Let's take a quick break," replied Henry. He needed to stretch his arms.

They lowered the cake box onto a large rock. Brisa sidled up against a groundhog that was sunning itself. It stared at her for a moment before darting across a fallen log and disappearing in the underbrush.

Henry joined her in the patch of sunlight and enjoyed a view of the valley through the small clearing. He had never seen it from above. He would recreate this view in his bakery.

The sparkling river ran past newly planted fields. It picked up speed as it rushed from the western lake where he, Brisa, and most of the other residents lived in log cabins. On a sunny day like today, many of the children liked to take the paddle boats out on the lake. They would fight over who got to use the single dragon boat and who was stuck with the dingy white swans.

Low mountains surrounded them on all sides, and the rotating blades of two wind turbines loomed over the valley. A safety perimeter of drones swayed back and forth above the ridges. They stood guard to warn against potential intruders, inclement weather, swarms of pests, and any other imaginable threat from without or within.

On quiet days, around dusk, Henry would stand outside as digital chirps mingled with those of real grasshoppers, taking long, deep breaths to relax.

"Can I ask you a question?" said Brisa.

"Ok."

"Why don't you ever accept my invitations?"

Henry hesitated. He could not believe she was calling him out like that.

"I'm trying to keep my head down," he said.

"I get that," said Brisa. "It's just—you seem lonely. I think you'd fit in well."

"I don't know."

"Just about everyone in the group is queer," she added.

Henry's face grew warm. He didn't realize she knew. It wasn't that he wanted to go back in the closet. Rather, he wasn't convinced Sediment Valley was a welcoming space. His criminal record would have been known when they hired him, but their willingness to overlook his past did not guarantee they would tolerate any future expressions of his sexuality. The valley was still located within the jurisdiction of the Militia, after all. Their guards patrolled the only viable entrance—the tunnel on the western edge—as well as all the roads and paths that connected the buildings like the threads of a spider's web.

Her brazen attitude surprised him. A small part of him worried Brisa was somehow a mole, sent to entrap him. He was probably being paranoid. Still, he looked away without acknowledging her last statement.

"You're always welcome." Brisa smiled and stretched her arms. "Shall we?"

Henry nodded, eager to return to the task at hand.

The final stretch was flatter, and only took a few minutes to cross, but after the break their arms felt weaker, drained by the mountain they had carried. By the time they could see the clearing and the rocky stairs at trail's end, Henry's arms shook visibly.

"Almost there," she said. "We can make it."

Her persistent cheerleading helped.

They climbed the half flight of stairs sideways. One little step after another, over and over again, until they made their way to the top. They set the delivery on the stone fence, and Henry rang the bell. Lady Duggery's mansion spread before them—a two-story log cabin with massive windows leading to the peaked roof in the center.

Henry regained some confidence in his work, seeing how accurately he had recreated the architectural details. The charm of his replica would rival the sparkling chandelier in the grand foyer. Lady Duggery would appear at the top of the stairwell in a glimmering sapphire gown with a slit up to her thigh. A hush would fall over the crowd. They would all marvel at her effortless grace as she glided down the stairs, and she would make a riveting speech while holding a slender flute of champagne beside his replica of her home. Henry hoped someone would record the event so he could watch it from the comfort of his bed later on.

The main door opened, and a man Henry assumed to be Colson poked his head outside. They had only spoken on the phone when he placed the order. His black hair, flecked with a few greys on the sides, was cropped short like his beard. Henry's cheeks flushed.

"You're almost late," said Colson. He gestured to the servant's entrance, visibly annoyed, and slipped inside.

Henry would have spent the following moment over-analyzing how he had offended the man, but Brisa interceded.

"I saw that," she said with a little grin.

"What?" asked Henry defensively as they picked up the massive cake box and walked through the front gate.

"He's attractive," she said and winked at him. "You two would make a cute couple."

Henry gave her an exaggerated quizzical look that only confirmed her suspicions. Colson was gorgeous but way out of Henry's league. He was in Lady Duggery's inner circle. Even if he were interested, the Militia would never allow it. The idea was too dangerous to consider.

Henry opened his mouth to contradict Brisa, but a faint buzzing in his ears distracted him. He had skipped breakfast, caught up in his creative anxiety, and his blood sugar had dropped. He'd snack on the cookies he had stored in his jacket on the way down the mountain. A few steps later, pinpricks crackled across his toes and heels.

"Hold on," he said, and he paused to shake his foot. It was not asleep. This was an altogether new sensation—and a rather unpleasant one at that. The static shocked him with increasing intensity, as if warning him to turn around, to run as far away as he could and never come back.

"Do you feel that?" he asked Brisa. His ears warmed, more intensely than when he saw Colson, and his pulse quickened.

"Feel what?"

Before he could explain, the sparking sensation coursed along his nervous system and erupted in a cluster of firecrackers behind his eyes.

Help! Henry!

Beware! Ahh! Restraints!

Henry!

Ahh! Fading!

Power!

Ahhhhhhh! Henry!

The isolated words popped into his brain. Each formed a distinct sound, some overlapping with others, but they never coalesced into a coherent voice. Instead, their meaning foamed like heavy cream poured into boiling sugar before fizzling out.

In the silence that followed, Henry grew dizzy, and his arms trembled. It was more than exhaustion. He was no stranger to panic attacks, but he had never heard voices before. He must be losing his grip on reality. He could feel the vibrations in his joints and behind his heart. Every bone in his rib cage buzzed at the same low frequency, the same energy shaking the cake in his hands, the stones under his feet, and the clay beneath those stones.

Critters rustled in nearby bushes, and flocks of sparrows took flight. Dead branches cracked and fell to the ground. A scream echoed up the ridge from the valley below. The massive windowpanes rattled. The entire mountain rumbled and rocked, threatening to shake the house down and fold the distant blue ridges in on themselves.

Henry had never experienced an earthquake before, not in the dormant ranges of the Appalachian Mountains where he'd spent his entire life. Even Brisa panicked as she coached him to remain calm. Standing in the open lawn, they bent their knees, instinctively lowering their center of gravity, still working to save the cake.

Then the big one hit.

The quake knocked them both over and took the cake with it. Henry fell backward, his hands and hips absorbing most of the shock. Brisa tumbled sideways and smashed her head directly into the stone wall. Henry braced his scraped palms and arms against the ground, in search of an impossible sense of security as the landscape rocked back and forth. Sediment Valley was indifferent, unresponsive, to his presence. The earth rippled beneath his body, turning solid stone into particle waves that Henry had no choice but to ride with uncertainty.

In time, the quake resided, the pines straightened their trunks, and the earth stood still once more.

Henry flattened himself against the ground in case of aftershocks and reminded himself to breathe. The familiar urge to flee returned. He needed to get off this mountaintop as fast as possible. Unable to stand, he got on all fours beside the cake, which laid in ruins. He was certain he would be fired for this sugary disaster and expelled from their little paradise.

His chest tightened. He looked away and caught sight of Brisa, which only compounded his dilemma. He needed to figure out a replacement for the cake. The clock kept ticking. But Brisa was lying on the ground, eyes closed, presumably unconscious.

"Brisa!" he shouted. She did not respond. He crawled toward her, confirmed she was still breathing and checked her head for blood. There was a bit of a scratch but nothing deep, as far as he could tell. The frantic thoughts banging around in his head blurred his vision.

This is why he preferred to work alone. Not to take all the credit. He could share praise where it was due. He preferred to work alone because he could not bear the responsibility of his actions if they resulted in—exactly a situation like this. Brisa had been harmed because of him.

Even though the ground had settled, his ears convinced him the world was still rolling and pitching. He had to get back to the bakery. He could not suffer the embarrassment of becoming the laughingstock of the entire Militia when Lady Duggery revealed his failure to them. Not to mention that his livelihood, his place in Sediment Valley, depended on his ability to perform the duty to which he was assigned. There would be a waiting list of highly-qualified bakers eager to take his place.

Henry thought he might throw up from the decision he was about to make. He would leave Brisa here. Colson or someone from the mansion would find her. It's not like he had any medical training, he rationalized. And he would alert the guards at the bottom of the trail.

"You're going to be alright," he whispered to her.

Henry crawled toward the gate, stood halfway, and ran down the mountain trail, careful not to fall over from the guilt weighing on his shoulders.

Chapter 4

Colson

When the quake subsided, Colson threw open the servant's door and rushed down the steps, but his head was still swimming. "Please, please, please, let the cake be in one piece," he chanted repeatedly.

He ignored the hunched-over baker stumbling toward the mountain path and the unconscious delivery person crumpled against the stone fence. He had eyes only for the ripped cake box on the lawn.

"No!" he shouted. "No, no, no, no, no!"

He darted over and dropped to his knees beside the ruins of Lady Duggery's replicated mansion. The dowels had ripped through the tiers of cake like fractured femurs and lemon curd sputtered from the wounds.

He dug his fingers into the mess. It was the fluffiest cake. The silkiest buttercream. The voluptuous crumb was flecked with poppyseed. The aroma of lemon zest and honeysuckle. Henry had exceeded Colson's expectations, but now the masterpiece was strewn in a tragic heap across the manicured lawn. He scooped some of the remains into the torn box like a child building a castle from handfuls of wet sand.

Then Colson noticed the miniature mansion resting on its side, relatively undisturbed. The excess of royal icing and tempered chocolate glued the edible details into a protective shell. He could rescue the maquette! He crawled toward it. He would have to remove it to the sideboard and fill the Brazilian mahogany entrance table with cut flowers, but he could make this work. He lifted it from the ground and inspected it. From the front and sides, it was undisturbed, but when he turned to the back, his shoulders sagged. It looked as if it had been blasted with a shotgun. Perhaps it was an illusion? Candies made to look like shale arranged in a meticulously haphazard manner?

Unlikely, but he was desperate for any bit of good news. He plucked a rocky shard from the ganache and placed it between his molars only to discover it was not cake, not confection, but solid rock.

He dropped the mini mansion from his sticky hands.

"This is an utter disaster," he mumbled to himself, still ignoring the delivery person groaning behind him.

Colson wiped his hands on the grass. He needed to think fast, to find a solution. He was so close to completing his life's mission, he could almost taste the glory of revenge. But no dessert meant no distraction. He needed all eyes on Lady Duggery's lily-white hands as she sliced through the layers and divvied it up to the power brokers of the Militia. Meanwhile, he would slip into the cellar, allowing them plenty of time to swallow the poppyseeds, and call on the full powers of the Earth. Gaia would make the poppies sprout in their bellies from the seeds in the cake. The roots would wind down into their rotten bowels, and elongated stalks would stuff their lying throats. He would step over their twitching bodies, searching for his main target—Agent Dixon—and hover over him. He would watch with righteous glee as crimson petals bloomed from each of their mouths, denying a final breath to the ecofascist fucks who had murdered his family and destroyed Levittown, his childhood home.

If he failed now, it could be years before he had another opportunity.

Colson closed his eyes and envisioned the blue ridges that spread out from his location in all directions. It would be dangerous to evoke his awakened powers out in the open. If one of the staff saw him, or even worse, if Lady Duggery were watching him on one of her cameras, his cover would be blown. He did not even know if Gaia would grant him the ability to reassemble a cake. His powers had mostly allowed him to grow and manipulate nearby vegetation, often as a protective barrier, and he was a bit out of practice.

Gaia had only spoken to him once since he arrived in the valley to protect his true identity. There had been no other way. One poorly timed spell to revive a dying houseplant witnessed by a wandering guard would have been enough to trigger interrogation and exile, if not worse. The general population might not believe much in the existence of the Awakened, but the Militia persecuted their enemies with inquisitorial fervor, and the Awakened were enemy number one.

He recalled the moment Gaia withdrew from him. He felt like his body was rent in two, torn to shreds, and left to rot alone. It was the second-worst night of his life, but the isolation was necessary. He quickly filled the void left by Gaia with the task of gaining Lady Duggery's trust. He had not risked evoking his powers ever since.

On the eve of his revenge, it was not the worst idea to get the juices flowing again, and in all likelihood, everyone would be distracted by the sudden quake. He would take the risk.

As he leaned forward, his fingertips reached for the earth. Colson furrowed his brow in concentration. He squeezed the ground and inhaled, as if preparing to be submerged. A hint of familiar energy fizzled in the palm of his hands before fading away. Something felt wrong. He relaxed his grip and tried again. He braced his knees on the rocky soil. "Come on," he whispered gently. He pulled and he tugged, but he was met with the banal laws of physics.

He clutched for the bonds that used to link him to Gaia. All he found were clumps of grass in his hands. He stood, defeated.

"Are you ok?" asked a groggy voice.

Colson jumped for he was not alone. The woman had managed to sit up with her head between her knees. He crossed his arms over his chest, soiling his clean white jacket. He worried how much she had seen.

"Yes," he said. She was not looking in his direction. The quake must have knocked her over. He hoped she was too stunned to have paid him any attention. "Are you the baker's assistant?"

She squinted toward him. "What?"

"I mean, are you ok?"

"A bit dizzy. But yes, I think so."

"Let me help you," he said as he reached out a dirty hand. "I'm Colson Dagwood."

"Brisa. Arroyo. Thanks. And no, I don't work for Henry. I happened to run into him as he was headed here, and he looked like he could use some help." She looked around. "Where did he go?"

"When I came out, I think he was running away."

"I better go look for him." Brisa took Colson's hand and stood slowly, bracing herself on the fence until she found her bearings. Then she noticed the cake. "Oh no, it's ruined!"

"If you catch him, tell him we'll still pay for the cake."

"Let's hope he's not injured first."

"Of course," said Colson, avoiding the judgment of Brisa's gaze, which threatened to cut him deeper than Lady Duggery ever could. He waved her goodbye with a closed-lip smile—fairly certain she did not suspect him of being an Awakened—and took one final look at the mess before his feet.

The cake was unsalvageable, by natural or supernatural abilities, and it did not bode well that he struggled to reconnect with Gaia. Then again, his powers tended not to be readily available outside of a true crisis. In the heat of the moment, Colson was sure Gaia would have his back. Gaia had never let him down so far. Still, he hoped they weren't upset with him for his almost total silence since he entered Sediment Valley. He did his best to put it out of his mind.

He went in search of a garbage bag, and as he cleaned up the cake, he formulated a new plan, one even more effective, more ruthless—more just. He would add heaps of seeds to every dish served at the party so that no bite would be without them. Colson could rescue his life's mission after all.

CHAPTER 5

LADY DUGGERY

LADY DUGGERY, STILL WRAPPED in her silk robe, surveyed the mess from the center of her foyer. She ordered Colson to change out of his stained clothes, while most of his staff slinked away to stave off any culinary crises. The first guests would arrive shortly for the Founder's Day celebrations.

The house had been built to withstand almost any geological disturbance, especially earthquakes. Still, a few loose trinkets had tumbled to the floor. She directed the remaining servants—*what a relief*, she thought, *to be able to call them "servants" again*—to opposite wings to ensure the entire residence was immaculate. As they hurried away, she made a grand display of picking up an unbroken vase and setting it back on the mahogany table in the center of the room.

In recent days, Lady Duggery had nudged items of little value near the edges of shelves, and she even weakened the leg on a credenza that reminded her of her grandmother's tacky décor. Had the mansion suffered no damage at all, the resulting whisper campaign might erode the foundations of her reign. She took a moment to appreciate her own forethought.

"Aren't you just a vision in white," boomed a voice behind her in an accent more at home in Muscle Shoals than up north.

"Damnit, man," she said, startled, as she faced Agent Dixon. The phrasing was uncharacteristic of her desired demeanor.

Agent Dixon's malted breath filled the empty space between them.

"You reek," she said. "It's a little early to be drinking, wouldn't you agree?" She pushed past him to close the door.

As she turned the latch, his sleeve grazed her ear. He reached above her shoulder and rested his hand on the door, boxing her in. Lady Duggery turned around and looked down at the man before her. His skin was artificially tan, and his boots had modest heels. He was self-conscious about his height and physical appearance. She could use that to her advantage. She stared him in his bloodshot eyes to exaggerate her disgust, but he remained unfazed. Since he was not the type to understand nuance, she grabbed his slender wrist, pinching the nerves, and pried his hand from the door. She then twisted his arm until he winced and slumped forward.

"Let's get one thing straight. Sediment Valley is my domain. You are here to do a job for me. Do you understand?"

Dixon grunted in affirmation.

She waited a beat before releasing him.

He took a step back, rubbing his forearm.

Though he put on a brave face, Lady Duggery did not miss the slight flush in his freshly shaved cheeks. He looked like a little boy who had been caught with his pants down tugging at his penis. How long had it been since someone had talked to him in this manner? Perhaps years. Or even decades.

In Sediment Valley, Dixon reported to Lady Duggery. In fact, earlier this morning, she had fortified her position. As the sun washed across her fine linen sheets to signal the culmination of a night of unbridled passion, Dixon's superior in the Militia had reiterated his support for her before his helicopter disappeared behind the mountain range. The Militia had near total control of the Commonwealth. But it was her fracking fortune, after all, that bankrolled SustainAble's expansion into crypto. Dixon and his men had been contracted to serve her interests.

Lady Duggery was no stranger to dealing with men like Dixon, but she was impressed by how quickly he swallowed his emotions, regained his composure, and nodded in agreement. There was no reason to belabor the point. Now they could get on to their actual business.

"I hear you have a gift for me," she said, restoring her disinterested tone.

Dixon loosened his bowtie and fished a chintzy gold chain from inside his tuxedo shirt. Two gemstones wrapped in the finest metal bands hung from the necklace. He fiddled with the clasp. "Can you help me with this?" He turned his back to Lady Duggery.

She unhooked the necklace, and some of his bronzer rubbed off on her hands. "You really ought to tone it down a bit with that tanning cream."

Dixon let out a dismissive grunt, and she wiped the residue on her silk robe. Colson would know how to remove the stain.

The amulets rested in the palm of her hand. At first glance, the gems appeared to be identical. When viewed from the front, they were two muddied green stones, cut into perfect squares; from the back, however, they were naturally ragged, as if the jeweler had completed only half of his work before burglars raided his studio. Metal filaments wrapped around the outer edges of the squares then stretched into the thinnest, most delicate chain. The rough backs of the stones were free of embellishments.

Lady Duggery adored bespoke jewelry, and yet she had a hard time making sense of how the band managed to hold onto each gem. They appeared to defy the laws of physics. The only distinction between the two stones was the direction of the nearly invisible spiral—one clockwise, one counter.

"The choice is yours," said Dixon. "These are made of east-onite, I'm told. Local stones are the key."

"I can't tell if these are gorgeous or the most hideous gems I've ever seen."

"The color is off-putting, especially in the unfinished stone. But you'll forget all about that once you take it for a spin."

Lady Duggery selected the amulet with the clockwise spiral—she was a forward-thinking woman, after all—slid it from the chain, and handed the necklace back to Dixon. He produced a second chain for her, which she hooked tightly around her neck like a choker. The stone rested in the small dip between her exposed clavicles.

"You might want to step outside," said Dixon.

Before he had finished his sentence, Lady Duggery had already closed her eyes. She had held power before. The power of her family's estate. The power of being the one whose fortunes could sway an election. The power of speaking to vast crowds and the even-greater power of whispering behind closed doors. She held such power naturally. It had always been available to her, even as other women lost their voice and their autonomy as a result of her preferred policies. Her social stature and eagerness to play the role of the woman who would climb the ladder built by other women granted her access to spheres of influence few would ever know in their lives. Especially after she pulled up the ladder behind her.

Still, despite this lifelong proximity to such worldly forces, she could never have anticipated the surge of energy that now flowed into her body through the gemstone. The wave, neither warm nor cold, washed over her nervous system, followed by a numbness that spread across her limbs and drew out a capacity for love that she had long ago buried alongside a hawkish impetus to conquer the world. Her mind was rent in half, torn between the extremes of envy and gratitude, between hopelessness and the certainty that she had never been more filled with joy.

Her physical body trembled, not unlike the Earth a mere hour ago, destabilized by the concentration of energy. Through this amulet, she conducted a force from deep below the valley floor.

Lady Duggery, splitting at the metaphysical seams, heard a faint voice call out to her. It was Agent Dixon.

"You have to stop resisting. It's going to rip you to pieces. Let the powers choose where to flow. They'll make the right choice in the moment."

Lady Duggery had to battle her instincts as well as four decades of experience directing, appointing, designating, and making the final cut. She did not want to let go, but the powers coursing through her could not be consumed by her will. They would consume her. She could feel the amulet winning. The more she struggled, the quicker it dragged her to her knees, strangled her, and flooded her bloodstream with oxygen.

She tried to push herself off the ground. She rose a few inches into the air, struggling against gravity, until the stone overpowered her again. It dragged her back to the Earth, and her ankles and knees popped when her heels dug into the hardwood.

The only way out would be to remain calm, like in all those stories about quicksand. As a child, she feared accidentally being sucked into its gurgling maw. The substance supposedly lurked in every forest and behind every rocky outcrop. She tried to take a deep breath, even though she had lost control of her involuntary systems, before finally granting this energy free reign over her mind.

Her body went slack before she had time to regret her choices, but she did not fall over. The equal but opposite forces warring within each of her organs and deep inside her psyche spun down, slowing their raging war, to establish a new equilibrium.

Lady Duggery raised her arms over her head. She had never been a dancer, but the gesture provided a sense of grandeur. She always put on a good show, even if it was just for this puny man standing in awe before her now.

The force of gravity loosened its hold, and the flow of air no longer affected the movement of her body. She levitated, slowly, getting a feel for this magic. Once it had a handle on her, and she on it, no longer clashing but working in tandem, she soared high above Dixon's head and twisted among the rafters.

"I could get used to this," she said, trying not to cackle. She tightened her robe and reasserted herself as the queen of this castle, the sorceress who commanded from on high. None would dare challenge her reign. She swayed back and forth, drifting to the various corners of the room, before returning to the floor. She wanted nothing more than to stay in the air, but a servant might burst into the room and spoil the surprise.

"Do you suppose this is what it feels like to be one of the Awakened?" she asked Dixon. Too many people ignored the myths of their existence, but she knew better.

"Miscreants, the lot of them," said Dixon, almost spitting at the mention of them.

"What about yours?" she asked in a whisper.

"Mine are a bit more . . . leaden, if you will." His arms and chest flexed as he responded.

"We can't have you thudding around on my new floors," she said, ensuring he would not ruin this special moment by firing up his amulet.

"I wouldn't dare," he replied with a bow.

"Good. And what about the volunteer for tonight?"

"I've got my sights set on someone already."

"That'll be all," she said dismissively. She preferred to leave some details to Dixon. She considered floating to the second floor to finish her preparations for the Founder's Day party, but she thought better of it. She pocketed the amulet inside her robe. When she reached the middle of the stairs, a knock sounded at the front door. The first guests had arrived.

"Oh, and Dixon?" she said coyly over her shoulder. She beckoned him closer. Her favorite sport was to play with the men in her orbit.

"Yes?" A sly smile spread across his face as he made his way toward the stairs.

"See to it that the guests are greeted, but only after I'm out of sight."

His smirk faded. "As you wish, ma'am."

Lady Duggery disappeared into the upper corridor feeling lighter than the breeze.

CHAPTER 6

BRISA

BRISA HAD NOT BEEN honest with Colson about searching for Henry after the quake. Henry had basically left her to fend for herself, but more importantly, her business at the mansion was far from over. The guards had already scanned her wristwatch at the gates as the baker's assistant, and that excuse should hold up until she located the cryptocurrency mines hiding under the mansion. Between the earthquake and the Founder's Day party, no one would even think of Brisa until she had made her escape and arrived safely back inside ChainBlock's stronghold with her wife and friends.

Once the last of the illustrious guests made their way up the mountain and into Lady Duggery's mansion, Brisa stepped out from her hiding spot among the trees. The uproarious chatter from the alcohol-soaked soiree leaked from an open window. Brisa knocked at the servant's entrance. Her skin was prickly from sitting still in her bike shorts and t-shirt all afternoon and into the early evening. She gripped the straps on her backpack and scrunched up her face, exaggerating to elicit sympathy.

Before the door even opened, an exasperated young woman said, "It's about time!" Clearly, she had been expecting someone else. "Oh, Brisa, what are you doing here? Come in."

It was Calla, a relatively new arrival to the valley. She wore a ridiculous maid's outfit and had braided her long hair with blue and black ribbons. ChainBlock's intel classified Calla as low risk, an unaware cog in the Sediment Valley machine. According to Brisa's files, Calla had been chosen by SustainAble's lottery system because of her almost pathological desire to fit in. Calla joined Brisa on every hike and bike ride she organized. She always brought leftovers from the mansion and kept squarely in the center of the pack.

Brisa rubbed her upper arms in the warmth of the mud room. She waited for Calla to speak first. She had learned this tactic during her training at ChainBlock. To let others choose the direction of the lie and then lean into it.

"Let me guess. You want to meet the big wigs, too?" asked Calla.

"You got me," said Brisa, laughing awkwardly to feign being caught. "I just couldn't stand sitting at home thinking how close our benefactors are. I had to try." She placed a hand on Calla's shoulder. "You're not going to report me, are you?"

"It's your lucky day, Brisa! One of the waitstaff never showed." Calla became serious and whispered in her ear. "You didn't hear this from me, but that Dixon guy is really hot." Calla's cheeks blushed as she pulled away and lowered her eyes to the floor.

Normally, Brisa would not hesitate to correct someone's assumptions about her sexuality, but she thought it best to keep mum. She was more concerned for the no-show member of the waitstaff. The civilian residents of Sediment Valley must understand the dangers of appearing useless or unreliable to the Militia. Brisa rubbed her shoulders again to change the topic.

"Sorry! You must be freezing! Let me get you a uniform." Calla disappeared into the busy kitchen.

Alone in the mud room, Brisa unzipped her bag to retrieve her recording glasses. The round frames were made of a slender black metal. After her extraction from Sediment Valley, she would share the footage with ChainBlock.

"Here you go," said Calla upon her return. She handed Brisa a maid's uniform just like her own. "I'll guard the door while you slip this on, and then I'll show you around."

Brisa stashed her bag near the outside door and pulled the maid's uniform over her clothes. It looked like it had been plucked from a costume bin, a parody of the 1950s, featuring frumpy, washed-out gray fabric with big, plastic buttons and rough-hewn beige trim on the collar. The suits transformed everyone working in the mansion from individual people into anonymous servants.

The Jim Crow era was all the rage these days, especially in Lady Duggery's circles. With the Militia's backing, they were well on their way to restoring that age in everything from architecture and design to legalized discrimination, all the while denying that racism ever existed. Lady Duggery probably kept someone like Colson by her side as proof of her inability to see color. Brisa had no idea what he got out of it.

"I'm ready," she said to Calla.

The directions were simple. Carry around a platter; don't look anyone in the eyes. Brisa's only concern was bumping into Colson. He might recognize her from earlier and get suspicious. Then again, as she came to on the lawn, he hadn't even glanced in her direction. Now Calla had helped her secure a way to go unnoticed. A Latina woman dressed as a maid—no one in tonight's crowd should pay her any attention at all. In fact, she was counting on it.

"Try one," said Calla. She shoved a prosciutto crostino into Brisa's palm and popped one in her own mouth as well. Then she wiped her mouth with the back of her hand and looked around the kitchen.

"You're not supposed to be eating on the job," whispered one of the waitstaff as he passed. He stopped just long enough to make eye contact with both Calla and Brisa, as if to let them know he saw their minor transgression. Then a knowing smirk crept across his face. He snatched a crostino from Calla's tray and pretended to snarl as he ripped it in half with his teeth.

Calla burst into laughter at her friend's antics. Brisa did not get the joke, but she smiled at him anyway. The man swallowed the rest of the prohibited snack, grabbed a serving platter, and headed for the party.

"A special friend?" asked Brisa.

"Who, Hiroshi? Oh, no. He's married with a little kid. We've become friends. He pokes fun at Colson's strict rules. Before you got here, Colson made a big deal about not eating any of the food. Like a *really* big deal. But why shouldn't we get at least a few bites, right? They're not going to eat all of this. They never do."

"That's true," said Brisa, nodding as she chewed. "This is delicious!"

The hors d'oeuvre was luxurious, and the sunflower seed garnish provided an unexpected twist. Before her, an assortment of platters waited to circulate throughout the grand foyer. Watermelon with feta, beef sliders on a sesame bun, chocolate chia pudding shooters.

Brisa had the urge to shove them all into her face after such a long day hauling that monstrous cake up the mountain and waiting for hours in the woods, but the many members of the kitchen staff, each in that hideous uniform, carried them away with haste.

No matter. She was on a mission: locate the server farm and install the back-door access so her accomplices at ChainBlock could skim profits from their cryptocurrency mines. For now, the proceeds would finance their underground organization until they had enough resources to shutter all of SustainAble's crypto mines once and for all.

Calla handed Brisa a platter of lobster canapés, sprinkled densely with poppyseeds—another unexpected combination, she thought, maybe a bit overboard—and they each sampled one. It was real lobster, not a plant-based substitute. *How did they even source these?* wondered Brisa. SustainAble's reach was incomprehensible to most, easily crossing national borders that actual people would never traverse, not legally anyway. The lobster, at first delightfully unctuous, now gurgled in her otherwise empty stomach.

Brisa tried to ignore her hunger, her splitting headache, and her worn-out muscles as she walked down the long corridor separating the kitchen from the grand foyer. Black and white time-lapsed images of the valley in different phases of construction hung along the walls. The earliest was an archival photo of the original strip mine with strapping young men in overalls, their unsmiling faces blackened with coal and dirt. The next showed the ruins of the mine awaiting rehabilitation in the final years of the United States, sometime in the late 2020s, when polluting operations like this temporarily lost their federal subsidies. As she walked by the remaining aerial photos, a deep pit became a foundation and from it rose the frame of a majestic log cabin, big enough to serve as a ski lodge, if only snow still powdered these ridges. Later came the landscaping, the security perimeter, and finally, a close-up of Lady Duggery standing with the keys to the mansion in hand as she took possession of her new domain.

The ceiling of the grand foyer vaulted to untold heights, and Brisa wondered if this was how astronauts felt when stepping onto a cloudless Mars. The chandelier twinkled among the rafters, and a pianist played renditions of twentieth-century country classics.

The civilian men from SustainAble wore navy pinstripe suits with floral bowties and bowler hats affixed with Militia insignia, and the officers sported their white dress uniforms. All their women wore subtle variations of floor length A-line dresses, with elongated waistlines and cap sleeves, in dark navy and shades of slate. The women, like the staff, were interchangeable.

Every surface burst with fresh-cut floral bouquets and white bows. Brisa had never seen so many different types of flowers. Some looked rather alien in their vibrant hues and prickly petals. The mahogany table at the foot of the grand stairwell housed multiple tiers of foliage and palm fronds. Tucked inside the leaves were crystal candy dishes filled to the brim with assorted nuts and seeds.

The grand foyer overflowed with opulence. Only Brisa and a few of the servants would notice the cake's absence.

A man whistled loudly to attract her attention, and a momentary hush fell over the room. He stood in a small group with a woman much younger than him and an older civilian man. He wore neither the requisite civilian attire nor the white dress uniform but a black tuxedo.

A poppyseed had lodged itself in one of Brisa's molars. She tried in vain to remove it with her tongue.

"Come here, miss." He waved her over in exasperation.

Brisa lowered her eyes. "Lobster canapé for the lady?"

The woman reached for one, but the man placed his hand on her gloved wrist and made a disapproving click. She looked over her shoulder, sighed, and swayed her hips to the piano, while the other man standing in their intimate circle piled three, four, and then five canapés onto a cocktail napkin in his swollen hands. Brisa identified him as one of SustainAble's head bankers. She made sure her camera caught ample footage of him in this room to potentially blackmail him later.

"Settle a bet for us," said the man who summoned her. "What are you?"

Brisa worried she had been discovered. She took a breath to steady her heart rate, while she tried to identify him. He was shorter than her, slender in build, and wore bronzer like a mask. She could tell by the undyed white skin peeking out from around his hairline. But she had never seen this man before. He was not one of the many white or white-passing faces she had memorized as SustainAble agents. Still, his location in the room, the way the other men lingered in his vicinity, his norm-busting attire, it all suggested he was the top dog. He must be an officer in the Militia. The Militia had been much more successful than SustainAble at erasing any and all traces of their members from the public record.

"Beg your pardon?" asked Brisa with a snap to her words.

"Are you a Mexican or an Indian?"

Brisa forced her pursing lips to maintain a polite smile. His casual racism was almost a relief because it meant her cover had not been blown. But the question still burned around her jawline.

"My mother was born in Puerto Rico, but her family relocated to Philadelphia after a hurricane in the 2010s. My father was third-generation Honduran-American."

"I didn't ask for your whole genealogy, girl." He turned to his accomplice, the banker, and gloated. "A Mexican, like I said. Pay up."

The banker rolled his eyes while he tapped on his wristwatch. "Yes, yes, Dixon, you win. A hundred ConFeds, as we agreed." It made a whooshing sound as the cryptocurrency transaction completed, and a vibrant gold check mark lit up the unknown officer's watch.

Brisa bit her lower lip and fantasized about slamming this Dixon against the wall, her forearm pressing into his neck until he slumped to the hardwood floors, before chasing the banker and gutting him like a walrus. But her mission was bigger than either man.

"Since you seem to have a number of opinions, answer us this. You see, my esteemed colleague here, Mr. Wilksburn, believes this valley would be best upheld if it were reserved for... How should I put it?"

"For the less melanated," said Mr. Wilksburn, drawing out those final vowels between open-mouthed bites of oily lobster and seed-studded cream cheese. Suddenly the food appealed less to Brisa.

"Whereas I think we're making the right choice in allowing you people to have some good jobs, like serving Lady Duggery in this here fine mansion." He gestured to the room around him as evidence of the luxury that, as long as he had his way, would only be accessible to Brisa dressed as she was.

His female companion—unlikely to be his wife, since neither wore a wedding band—nodded in Brisa's direction. "We've got to put you somewhere," she said.

"It's a fine job," said Brisa through gritted teeth. She fixated on the gaping pores on the woman's nose that no amount of foundation or powder could conceal. Then she took a step backwards.

Dixon grabbed her wrist, and the canapé platter wobbled as he pulled her close. Her arms still ached from this afternoon's hike, and the spot where she hit her head pounded, but she prevented the platter from crashing to the ground.

The gloved mistress snatched a canapé that almost slipped off the side and, in defiance of her date, ate it before he could stop her.

"Careful now," he said. He leaned in to whisper into her ear. "Be a good girl and fetch me a whiskey, won't you? Bring it to my room right after the fine lady of the house gives her speech."

Brisa nodded, knowing it would be easier to get away if she lied and said yes. He released her wrist. A venomous chill rushed down her spine. She needed to bottle up her rage, but she desired nothing more than to dismember him, one small body part at a time. *Later*, she thought. *I'll take care of him later.* Right now, she had to finish the job and slip out the servant's entrance before he demanded his pound of flesh.

So much for going unnoticed.

The data servers would be underground, perhaps even directly under her feet, hidden in the basement or in a deeper chamber beneath the mansion. According to her schematics, there should be an entrance somewhere off the kitchen. She returned to the long corridor, holding the empty platter at her side. As she approached the swinging door, hushed shouting overtook the sound of clinking dishes and the exhaust fans. Inside, Colson was pointing at the mud room door.

"Go. Right now. You need to get the *fuck* out of here," he said to the man standing before him. Colson's voice was quiet but harsh, as if he were embarrassed to be seen with the other man. The staff members gawked and giggled under their breath. He pushed the other man toward the door, and as he turned around, Brisa recognized him as Henry.

What is he doing here? She was relieved to find him standing without any bruises or obvious scars under the harsh lighting. Only tears welled up behind his eyes as Colson publicly humiliated him.

On the stainless-steel island sat a pile of gingersnap cookies. He must have rushed back to the bakery to whip up a substitute dessert for Colson, and in return, Colson had treated him like a misbehaving puppy. Maybe she had been wrong to encourage Henry. She had been working an angle, and even though she didn't know anything about Colson's true identity, she couldn't resist a little matchmaking. *Too bad*, she thought.

Brisa took a step backward into the hallway to hide, while Colson pushed past his staff toward the back of the kitchen. On his way, he dumped all of the cookies into the trash, and the platter clanged on the floor. She was determined to find out what he was up to or, at the very least, force him to tell her how to access the server farm. He would know every secret entrance and hidden room in this place.

She waited a moment, entered the kitchen, and rested her empty platter on the island. The other staff were too busy whispering about Colson's outburst to notice her following him into the narrow space in the back. Fully stocked floor-to-ceiling shelves blocked her path, and Colson was nowhere to be found. She spun in a little circle, confused, until she noticed a subtle line of light running vertically along the back wall. She pressed her hand on it, and the false wall gave way. It swung back on well-oiled hinges to reveal a hidden staircase.

"Bingo," she whispered.

The yellow lights flickered mere inches above her head, and the concrete stairs turned three times at ninety-degree angles. She was careful not to make too much noise, while hurrying in case she had to follow Colson through an underground maze. She stopped on the bottom step.

In the center of the expansive basement, Colson kneeled on the ground before a towel and a pitcher. Plastic tubs lined the back wall, some junk piled in the corner. A metal rack had fallen over, probably during the quake. But there were no servers to be found, no remnants of expansive cooling systems or visible doors leading to other rooms. This was no secret lair, just an unfinished basement. Brisa had made some serious miscalculations. She needed to think fast. She wouldn't get another chance to roam freely around the mansion.

The exposed rafters creaked under the weight of the partygoers. A muffled piano tinkled through the floorboards. Before Brisa could formulate a new plan, the pianist stopped mid-song. The room above came to a standstill. Only the appearance of Lady Duggery could explain the sudden silence.

"Right on time," said Colson to himself. He sat with his back to Brisa and fixated on the space before him. He pulled back the towel. A crude hole had been dug in the cement floor, exposing the dirt under the foundation. He poured water into the hole and plunged his fingertips into the muddy earth. The scene was eerily familiar to whatever mystical ritual he was performing when she regained her senses after the quake.

Something moved in the shadows near Brisa's feet. It startled her, but it was only a field mouse. She tried to shoo it away, quietly, but it nipped at her laces and pulled at them, as if trying to drag her upstairs.

Don't be silly, she thought. *You're imagining things. It's just hungry or something.* She swiped her shoes, careful not to harm it, and it scampered back to the shadows.

Brisa flicked her tongue over the nagging poppyseed lodged in her molar to no avail.

Now Colson rocked back and forth on his knees, undulating as if to harness some unseen rhythm from within the mountain. He pushed and pulled, almost kneading the soil. He slowed down, then shook his head and took a deep breath. The sound of heels descending the grand stairwell tapped out a muffled beat overhead, and he began rocking again with an increased sense of desperation and enlightened rage.

The knot in Brisa's stomach begged her to flee, but she clenched and resisted the urge. This was not the mystery she had come to discover. She had expected server farms and crypto-mining in SustainAble's greenwashed village. The same as she had unearthed in two other corporate-owned refuges dotting the Appalachians. But this was far stranger, and she could not shake the sense that something even more insidious was taking place in this happy little valley.

She had been wrong about Colson. Surely, he was not working with Lady Duggery. The pieces of this puzzle did not line up.

"Don't fail me now, Gaia," said Colson. "Come on!"

Gaia, thought Brisa, *such an odd name*. Brisa could hack her way through most systems, but when it came to all the new wave spiritualities that had flourished in the wake of the climate crises, her brain shut off. It was all too confusing and irrational to her.

Colson plucked his muddied fingers from the soil, cracked his knuckles, and tried once more. As his hands entered the earth, the lights blinked off and back on.

"Easy now," he said.

That had to be a coincidence, thought Brisa.

The flickering intensified, and Colson's entire body, hunched over the hole, slackened as if a wave of relief had washed over him. A slender shadow rose from the soil beneath his hands. The small stalk wavered, searching for the non-existent sunlight, as its tip slowly uncoiled.

Brisa gripped the handrail to steady herself, while the plant suddenly bloomed before Colson's entranced body. Her knees locked up, and pressure built between her teeth. She reached her tongue toward the stubborn poppyseed, but in its place a thin, vegetal thread sprouted and thickened at an unnatural pace. At the same time, something other than the rich canapé writhed in her gut. She plucked the sprout from her teeth, and as she examined it, she felt nauseated and frightened. *How many seeds had she eaten?*

The basement went dark as she bent down to wretch. The lights stayed out for a second, and then another. Between Brisa's dry heaves, a soft glow returned to the room. The electric hum grew louder as the lights intensified, and the buzzing reverberated behind the bump on her forehead. The lights burned brighter than ever, searing her eyes but also calming the turbulence in her intestines. In the last flash of white, Colson and the stalk slackened, slumped, and fell limply to the side.

In the darkness, the ground began to shake. Brisa braced herself against the stairwell, but her legs compelled her toward Colson's helpless body. She stumbled and, as the lights flickered, fell on top of Colson. He was still breathing. The house rumbled above them. Men and women shouted from upstairs. She splashed his face with the remaining water in the pitcher. He slowly came to.

"What are *you* doing here?"

"We've got to run. It's not safe."

"It doesn't matter. I failed." He rolled onto his side.

"Get up!" Brisa did not have time for theatrics. She tried to stand, preparing to drag him up the rocking stairwell if she had to. But another shock planted her back on the ground.

She stood again, bending her knees, feeling out the rhythm, but just as she was gaining a sense of stability, the quake subsided. The mansion stopped shaking. She stumbled once more as the world went still, and the lights returned to their original yellow glow.

Through the rafters, the attendees clapped and cheered. As if relieved to be alive like the passengers on a plane that had landed during a storm, nauseated and a bit lucky. They stamped the floor above her head in triumph.

Brisa stood there, in utter confusion, doubting everything she knew about SustainAble's archipelago of crypto-mining valleys. And everything she denied about the existence of the Awakened.

"Go! Now! It's not safe if they catch you here," said Colson. "They'll be looking for someone to blame, and you'll be an easy target."

"And you're not? Let me help you."

"It's less suspicious if I stay."

"I don't understand."

"Just get out of here, please."

"Ok," she said. "But you and I are going to have a long talk." Brisa headed back up the stairwell. With all the confusion and the chaos, she managed to grab her bag, sneak out the servant's entrance, and past the empty guard station without being noticed.

As she hurried back to her cabin, she sent a message to ChainBlock to delay their rendezvous. Brisa would spend the night detailing a new plan to break open this valley, one way or another.

PART TWO

TO TETHER

Chapter 7

Henry

Henry was in a piss poor mood when the first rays of dawn spilled across the quilt of his twin-sized bed. Dust motes whirled in the beam, and the pothos and peperomia stretched from his refurbished bamboo shelving to catch the springtime sun. He had not slept a wink.

Tremors persisted throughout the night at irregular intervals. Each one re-upped his state of panic. He tried clinging to the rattling bedframe, sitting with his head between his knees in the corner of the room, hiding under the desk, and even standing in the stout doorway.

In theory, he had trained for this in elementary school. But he couldn't recall which place was safest for earthquakes instead of tornadoes or active shooters. What did it matter if none of them made him feel safer? That was always the point, wasn't it? To provide a false sense of security when, truly, everyone was in grave danger.

If only he were more amenable to placebos or less prone to catastrophic thoughts, his life might have turned out differently. He might not be alone. He might not be a total fucking fraud running a bakery while the rest of the world burned. He might not have wasted his entire life. But where else could he go?

He had no one. His parents were long dead—his dad from lung cancer, and his mom, she had been arrested while protesting a new pipeline. They found her hanging in her cell. He never believed she would do that to herself—or to him. Once the officer delivered the bad news, that was it. Case closed. He had resigned himself to never getting answers. Meanwhile, his older brother, jacked up on conspiracy theories about government camps and a global war, had run off to join a heavily armed disaster assistance squad with all the other macho dudes his age. Henry hadn't heard from him since.

Henry wanted to be more grateful. He had a house, a job, water, and food, but he also had enough anxiety without adding earthquakes to the mix. Before resettling to Sediment Valley, he suffered through a heightened state of alert, always on the lookout for the next threat. For a few hours each night, he could press pause on the ringing alarms and fall into a deep, dreamless sleep. His brain might be broken, but at least it did not produce horror-riddled nightmares. It saved those for the waking hours.

Now even his sleep had been taken from him.

Each new tremor he hoped would be the last. The seconds ticked by on his wristwatch as alternating scenes played out in his mind. In the still moments, Colson's voice scolded him over and again, while the staff members stood by, judging him as they snickered. Only a fresh tremor could interrupt the cycle of humiliation as it conjured images of the roof caving in on him. Perhaps being crushed under the rubble was not the worst outcome after all. With a massive log from his rustic cabin bearing down on his chest, his breath would slow, and his limbs would numb.

The smell of cedar and dust, irritating his nose.

A bit of blue sky, visible above his head.

When the ringing stopped, voices would call out to him, shouting his name, telling him to hold on, that help was coming. That someone cared about him. Then Colson would lift the heavy beam from his chest and pull him up and apologize. Henry, a master at holding a grudge, would refuse him and limp past the gossiping bystanders. *Now who's the one being publicly disgraced?*

He tried it on for a moment, this public humiliation fantasy, but it didn't make him feel any better. Colson had been so pleasant to him when he placed the order, calling him on the old-timey landlines that had replaced their cell phones. The Militia insisted on banning any devices they could not wiretap or turn off with a single switch. Even their wristwatches had been downgraded from all-encompassing communication devices to glorified ID cards that pushed out official messages.

As Colson described the flavors he wanted, his enthusiasm for all things poppyseed had been contagious. Henry had tried to convince himself his efforts were all for Lady Duggery, but that was not the entire story. He felt so dumb now, having gone all in on that stupid cake to impress a boy. Thirty-two felt too old to be acting like this. Lovesick behavior was for teens.

I'm such a mess.

Still, Henry could not figure out why Colson had been so cruel. The gingersnaps were his best-selling recipe, humble but a total crowd-pleaser. He had rushed back to make them and even abandoned Brisa on the ridge. *Oh wow, how could I do that?* He had practically forgotten about her given everything that had happened since. He did not even know if she was alright. *I suck.* Henry rolled over in his bed, wrapped himself in his shame and loneliness, and squeezed the downy pillow around his ears to mute the screaming world. He wanted to disappear.

When a push notification from Lady Duggery vibrated his wristwatch, Henry let out a deep sigh of relief. Certainly she would offer an explanation and a plan of action.

COMMUNITY ALERT: *Please be advised we are aware of the current situation. The climate crisis has created the most unpredictable scenarios. By our reports, earthquakes can be expected to persist in the days and weeks ahead. They will decrease in frequency over time and may disappear altogether. By no means should these minor disruptions prevent you from going about your routine activities. Watch for falling debris.*

Her message disappointed, to say the least. Henry expected better from Lady Duggery. How could they not know what is going on and have a prediction for future seismic activity? He was no seismologist, or climatologist, but he was pretty sure climate change could not set off an unending yet scheduled barrage of earthquakes. Who was he to say? Regardless, the message was clear: report to work despite the dangers.

Guilt soon gave way to frustration. Henry sat up too quickly. His brain turned somersaults, demanding he retreat to the underside of his pillow, but his bladder forced him to the toilet. He stumbled toward the doorframe wearing only boxer briefs. Deep red and purple bruises spread up his right hip from where he had fallen. He checked his tender buttocks in the bathroom mirror to find it covered in splotches. At least no one else would see his naked body. He lifted the toilet seat. It took him a few seconds, even when he was alone, to start going.

A familiar but distant voice vibrated in his head, distracting him.

Henry

Kindness.

Not alone.

Help!

That voice again. The one he heard just before the first earthquake. It sounded deeper now, like an echo from the bottom of a ravine.

Find me

grant you—

The voice cut off mid-sentence. Henry thought he was losing his mind. Hearing voices was not a sign of mental health. He shook the thought away to attend to his full bladder.

Just as he began to relieve himself, the room rocked sideways. "You've got to be kidding me," he said. He braced one hand against the wall and, unable to stop the flow, used the other to steady his aim. All was well until the toilet seat and lid clapped shut, splashing urine onto Henry's thighs and the wall. The final jolt stopped him from peeing, but not before he soaked the floors and drenched a new roll of toilet paper.

In that moment, his bottled-up angst burst into anger. He ripped off his underwear and threw them in the trash. Then he stomped to the kitchen to find the cleaning supplies, trailing wet footprints down the hallway.

While he sopped up his own piss with a towel, Henry wanted to shout at the world to make it all stop. The shaking, the corruption, the pollution, the abandonment, the unbearable losses. It was all so infuriating and unfair, these past few decades. His entire life. He had the poor luck to be born into a comfy world on the brink of collapse, just long enough to be keenly aware of how far things had fallen. Sediment Valley was supposed to get him back to that middle-class stability of his childhood. Nothing too luxurious—he wasn't greedy. Just enough to forget the outside world. And he had worked hard, dammit. He deserved this one little thing.

If only I had run away with Jonny, he thought. He rung out urine-soaked towels under the faucet and hung them to dry. It's not that he hated being by himself. He never had more than one or two close friends at a time, but he'd become deeply attached to each of them. The downside was, when they inevitably moved away, or got married, or decided they could no longer live in this world, Henry ended up alone once more.

Jonny was the last friend to abandon him before he won the Sediment Valley lottery. Jonny had run off with a cult, worshipping the Earth and some nonsense about people waking up with superpowers. The Awakened. *People will believe anything*, thought Henry. He hadn't expected Jonny of all people to fall for the fake news.

He and Jonny parted on harsh words—Henry's harsh words—when Jonny invited him to a refuge in the Northwoods of Wisconsin. Henry refused to go. He had convinced himself that Jonny and his new friends extended the invitation out of pity, so he pretended not to be home when his best friend in the world begged him to at least say good-bye.

Jonny banged on the rusty door for an hour. He sobbed and pleaded for Henry not to turn his back on him. Their friendship had been the one constant in both of their lives. They had come out to one another. They were each other's wingman at underground house parties. They shared every detail of their bad hook-ups, all the sloppy kissers and toothy blowjobs. They built a little world together. But neither of them had set down roots in Pittsburgh. They had shitty jobs at a SustainAble factory they could get anywhere, and they squatted in the husk of an old mill that had been transformed into lofts before falling once more into disrepair.

On that day, Henry sat in silence—out of fear, he realized now—until the man on the other side of the door gave up, grew angry, and told Henry to "fuck off, then, if their friendship meant so little."

Colson's "get the *fuck* out of here" echoed alongside Jonny's retreating footsteps in his mind.

And that was the end of it. Jonny became yet another person who simply disappeared from his life with no trace. He wondered if Jonny ever thought about him now.

Henry sprayed cleaner across every surface in the bathroom and wiped them vigorously. Once finished, he wanted a drink. He never started this early, but what did it matter? Standing naked in the kitchen, he threw back a shot of whiskey, slammed the shot glass on the butcher-block countertop, and poured another.

He soon realized his mistake. The alcohol only increased the frequency of palpitations rattling inside his chest, which sent him spiraling about heart attacks and aneurisms, creating more palpitations. He leaned over the counter and closed his eyes. If only he knew how to take charge, to take some fucking action, instead of always keeping his head down. He felt scared and useless locked inside his dark little cabin, but the outside world had never been more terrifying. Maybe a shower would help.

The hot water ran down his back, soothing his aching muscles. He inhaled deep drags of the steam to release the tightness in his chest, while the memory of a foggy night out with Jonny resurfaced.

Henry had never attended a leather bar. In a dark alley under a dim, yellow bulb, Henry looked over his shoulder while Jonny whispered a password through a sheet metal door. The attendant buzzed them inside but charged them a cover fee because they were not wearing any gear. The beefier, hairier men in leather vests and chaps practically ignored the newbies in raggedy t-shirts and hand-me-down shorts.

Instead of the big game, pornographic photos streamed on the televisions above the bar. Henry could not peel his eyes away. Gay porn had been blocked on all social media sites since he was a teen. A few clandestine pamphlets passed through his hands from time to time. It always felt forbidden and dangerous, but not in a sexy way. In this bar, his sexuality was on display, and the banal irreverence of it made him feel like he was no longer the oddity in the room.

Meanwhile, Jonny had struck up a conversation with two men clad in head-to-toe gear. The shorter one could have hopped on a motorcycle and blended in with a roving biker gang. The taller one paired a leather harness and jockstrap with industrial boots. Wide, studded straps crossed his chest, and Henry had a sudden urge to grab on and never let go. Before he knew it, the man removed his harness, while Jonny pulled off Henry's shirt. The former stranger—his name now slipped Henry's recollection, the memory growing foggier—placed the harness over Henry's bare shoulders and tightened the wide straps that were better suited to barrel-chested men. "You look good, kid," said the man. He cocked his head to the side and nodded.

In that moment, Henry felt powerful.

"That's it!" said Henry out loud and shut off the water. If he was going to make it through the days ahead, he needed something to tie him down while the earth shook.

A *harness*, he thought. A harness would do the trick.

Chapter 8

Brisa

"Plausible Owl, this is Wendy River. Do you read?" Brisa spoke into the satphone she kept hidden under a floorboard in her bedroom while drawing the shades. She sat on a stool, parting the blinds at random intervals. The room was empty except for the recycled plastics furnishings, a canteen of water on the nightstand, and her go-bag.

Brisa barely slept through the night and not just because of the earthquakes. She replayed the footage from her camera, trying to piece together the unexpected mysteries in between splitting headaches. By the time the sun rose, she had spiraled around the same few points with no way to make sense of it all. She needed an outsider's perspective, and if she was being honest, a bit of emotional support as well.

The call implied a major risk. ChainBlock's telecommunication infrastructure had superior encryption, but all bets were off given the extraordinary circumstances of Sediment Valley.

"Plausible Owl reads. Confirm ID," replied an altered voice.

Brisa rambled off a string of letters and numbers that ended in the phrase, "Acaso hubo búhos acá." Brisa loved a palindrome, each letter in its proper place, a pattern that made sense from every angle. This one was her favorite and also the origin of her wife's code name, Plausible Owl.

"Thank the stars, babe! I was worried when you postponed your rendezvous."

The sound of Val's voice almost brought Brisa to tears. She felt a lump in her throat, but she steadied herself. She exhaled loudly. "I am. Just needed to hear from you."

"What's wrong? Are you hurt?"

Brisa never could hide anything from Val. Not her plans to throw a surprise thirty-fifth birthday party. Not her secret perusal of puppy adoption agencies. And definitely not her stress related to their shared work at ChainBlock.

Brisa let it all out at once. "This place is fucked, Val. I can't find the server farm. The Militia is playing a much larger role here than we had anticipated, and their leader, a guy named Dixon, was not on our radar. There are earthquakes and, I can't believe I'm saying this, some kind of magic?"

"You never believed in the Awakened," said Val.

"I didn't. Or I don't. It's complicated." Brisa stumbled over her own words. "It's not like the fake news stories. This guy Colson, he made a plant grow, and a bunch of seeds that we had eaten, and I almost choked to death. Then the quake hit, and it all shriveled up. It messed up all the footage I took of his ritual."

"Slow down, Brisa. You're not making any sense." Val laughed under her breath, as if expecting her to jump out from behind her in the office and reveal it was all a prank even though they were hundreds of miles apart.

Brisa paused for a beat to reorganize her thoughts. She needed to start from the beginning and recreate the last twenty-four hours in sequence. Val would see some detail Brisa had missed. She always had a keen sense for lopping off the excess and getting to the core of an issue. "It started when I infiltrated the mansion by helping Henry, who I tried to set up with the butler—".

"You're matchmaking during a mission again?"

"Yes, dear. We can't wait for the world to be perfect before we allow ourselves to find love."

"Always the romantic," said Val, still bemused.

"It backfired," admitted Brisa. For a brief moment, she felt like she was back at home, sitting on their couch with one dog nestled behind her back and another curled up beside her, while her wife became enraptured by the messy details of the latest gossip.

"You pushed too hard?"

"No. Ok, maybe. Henry wasn't quite ready."

"And that's when he choked you with his magic powers?"

"You're not paying attention. Henry doesn't have powers. Colson does. But they're not that strong."

"They say the Awakened can conjure walls of burning tar and calm the churning seas with help from the Earth. But this guy just made some seeds sprout?"

"That's where it all gets weird."

"Walk me through it." Val adopted a more serious tone. She was ready to get to work.

"I replayed the footage that survived. During the party, the room was packed with SustainAble execs and officers from the Militia. The mic picked up jealous small talk, rumors about Lady Duggery sleeping her way up the chain of command, snide remarks about the tacky décor. Typical stuff. But before I got called over to this Dixon guy, the mic recorded a few lines about the processing power of human brains outpacing even the fastest quantum computers."

"Is that some new ecofascist talking point about their innate abilities?"

"Could be."

"They never cease to amaze, do they?"

"It's always the same idea. Anyway, later I followed Colson to the basement looking for the server farm. The other crypto valleys built them underneath the mansion where they would be most heavily guarded. But there was nothing in the basement."

"That's where Colson did his Awakened ritual?"

"I know how it sounds. Trust me. But I watched this seed grow into a snaking vine from a hole in the ground within seconds. The seeds I had eaten also began to sprout in my teeth and my belly. Then the lights went out and an earthquake struck. Both Colson and the vine fell over. It was as if the quake had been timed to prevent him from using his powers."

"Hold on. I'm looking it up." Brisa could picture Val sitting before two massive screens, her back arched in perfect posture, typing furiously as she trawled ChainBlock's databases for any possible information. "The Poconos don't get major earthquakes. The last one was back in the late twentieth century. One every few decades might be justifiable, a bit more if they're actively fracking."

"But six or seven in one day? Something feels off. There are too many coincidences."

"You think it's all connected?"

"What am I missing here? Anything on Dixon or the others?"

"I'm pulling up their files now. I see Henry Townsend. Pittsburgh. Worked for a SustainAble factory in the kitchen. Not much here. He was arrested for indecency."

"So he got caught in a raid at a gay bar."

"Yeah. And, oh! He only served one night in jail. Interesting. The records are censored, but someone got him out early. A few days later, his application to the so-called lottery was selected."

"We know the lottery is rigged. I assumed they were looking for particular skill sets to build and maintain Sediment Valley, but Henry doesn't fully fit the pattern. Most of the people I've met during our hikes and bike rides lived in relative isolation, or their extended families got separated on opposite sides of the new national borders. They don't have anyone on the outside who would come looking for them. Henry acts like a loner here, but this makes it sound like he has connections. Who do you think it was?"

"I'll look into it, but you should keep an eye on him in the meantime."

"What do you have on Colson Dagwood? He was in my files, but he's not who he says he is."

"Definitely not. He has gone from trash boy to Lady Duggery's trusted confidant. His records prior to that are practically non-existent. Either Lady Duggery's people at SustainAble scrubbed them to protect one of their own, or he assumed a fake identity to infiltrate the valley."

"I suspect the latter. He has a mission of his own. I have no idea who he might be working for, but it's not for SustainAble or the Militia."

"You'd have a better chance getting it out of him directly. I've got nothing over here."

"I'm pretty sure he was trying to murder everyone last night."

"Murder?"

"Yeah, with his magic, but it failed. I got lucky."

"You're acting awfully nonchalant."

"I wasn't his intended target. He helped me escape. If it weren't for him, I might not be calling you right now."

"I don't like this one bit, Brisa."

"It's ok. I just don't know what his deal is yet. What about Dixon?"

"Dixon, let me see. First name Mason."

"Fuck you, his name is *not* Mason Dixon."

Val just laughed and laughed. "No, silly. I'm trying to lighten the mood, because frankly, I'm not liking this scenario."

"Me neither. This is not what we planned for."

"We will figure this out. As for Dixon, I found a Gerrard Dixon who led the charge at the Levittown massacre. A lot of redacted files from the early days of the Militia. His parents held major stocks in SustainAble. Sounds like your guy. Hmmm, and there is more recent chatter about an engineering project. Some sort of renewable energy grid. The details are hazy."

Before the new information registered, Brisa felt the first tremors announcing another quake. "Val, it's starting again."

"What is?"

"The earthquakes."

"Brisa, you need to get out of—"

With no further warning, Val's signal was cut off. She was gone, their connection severed, and Brisa's awareness snapped back to her stark surroundings.

Brisa was alone in a corporate-owned valley patrolled by ecofascists.

Instead of leaving the call with a renewed sense of purpose, the isolation and danger at the heart of each mission sat in the front of her mind.

The cabin lurched side to side. Brisa braced herself and turned the satphone off and on repeatedly. She opened the blinds and held the device high in the air, even though the mountains were not to blame for the lost connection. She fiddled with every setting and ran a diagnostic test, but upon every reboot a blinking message on the screen read, "Signal Not Found."

She threw the piece of junk on the rattling bed and slammed her fist on the desk. In resignation, she shouted, "I've got to get out of here!"

The mission was no longer viable, and she risked putting herself in real danger if she stayed any longer. The best option was to report back in person and reassess the situation. She or another undercover agent could return once ChainBlock had a better idea of what they were up against.

When the shaking subsided, Brisa retrieved her go-bag from under the bed, stuffed a few extra protein bars in its side pockets, and left the front door wide open. She headed around the lake on the mulched rubber pathways toward the gated tunnel of Sediment Valley. Once beyond the security perimeter, she could reconnect with her wife and arrange for her own rescue. It would only be two days, three tops, foraging and camping in the Poconos.

No problem.

CHAPTER 9

COLSON

IF THE NIGHT HAD gone as hoped, Colson would be raising spiky vines from the depths of the Earth to bind and bury the choked bodies of his enemies. He should be setting them on fire and growing wildflowers to mark the regeneration, the new growth, the potential for expansion in a purged Sediment Valley. The staff would move his few belongings into Lady Duggery's mountaintop chambers, anointing him their new leader for having freed Sediment Valley from the malicious ploys of the Militia. People told stories of similar communities dotting the Appalachians, and he intended to build a version for himself.

Instead, he was leading the morning staff meeting as if nothing had happened. Except now he heard whispers around every corner and spied shadows whipping down corridors. He found the cleaning supplies rearranged with half the labels turned away from him. Although it was probably the fault of a sloppy staff member, his sleep-deprived brain insisted on discovering a secret sign of impending ouster or arrest.

Lady Duggery, usually a chatterbox when receiving her espresso, only reminded him to clean behind the furniture and under the rugs after the party. He had no idea if she suspected his trespasses or if she remained oblivious to the indirect attempt on her life.

She had never been his primary target. Dixon and the leaders of the Militia were. He assumed Lady Duggery would not eat during the party, meaning she would only have been witness to the horrific deaths. Though he had considered her death acceptable collateral in the grand scheme, he was relieved she was still alive. His relationship with her was complicated.

Once the staff were busied with cleaning and prepping lunch, Colson double-checked his surroundings and even spoke to the empty room to see if anyone responded. When no one did, he slipped out the sliding glass door and ran down the deck stairs into the woods.

Despite his best efforts to cultivate an escape route from the mansion, the forest undergrowth worked tirelessly to reclaim its land. He trudged over slick mosses as thorned brush scraped at his forearms. It did not matter. He would endure anything to hear Gaia's voice in his time of need.

Where did I go wrong? he asked himself on a loop.

As he hiked through the underbrush, his uncertainty morphed into paranoia. Colson felt like a target in the night, seen only out of the corner of the eye, knowing soon the light of dawn would reveal him to his hunters. He was powerless in this magicless state.

More than being caught, Colson's deepest fear was that Gaia had shaken themself free of him like a wet dog coming in from the rain. Gaia had protected him for so long. They had been the one constant since the massacre, the only friend or family in his life on the run. The loss had been so tremendous, so foundational to his sense of self, that he avoided forming new relationships for most of his teenage and adult life. Instead, he carried the memories of his family with him, and when he sought companionship, he turned to Gaia. They could be distant, communicating only through vague impressions in his mind, and unmoved by his tiny, human thoughts. But they always reappeared in the darkest hours to comfort him.

Until yesterday.

In order to infiltrate the mansion and gain Lady Duggery's trust, Colson had to befriend the enemy. Acting like a true believer in her plans had not been difficult. She was a hoot and a holler once the two of them were alone. She delivered devastating takedowns of the petty men in her social circles. She kept him dressed in the finest clothes, so he never wore the threadbare rags that rolled out of sweatshops. And she could drink him under the table during games of two truths and a lie, in which they both artfully avoided revealing anything substantial about their past or present lives. In different circumstances, they might have become inseparable and needed to convince any of Lady Duggery's suitors that Colson posed no threat to their nuptial vows. Not that Lady Duggery expressed any interest in getting married. No, she might uphold the return to traditional marriages for others, but she would never submit before any man.

For the past few years, Colson had tucked his real identity so deep within himself that he had almost become this other Colson, the gay best friend, the grateful house servant, the proof that Lady Duggery was neither racist nor homophobic. How could she be? Her best friend was both Black and gay.

The deceit had proven detrimental to his own wellbeing.

Maybe that was the problem. After so much time becoming this other person, his bonds with Gaia had weakened, or perhaps they no longer felt he deserved their power, their attention—their love. Perhaps such proximity to the enemy came at a cost. Gaia could be fickle and withholding in granting powers even in the clearest of moral scenarios, often awakening their vessels only at the eleventh hour, when all was lost.

Neither he nor the other Awakened possessed magical abilities. They were neither masters of the occult nor incorruptible stewards of unbridled power. The Awakened were Gaia's agents. Their powers, on loan in small doses. Colson liked to think of himself as a voltage converter, tampering raw volcanic power into vital streams of energy that he could direct with utmost care into the plant life around him.

Gaia could defend themself better with allies, but humans could not be trusted indefinitely. Power corrupted too easily. Comfort tempered the most ardent minds into complacency. A small token or a fictional bogeyman could suffice to turn the most desperate individuals against their own interests and communities. Had the Militia disappeared, he might have simply become this other Colson, the faithful companion to Lady Duggery. This inconvenient truth, Colson had to admit, might have cost him everything.

Colson wiped the sweat from his brow. It was another scorching spring day in Sediment Valley. The green glow cast by the canopy provided no relief. Warblers rested silently in trees, and a distant woodpecker tapped a sullen song that echoed up the ridge. Only the ferns, growing at an unusually high elevation, remained perky in this steam bath.

Inside the grotto, he could find the quiet and calm to reconnect with Gaia, to remind them he had not abandoned their plans. He was still committed to getting revenge on the Militia for their attacks, both personal and planetary. He would beg for forgiveness if he had to. This failure did not have to be the end of their relationship.

He would get Gaia back today.

A pine had fallen over the trail near the valley floor. Colson picked up his pace, planted his left hand on the trunk, and vaulted over the hurdle. *I've still got it*, he thought mid-air, feeling a slightly renewed connection to nature.

His feet hit the ground, but he slipped on the dewy foliage. He landed hard on his hip, his jaws snapping shut as his molars absorbed the shock. Mud and green gunk streaked across his new pants.

"Dammit!" he shouted, and his words echoed through the soupy air. He picked himself up and used leaves to wipe his hands. They were scraped but not bleeding. He was frustrated and losing control of his temper. He wanted to rage at the world. At himself. At all the people who had wronged him. But if he did not calm down soon, he was going to keep making errors.

Or putting someone else—Henry, in particular—in harm's way. *That cute idiot almost got himself killed.* Colson's rib cage tightened around his lungs as he stepped into a clearing. *Why did he come back? And with that tray of cookies. I couldn't have served that. Lady Duggery would have fired me on the spot for such a paltry display.*

He gritted his teeth but had to relax his jaw. It was still sore. He took a deep breath.

I know he meant well. He was so timid and flustered. And I was such a dick to him. "Get the fuck out of here!" *Why did I say it like that? I was too harsh. But I had to get him out of there. I had no other choice. If I hadn't been so mean, he might not have gotten far enough away.*

Colson arrived at the sinkhole near the eastern border of the valley. In the distance, the river spread out, diving into underground tunnels and tumbling over shale shelves that led to a steep cataract. The Militia quickly fashioned a steel cage patrolled by drones to deter anyone who thought they might follow the river to freedom. Colson doubted the quality of the

Militia's work. He convinced himself he could slip through the security perimeter if he put his mind to it.

Before he made any decisions about whether to walk away or stay and fight, he would call out to Gaia one last time.

CHAPTER 10

BRISA

"A QUICK TWO-DAY TRIP," she told the guard stationed at the westernmost edge of the valley. They stood at a military barricade on an elevated highway that burrowed through the mountain. Stone arches limned the gated entrance, and subway tiles covered the tunnel walls. She squinted but could not glimpse daylight from the other side of the misty, evergreen mountain. "My mother is ill."

"Wait here," said the guard. The glare reflecting off his helmet left an imprint in her vision. He consulted with another guard, who shrugged, before calling his superior.

It wasn't a lie, Brisa reminded herself while waiting. Her mother had been ill, but her mother also told her to never visit again. She had accepted that Brisa was a lesbian. That had never been an issue. Val had been invited to every family gathering and even earned her mother-in-law's trust to lend a hand in the kitchen. But when her mother intuited Brisa had been involved in an explosion at a SustainAble plant, she turned her back on her child.

Brisa thought of her actions as victimless crimes, working to take down the predatory systems that had devasted so many regions in the wake of natural disasters. Puerto Rico had been one of the testing grounds for the crypto bros who went on to invest in corporations like SustainAble. They called themselves the Puertopians. They promised jobs, modernization, and prosperity—disruption. In return, they demanded tax exemptions and priority use of the island's taxpayer-funded electric grids, which relied on imported fuel, to power their server farms. They drained the sun-soaked island of its resources and hopped on their jets whenever the slightest breeze mussed their unruly hair.

Over the next few decades, SustainAble perfected the Puertopian model and implemented it wherever a natural disaster struck, filling in for the federal government after the collapse of the United States. While the citizens mourned their losses and picked through the rubble, SustainAble rewrote the tax code and bought up land on the cheap with lightning speed. By the time the dust settled, entire communities had been ransacked, public education systems defunded, and infrastructure privatized. People's only option would be to work for the new corporate master in town.

ChainBlock, where Brisa and Val worked, had been established to target any organization that relied on cryptocurrency. It originated in Central America around the time El Salvador adopted bitcoin as a national currency alongside the dollar. When ChainBlock's public efforts failed to convince the Bukele administration to repeal the new finance laws, they went underground in fear of retaliation.

Over the following decades, ChainBlock went international and grew by accepting funding from diverse stakeholders who saw in crypto a common enemy. The International Socialist Party and Greenpeace, despite some internal divisions, both publicly stated opposition to all cryptocurrencies due to their reliance on coal-powered energy grids. Meanwhile, the International Monetary Fund hedged its bets. With one arm, they funded clandestine groups to destabilize emerging crypto farms throughout the Global South, because they feared losing the iron grip they had secured over those economies during the anti-democratic coups of the last century. With the other, the IMF shored up their own reserves of major crypto currencies, seeking to regulate, or at least own, as much of the decentralized infrastructure as possible. ChainBlock also counted on private donors, some committed to the cause of banning cryptocurrency, others looking to greenwash their business practices through charitable donations.

Brisa and Val often reminded one another that ChainBlock was not a perfect organization. But they agreed that its leaders put that dubiously sourced cash to good use. She and Val saw the work as a needed countermeasure to the hidden violence on which crypto depended.

Brisa's mother, however, only saw the spectacular explosion at the plant where her second husband had earned not only a living, but also the retirement plan that paid for her doctor's visits.

"I'm sorry, miss," said the guard as he walked toward her. "We are under strict orders not to allow anyone passage through this gate today."

"I'm sure you can make an exception, Mister— what's your name?" Brisa's expression remained inscrutable, but underneath her façade the tension was rising. She knew of no other way out. If she tried to scale the mountains and cross the security perimeter, she would be pursued as a runaway. Her escape plan of hiking through the Poconos until she reached a suitable extraction point did not include countermeasures to evade Militia drones.

"No exceptions. Return to your quarters," he said sternly. Then, he leaned in, placed his hand on her waist, causing her to recoil, and whispered in her ear. "Be careful." Then he stepped back and shifted the reflective gaze of his helmet to the valley in the distance.

Brisa stood there, dazed, as the words sank in. She had no choice but to turn around. She was trapped in Sediment Valley with no way home.

Chapter II

Henry

Next to the workbench on the side of Henry's house, a long mirror leaned against the exterior wall. Henry stooped down, holding strips of faux leather against his chest, and draped them over his shoulders. He could barter for anything with a half dozen cupcakes. He was crafting a harness with a retractable leash that he could clip to anchors on the wall or tie around the bed or any post. He was stuck on this rickety rollercoaster for the foreseeable future, so he might as well strap himself in for the ride.

As he worked, sunlight filtered through the blooming dogwoods. He kept his back turned toward the neighbor's children, but in the mirror, he caught glimpses of them playing king of the hill in their sandbox. The littlest one, what was he, five, eight, ten? Henry could never tell how old. Kids were a mystery to him, even when he had been one. The little rascal had worked his way into the center, and he staved off sustained attacks from all three of his siblings. He kept his center of gravity low and dodged as they rushed him from all sides, crashing into one another instead. He let them wear themselves out while barely expending any energy of his own.

The little fellow was lithe and clever. The kid would not be deterred by the tremors. He wouldn't remember a world other than this one, and he was training from the start to ride out the waves while fending off aggressors. In another era, he might have gone on to Olympic fame, or more likely, to steer a hedge fund through the wild swings of the crypto markets. In this era, he'd probably rise through the ranks of the Militia and one day issue orders to Henry and the other old folks stumbling around and daydreaming of a world in which the ground never shook.

Henry envied that kid.

"Dammit." The tip of the utility blade lodged itself in his fingernail. It stung when he pulled it out, but it wasn't bleeding. He needed to pay attention. He measured and cut the straps of his harness, double- and triple-checking in the mirror each time.

He did feel somewhat selfish. Instead of cleaning up the debris from the past twelve hours at the various lakeside cabins, here he was fashioning a safety net for himself. Hadn't the rule been to secure your own oxygen mask before helping others?

Across the lake, Militia guards inspected a tree that had fallen on one of the refurbished campers, smashing the solar panels to bits. A few cabins had broken windowpanes and cracked sidewalks. Most of the swan paddle boats bobbed in the middle of the lake, but the coveted green dragon remained tied to its port.

His neighbors talked about greater damage to the auto-fertilizers and irrigation systems on the other side of the Square. Apparently, all the shops remained intact, and the electrical grid still lit everything up. He took their word for it. Even if he had a mess to clean up, the bakery would still be standing, and his ingredients kept fresh. He would attend to that later today.

Luckily, no one had been seriously injured.

As he worked, Lady Duggery continued to push notifications to him and his fellow residents. She made suggestions to stave off further property damage and circulated a priority list for repairs. His neighbors had woken early to tidy their surroundings before heading off to the fields, while he worked diligently on his harness. He hoped his benefactor would not learn of his minor trespasses.

Sweat formed on his brow on this cloudless morning. He punched holes and hammered grommets in between bites of cookies and day-old pastries. He had needed something to soak up the sunrise shots. By the time the neighbor's kids were called in for lunch, Henry was ready to try on the harness over his t-shirt.

He stooped once more before the mirror. In the front, narrow diagonal straps crossed his chest and were joined by a metal ring. Other straps fit snug over his shoulders and around his sides, meeting in the back. He gave it a tug. It held up, so he yanked a bit harder. It was a little tight, especially if he were to wear it over his apron, but he could adjust that. He turned side to side in the mirror to see the back. It looked good. Better proportioned to his slender frame than the one he had tried on back in Pittsburgh. The faux leather harness would be his private homage to what was—and to what could have been.

Henry caught his own smile reflecting back at him. It made him feel more confident, powerful even. He liked it so much he ignored the judgmental glare of his neighbor also staring at him in the mirror from her front porch. He paid her no mind when she slammed the door and drew the blinds.

For the time being, he clipped into the retractable leash anchored on the workbench. He took a few steps forward, getting a feel for the tension. It would take some getting used to. Even standing still required him to brace against the ground. Then he let it pull him backwards and hold him steady against the workbench. It was the closest thing to a heroic hand reaching out to grab his forearm and pull him to safety as he tumbled into a pit of despair.

Maybe a few little quakes would not be so bad. Henry was ready to ride out the future all on his own. With a little effort, he could turn this place around.

CHAPTER 12

COLSON

THE OPENING OF THE grotto was the size of an above ground swimming pool. Colson had visited only once before. When he first arrived in Sediment Valley, he sought Gaia's advice here for gaining Lady Duggery's trust.

That was what didn't make any sense. Gaia helped him develop his plans. The more his rational brain edged out his paranoia, the more Gaia's silence befuddled him.

He dangled his legs over the side of the grotto and hopped down onto a large stone that formed a natural staircase. The impact bothered his hip from the tumble earlier. He took care not to slip and fall again as he scrambled down the cool, rocky ledges. If he broke a foot down here, there would be no way out.

At the sandy base of the sink hole, the scent of wet clay permeated the air. Layers of shale fanned out above his head. They formed a natural dome over much of the grotto, many times larger than what it appeared from above. A sunbeam pierced the cavernous darkness. Fuzzy dandelion seeds danced in the ray that lighted up an outcropping. It held space like an ancient altar. Water trickled over the ledge and pooled near the center of the sink hole. Purple and white wildflowers blossomed near the miniature pond. In another age, honeybees might have swept up the sweet pollen on their tiny bodies while croaking toads bellyflopped in the clear waters. But even in their absence, the grotto remained a sight for weary eyes.

Colson took a seat on one of the flatter stones and crossed his legs. He closed his eyes, turned his head toward the light, and rested his stinging palms on the rock. He inhaled the damp air and unbottled the memory of his first encounter with Gaia.

Colson was ten years old. He had been hanging upside down from the jungle gym in a park near his house when the first shots rang out. It was dusk, and the other kids had already run home for dinner, but he enjoyed being the last to leave, pretending to rule the playground in their absence.

As the gun shots grew closer, he dropped from the jungle gym. He fought against his disorientation to crawl through the triangular holes in the cheerful metal dome. He hid behind the public bathroom. He leaned against the exterior wall that faced a small wooden patch of land. The older kids usually claimed the space to smoke or explore their bodies. Here he felt out of place and far from home.

He slid to the ground and tucked his knees to his chest. A series of explosions reverberated for minutes—or for hours, he could not tell. Time held no meaning in the apocalypse. The screams of children and adults alike were silenced by gunshot. He pulled his shirt across his mouth to stop himself from choking too loudly on sulfurous smoke and gasoline fumes.

Three or four of the attackers spread out across the playground in search of survivors. Colson gripped the soil with his fingers to ground him in his final moments. He clung to the earth. As he dug deeper, green shoots pushed through the dirt around him. Their tendrils waved through the air, searching, until they tapped his ankles and shoelaces. Then the vines pulsed, and a dense thicket sprung from the dirt. It enclosed him in a thorny bubble of fresh growth. *Am I dead? Is this what the afterlife looks like?* He could not comprehend his new reality.

A voice, deep and geologic, comforted him.

I'm here. To mend.

He focused on those words as a surge in energy flowed through his fingers, up his arms, and across his nervous system. When it reached that space behind his eyes, he blacked out.

He awoke sometime later still tucked inside the verdant bubble that shielded him from the bloodshed.

Wake. Leave now.

The stony voice spoke in his mind.

He was sore and wiped dried blood from his brow. The rigid branches parted at his touch like seaweed in the current. Gaia guided him to safety far from the smoldering ruins.

As far as he knew, no one else had been saved by Gaia the day a mob of angry white men stormed his hometown and torched it, claiming to retake Levittown from the Black transplants who "invaded" it generations ago. No one survived. Not his parents. Not his neighbors or his friends. Not his aunts or cousins, nor the handful of white families who stood in the Militia's way.

He never asked why Gaia had chosen him, too afraid that it had all been an accident, a wasted effort, a salvation meant for another more deserving than he. Afraid to be abandoned again, Colson pledged to Gaia he would seek vengeance at any cost.

Sitting atop the altar in the grotto, tears streaming down his face, Colson repeated this promise to Gaia.

This time there was no answer.

In the silence, he tried to contain his grief, to bury it deep underground. He imagined himself drying and hardening, as the living pain in his limbs and the pressure in his chest drained into dirt and pebbles, into ridges and tectonic plates, as he became impervious to human forces and emotions.

Only the stars could alter his course now. Only dark matter could penetrate his calcifying bones.

Colson released the tension in his body as he drew inward, crunching, cracking, and petrifying until his identity faded away and he became an extension of the altar.

An emptiness surrounded him, became him. Neither alone nor feeling—he was blissful stone.

In this void, as the void, he summoned a wisp of consciousness, a slim, snaking, vine-like thought. Created to invoke the forces of Gaia that had once protected him, it had flowed so many times through his hands and into fallow, contaminated soil. He had been capable of bringing forth life from any seed and protecting it until it flourished as flowers, fruits, vegetables—as sustenance for those in need.

His thought vine extended into a staticky region crackling like power lines. He hoped it was Gaia. It had to be. As he felt around, a familiar force buzzed through the tip of his probing vine. The static amplified, almost humming, into a sizzling bundle of energy. He pushed further into the region, and Gaia's forces vibrated at an ever-increasing frequency as if building toward release.

Gaia felt so close yet so far away. It had never been this difficult to find them, not in times as desperate as these.

Colson reached out again. Something tickled him. He thought he had found them. Without warning, the bundle yanked away, becoming a point of light that streaked before him until it disappeared altogether.

In its wake, his tentacle writhed alone within a pit-shaped nothingness, an inverted staircase sheathed by impenetrable walls, a well that deepened as the water drained from below. That stony voice grating in the back of his mind, who guided him toward Sediment Valley, his only reliable companion in years, had fled.

Once, they had encouraged revenge. Their voice supported him, held him together, offered him a way forward though the grief, the flashbacks, the terror. But now in his time of need, Gaia abandoned him.

Colson felt the isolation and rage rippling through his solidified body, almost as if he were back there, in the aftermath of the assault, as furiously impotent as he had been at the age of ten. Except now he could no longer bury his emotions. He became as brittle as the surrounding shale. His neck threatened to shear along a horizontal plane. A single gust of wind could have eroded his crumbling knees within seconds. Directionless and angry, he felt like a total failure, unwanted by all and deserving of no one, adrift in the void.

The last time Colson felt this despondent was when he had returned to his former hometown. It still laid in ruins. The waters of the Delaware River had been on the rise, and the whiplash the region experienced when summer-long droughts were followed by churning hurricanes meant even the families who spent decades fantasizing about re-segregating their town were unwilling to rebuild.

In the end, it had not mattered to those in the Militia. They got their long-awaited reckoning, and they rode the wave of that first assault to regional power as the state of Pennsylvania fractured. Philadelphia and some of the suburbs joined the Coastal Republic of America, while the rest of the state, including Pittsburgh after the siege, fell under the control of the Militia. They allied themselves with the Midwestern Federation, wagering that the legislative leadership in Michigan and Wisconsin would pay little attention to what took place east of the Ohio River. If they did, the Militia would not hesitate to break their ties.

As Colson's mind spiraled, a visage rose from the void to greet him.

Colson saw Henry's face. His round, clean-shaven cheeks. The burgeoning stripe of silver in his wavy hair. The timid twinkle in his eye. The way his entire face flushed when Colson had placed a hand on his shoulder.

For a moment, Colson's rock-heavy body drifted weightless; his disjointed spirit felt grounded, tethered to another person in this forsaken valley.

Then Henry's face flickered with the image of another man whose features were all too familiar. An angry, rabid face he had glimpsed from within Gaia's shield in Levittown. Its mouth opened wide, shouting obscenities, as it lurched past him.

Colson returned the insults, but the face flickered again. Henry's expression drooped like a sad puppy as Colson called him a back-country moron—an insult intended for the other man. Before Henry could run away, he coughed, and his eyes widened into a panic. Struggling to breathe, he clawed at his throat. The pink rush of anticipation shifted to blue as the oxygen drained from his cheeks. Sprouts burst from his nostrils, and new growth crawled like snakes across his tongue.

Colson saw Henry's face, fearful, begging for answers and salvation. The corners of his mouth split open as the stalks grew thicker and red poppies bloomed in place of blood from every wound.

The gory vision of Henry's face, frozen in death, sank into the void.

Colson ripped himself away from that emptiest of places and returned to the reality of the grotto. He lifted his tingling hands from the unfeeling stone and pulled his legs into his chest. He sobbed with his head between his knees, rocking in the patch of sun. His body trembled even as the ground remained still.

But no vines rose to shield him. No stony voice reached out.

After a moment, he took a deep breath to temper the explosion of grief, and he wiped his nose on his sleeve to recompose himself.

There were a few things that Colson now knew. First, he could not count on Gaia moving forward. Second, he could not continue to work alone. Third, he needed to apologize to Henry and tell him the truth. Or at least some of the truth. Maybe Henry could forgive him.

Colson slowly gathered himself atop the altar and hopped off. He would visit the bakery as a first step toward making amends. Only after could he begin to chart a new course.

Chapter 13

Brisa

Brisa meandered on the long walk back to the lake.

She took deep breaths of the fresh mountain air to keep herself from hyperventilating. She had no satphone connection to request an emergency extraction. No back-up at all. Not even the comfort of hearing her wife tell her it would all be ok. Brisa was not one to wallow, but Sediment Valley was pushing her to her limits.

I will find a way through, she repeated to herself. Maybe if she said it enough times, she would believe it.

As the lake came into view, Brisa sat on a rock to formulate her next steps. A squirrel crossed her path. "This place is unbelievable," she said to the little guy. "What I would give to switch places with you."

The squirrel cocked its fuzzy head to the side. She leaned down and opened her hand to call it over. It took a hesitant leap in her direction, paused, looked around, and then hopped even closer. Brisa reached out and gently rubbed the space between its ears. She missed her dogs so much, and if she didn't think too hard, he made for a decent stand-in. He even made her regret all those times she encouraged her pups to chase them through the woods.

The squirrel nuzzled her hand, but something caught its attention. Brisa looked for a hawk in the clear blue skies. There was not a cloud to be found. The squirrel squeaked—as if in distress, she thought—though maybe she was projecting her emotions onto it.

Out of the blue, a high-pitched shriek echoed across the lake. Then metal grated against stone. One sound was as shrill as the next.

Brisa instinctively ran toward the danger, while her squirrel friend darted into the underbrush. After a few steps, she reconsidered and followed the critter toward saplings lining the trail. She could approach the danger, but it was in her best interest to lie low. Before she got close enough to see what caused the commotion, a second, blood-curdling scream was quickly muffled, followed by a small, rumbling tremor. The person in distress was very near her own cabin.

Brisa's relief at seeing four guards standing around her neighbor's porch, instead of her own, soon gave way. Dixon was kneeling over a body lying in the grass. At first glance, she thought he was holding a sledgehammer in both hands. She immediately recognized the bleached blonde hair.

The woman lying on the ground was Calla.

Brisa's expression turned blank. She looked away, fearful of spotting a pool of blood, and slowed her approach. Her head suddenly thumped. She needed to hang back. She stepped into the shadows. There were too many variables at play right now.

A wave of guilt washed over her. She reprimanded herself for not warning Calla to stay away from Dixon when she had fawned over him at the party last night. That man oozed with poison. Yet Brisa practically encouraged Calla to pursue him just to distract from her own agenda. She smiled as Calla skipped toward the viper's nest and then left her to fend for herself.

In the back of her mind, her mother's voice asked what had become of her baby girl.

Her behavior was reprehensible. And not unlike the way Henry had left her unconscious after the first quake. The realization stung.

She tried to release the tension around her temples and in her shoulders. This was not the ideal time to reprimand herself. She needed to do something.

When she looked back at the scene of the attack, Dixon's hands were now empty, and he was tucking a necklace inside his shirt. The sledgehammer was gone. Not resting on the ground or passed to one of the guards for safekeeping. But vanished. Nowhere to be seen.

Had she imagined it? She was out of sorts, but this was beyond explanation.

A distant voice called her name from the water's edge.

"Brisa, you're ok," shouted Henry. He was panting, dragging a faded green plastic dragon paddle boat to shore while wearing a harness over his t-shirt.

She shook her head in disbelief. *I didn't think he'd be into that. The quiet ones always surprise you.* The image silenced her shame spiral.

Henry was dripping from the waist down and running on pure adrenaline. "I came as soon as I saw Dixon marching toward the cabins. What happened?" He mumbled the final words as he caught sight of Calla's body being lifted onto a stretcher by the guards.

Brisa thought he might cause a scene, so she pulled him behind the nearest cabin to evade Dixon's attention.

"I'm as confused as you," she said. Her voice was stern. "Why are you here?"

Henry blushed. "I don't know. I just sort of reacted." He looked back at Calla. "Oh, she comes into the bakery. What's her name?"

Typical Henry. He'd lived here for months, but he barely knew who anyone was. "Calla. She works with Colson." *Damnit,* she thought, *why'd you have to mention Colson right now?* Henry could be so skittish. Bringing up last night's embarrassing moment in the kitchen just might send him running away again.

He turned his head from her momentarily and gathered his thoughts. They spoke in hushed tones. "I'm sorry I left you yesterday. I did make sure you were breathing, and I asked the guards to check on you."

Like that makes it any better, she thought. She could be mad at him, even if she hadn't behaved much better. "Let's not worry about that now," she said. "There are too many oddities taking place here. I'm probably going to regret this, but right now I need an ally."

"You can trust me," he said, as if he had not expected her to doubt his character. "Are you hearing that voice, too?"

"Voice?" Brisa had to clasp her hands over her mouth to stifle her outburst. Quieter she said, "What do you mean you're hearing voices?"

"Just before the first earthquake yesterday. I got this electric tingling in my toes, and a disembodied voice called out to me, saying, 'Henry, help me.' Or something like that. I don't know. The words weren't fully formed. More like the sensation of words in my mind?" He remained calm and steady as he spoke, not nervous like he had been the day before. Brisa felt certain he was telling the truth. He continued. "Just now, as I crossed the lake, I heard it again. It told me to save the girl. The words sputtered like water in hot grease. I assumed it was talking about you."

Brisa sighed. She did not need a white knight to rescue her, and frankly, she was surprised Henry, of all people, would be this concerned about her or anyone else.

"I wouldn't believe me either if I were you," he admitted. He looked despondent.

"You know, any other day, I'd suggest you find a therapist. But something is going on here. They've blocked all external communications. Locked down the tunnel. No one can come or go. Lady Duggery never explained why there were suddenly ongoing earthquakes. And I don't want to rub salt in open wounds, but I saw Colson attempting some sort of ritual in the basement during the party."

"You were at the party?"

"Yeah, Henry. I'm not who you think I am."

"Then who are you?"

"I can't believe I'm saying this, but you've caught me at a tricky crossroads. Have you heard of ChainBlock?"

He shook his head.

"Let's just say, I've been surveying SustainAble's fake utopian settlements. There are three of them so far, and the first two were simple, in-and-out jobs. I was looking for the server farm in the mansion last night."

"It wasn't a coincidence that you ran into me?"

"No, I planned that," she admitted. He was less oblivious that she had assumed. "I'm sorry for tricking you. I truly am. But this is serious stuff. I never imagined anything like what's been going on."

"I guess we're both sorry." Henry laughed uncomfortably. "What kind of stuff?"

"Usually, these settlements are easy to infiltrate. The local leaders leave gaping holes in their security perimeters, and the energy grids are wildly obvious to chart. The reality is that these locals have nothing to hide. The Midwestern Federation, though technically overseeing Pennsylvania as well, has a hard time mounting serious control east of the Ohio River. The Militia is the de facto force of law in these parts, and they have no objections to mining, be it coal, shale, or crypto, nor to these walled-in lifeboats being built for the wealthy to weather the worst of the climate crisis. All I needed was to pinpoint the locations of the underground data centers in each of the corporate towns, set up some back doors for easy access, and then my organization would begin their assault."

"But all of these people would be cast back out into the world. Why would you do that?"

The righteousness almost exploded from her. She was sick and tired of people doubting her intentions, especially those too near-sighted to understand the issue was bigger than their own personal sense of security.

"Because SustainAble is actively making the planet worse," she said tersely. "They are the reason you were displaced to begin with. You're from Pittsburgh, right?"

"I didn't grow up there, but yeah. How'd you know?"

"We have files on almost everyone here."

Henry's eyes bulged at the revelation. He seemed so naïve to her, despite the streak of grey in his wavy hair.

"I know," she said, admitting the invasion of privacy. "Look, SustainAble is the reason Pittsburgh remains a charred husk. They own every block, every local politician, every school, and every workplace. They have a stranglehold on that city, and so many others like it."

"And you're going to stop them?"

"I'm trying."

"What happens when you succeed? Where do all these people go?"

"We'll figure that out when the time comes."

Henry raised his eyebrows. He seemed suspicious. "What about the voice?"

"Maybe you're becoming one of the Awakened," said Brisa as a joke.

"That crap? Come on, you don't believe in that."

"I didn't," she said. The echo of her conversation with Val interrupted her train of thought. She could not think of Val right now, or she would lose in her struggle against a full-blown panic attack.

"I'll distract them," said Henry. "You can sneak closer and figure out where they're taking Calla."

Before she could consider the implications of this plan, Henry ran toward the dragon boat.

"Stop right there," said one of the guards.

Henry stopped in his tracks. "Is she alright?" He pointed to Calla.

"What does it look like?" replied the guard through the speakers in his helmet. "Hey boss, check out this pervert."

Brisa ducked behind a flowering shrub.

"On your way to a naughty little afternoon delight, are we?" asked Dixon.

Brisa could not see any of them, but she imagined Henry becoming suddenly aware of the harness he was wearing in broad daylight while climbing into a child's paddle boat. He had seemed uncharacteristically confident, triumphant really, when he first approached her, but she suspected Dixon was about to burst Henry's bubble. She quickly snuck behind her own cabin and across the unkempt lawn toward Calla's.

"No, I just—"

"Go home, pedo. And keep that smut indoors," said Dixon, dismissing him.

Once more, Brisa had used a mostly innocent bystander as her shield. Henry was lucky Dixon didn't take him out as well. He got away with a bruised ego, but Calla, poor Calla. This was getting ugly. Two of the guards lifted the stretcher from the ground, but Calla's chest still rose and fell. *Please be ok*, she said to herself.

Brisa had crossed a line today. She had justified her actions because she had not been part of this community. These were not her people. In the end, she would be saving them, too. Or so she told herself. But now she was stuck here. She had gotten to know some of them. She could not carry on with such reckless abandon and come out the other side of this, if there was going to be another side of this, with her sense of justice intact.

Once Dixon gave the orders to march, Brisa took meticulous pains to track them. She would follow them anywhere. She had to get Calla back and find a way to stop Dixon from ever doing anything like this again.

CHAPTER 14

COLSON

COLSON WAS ALMOST TO the top of the grotto when the lock-step march of Militia guards resounded in the distance. He craned his neck and, though the foliage, four guards approached, carrying a stretcher. Behind them Agent Dixon barked orders. It was too late to climb out and run away, so he retreated to the sandy floor and sought a hiding spot behind a rock among the shadows.

Two of the helmeted guards scrambled down the grotto walls, while the other two lowered the stretcher through the opening with a hastily assembled pulley system. As it descended, the victim's face became illuminated in the sunbeam. Colson sneaked a look. He recognized the young woman. She worked for him, he realized, in the kitchen. *She must be new*, he told himself. This was no time to confront his narrowminded pursuit of vengeance.

"Faster!" ordered Dixon. "She's unconscious. No need to be gentle."

Obediently, the guards above allowed her to plummet the final feet toward the grotto floor. They stopped it abruptly, mere inches above the ground, and the body almost tumbled out of the stretcher. One of the guards below repositioned her, while Dixon and the two guards above climbed down.

Colson feared for what these five men planned to do to an unconscious woman in this sacred space. He prepared to rush them, but he considered the odds. Five to one, and all of them had tasers and nightsticks, while he was unarmed and, quite literally, powerless. He had no way of stopping them, but he considered whether it would be better to try and fail or to do nothing at all. The first scenario resulted in him bloodied, imprisoned, or dead; the second, riddled with the crushing guilt of having allowed this grotesque scene to play out with no resistance.

For better or for worse, Colson chose to stay hidden among the shadows.

Meanwhile, Dixon stepped into the light and fiddled with a chain around his neck. He revealed an amulet that, to Colson's eyes, appeared to drain the sunbeam of all warmth. Colson's arm reached out toward the gemstone involuntarily. Something in that stone attracted the very fiber of his being. His fingers snaked up and over the jagged rock that shielded him, even though he risked being seen by one of the guards. Only when Dixon enclosed the amulet in his fist did Colson yank his hand back into the shadows.

The ground beneath Dixon's boots compressed with a low thud. He hunched over somewhat, as if straining against gravity to remain fully erect, and he bent his knees for stability. He placed his hands on the stone altar, braced himself with one foot in front of the other, and slowly pushed the boulder to the side with extra-human strength. A stairwell opened where the altar had once sat, and the five men climbed further underground carrying the woman they had captured.

Colson's eyes about popped from his head. He instinctively recognized that sort of power because it was the power he once possessed. But he could not reach it any more than he could reach that electrified bundle deep in meditation. *Dixon should not have access to Gaia's power*, thought Colson. Everything about the scenario felt wrong. Dixon commanded an authoritarian militia that used the climate crisis to overthrow democratic institutions. The Gaia Colson knew would never allow an officer in the Militia to become one of the Awakened.

Once they were gone, Colson ran to the secret stairwell. Staring into the depths, doubt ate at Colson's beliefs like root rot on a waterlogged plant. *Is Gaia now siding with the ecofascists? Have they become so desperate that they could fall for the Militia's greenwashed propaganda?* It made no sense at all. Then again, there was something about that gemstone. And he had no idea how that woman's body fit into it all.

Before he could gather his thoughts, a hand landed on his shoulder. He jumped, spun around, and almost fell backward into the stairwell. "You almost gave me heart attack," he said to Brisa, who had snuck up on him inexplicably.

"You never seem to notice me," she said with a smirk.

"Ouch," said Colson. "You got me there." He had deserved that. He had not been subtle in his lack of concern for her when she was the unconscious woman lying nearby. His behaviors formed an unflattering pattern.

"Did they take Calla down there?" asked Brisa.

Calla. That was her name, thought Colson. He felt terrible. Brisa had a way of shining a light on his selfishness that made him want to slink away. At the same time, her resoluteness showed him another way to be in the world. She made him want to do better. "Yes, Dixon took her. What are they going to do with her down there?"

"I was hoping you could answer that, since you seem to know a lot more about what is going on in this valley than I do. What were you even doing here?"

He didn't know if it was because of his spate of failures or because he could not imagine going one more second alone through this world, but he desired nothing more than to explain everything to Brisa. He no longer cared if she was here to trick him. He had to risk telling another living being what he knew if he wanted to save Calla and shut down whatever Dixon, the others, and maybe even Gaia, were up to.

Colson revealed everything he had learned so far to Brisa as they climbed out of the grotto and retreated into the nearby tree line. He explained the origin of his now-missing powers to grow plant life at will and how he had planned to use those powers to get revenge on the Militia. He even admitted his concern that Gaia had abandoned them all after seeing Dixon reveal the stairwell with the amulet.

Brisa knitted her brow.

"You don't believe me about the magic part, do you?" he asked.

For once Brisa did not have a quick retort. She hesitated. "I'm . . . struggling with that to be honest. I always assumed the Awakened thing was a massive hoax. A collective hallucination in a rapidly changing world. But I'm open to the idea. There are things happening here that remain beyond my understanding."

"That's fair. Tell me then, what are you doing here?"

Brisa revealed her work with ChainBlock to destabilize SustainAble's crypto servers, which towns like Sediment Valley were being used to hide. It turned out that SustainAble and the Militia were inextricably linked. Taking down only one or the other would not solve either of their problems.

"I have to admit the whole crypto thing always sounded like magic to me," said Colson.

"More like a high-tech parlor trick," said Brisa. "Blockchain technology is used primarily to create vast sums of wealth through exploitation. It funds authoritarian regimes, human trafficking rings, the worst of human desires, while burning through fossil fuels at an unprecedented rate. Only AI servers rival its overconsumption of energy. The problem is that understanding how crypto works requires a deep dive into esoteric jargon that drives people to boredom long before they make sense of it. At the same time, its apologists flood the media with dumbed-down arguments about all the grey areas, all the potentially utopian uses this new tech could usher into the world. They sow just enough doubt to allow the majority of people to turn a cheek."

"It's a clever trick. I wonder why you were never chosen to be one of the Awakened," said Colson. "Then again, sounds like you haven't needed much help."

"Sounds to me like neither of us have."

"That's where we both went wrong, huh?"

"I see that now," said Brisa. "But there's something I don't buy."

"I'm not making up the magic powers. They're real."

"Not that," she said, shaking her head. "The bit about Gaia. There's no way they sided with the Militia. You said something about an amulet?"

"He wears it as a necklace. It radiated an energy that felt like Gaia just before he pushed the stone altar away."

"I thought my eyes were playing tricks on me earlier today. I thought he was holding a sledgehammer that disappeared. Now I'm thinking it's part of his powers."

She looked directly at Colson with a compassion and understanding he hadn't experienced in years, since he was accustomed to treating everyone like a potential threat to his mission. He met her warmth with a genuine smile, a first step toward their tentative partnership.

They might have hugged in the green glow of the canopy, if not for the sound of rustling foliage in the still air. Brisa pulled Colson to the ground.

"What's she doing here?" whispered Colson.

Brisa did not respond. She fixed her gaze on Lady Duggery who glided toward the edge of the grotto's opening and, without slowing down, hopped off the ledge. Colson instinctively stood as if to catch her. There had been no need. Lady Duggery soared above the opening. Like a ballerina leaping with her legs unbelievably extended, she appeared to hang in the air for a moment. Colson thought his eyes were playing tricks on him. Yet, Lady Duggery did not fall. She drifted gently downward and disappeared into the grotto.

"There's no more denying it then," said Brisa with a deadpan tone and wide, horrorstruck eyes.

"She shouldn't be able to do that," said Colson, equally in disbelief.

"No she should not."

"Do you think she has an amulet, too?"

"Seems likely."

"We've got to do something."

"I agree," said Brisa. "But there's no good way for us to infiltrate whatever they have down there. It's too dangerous. We don't know enough, and if we fuck this up, Calla could be lost forever. Let's get back before we get caught here and see what we can figure out in the coming days."

Colson agreed to contact Brisa the minute he found anything new. They shook hands, walked together for a bit, and then parted, returning to the separate paths that had led them to their unexpected encounter in the grotto.

CHAPTER 15

HENRY

THE SHOP BELL CHIMED while Henry wrapped his spiraling thoughts into the meticulously even swirls of cinnamon, sugar, and melted margarine. After the electrifying encounter with Dixon and the guards, he scurried back but kept his harness strapped tight around his chest. He wasn't sure where that show of bravado had come from, but it had been both exhilarating and terrifying.

"I'll be right out," he shouted with his back still to the door. He hoped it was Brisa, safe and sound, with some good news. He placed the baking sheet in the roaring oven and wiped the sweat from his brow.

"Do I smell cinnamon rolls?" asked a familiar voice.

Henry whipped around, shocked to find Colson hovering over the refrigerated display case. He scanned rows of the infamous gingersnap cookies, cupcakes decorated with the colors of the Militia, and homemade bear claws. Colson was the last person Henry expected to see today. Henry stumbled as his harness yanked him away from the oven and toward the middle of the kitchen. He was not used to the added tension.

"How can I help you?" He used his formal shopkeeper tone, an octave lower than normal. Earlier, he kept his head high in the face of Agent Dixon's insults, but he could not bear to look directly at Colson after being so publicly shamed.

"Henry. How are you?" replied Colson, delightfully.

"Fine, thanks. What can I get for you?"

"I was hoping we could talk."

"I'm pretty busy," he said and gestured to the pile of dishes in the bubbling sink.

"About last night, at the mansion."

Henry studied the faux Formica countertop and fiddled with the perfectly arranged boxes of assorted chocolates. This was a conversation he did not want to have. The wounds were too fresh. He was still embarrassed and preferred to retreat into his shell.

"It's ok. Really." Henry hoped to avoid further conflict.

"No, it's not. I wasn't being myself last night. Or, I was, but that's not an excuse. I came to say I'm sorry."

Henry kept his head down. He had a chance to turn the tables, to launch a thousand insults, to send Colson running for cover. But all he managed to eke out was a quiet "Ok."

"It wasn't anything you did. I should have been grateful to you. That cake you made—it was stunning. I've never seen anything like it."

That still didn't explain the sudden outburst. Henry had left the mansion humiliated, unable to figure out where he had gone wrong, what he had said or done to offend Colson. "You only saw it smashed on the ground."

"That mini mansion held perfectly together. You couldn't have predicted it needed to withstand an earthquake."

"You do try to reinforce show pieces, so nothing falls off halfway through a dinner party." He cautiously met Colson's eyes as he explained the technicalities of his craft. He could talk about baking forever.

"The cookies were delicious, too."

Henry's stomach sank again. He ran his fingers around the edges of the cashier's tablet. Neon blue light raced around the edges, and static hummed in the space between glass and flesh. The screen lit up, anticipating an exchange.

"I wanted to explain—" As he started to speak, Henry cut him off.

"We're closing up, and I've got to finish here." He pointed to the sink again.

"Can I lend you a hand?"

Henry hesitated. A part of him wanted to turn Colson away, to shout at him, to even the playing field and make sure they never spoke again. But this was not a big city, where he could cut someone off. He and Colson would bump into each other all the time whether he liked it or not. Making matters worse, his job required them to cross paths on a regular basis.

"You're busy," said Colson. "I'll get out of your hair." He touched the counter, mere inches from Henry's forearm, and backed away.

The cashier's tablet suddenly sparked, and the screen blinked on and off before resetting itself. Henry jerked his hand back. It only stung a little, but somehow the jolt re-opened a Jonny-sized hole in the pit of stomach, as if warning him not to fall back on old patterns. Why did he find it so hard to just open his mouth and say what he wanted to say?

Colson reached slowly for the doorknob, and the little bell beside Lady Duggery's portrait chimed. He flashed Henry a remorseful smile.

"Wait," said Henry. "I could use some help."

"Yeah?"

"Turn the closed sign around, will you?"

"Sure thing."

Henry nodded, biting his lower lip, and Colson locked the door from the inside. Henry lifted the section of the countertop that allowed Colson to pass into the back of the shop. "You can dry the dishes while I wash."

"Deal," said Colson. They danced around one another, figuring out who should go which way first, because Henry was still clipped to the wall. "What are you wearing?"

"It's a harness. I made it this morning. For the quakes."

"You don't get caught on things?"

"I'm still getting used to it. When a quake hits, I should be able to brace myself against the wall. It's a silly idea."

"It looks well made." Colson ran his fingers over the shoulder strap.

"Thanks," said Henry, trying not to let a shiver run down his spine. As he followed Colson into the back, he noticed the mud stains on his butt and hips. "What happened to you?"

"This? I slipped and fell earlier."

"Here," said Henry. He ran a clean dish towel under the faucet. He almost took it upon himself to wipe off the mud, but he stopped himself and handed the towel to Colson.

"Thanks! Did I ever ask you where you're from?"

"Pittsburgh. Well, I moved there for culinary school. Grew up in South Central Pennsylvania. You?"

"Near Hagerstown," he said. He held up the muddied towel after cleaning himself off, and Henry gestured for him to throw it in the corner with the other dirty laundry. "In Maryland, probably not too far from you, but I always thought I'd move to the coast, you know? One of the big cities. Not New York, but Philly or Boston. Being Black or gay in my hometown, either one made you stand out too much, and to be both—I was either the only gay guy or the only Black person in the room, no matter where I went."

Henry plunged his hands into the soapy dishwater. He found Colson very attractive, and Brisa had insinuated they date, but he had not known for sure if Colson was actually gay. He cleared his throat to buy himself an extra second or two. "I couldn't stand that much attention on me all the time."

"But in elementary school we moved to Levittown."

"Oh," was all Henry said, recalling the reports. It was one of the last major stories before the Militia enacted its widespread censorship of reliable journalism. Photographs documented the before and after of the once wealthy and diverse neighborhood. Victorian-style homes turned into burned out husks. Flowering, tree-lined streets felled to ash. Family portraits piled among unidentifiable human remains. Video footage showed the early Militia, almost exclusively white men, clad in black, white, and blue camo. They always had a token light-skinned person of color or a transphobic gay man who they could place in photo ops to earn the benefit of the doubt from the middle class. Before Levittown, they covered their faces with balaclavas or bandannas, but afterward, they smiled for the cameras and flashed neo-fascist hand signs while occupying the ruins. All traces of the massacre disappeared within days and were replaced with propaganda showing the same Militia setting up field hospitals, distributing water to white residents in the nearby suburbs, and planting trees in the charred soil.

"I could have sworn the reports, the real ones before it all got shut down, said there were no survivors." As they talked, Henry washed and rinsed, while Colson dried and stacked the various utensils and bowls. "Sorry, I just mean I had no idea you lived through that. And as a kid, no less." Colson must carry that rage and loss with him every day.

"Yeah, it was great until it wasn't."

"Kinda like this place." Henry regretted the comparison as soon as it slipped from his lips, but Colson let it pass without further comment.

"My mother always used to say, 'What happened to me and my family prepared us for who we are now—stronger human beings.'"

"I really like that."

"It's funny, I haven't thought of those words in a long time. They're from Daisy Myers."

Henry shook his head in ignorance. "Why does that name sound familiar?"

"She, her husband, and their three children were the first Black family to move to Levittown in 1957. The assault in 2037 was meant to finish the work begun by the riots from eighty years earlier."

"What happened back then?" asked Henry. He knew of the horrors of segregation, but he had never heard of a longer history behind the massacre at Levittown.

Colson took a deep breath. "It goes way back. The Levitts founded numerous suburbs after World War II. The G.I. Bill was supposed to guarantee mortgages and small business loans to all veterans returning from the war to rebuild the United States. But there were a thousand tricks that segregationists used to make sure those benefits rarely made it into the hands of the Black, Latino, and Asian-American soldiers who often fought on the front lines in the fight against fascism. Levitt and Sons, when they wrote the deeds to the properties they built, included a clause stating that it could only ever be sold to members of the 'Caucasian race.'" He made air quotes with his free hand.

"That's fucked up. Was that even legal?"

"Probably not, but it was a huge selling point for most of the white families who moved there."

"Until the Myers family moved in."

"Exactly," said Colson. "Within the hour, angry neighbors were patrolling Deepgreen Lane, while others circulated a petition to protect their right to live in a lily-white town. By the evening, an angry mob had formed outside, threatening to blast the place to bits. They smashed their picture window and burned crosses on the lawns of the neighbors who showed support of the new family. Mostly it was Jewish families who stood up for them."

"I'm guessing the police were of no help."

"It's worse," said Colson with a scoff. "The local Protestant and Catholic churches helped organize against the Myers family, and some even worked with the Ku Klux Klan. It was a nightmare. They were so worried their kids would grow up thinking those Black kids were no different than they were."

"Or that they might start dating."

"Interracial marriage was still illegal then, but yeah."

"It's easy to forget it wasn't that long ago."

"I know what you mean. But they never forgot. The Levittown massacre was the long-delayed reckoning."

Henry exhaled loudly as he took it all in. "Wait. What happened to Daisy Myers and her family? Did they drive them out?"

"No! That's the one good thing. It took a year and two days—which is fucking ridiculous—but the courts finally granted a permanent injunction against harassing the Myers family. The worst offenders got a slap on the wrist with a fine, and the tension remained palpable. But the Myers stayed in their home for five years before moving out of town for a new job. They never backed down."

Henry and Colson both stopped what they were doing to exchange hopeful smiles.

"I can see why your mom loved that quote."

"She made sure we knew the price our forbearers paid to live in a place like Levittown."

Henry and Colson fell into a moment of silence except for the sound of the scrub brush against metal bowls.

"You were from a small town, too?" Colson shifted the conversation from such heavy topics.

"Yeah, but I had gay uncles. I was the ring bearer in their wedding. Everyone seemed to know I was gay before I did. My uncles were the ones who had to deal with all the fights and the stupid remarks about grandkids and the 'jokes' about not having found the right woman to turn them straight. It was different for me. Kids at school were mean, but they were mean to everyone. I got good at keeping my head down and staying out of sight until I could move away."

"Sounds lonely." Colson stopped drying to look at Henry, who kept his focus on the dishes.

"I'm used to it," admitted Henry, before realizing Colson was talking about Henry's youth, not his present predicament.

"Not me," said Colson. Henry was grateful he didn't linger on that slip of the tongue. "As a kid, my strategy was to befriend everyone. Superficially at least, you know? Make everybody happy. Never let them see the real you."

"That sounds exhausting." He had thought Colson to be his polar opposite, but when it came down to it, the only real difference was the specific tactic each used to survive.

"We do what we can to get by."

"We do."

Henry rinsed off a baking tray and handed it to Colson. Their fingers grazed one another and sparked.

"You shocked me," said Colson.

Henry let out a nervous laugh and dipped his hands back in the soapy water. "Sorry, I'm always doing that in here. Something with the wiring."

Yes!

Connect!

That voice again. First with the cake. Then with Calla. It was clearer this time, but just as urgent, as if asking him to take action on its behalf. Henry suspected it was all in his head. Brisa told him she couldn't hear it, and Colson's expression did not suggest any mental disturbances by disembodied voices. Henry tried to mask his distress.

"Look, I am sorry," Colson said, while drying the tray. "There was a lot going on last night, and I don't know how to explain it all." He looked for a place to rest the tray, and Henry pointed him to the proper shelf.

Colson severed.

Henry bridge.

Henry ignored the voice while Colson continued speaking as if nothing out of the ordinary was happening. "No, I get it. Working for Lady Duggery has to be intense."
"It is, but that's not the whole story."

Listen to Colson!

Listen!

Listen listen listen!

I'm trying to listen, but I can't with you in my head, Henry thought to the voice. He had no idea if it could read his mind or not. He refocused to ask Colson, "What do you mean?"
"This is going to sound dumb and probably patronizing, but I was trying to protect you."

Help you! Listen!

"I can handle myself," said Henry out loud. He dropped the last dirty bowl into the sink and suds splashed across his apron and harness. He had meant to keep that thought inside his head. It was intended for the intrusive voice, not for Colson. But he did not want to explain himself, even if he could.
"Yeah, sorry." Colson paused.

Breathe Henry.

Calm Henry.

"I didn't mean it like that," said Henry to Colson. He rinsed the bowl three times over.

"The Militia burned my hometown." Colson blurted out the words.

Henry did not expect the sudden shift back to that topic. He turned off the water and pulled the plug from the drain. "You must be so—" he started to say, but he didn't know how to finish that sentence. He took a small step toward Colson, the dripping bowl still in his hand.

"They burned all our homes and our businesses. I was lucky. I survived, somehow. It's all so blurry. I remember the intense heat and broken glass, the ringing in my ears, the taste of burnt hair in every breath. I woke up in the park down the street while the town was still smoldering."

"That's terrible." Henry wondered how Colson had managed to hide unlike everyone else, but now was not the time to pry.

"Anyway, I shouted at you last night because my plans were falling apart. The official who led the assault, Agent Dixon, attended the Founder's Day party, and I—" Colson's voice cracked.

DIIIXXXXXXOOOOOOOOOOON!!!!

The voice roiled inside Henry's head along with Colson's revelation. He must be the only one to hear it, because Colson would have reacted to the outpouring of rage that erupted in those two simple syllables. As quickly as it resounded in his head, it fell into silence, as if the power had been cut off in the middle of a radio transmission.

"Let's just say . . ." Colson leaned in close and whispered, "I might have been trying to get revenge." He leaned back, took the wet bowl, and dried it. Henry placed a sympathetic hand on Colson's shoulder encouraging him to continue. "Then the quake hit, and my plans got messed up. When you returned with the cookies, I was scrambling. They murdered my family and my friends! I just—I needed you to leave because I didn't want you to get caught in the middle of it." The metal bowl trembled in Colson's hand, and he stacked in on the shelf. "It was horrible how I treated you, and I'm so sorry."

Henry stood there in awe. The real story behind Colson's actions was nothing Henry could have even remotely imagined. It was all too easy to forget that everyone in the valley had a life before they got here. An entire life out there, where the world had not just fallen apart but had been destroyed, one action at a time, by militias and governments and banks and corporations and voters, all of them making choices, granting cover for the worst people to take advantage of the chaos, compounding the pain for profit.

Or simply because they liked to make others suffer.

Still, there had to be more to the story than what Colson shared. Henry never imagined Colson might try to—to do what, exactly? Hurt them? Or something worse? Then again, Dixon was directly responsible for the death of Colson's entire family. Henry would want to get revenge, too, if he knew who was responsible for his mother's death. But he learned a long time ago not to get his hopes up of finding out what actually happened to her.

Not to mention, Henry rarely stepped out of his safe routines. Especially not after he arrived in the valley. Here he had tried to expunge the memories of the past from his mind. He buried himself in his little jobs, erasing the outside world as if Sediment Valley were surrounded by a void, pretending everything was okay.

Nothing is okay, Henry! Help me!

The voice, no longer patient or comforting, burst into his consciousness once more. It was coherent this time. Henry could feel the frustrations of his former life coursing through his veins like lightning. He could see Colson becoming visibly upset as his own traumatic memories flooded back.

Out of nowhere, the entire shop jolted to the side, and a few of the clean plates shattered on the tile floor. Colson fell forward and crashed into Henry. Henry grabbed onto him, and the retractable cable guided them both against the shaking wall. The cinder blocks felt cool even through Henry's apron. Colson wrapped his arms around Henry and gripped the straps of the harness that ran across his shoulder blades. The scruff on Colson's cheeks brushed Henry's ear, sending goosebumps down his neck, and Henry squeezed him tight.

They rode out the tremor, hip to hip, wrapped in each other's arms.

Despite it all, Henry had never felt more at ease, more protected and seen, more prepared to hold someone else up, than he did in that moment.

Henry expected the voice to boom inside his head again. Instead, the buzzing sensation in his palms dissipated.

He and Colson stood in a tight embrace, having remained upright through it all, not ready to move away from the wall or from each other. Henry could feel Colson's heart beating against his own chest. He tried to sync his breath with Colson's. They inhaled deeply and let out their breath in unison, gradually regaining a sense of stability, moving together and with the quake.

The ground shook once more, and then again, and then it stopped.

When Colson finally loosened his grip and looked Henry in the eyes, he said, "I get it if you don't want to speak to me again."

It was scary—what Colson had revealed, this proximity, this potential intimacy—but Henry was not in a position to judge. "No, that's not it," said Henry. "It's a lot to take in. I didn't know any of that."

"I didn't go through with it, you know."

"The . . . revenge?" He didn't want to specify any further. Not after getting that close. Some other time.

"Yeah."

"That's probably for the best," said Henry. A small doubt crept across his mind. Had Colson not gone through with it, or had his plans been messed up by the second earthquake last night? What was it that Brisa had said about catching Colson performing a funky ritual? Henry wanted to trust Colson, he wanted to squeeze him tight and fall asleep in his embrace, but old patterns died hard.

"Probably," said Colson. "I just hope you can forgive me. For all of it. But especially for the way I treated you."

"I can," said Henry, and he meant it.

"Thank you. I better get going. They'll be expecting me at the mansion." Colson squeezed Henry's shoulder before backing away. "Save me a cinnamon roll, will you?"

"You bet," said Henry. The harness held him against the wall as Colson waved once more from the front door. Henry now had a new conversation to replay in his head, trying to decipher Colson's words. Was Colson lying or was there simply more to the story that would make it all make sense? Or maybe he was losing his grip on reality. He wanted to hold out for hope, but he wasn't ready to open himself to the possibility of more pain.

The timer went off on the oven. Henry busied his brain again with his work. He removed the rolls to a cooling rack, whipped up a batch of fluffy icing, and individually packaged each one to sell during the morning rush.

Chapter 16

Lady Duggery

Lady Duggery alighted ever so gracefully on the grotto floor. The amulet hummed in the indentation of her exposed clavicle as naturally as if she had been born wearing it. Not a single sign of the tug of war that had raged in her mind persisted less than twenty-four hours after receiving her powers. She always impressed herself with how quickly she adapted to new scenarios and rose to the top. More than soaring through the air or gliding into the depths of this mildew-encrusted grotto, her drive was her true superpower. But she had to admit these most recent innovations were quite delightful.

Less exciting was the way the gritty soil stuck to the bottom of her chiffon pants. *Colson, poor thing, is going to be chasing down grains of sand for weeks*, she thought.

She was proud to have gambled on him. He appeared out of the blue, but from the start, she sensed that same drive in him to excel, no matter the cost. Still, she remained vigilant, lest he outshine her one day like she did her own father. But she wasn't seriously concerned. She had command of an entire army and could have any usurper cuffed and carried away. She knew better than to repeat her father's mistakes.

The spiraling stone steps echoed beneath her pumps. This was the last place she wanted to be. The events taking place underground were located there on purpose—so she did not have to witness them. She placed one hand on the walls to brace herself, but she recoiled at the slime. This hidden entrance seemed so medieval, so impractical. It was the antithesis of the well-oiled machine being assembled in the depths of her kingdom.

She wished they had left the entrance behind the Square exposed. Those steps were a bit terrifying, but at least they were not covered in filth. Of course, she understood better than anyone the importance of keeping the true purpose of Sediment Valley a secret from its current inhabitants. Otherwise, her temporary subjects would never give her a moment's peace to harness their little lives for the benefit of the wealthy supporters who waited in the wings.

Deep beneath the grotto, the stairwell opened into a wide tunnel. The geometric designs of the concrete cathedral glowed in a saturated azure ombre that gently pulsed from one end of the tunnel to another as if it were breathing. The floor looked a bit wet, so she drifted toward the laboratory.

At the far end, the tunnel forked. One branch led toward the now-barricaded shaft. The other ended in a sprawling concave wall of wide windows that framed the overwrought metal door to the underground laboratory. To confirm her identity, Lady Duggery held her watch to a scanner.

"Lady Duggery," said Dixon, with reverence, as the door whooshed opened. He bowed ever so slightly. "Please, by all means, enter."

She was not sure if he had learned his lesson or if he was up to no good. "I cannot imagine what was so important for you to insist I come all the way down here."

"You're in for a treat." He acted giddy, like an over-eager puppy dragging home the carcass of a groundhog for his master. "Just one moment. Please, have a seat."

One of the guards stood from his rolling chair at the control panel. Normally, they overlooked a vast cavern, but today the windows were covered in cheap drapes. Dixon was putting on a show. She crossed one leg over the other, shaking it to exaggerate her exhaustion. She was the one who made others wait. Not the other way around.

"Remove the drapes on my signal," he said to a guard. Then Dixon exited the control room for the cavern below.

As the minutes passed, the amulet hanging from Lady Duggery's neck began to pulse. A mechanical whirring vibrated the glass, and the lights in the entire lab faded to pitch black. The rustling of fabric suggested to Lady Duggery that the drapes were being whisked away for Dixon's grand reveal.

Through the windows, a golden spotlight shone on Dixon from the ground, casting the features of his face into sharp relief. He looked even smaller from Lady Duggery's position in the lab. Just beyond the edge of the light, two metallic, glimmering rings, spun around a fixed point. She had seen the schematics, briefly, but they were larger than expected.

"Today we embark on an unprecedented journey toward our ultimate mastery over nature," said Dixon. His voice emanated from the speakers in the control panel before Lady Duggery.

"Mankind has spent centuries learning to cultivate the soil, scale the highest peaks, and traverse the raging seas."

His intentional use of the word "mankind" rankled. But she would let it slide if it meant getting out of here sooner.

"We have plumbed the depths of this planet and stepped into the great void beyond our atmosphere. Our forbearers have made tremendous strides toward taming the wild beast we call home through technological innovation. However, the Earth has surprised us in recent decades with a new power. The Awakened. Those whiny nobodies who acted out in jealousy at the hard-earned success of others somehow convinced the Earth to aid them in their attacks on the greatest men among us. We admit it caught us unprepared. Many denied the possibility the Earth could grant those snowflakes actual powers. It took real insight to not only accept that magic can exist but, importantly, to conceive of a way to harness the Earth itself, to restrict its ability to choose who may and may not call upon its powers, and to siphon its most secret source of limitless energy for ourselves."

Agent Dixon paused and gestured to the guard standing by his side. "Lady Duggery, it is my greatest honor to welcome you to witness the final phase of Sediment Valley. Hit it."

The rings came into focus. Lady Duggery's first impression was of a giant's bracelet woven together with thin, golden threads, just like the ones coiled around her amulet. Each was easily six feet in circumference and two feet wide from top to bottom, yet the fine threads suggested an impossible weightlessness as each floated horizontally and rotated around an orb of green-white light. A rippling beam of that same light shot vertically from each orb toward two nodes. Thousands of verdant threads snaked their way from those nodes into the natural rock that formed both the ceiling and the floor. This was no sterile lab, but an ancient cavern dripping with stalactites. Dozens of node pairs spread across the entire chamber, each with their own bracelet resting on the ground, waiting to be activated.

"Join us, if you'd like," said Dixon.

The guard in the lab offered Lady Duggery his hand, but she refused his assistance. "I can handle a few flights of stairs." He still opened the door for her. The corrugated steel steps were rickety. She had no intention of walking down two more flights, so she rose above the banister and glided masterfully to Dixon's side.

"My superior activated the first ring some time ago. And over here," said Dixon, directing Lady Duggery toward the second ring. "This is the one we activated during the party last night. It has been running smoothly ever since."

"Smoothly, you say?" The tremors were a necessary side-effect of these devices, but she relished the opportunity to take a jab at Dixon.

"The seismic activity is all within expected parameters," he replied. "The Earth is rather unhappy with us, and it convulses to loosen our grip from its throat whenever it can. The shaking will continue at unpredictable moments, as the Earth builds up and releases whatever bits of energy it can withhold from us. But rest assured, with just two of these rings we predict a 92% success rate of blocking the Earth from contacting those it had already awakened. And a substantially diminished ability to awaken any new foes. As we continue to bring the others online, our stranglehold on the entire valley will reinforce itself. Once we activate the third ring, our crypto servers will go live. We scale up until all thirty-six are purring like a kitten."

The operation was running ahead of schedule. Lady Duggery was impressed, but she preferred to keep a poker face. "I have to admit, I thought the servers would be up and running. I gave you permission to find our little volunteers yesterday, did I not?"

"You are correct. In fact, that's why I asked for your presence. I thought you might like to witness the activation procedures." Dixon whistled to his guards. "If you look closely." He invited Lady Duggery toward the original ring.

The air became humid, and she stepped forward, shielding her eyes from the intense green light. Something clung to the insides of the bracelet as it spun. The fleshy lump gradually assumed the figure of a human body.

Lady Duggery gasped. It was all fine and well on paper, knowing volunteers would be needed to harness and redirect the powers intended for the Awakened, but seeing an actual human body unsettled her.

"Who was it?" she asked, using the past tense, even though the machines needed living bodies to function. She would have to confront the naked truth of the devices now that Dixon had seen her flinch. She recomposed herself to stare it down. She could not falter again.

"One of the engineers, Dr. Douglas Eaves. He and his colleague, Dr. Clive Gillum turned on us and destroyed the Easton lab. They tried to make off with the amulets. Dr. Gillum evaded us, along with his husband. We believe they've been granted refuge in the Bent Greens, which makes it considerably more difficult to capture them. Still, we keep tabs on them, and they seem unlikely to leave those tree-huggers anytime soon. Dr. Eaves, however, wasn't so smart. He thought he could pour a bucket of cold water on our plans. But we got the last word."

"Very well," she said, finding it somewhat easier to swallow knowing it was the body of someone who had intended to topple her empire. She did not inquire about the identity of the person in the second ring while two guards carried a young woman on a stretcher.

"Would you like to see how it's activated? It's fascinating."

Lady Duggery could not refuse now. He was testing her resolve. "Yes, I'd like nothing more." She stared intently as the guards lifted the unconscious woman off the stretcher and swallowed the bile rising in her throat.

Nevertheless, Lady Duggery did nothing to stop Dixon's men as they bound her ankles and wrists, nor as they tied her long, blonde hair in a tight ponytail. Lady Duggery simply watched the two guards align her body against the inside walls of the bracelet. They strapped her down to keep her in place until the centrifugal force of the rotations took over. Then they inserted feeding and waste tubes into valves already affixed to her abdomen. The three guards struggled to tip the bracelet horizontally and hold it steady between the nodes. On Dixon's signal, the fourth guard activated the machine from a workstation in the control room.

Any lingering sense of guilt washing over Lady Duggery receded at that moment. She levitated involuntarily, and Dixon appeared to brace his knees against the ground and hunch over. Two writhing green lights pushed their way from the center of the nodes, searching for one another like fresh sprouts reaching for the sun. They approached the bracelet and elongated in agonizing need of one another. Lady Duggery wondered if they would fall short, mere inches apart, yet the wiggling tendrils tightened into perfectly vertical rods of light.

Meanwhile, the guards walked clockwise, still holding up the bracelet with the woman chained inside, setting it in motion. The light beams kissed, delicately, forming a tight bond. Lady Duggery's body flowed toward the device, desiring to feel that connection, but Dixon's heavy hand pulled her back to the ground.

A shock of green light rippled outward before being dragged back toward the center, spiraling inward on itself. The guards carefully released their hands as the bracelet supported its own weight and increased its speed to match the newly formed orb in its center. They took one step back, then another, making sure the device reached full power before returning to their station.

"Is that everything?" asked Lady Duggery. She would only offer him a deadpan reaction to this stunning integration of magic and technology.

Dixon laughed under his breath. "Yes," he said. "That is all we wanted to show you today. Are you satisfied with the results?"

Dixon had walked into her final trap, admitting his desire to please his superior, to please a woman—to please her. She would accept his defeat by throwing him a bone. "For now, Dixon. Keep it up. But cut the theatrics. I could hear the commotion you caused to acquire that girl from my mansion, and we cannot have you scaring off all the volunteers before we get them installed."

"Of course, Lady Duggery. I'll be more discreet." He smiled. "Would you like an escort home?"

Lady Duggery rose from the floor, her chiffon pants flowing as she soared toward the lab door. She paused mid-air between magnificent stalactites. "I can manage," she said, looking down upon him one last time. She flew into the control room, across the threshold, down the long, glowing corridors, up the spiral staircase, and out of the grotto as fast as the amulet could carry her.

That grotesque scene in the cavern had been too much to stomach. She would not return to that site. Never again. She would purge the images of the bodies she exploited from her mind and leave Dixon to deal with the human element. Why have this much money if she could not insulate herself from the dirty work?

Lady Duggery gathered herself, and as another tremor hit, she glided just above the ground all the way back to her mansion, unbothered by such earthly concerns.

PART THREE

TO ARM

Chapter 17

Henry

THE SQUARE HAD NEVER been quieter. For the third day in a row, Henry had to throw away a substantial portion of his freshly baked goods. He emptied a full tray of bear claws, half the cinnamon buns, and even a few gingersnap cookies into the trash. It pained him to see his creations turn stale and go uneaten after perfecting the recipes.

Then again, he had probably baked too many products, given the circumstances. Lady Duggery's promise that the quakes would become less frequent had yet to be fulfilled. They had only become less severe. Still, the damage had been done. Shattered windows, cracked cement, leaking septic tanks—nowhere felt like home. Even the trees and bushes that had been in full bloom were turning brown and wilting, as if drained of some vital energy. Only the flapping black and blue banners used to decorate the valley for Founder's Day withstood the relentless onslaught.

In the time usually spent serving customers, Henry had taken to shake-proofing as much of the bakery as possible. He tied the display-case baskets in place with rope, so the assorted pastries wouldn't tumble out of their bins. He wrapped the silverware in cloth napkins and tucked sharp knives and heavy gadgets inside closed plastic containers. He padded trays with woven strips of stained dish towels for the ceramic plates and platters, which he never stacked more than four high. After being smacked in the back of the head by a cast iron skillet, he relocated all of the pots and pans that used to hang from hooks over the island onto rugs against the wall, creating little pathways he now had to navigate in his harness.

Even a task as simple as brewing fresh coffee had proven too dangerous. Now he only served cold-brew from a ten-gallon, orange plastic beverage dispenser that hung from a series of bungees under one of the counters. Whenever the shaking began, the coffee swayed to the rhythm of the valley like a counterweight instead of spilling onto the floor. Meanwhile, Henry backed himself against the wall in his harness and focused on taking long, even breaths. The solution was inelegant but effective for keeping his bakery intact and stopping himself from having a full-blown meltdown.

Henry understood the dip in sales. It was one thing to survive a quake; it was another entirely to get hit over and over. When not busy cleaning up the debris, everyone hesitated to leave their houses. They only ventured out for their jobs lest they be smushed under a felled tree or sucked into a sinkhole. Henry even took to sleeping in the bakery.

But the tremors alone could not explain the mass trepidation. The sight of Calla being carted away still haunted him. When her best friend, Hiroshi, came asking about her, he did not want to relive the memory. Henry told him to keep his head down and sent him on his way with a bag of day-old cinnamon rolls. He suspected others were just as jittery from the abduction, and rumors abounded that more people had begun to go missing in the days since. If the gossip was true, then Agent Dixon had chosen to be more discreet about disappearing the residents of Sediment Valley.

When not replaying his recent conversations with Brisa and Colson, Henry's overactive imagination conjured scenarios of helmeted guards sneaking up behind him on the long walk home, throwing a bag over his head, and carting him off to who knows where. He would not be leaving the bakery unless absolutely necessary. He had everything he needed right here. Food, hot water, a toilet, the harness, and even the mattress from his cabin. With no health inspectors to regulate his business, he was free to do as he pleased.

While Henry tested the new coffee dispenser, two guards knocked on the bakery window. He considered making a run for the back door, but they had already seen him. *This is it*, he thought. *I'm done for.* The panic froze him in place.

The guards, however, simply set the large box they carried outside the door and walked away.

Once they were out of sight, Henry cautiously brought the package inside. This was some sort of trap. His fingers trembled as he cut through the packing tape. He took a step back, shielded his eyes with his forearm, and flipped open the top flap. He jumped backward and let out a muffled yelp, but the box was not full of explosives or anthrax. Inside he found big blocks of real butter. At least he could laugh at himself for overreacting.

Inside, a letter from Lady Duggery explained her aching sweet tooth and a desire for something decadent. *Colson has done nothing but rave about your skills,* her letter read, *and he assured me the cake had been beautiful before its unfortunate demise, for which no one blames you.* Her gracious acknowledgment lifted a huge weight from his shoulders. Not to mention the way he blushed at the thought of Colson speaking so kindly of him.

He knew immediately what to make. Mille-feuille, with their thousand delicate sheets of butter-flaked dough, should satisfy his benefactor's cravings and his own need for redemption.

This was a once-in-a-lifetime opportunity. Almost no one had butter these days. Butter required cows, and SustainAble had built their business on promises to eliminate the carbon footprint of the cattle industry. Henry recalled faint details of an explosion at one of their plants, rumors of hidden factory farms, whispers about reclassifying the undesirable bits of livestock as something other than meat so it could be marketed as plant-based products. Cows only ate grains, hay, and corn, the lobbyists argued, and You-Are-What-You-Eat arguments became enshrined in the legal code.

That's what people said, anyway, on the outside, whispering while they collected their food boxes after twelve-hour shifts at the SustainAble plants.

There were so many stories flooding every Militia-controlled media outlet and potable water queue that it was nearly impossible to decipher fact from misinterpreted data and straight up lie. On any given day, Henry had been too consumed by other basic existential concerns, like not getting arrested again for violating the Two Gender Act, to do his own research. It wasn't like he had access to another source of food if he lost his job. Henry kept his head down and his mouth shut, and he thought everyone else would be better off doing the same.

Despite everything he had learned from Brisa and Colson in recent days, he hesitated to poke the bear that provided him stability, albeit of the shaking ground variety. Brisa seemed like she could handle most problems on her own. Henry admired her for that. He also found her a bit intimidating. She liked to rock the boat a bit too much, and he worried it would come back to bite her. Still, he had helped her the other day, and that was all the excitement he could handle.

Things with Colson were more complicated. Henry felt a deeper connection to Colson, but somehow, the more Henry thought back on their conversation, the more Colson's story did not fully add up. Colson had breezed past some key details, like how exactly he had planned to get revenge. A small part of him worried this was all some elaborate scheme to catch him betraying Lady Duggery or breaking the law.

But one question sat above the rest: when the quake hit, had their embrace meant anything? Or was it purely about staying safe?

It had all become too much to untangle.

I've got actual, real butter, he reasoned with himself. *At this point, the true crime would be to let it go to waste.*

Puff pastry required a shocking amount of butter, in the *beurrage* and in the—what was the proper French word his instructor, Chef Carême, had made him memorize? It slowly came back to him—the *detrempe.* While he rolled and folded the butter block and dough, he repeated the words, echoing his instructor's breathy, guttural Rs. His pronunciation was as bad an imitation as the shoddy, misshapen slab before him now.

The recipe turned out to be significantly more difficult than he had imagined. In culinary school, Chef Carême had made it sound so easy. Since butter had been unavailable during his training, and his Paris-born instructor absolutely refused all substitutions when it came to puff pastry, Henry had never actually attempted the recipe before. Instead of demonstrating the technique firsthand, she taught them the basic principles through a series of lectures, belaboring her critique of lazy ruff puff doughs, with the hope that one of her esteemed students might continue the tradition of classic French pastry in some remote future.

Henry thought she might be pleased that the future was now, assuming she had survived. Though she would be unlikely to take solace in the fact that he was the one to pick up the mantle. Despite his best efforts, Henry had only ever performed in the middle of the pack.

On his first attempt, he moved too slow. The butter block softened and oozed out the sides as he rolled the dough. "This has to work!" he exclaimed under his breath, but the dough was ruined. If only he knew how to repurpose it. But the pressure to perform unnerved him. He balled up the squishy mess and tossed it in the trash alongside yesterday's pastries, hoping Lady Duggery would never learn of this gross misuse of a precious resource. Then he began again.

For the second batch, he let everything chill as required, including himself, but still, he had to learn to use a rolling pin while strapped in his harness. The retractable leash bolted to the wall resisted his forward momentum, and instead of rolling evenly, he miscalculated the force. After irretrievably denting the dough for the third consecutive time, he slammed the rolling pin on the stainless-steel countertop until it sparked.

The sound of the shop door opening and closing, as a customer slowly backed away to avoid getting caught up in his tantrum, barely registered through all the negative self-talk. He felt like a failure, a hack, an imposter taking a space from a more seasoned baker still stuck under the smog-filled skies of Pittsburgh. He had to try again and again to maintain his place in Sediment Valley.

He took a deep breath, recalled the tight grip of Colson's arms around his waist, the same memory he replayed to lull himself to sleep for short intervals over the last three nights, and focused. By the time he finished rolling and turning batch five, Henry had gained some confidence in the basic technique. Now he just had to remember which dough in the freezer was on what step of the process.

The ground had been unusually quiet today. Six hours of peace was the record. He hadn't set a timer, but they must be approaching that benchmark. Maybe Lady Duggery had been right all along, and things were improving. After lunch, while cutting the dough into a hundred perfect rectangles, he was tempted to remove the harness. The straps fit well enough after some trial and error. Too loose, and the tension from the retractable cord made the leather chafe his armpits. Too tight, and the cramping in his rib cage became indistinguishable from his panic attacks, offsetting the intended use of the entire device. The trickiest bit was to avoid looping himself around the workbench in the center of the kitchen as he navigated the piles of pots and pans on the floor. More than once the cord snagged and yanked him backward.

The shop door chimed later that afternoon, while Henry placed the final touches on his mille-feuille. The last few batches of puff pastry exceeded his expectations. He cleared his mind to pipe hundreds of dollops of cream between the layers, squeezing and swirling the pastry bag with the precision of a machine. He called out to his customer, letting them know he would be right out. He could almost imagine the bliss radiating across Lady Duggery's face, eyes closed, corners of her mouth relaxed, head reclined and letting out a subtle moan, as she sunk her teeth into his dessert.

Henry laid the pastry bag on the counter and wiped some cream from his fingertips. The harness resisted him, and then a warm hand gripped his shoulders from behind.

"You scared me, handsome," he said, expecting to find Colson.

"You might want to rethink those words," said a gruff voice that belonged to someone else.

Henry's heart jumped into his throat and he whipped his head around to identify the strange voice. He stumbled backwards when he found himself standing face-to-face with Agent Dixon.

CHAPTER 18

BRISA

BRISA SAT IN THE park beside the river, banging her satphone against a rock and holding it over her head to no effect. The device searched uselessly for a signal that would never penetrate the Militia's jamming frequencies.

Of course, it was dangerous to be seen with a satphone in broad daylight. Communication with the outside world had been strictly prohibited from the start in Sediment Valley. Before the lockdown, violations meant expulsion. These days, there was no way the Militia would let anyone leave. The news of Calla's abduction had spread like wildfire, and the Militia would not want that information leaking beyond these mountains. Certainly, any future violators would become the next victims to disappear underground.

The string of failures, the relentless barrage of earthquakes, and the fading echo of Val's voice—it all wore her down. Her discouragement, unfamiliar as it was, loosened the restraints on self-destructive behaviors. She was barely eating. She hadn't talked to anyone in a few days. She just paced inside her cabin, half-heartedly cleaning up fallen debris around the lake, and wound herself up with harebrained schemes to rescue Calla. Sometimes she moped, and at others, she prepared to storm the mansion gates, armed only with her righteousness, to demand the prisoner's release. Typically she could plot infiltration and escape routes with a disinterested nonchalance, but her executive functioning simply refused to cooperate.

Worst of all, Brisa no longer cared if she got caught with contraband tech. In fact, she welcomed it, stuck as she was between impotence and rage. She would relish the opportunity to shout down an anonymous guard, to chafe and bleed her wrists against zip ties as they carted her away.

Anything would be better than complacency.

She feared slipping into the mindset of the other residents of Sediment Valley. They would recycle and farm as dictated by Lady Duggery, but not out of conviction. These were not people who had dedicated their lives to reversing climate change or to building a better world. At first, she judged them all harshly. But as she confronted the possibility of being imprisoned here, she sympathized with the difficult decisions each of them had been forced to make to simply survive. They moved here to build a better life for themselves. That meant not questioning the status quo, because it was better to be in here than out there. She had no idea if they would feel different now, given the earthquakes and the abduction. Or if they would accept that a few people had to be sacrificed for the greater good.

Brisa dug her fingernails into the sides of the satphone and focused on the fish swimming against the current. She had been relatively lucky in her missions with ChainBlock so far, infiltrating other valleys to collect intel and escaping before anyone noticed her presence. She had incapacitated a few unsuspecting passersby with mostly harmless chloroform. She once stole a security guard's taser to peek into some encrypted documents. A close call, if she was honest with herself, but it had all worked out in the end. Those missions lasted a few days, a week tops, and she got to return home and fall asleep in the arms of her wife while their dogs burrowed into the not-quite-empty space on the couch.

Here in Sediment Valley, Brisa sensed an absence in the world. Calla was only a part of it. Something else was missing. While she focused on the school of fish struggling against the current, she let her mind's eye wander. That absence was not quite a ghost. It was more like a sunken shell tucked into a tuft of seaweed that used to house a snail. Every time she reached for that shell, it slipped between her fingers and got carried away by the current. Until her luck shifted, she would be incapable of picking herself up.

A gentle breeze rustled the tall grass on the slope behind her. She let her head fall backward and closed her eyes while she soaked up the sun. How long had it been since she last rested like this? She recalled sitting on a dock and, despite all the warning signs, dipping her toes into the warm waters of some lake. Beside her, Val thumbed a chunky paperback. Brisa peered below the lake's surface, halfway hopeful for any sign of life, halfway fearful of what disfigured monstrosity might rise up from the depths and take a bite of her big toe. She longed to dive into that lake. She wanted nothing more than to rile up Val by splashing her relentlessly until she dove headfirst into the waters and chased her while they both screamed in laughter.

But the risk of infection had been too high. So Brisa deciphered the various cadences of birdsong floating on the breeze, while Val devoured a plot that made her audibly gasp on more than one occasion. *What was the name of that lake?* Brisa felt ashamed to have let such a perfect moment slip into the fog of memory. She recalled the electric car they rented, the tropical pattern of their vibrant beach towels that contrasted with the locale, the moldy smell hanging in the air when they opened the cabin door. She could remember so many tiny details but not the name of that lake. *Could it be a lake fed by the same river before her now?* For a fleeting second, she thought she could call Val on her satphone before reality caught up with her.

A passing cloud cast a shadow over Brisa, and she opened her eyes.

Her stomach jumped into her throat. The silhouette of a woman stood before her clutching something in her fist. Brisa scrambled backward but was slowed by the steep slope. The woman took a step toward her and leaned down.

"Stay right where you are," Brisa shouted in a stern, deep voice.

"I was hoping you could help me," said the stranger. The woman's words, dripping with desperation, allowed Brisa to lower her guard—only slightly. "But you might want to hide that satphone before someone sees," she added under her breath.

Brisa tucked the satphone into her bag and shielded her eyes. The woman looked familiar but in a generic sense. Brisa gestured for her to take a seat. Her lower arms were only a few shades lighter than Brisa's natural skin tone, while her upper arms revealed a pinkish white. Her slender legs contrasted with the hint of a belly peeking out from a faded t-shirt a size too small. After a lifetime of table scraps, she must have allowed herself to indulge in Sediment Valley. The extra pounds looked good on her.

The woman took a deep breath, as if gathering the courage to reveal a secret for the first time.

"Can I trust you?" she asked.

"I don't know how to answer that," said Brisa. She exhaled through her nostrils, evaluating the scenario. The woman tapped her thumbs on her knees and rocked back and forth. She was brimming with nervous energy. If this was some sort of trap, it was convincing. "I think you just have to tell me what you came here to say, and we can go from there."

"I've been watching you."

Here we go, Brisa thought. She crossed her arms.

"You were there when they took Calla."

Brisa did not reply one way or the other, but the woman must have noticed how she recoiled at the accusation.

"This is coming out all wrong," she said. She shook her head. Then the words tumbled out. "It's my husband, Hiroshi. He didn't come home last night. He worked in the kitchen with Calla, and at first, I thought, it's ok. Sometimes they have to stay late to prep food for the next day or whatever. But when I woke up this morning, he still wasn't back. I called up to the mansion. Colson said he didn't see him yesterday and hung up the phone before I could ask him anything else. I don't know what to do. I had to leave our kid with the neighbor. I need to report to work, and we don't have anything prepared for dinner. The window's still broken from one of the earthquakes, and some birds got caught in the rafters."

Brisa could tell this woman's list of problems was far from over, but somehow, she managed to close her mouth like one does an overflowing junk drawer.

A breathy plea escaped her lips before she started to cry. She hid in the crook of her own elbow.

Brisa, at first, wanted to give her some space, but then she let her guard drop. "It's going to be ok," she said assuredly, even though she did not believe it. Brisa felt some sense of relief as she reprised her role as the compassionate leader.

At the same time, this new information set the gears of her atrophying mind back in motion. Is this what Brisa had been sensing? That Calla was only one victim in a string of abductions? Come to think of it, the valley had become quieter by the day. Brisa had chalked it up to the earthquakes driving everyone indoors, but they had all been required to report to work, nonetheless. Some part of her had only been so reckless with the satphone on display because the park had been uncharacteristically empty. The chances of being spotted were low.

Dixon had been messy that day, too. He made a spectacle of the event, terrorizing everyone into submission, by simply carting off an unconscious young woman in broad daylight. This woman's husband must not be the only one to have disappeared in recent days, and if Brisa was right, he certainly would not be the last.

"Tell me what you can about your husband. Did he rub anyone the wrong way or seem different in recent days?"

"No, he always got along with everyone at work. He's kinda goofy. Makes you feel at ease in his presence. It's what drew me to him in the first place. I can be so on edge all the time, but he always made me feel safe. He wasn't one of those macho guys running around waving a gun in the air at every little inconvenience. I know he would never have said anything unwarranted. I mean, he was concerned for Calla. That was clear. They liked to meet at the bakery for a coffee before work. After everything happened, he started asking around about her, but most people just shut their doors in his face. He said the baker, Henry, got really awkward when he brought up the topic and told him to keep his thoughts to himself."

The mystery evading Brisa, a tendril of smoke in a glass vase, began to take shape in her mind. "What's your husband's name again? What does he look like?"

The woman retrieved a family photo from her pocket. "I'm Jeannine. This here is Hiroshi and our kid, Satoru. The photo is a few years old, but he mostly looks the same."

Brisa cupped the photo in her hands, protecting it from a sudden gust. Despite the wear and tear, she immediately recalled one of the men working in the kitchen. Jet black hair, all skin and bones. Hiroshi had been the one to pretend to chide Calla and Brisa for sneaking a canapé during the Founder's Day party.

"I remember your husband. I met him briefly." Brisa almost revealed where, but then she snapped back into spy mode with a renewed vigor and stopped herself from saying anything more to be safe.

Jeannine almost choked on her own breath. Her husband's disappearance had become real now that another person acknowledged it. She stumbled over her own tongue a few times before she gathered herself. "So you'll help me?"

"Go to work. Tell your kid their dad is on a special duty at the mansion. Fix your broken window. Don't talk about Hiroshi to anyone else. Understand?"

Jeannine's lip trembled as she held back tears, but she nodded.

"I'm on it," Brisa said. She should not have been so direct, but sad sap Brisa was not a good look on her. Her instincts told her to trust Jeannine. It was too early to tell if Dixon was targeting Lady Duggery's staff or if the victims were chosen at random or if Hiroshi had been taken simply because he inquired into his missing friend's whereabouts. Two does not a pattern make. Brisa needed to gather more intel. But she had a lead now. She knew how to work with that.

Brisa stood and lent the woman her hand. She took one more risk and hugged Jeannine. Then she sent her on her way so she could finally get back to work.

CHAPTER 19

HENRY

HENRY GRIPPED THE COUNTER, knocking a few mille-feuille out of alignment. Pastry cream smeared across his forearm. He was a good six inches taller than Dixon, but somehow, he felt small in the officer's presence. He desired nothing more than to crawl under his workbench and wait out the coming storm.

"Agent Dixon," said Henry, his voice audibly trembling and an octave lower than normal. "I'm s-sorry to have left you waiting."

"You're lucky you're in Sediment Valley, Henry." Dixon took a step closer, narrowing the only path between Henry and the back door. He cracked his knuckles and squinted. "Otherwise, I might have to take you in for questioning. Publicly displaying affection for a member of the same sex is a crime. But I don't have to tell you that, do I?"

Henry closed his mouth and lowered his eyes as he retreated inside himself. He questioned why they gave him a free pass today. But those thoughts were short-lived. His pulse thrummed against the straps of the harness. It no longer provided a source of comfort and empowerment. Instead, it felt like a glowing neon sign that read "faggot." He was over-exposed and tied down.

Dixon's nightstick, the chipped blue paint revealing a black polycarbonate core, poked out from his waist. Henry recalled the sudden crack of a similar one against his lower back while he and Jonny struggled to remove the harnesses their new friends had lent them for the night. Sirens blaring. Red and blue lights painted them as criminals while they were shoved into an armored van. Dried blood on the seats and day-old vomit in the air.

"I told Lady Duggery she was too soft on crime, but it's her money she's gambling with," said Dixon, shaking his head in disapproval. He took another step toward Henry. The smell of cigarettes and plaque wrinkled Henry's nose. "That'll all be over soon. But that's not why I've come."

All thoughts vacated Henry's mind in anticipation. He felt emptied of all emotion and sustenance, a hollowed-out shell, except for a fizzling whisper he tried to ignore. *Worry not*, it said. *Still . . . holding . . . on . . .* Something was different about the voice now. It sounded softer, more strained than before, and less demanding. More like a trickling stream than grinding bedrock. Less capable of protecting him.

Meanwhile, Dixon closed in on him and took a swipe at the mille-feuille, knocking two to the ground. "Look at the mess in here. Aren't you going to clean that up?"

Henry grabbed a towel and dropped to his knees to wipe up the splattered desserts he had spent hours making. When he tried to stand, Dixon held him down by the shoulders, as if to say, "*Stay right there.*" Henry felt his chest tighten, but not from the harness. If there was ever a time for that voice to distract him or suggest a plan of action, it would be now. *Please, please, please*, he begged.

In its prolonged absence, he focused on the pots and pans stacked beside him.

"I find that you're in an ideal position to lend me a hand. You see, Henry, Sediment Valley is on the cusp on an enormous breakthrough. Something that even a swishing little deviant like you could come to appreciate. Within days, we will unveil a new source of energy that is not only renewable but limitless and reproducible at scale around the world, and it's perfectly clean. No carbon footprint. No emissions."

A mindboggling confluence of ecological concern and genocidal violence coexisted on the branch of the far-right that rose to power during his teenage years. The Militia promised to restore order in a world upended, according to one angle of their messaging, by overpopulation and the unnatural breakdown of racial barriers and gender norms. They demanded assimilation into their culture, yet they decried anything that approached miscegenation. It was the perfect trap against their perceived enemies.

Henry lifted his eyes. He could feel his arms trembling in fear. Dixon now stood before Henry, hands on his hips, thrusting his pelvis forward and backward as he rambled on about the glorious future he was building. The enormous belt buckle represented a bald eagle clutching five arrows. It tugged at the waist of Dixon's pants, heavy and leaden.

"I see I've caught your interest," said Dixon.

Henry stared in horror at the man above him. His skin crawled. He would agree to almost anything if it meant Dixon would leave the shop without touching him. Henry nodded ever so slightly, trying not to awaken the monster in the room.

"Good. From what I gather, people implicitly trust you, Henry. You keep your head down. You don't run around gossiping to the high heavens. You don't generate much of an opinion, neither good nor bad, from the others. That means they'll open up to you, tell you things they can't tell their loved ones. Little secrets, minor peccadillos, maybe even devious plans."

"I don't understand," mumbled Henry. It was the truth. It didn't make sense that Dixon would want to team up with him. The Militia was known for excommunicating its members for even the slightest violation of the Two Gender Act.

"It's simple. There's a fraud amongst us. Someone plotting to destroy Sediment Valley before it has a chance to succeed."

Not one suspect, but two, crossed Henry's mind, and he burned hot. He was so terrible at keeping his face from betraying his emotional state. Luckily, Dixon had become distracted. He reached for one of the mille-feuille, opened his mouth wide, and tore through the delicate treat like a bear trap crushing a cub's hind leg. The pastry cream spurted out the back and dripped onto Henry's forehead.

Henry dared not wipe the cream.

Keep . . . chsss . . .

Dixon . . . cannot . . . akkksss . . .

The voice had become staticky and incomprehensible. Whatever its origin, it had encouraged him to trust Colson in the past and now appeared to hold something against Dixon.

Was it related to Colson? To the quakes? To the new technology Dixon described? The voice gurgled gibberish, as if imitating the fear that currently prevented Henry from thinking straight while Dixon had him cornered.

"An impostor, I tell you," Dixon said while chewing. "Someone who has faked their way through the front gates and is trying to sabotage our plans. I always knew this would be the risk of working with a desegregated population in phase one, but you, Henry, you can be brought around to our side. I have it on good word from the higher ups. I sense it, too. We need to show you how much happier you'll be when you lean into your God-given masculinity and the natural benefits of being born of pure blood. But one step at a time, my boy. For now, I just need you to listen. Keep your ears open and gather intel. You hear anything suspicious, you let me know. Think you can handle that?"

What had Agent Dixon meant about the higher ups speaking on behalf of Henry? He was not connected to the Militia in any way that he could think of. Not unless? No, he hadn't heard from his older brother in ages.

Before Henry could answer, the voice whispered like the wind.

sssssstoooooooooooooop

Henry wanted to refuse Dixon, but what choice did he have? This was not a negotiation. Henry was literally kneeling before his captor. His only option was to accept the mission. "Yes, sir."

"Good boy," said Dixon. He grabbed another pastry.

NOOOOOOOOOOOOOOOOOOOOOOOOOOO

The voice seared Henry's mind from the inside. Every synapse, every fiber of muscle in his gangly body, rippled with electricity, as the voice shouted at him for agreeing to Dixon's plan. Henry teared up and cupped his ears to no effect. He tried to rationalize his actions, but the voice just kept raging. Henry might pass out from the sublime force that only he could hear. Until suddenly, the howling came to a halt. Maybe it had understood his predicament.

An alarm sounded on Dixon's wristwatch. He stepped to the side. "Dixon, go ahead."

The tinny voice of one of his subordinates delivered the bad news uneasily. "Uhhh, we're seeing signs of spiking activity down here."

Dixon was the type of leader who would shoot the messenger in a fit of pique. He encouraged fear instead of loyalty. *Maybe that could be exploited one day*, thought Henry.

Yes . . . Henry . . . good.

"Do something about it!" barked Dixon.

"On it, sir. Yes, sir."

"Don't bother me with this shit again." He tapped his watch to end the call.

Henry took note that Dixon also required having the last word.

Dixon turned his attention back to Henry and said, "Glad I can count on you. Now stand up. Let's see what that harness can actually do. In five, four, three." Dixon devoured the rest of the dessert instead of counting down to two, wiped his mouth on his sleeve on one, and grabbed onto the countertop as the first tremor of a minor quake rippled through the bakery.

Henry crawled across the floor, embraced by the tension of the retractable cord, until he reached the wall. The last thing he wanted to do now was show a moment of weakness. By the time he was upright, the shaking stopped.

"Not bad," Dixon said with a mouthful and swallowed on his way to the door. "Not bad at all, my little friend. I'll take a box to go."

"Of course." Henry immediately packaged a dozen of his most impeccable pastries and handed them to Dixon from behind the register. "On the house."

"See, this can work out well for you, if you play your cards right. I hope you'll recall just how well I've treated you in the future."

The door chimed as Dixon finally left the bakery. Henry waited a beat to make sure he wouldn't return. Then he locked the front door, retreated to the kitchen out of sight of anyone looking through the windows, and tightened the harness around his shoulders. He sank to the floor and buried his head between his knees.

He had a million questions. How did Dixon know a quake would happen at that exact moment? Could he betray Brisa and Colson to a man like Dixon? What would happen to him if the Militia discovered his duplicity? Who even was the good guy in a place like this? Answers could not break through the chaos.

Terror churned in his stomach as he sobbed into a dish towel. He could not stop the image of Dixon's shining belt buckle from flashing over and over in his mind. He had never been more scared in his life. He ran to the sink, heaving and gasping for air in between retches that emptied his stomach.

Sometime later, the sheer panic released its grip. He laid on the mattress on the floor, curled up in the fetal position, and fell into a deep, dissociative sleep.

Chapter 20

BRISA

THE FRONT DOOR TO the bakery resisted Brisa. She jiggled the handle, and despite the Open sign, the door was locked. She pressed her nose to the glass. The bakery was bright and cheery, like an old-timey soda fountain that had been retrofitted with modern technology. For midday, the display case was filled with treats, but no other customers sat at the small tables.

She could not find any trace of Henry either, only something odd just beyond the counter. She moved to the large window and stood on her toes to get a better look. If she was not mistaken, Henry was curled up on a mattress on the floor.

Had it not been for her bout of misery and dejection the past few days she might have judged him. Instead, she rapped on the window to get his attention. She would try to shake him out of his depression like Jeannine had helped her earlier today.

A groggy Henry poked his head above the counter, quickly ducked back down as if to hide, before standing. He was still wearing his harness.

"What—what are you doing here?" asked Henry as he unlocked the door. He wiped the dried saliva from the corners of his mouth. His eyes were dark and puffy. He must have been crying. Good thing she stopped by. They could both use some cheering up.

"You know, I don't think I've even been inside. It's cute," she said. The shop bell chimed behind her, and she took a deep breath of the cool, sweet aroma in the air. "Want to join me for afternoon tea?"

Henry looked perplexed. She recognized that look. It was the same one he'd given her when she offered to help with the cake. She expected him to hurry her along, but then he reconsidered.

"Yeah," he said. "That sounds nice. I've got fresh, well, everything." He gestured to the fully-stocked display case.

"Slow day?"

"Slow week," he replied. He opened the case and pointed to the bear claws. Brisa nodded, and he retrieved one with the most delicate set of tongs and placed it on a small plate lined with a paper doily.

Brisa positioned her wristwatch over the scanner. The neon blue lights raced around the screen.

"It's on the house," said Henry.

"I'm happy to pay." She held her wrist in place.

"Honestly, I don't even know what purpose paying serves here. I don't keep track of my expenses, and Lady Duggery keeps everything stocked." He lowered his voice. "I think it's all fake."

"Or a test run for some later phase," said Brisa reflexively. She was not sure where that idea had come from, but sometimes the clearest thoughts came while the brain was distracted.

"I'd rather not consider that," admitted Henry. He joined her at the window table with a stack of gingersnaps. "What do you think?"

The bear claw was bigger than her hand and made her feel like a little kid again. She held it up and pretended to scratch at Henry's face. He laughed politely at her silliness while she savored the burst of almond paste. "Oh my, Henry. I've never tasted one like this before."

"That's because you've never had it made with real almonds or butter. Only extract and margarine."

Brisa intended to reiterate just how delicious it was, but her words came out a garbled mess in between bites. Sitting with Henry was nice. She had been so lonely the past few days, and now maybe things were starting to take a turn for the better. Time to get down to business. After one last bite.

"I wanted to talk to you about something," she said while licking the icing from her fingertips.

Henry sat upright in his chair, suddenly more serious than before. He narrowed his eyes in silence and put his half-eaten cookie back on the plate.

"It's about Calla." Brisa cleared her throat.

"Did you learn anything new?" he asked as he went into the back. He lifted his retractable tether to avoid getting snagged on the counter and ducked down. His getup seemed like more work than it was worth.

"Maybe," she replied. Something told her to put her guard back up. She hated that feeling, but old habits died hard. She waited for Henry to reemerge, and he carried over two iced coffees. "Let's just say I have some new leads. I've been stuck the past few days. I couldn't figure out what I was missing. Until a bit ago when Jeannine—you know her? Hiroshi's wife—came over to me in the park."

"I told him not to go making a lot of noise about Calla." Henry shook his head disapprovingly.

"So you did speak with him?" Brisa did not intend to interrogate Henry today, but she found herself staring him in the eyes to gauge his reaction.

Henry sipped his coffee and craned his neck. He swallowed hard before mumbling under his breath. "Hiroshi came in the other day wanting to know if I had heard about Calla. He looked distraught. They used to have breakfast here most mornings. Nothing scandalous, as far as I could tell, just good friends. I told him I had seen what happened. Figured there was no reason to lie. Dixon—" Henry paused awkwardly when he mentioned his name. His jaw clenched before he gathered himself. "Dixon saw me there. But then I told Hiroshi he should be careful unless he wanted to end up like her."

"That was the right advice, unfortunately." Brisa sighed. She disliked advising inaction in the face of injustice, but these circumstances dictated other tactics.

"They took him, too?"

"I was hoping you could confirm that, but it seems so. The problem is no one saw anything. Or no one is willing to talk about it. You haven't heard from other customers?"

"Look around," said Henry. His concern shifted into agitation at her questioning. "Barely anyone has stopped by in the past few days. The only reason I keep baking is because I need to keep my hands busy. I've been dropping bags of leftovers at different neighbors' homes hoping it doesn't all go bad. Even so I'm throwing out a ton."

"You haven't heard anything suspicious while making those deliveries?"

Henry chose his words carefully. "Let's say I don't think Hiroshi and Calla are the only ones to have gone missing."

"What do you mean?" she asked, even though she suspected the same.

"There are people I haven't seen in days. Our cabins are so small. It's not easy to hide in there all day every day. The Militia are taking people. I don't know how or when, but they're being more careful than before."

"Then we're on the same page," replied Brisa. She shuddered as the weight of their new reality settled on her shoulders. "In that case, I need to ask you a favor."

"What do you have planned?" he asked, flipping their roles.

"A protest." She blurted out the words, worrying immediately if that had been a mistake. It was too late now, and she would have to confide in others if her plans were going to work. "Two days from now. I want us all to gather by the lake and march down to the mansion gates where we will demand answers."

"Are you sure you want to do that?" Henry's eyes were wide with nervous energy. The coffee mug clinked as his shaking hands set it on the saucer.

"It's the only way," said Brisa. "If we sit back in silence, they'll keep abducting people while we're distracted by the earthquakes. But we can take advantage of this collective fear and anxiety. If you give people an outlet, a way to vent their pent-up emotions, you can turn it into a powerful movement."

He shook his head.

"Trust me. It's the only way," said Brisa.

Henry bit his lower lip but he stayed in the moment.

"You don't need to do much. Keep delivering the leftovers, but let me slip in a note to alert people to our plans."

"Is Colson in on this, too?"

"No. Not yet at least. Actually, you're the first person I've told. Wait, are you two talking again?" Brisa shot him a sly grin.

"It's . . . complicated," said Henry, blushing. "I'm supposed to see him tomorrow. Maybe. We'll see."

"Come on, now. It's me you're talking to."

"We're having a picnic."

"So it's a date, then." Brisa could not mask the glee in her voice. Nothing like a budding romance on the eve of a historic march to pick up her spirits. Things were looking up.

"I don't know about all that."

"Call it what you like, but I'm glad to hear it."

"Do you have the notes?" asked Henry.

Brisa could read the room. The obvious non-sequitur politely changed the topic. "Not yet. I'll be back later with them."

"You know where to find me."

"Thanks, Henry. Don't stress." He could use the encouragement. The simplicity of the task did not make it any less dangerous, and she had a newfound understanding for Henry's hesitation to get more involved. "You're just making the same deliveries as before. I'll take care of all the rest."

"If you say so."

Brisa picked up her plate to take it to the dish tub.

"I'll clean up. I'm not exactly strapped for time."

"Just strapped in," she said. "Aren't you worried about being chained to a wall inside a collapsing building?"

Henry looked suddenly terrified. "I had never thought of it like that."

"Sorry! It's a cute look though," she said, trying to pull her foot back out of her mouth.

"It's dumb, but it helps, you know?"

"I get it," she said. Not that long ago she had been waving her satphone around out in the open as if asking to get caught. Sediment Valley was not the shining image of a stable community. "Thanks again. I'll swing by later with the pamphlets." Brisa gave Henry a half hug.

As she left, she caught a glimpse of Lady Duggery's framed portrait hanging over the door. *That woman is always watching,* she thought. She took it as a reminder to keep her guard up.

On the walk home, Brisa felt securely back in her element, planning political rallies and knocking at the gates of power. She had two days to prepare. It would be tight, but she thrived under pressure.

CHAPTER 21

COLSON

HENRY WAS TWENTY MINUTES late for their—was Colson willing to call it a date? The world felt turned upside down. The forces arrayed against him appeared to be growing stronger by the day. He had even confirmed his inability to reconnect with Gaia. Despite it all, Colson knew one thing for certain. The fleeting embrace with Henry backed against the bakery wall was the safest he had felt in ages. Their untimely connection, inconvenient as hell, was undeniable.

He fiddled with the fringed edge of the picnic blanket. Wanting everything to be perfect, he had picked a discreet spot in the park where they would be mostly hidden behind a row of browning hedges.

In recent days, Sediment Valley had taken on the appearance of a ghost town. Except for the odd person who skittishly power walked between errands, the formerly ebullient public spaces had become vacant. The park in front of the square usually buzzed with people. Children used to chase one another in a game of tag while their parents shared cocktails and confections after a hard day's work.

Now, the grass was overgrown and drying out. Once luscious flowerbeds of hydrangeas and daisies sagged as if the life had been slowly drained from their petals and leaves. An ancient oak tree had crashed to the ground, its exposed roots desiccating in the harsh sun. The sprawling canopy knocked out a few solar umbrellas and cracked a picnic table, which remained in disrepair in the wake of all the other disaster zones that took priority. Even the squirrels and rabbits, who used to roam without a care in the world, unafraid of their human neighbors, were nowhere to be found. The park had decayed at an alarming, unnatural rate.

After checking his watch for the hundredth time, Colson began to doubt his own memory. Maybe he had said 12:30 instead of noon? But that wasn't right. He had said noon. Henry said it was the perfect time for a break because he would need to let his pie doughs rest in the walk-in cooler. Maybe Henry had slipped into a baking tunnel and lost track of time? Colson was not used to going on dates, closed-off as he had been to everyone except Gaia, and the doubts spiraling in his mind were not a feeling he wanted to normalize.

Colson stood to get a glimpse of the bakery. Not wanting to appear desperate, he pretended to search for something in the picnic basket. It was hard to see anything through the wooded park, but the bakeshop appeared closed with the lights off. Maybe Henry was just locking up?

As the minutes crept by, Colson felt his impatience shifting toward frustration, and it didn't help that his stomach began gurgling. The kitchen had packed a decent spread, and he decided not to let it go to waste just because some boy he barely knew was ghosting him in a town of three hundred.

Before that thought had time to root itself too deeply his mind, he heard footsteps crossing the park behind him. He was torn, caught between the desire to lash out and the relief that Henry had shown up after all. He hated this feeling. He decided to play it cool. He dipped a carrot stick in hummus without turning around.

"Sorry for the delay!" said Henry. He came running around the row of hedges. "The past few days have been hectic. Lady Duggery had that huge order of mille-feuille yesterday. Here," he said as he held out an enormous cinnamon roll.

Henry's immediate apology disarmed Colson. He decided not to hold a grudge for once in his life and set the cinnamon roll aside for later. "You should've seen her," said Colson. "She came running into my room with sticky hands and practically shoved one down my throat."

"Sounds hot," replied Henry with an ironic wink.

A sly smile slipped from Colson's lips. "She's a big fan of yours. That's for sure." He was relieved to have Lady Duggery talking to him like old times again. Apparently, she didn't suspect him of treason, at least not yet. He patted the blanket next to him, inviting Henry to sit.

"I've recently learned what it's like to have her heap attention on me. She wanted a berry pie. Easy as can be, I thought. But right as I was crimping the lattice crust, she called and changed her mind. Now she wants a chocolate croissant, and she wants it with her afternoon tea. I only just got to a stopping point." Henry sighed.

"It's ok," said Colson, and he meant it. "More than once I've had to drop everything and shift gears, regardless of how that would affect my schedule." It felt good to commiserate with someone who wasn't technically a staff member. He poured Henry a glass of rosé and arranged other containers of food on the picnic blanket.

"Cheers!" said Henry. They clinked glasses and locked eyes until both had taken a sip. "Shall we?"

Colson nodded and handed Henry a plate. But all he wanted to do was kiss him. He felt like a teenager. It was almost embarrassing.

"This is delicious." Henry licked his lips and downed half the glass of wine in a single swig. "I really like this color on you," he said with an uncharacteristic nonchalance.

Colson wore a new outfit he found tucked in his closet that very morning. "I wasn't sure about the purple."

Up to this point, Henry had been avoidant at best. The kind of guy who looked nervously around the room while in the middle of a conversation. Now he stared into Colson's eyes without blushing.

"You seem different today," said Colson.

"How so?" Henry dipped a carrot stick into the hummus. It crunched loudly when he bit into it.

"More confident? I wasn't sure you'd show up."

Henry hesitated, as if holding himself back from speaking. He turned his head to the side, and Colson could have sworn Henry was mouthing words to himself. He was timid and skittish, so he gave Henry the space to gather his thoughts. He didn't want to send him running away when he had shown up in such a good mood.

"Sorry, I'm not trying to make you feel bad," said Colson, backing down from the interrogation.

"It's ok. I wasn't sure we should do this either," admitted Henry.

"What do you mean?" Even though Colson had similar doubts, the words stung. He let Henry explain first.

"Lady Duggery's order did delay me just now, but if I'm being honest, I almost called to cancel." Henry paused again, visibly mulling his words. "I guess I thought that part of my life was over. That I should just be happy I get to bake. It seemed selfish to want more."

"I know what you mean. I've been so focused on one goal for years now."

"You mean, getting back at the Militia?" Henry whispered the last few words.

"Yeah." When he thought about it alone, his plans felt justified, even normal. In conversation, however, his own detached, relentless pursuit of vengeance cut through him.

Henry poured himself another glass of rosé.

The silence spread before the two of them as Colson retreated into his memories of the massacre. He recalled hearing Dixon's amplified voice ordering any survivors to surrender while Gaia guided his escape through the tree line. A few blocks from his home, he listened from the shadows as a door creaked open, revealing a few survivors. He knew that family, the Andrews, an interracial couple and their two-year-old daughter. He heard them call out, proclaiming their surrender, if they could just leave in peace. They promised to never come back. Colson strained to hear their pleas, their throats erupting in grief. Then the deafening gunshot, followed by two more. He almost screamed, but the vegetation grew across his mouth to silence him. It held him back as he prepared to lunge, unarmed, toward the vile man holding the gun.

Every time Dixon spoke, even after all these years, Colson heard those bullets tearing fresh holes in the few remaining memories of his childhood.

Henry's hand crept across Colson's knee and brought him back to reality.

"Sorry, sometimes I get flashbacks."

Henry withdrew his hand, but before he got too far away, Colson locked his fingers around Henry's. Something about his touch helped him feel grounded again.

"Your hands are cold," said Henry.

"It's a bit chilly today."

Henry set his wine glass down and sidled up alongside Colson. His knee grazed Colson's, tentatively, and Colson took a deep breath to calm his beating heart. He relaxed his own thighs and rested against Henry's, inviting more contact. He turned toward Henry's lips, then briefly downward. He wasn't *not* looking at the way Henry's pants bunched up in the crotch, but he also didn't want Henry to think him too eager.

"Hey," said Henry, gently and inviting.

Colson raised his head, and Henry leaned in for a kiss.

Colson closed his eyes, and he released the tension he had been carrying around his temples and in his shoulders. He returned the kiss, holding himself against Henry for a nervous moment, before allowing his tongue to tempt Henry's lips. He took a deep breath in through his nose and held the back of Henry's head. He ran his fingers through Henry's wavy locks and pulled him in tighter.

Henry's tongue responded, and his hands gripped Colson's shoulder blades, while lowering him onto the picnic blanket. Colson felt the weight of Henry's chest on top of his, of one of Henry's legs sneaking in between his own. He worried for a brief second about getting caught, but the risk heightened the thrill.

It had been years since he'd been intimate with someone, and back then, it had always been a stranger in the night. This felt different, more than the passing rush of throwing himself against another. Adrenaline coursed through his stiffening body, eager and willing—not just for sex, rather for Henry.

He placed both of his hands around the side of Henry's face, and the two smiled at one another. It was Colson's first moment of joy in the valley, the first few seconds of relief he had known in years. His arms trembled in anticipation of what he and Henry could become.

But that break from reality did not, could not, last.

Colson stared into Henry's eyes, but he began to see another face before his own. The features were similar enough to merge in and out of one another. That other face rippled and pushed toward the surface of Henry's skin, fighting to take over. He knew that other face. It was the same one he had seen during his trance in the grotto. Colson blinked, but he could not shake this hallucination from his mind. The memory flooded back after all these years. Suddenly, Colson was mere inches from the only man who gave orders to Dixon in Levittown, a man whose identity he had been unable to confirm in the aftermath. This ghostly visage, one he had almost forgotten about, now leered above him.

Then Colson remembered Calla and the emptiness where Gaia had abandoned him. His blood ran cold, and he freaked out. He sat up abruptly, pushing Henry to the side, and tipped over a tub of salsa. "Shit!"

"It's just a little spill." Henry scooped the salsa back into its container and set it aside, while Colson tried to wipe the stain from the blanket. "Did I do something wrong?"

"No, it's nothing," said Colson. He couldn't believe he had made such a mess when, for one second, things had been going so well. Where had the memory come from? And why did it have to jump out at him right then? "It's not you," he said, even though, deep down, he sensed it did have something to do with Henry.

"You can tell me," said Henry. He placed a comforting hand on Colson's shoulder.

Colson felt a current ripple across his collar bone and down his rib cage, as if Henry's touch were an electric charge. He considered evading the question, excusing himself, and packing up. It's not that he wanted to run away. It's not that he thought Henry didn't actually like him. He could see the attraction. He felt it, undeniably, just moments ago. Henry's stance reinforced it just now. Yet he struggled to look at Henry for fear of seeing that other man. A man all too similar to Henry.

He wanted nothing more than to pretend none of this was real. He wanted to give up his plan to exact revenge and live out some pastoral fantasy with Henry in one of the lakeside cottages. But the Militia would never allow them to live in peace. He had seen Dixon's violence before, and that man's unbounded hatred only found restraint at present by needing to appease Lady Duggery. Colson couldn't keep playing at having a boyfriend while trying to take down an officer in the Militia.

"If you're worried someone might see us—" Henry offered.

"No, I'm distracted."

"By what?"

"You." The word slipped from Colson's lips.

Henry withdrew his hand and slid away.

"That came out wrong," Colson said. He gathered his thoughts. "What I mean is that I shouldn't be doing any of this. I'm so lost. My plans failed. Things are worse than I ever imagined here. These memories. They keep coming back. I don't know if I can fix it or if I'm about to get caught or if I should just pack my things and try to run away with you. It's all too real."

"I've thought about that as well."

"I know it's not possible. They've got the valley locked down."

"Right," said Henry. "Have you, I don't know, come up with another plan?"

"Kind of." Colson hesitated to say any more. He wanted to trust Henry, but that strange vision held him back.

"Do you want to run it by me?" offered Henry.

"I don't know if I should."

"Is it related to the protest Brisa is organizing? Maybe I can help out."

Colson weighed his options. He and Brisa had agreed not to tell anyone else. *Still,* Colson thought, *it's Henry we're talking about. He's harmless.* "Do you know the grotto on the eastern side of the valley?"

"I don't," said Henry.

"Let's just say, Brisa and I found a secret stairwell. It's where they took Calla. The other day when I stopped by, I had just come from there. I got interrupted by Dixon and his guards. I hid until they went underground, and then I bumped into Brisa."

"Yeah, I tried to distract Dixon so she could trail them. Is Calla alright?"

"I don't think so. She was unconscious when they carried her underground, but Lady Duggery appeared before Brisa or I could follow them. People are getting restless. It's not just Calla. Others have gone missing, and we're certain Dixon has carted them off into the grotto for who knows what. It's something to do with the magical amulets. They seem to have stolen the powers of the Awakened. It's related to why I can't evoke those powers anymore."

Henry's eyes might have popped from their sockets. "You are one of the Awakened?"

"I . . . was," said Colson. "But that seems to be over now."

"Wow," is all Henry said at first. "Umm, do you need me to do anything?"

"Not for now, but if you hear anything suspicious, let me know."

Henry paused. He turned to the side again and mouthed something to the air.

"What's that?" asked Colson.

"Hmm? Nothing, umm, just worried about Calla and everything. I'll let you know if I hear anything. But these days almost no one comes into the bakery."

Colson squinted in disbelief. Something was off. He hadn't noticed it before since he was caught up in the romance of it all. It felt like Henry wasn't telling him the fully story. Like the tables had been flipped. He didn't know if he could add one more thing to his list of concerns right now. "I guess we better get back to work, huh?"

"Don't want to leave Lady Duggery waiting."

"No, we do not."

Henry helped him pack up what remained of the picnic. Colson folded the blanket and tucked it inside his knapsack. They stood, staring at one another for a beat. Colson almost leaned in to give Henry a little good-bye kiss, but he thought twice of it, and they parted ways without any physical contact.

Chapter 22

Brisa

As Brisa sipped from a steaming mug of coffee, two chipmunks hopped onto her small kitchen windowsill. "Hey little buddies," she said through the glass. One of them turned toward her. The other picked up a twig. The first one squealed a bit, and the second one echoed the same noises, this time holding the twig in the air. It swung the twig toward the first one, who just barely jumped out of the way. "Whoa, watch it!" she called out to the one with the weapon in its hand. The chipmunks squeaked a bunch more before hopping back into the brush.

Brisa loved visits from little critters. Something about her attracted them to her side, ever since she was a little girl. She imagined Colson reading all sorts of auguries and forewarnings into their frantic actions. But her rational brain intervened. These were simple chipmunks playing on a windowsill, mostly unaware of her presence, not oracles delivering visions of fire and brimstone on the day she would lead a march toward the gates of Lady Duggery's mansion.

The plan to take action had restored her sense of purpose over the prior two days. She had all the puzzle pieces lined up, even though she could not see the whole picture. The crypto servers were not where they were supposed to be under the mansion, and the Militia was carting people into the grotto at an increasingly alarming rate. Dixon had committed atrocities while blaming climate change on overpopulation among communities of color, and he was likely to continue down this genocidal path as his power grew. Even though she did not want to believe it, Colson had been one of the Awakened. Now, inexplicably, Lady Duggery possessed those same powers, and Henry was hearing a strange voice.

The disappearances, the crypto servers, the shift in magic. It all had to be connected. Today she would demand answers, even if Colson had reason to urge caution. Plausible deniability and hesitation only gave the architects of genocide more room to maneuver, more time to plan grander acts of terror and destruction.

She finished her coffee just as Jeannine and three other neighbors knocked at her door.

"Bad news," Jeannine said in lieu of a greeting.

"Good morning to you, too," replied Brisa.

"Sorry, are you ready for this?"

Brisa stepped outside and nodded.

"Only a small handful of people say they received your messages in the bakery bags."

"Hold on. Did they not receive them, or are they afraid to admit it?"

"That part is unclear," replied Brady. He lived next door to Jeannine and had been Hiroshi's closest friend since they moved to the valley.

"And the good news?" asked Brisa optimistically.

"The good news," said Jeannine, "is that we managed to knock on almost every door on this side of the Square. The residents are on edge, for sure. They're not happy with how things have turned out here, but they worry about what happens once they cross this line in the sand. I'm sure if you squint, you will see anxious people peeking out from their own windows. No one wants to be the first one out their door."

"That's normal," said Brisa. She shook hands with the other two people accompanying Jeannine and Brady. The five of them hopped on their bikes toward the bridge that spanned the rapids where the lake narrowed into the river. If they led, the others would follow.

Once they were in position, a few residents poked their head out of their doors to make sure no guards were patrolling the immediate area. Little by little, they emerged carrying pots, pans, baking sheets, anything metal from their homes, and they banged on them with serving wares and garden tools.

Some of them rode their bikes, and as instructed, all wore helmets or bandanas. Many of the residents had coordinated, taking the deep blue arm bands the men had been forced to wear on Founder's Day, and shredded them into a fringed rag now tied to their belts. The symbolism would not be missed by the Militia, who treated their insignia with more respect than most human lives.

The more people joined, the quicker the stream of first-time protesters grew into a critical mass prepared to demand justice by putting their bodies on the line.

After all those days in a slump, twiddling her fingers and dreaming of home, Brisa was back in her element. She had spent her early twenties organizing, protesting, and even scheming to blow up a pipeline once. Nothing could compare to the rush of taking direct action, occupying airports, handcuffing herself to trains, and picketing outside the homes of unelected fascist judges. In the last few years, her attention had shifted to building up ChainBlock into a clandestine organization. Even though her efforts at ChainBlock had seen more success in actually shuttering crypto mines around the hemisphere, in actually effecting change, nothing could compare to the fire she felt when otherwise passive citizens awoke.

Before they set out, Brisa riled up the residents even further with a series of chants. Some in the group began to cheer, while others, overcome with emotion from the collective outpouring, yelled from deep within themselves. Their collective grief for a world in crisis and for the missing commingled with a rage they now believed could transform Sediment Valley into the happy refuge it was always supposed to be.

On Brisa's signal, the throng of protesters banged their pots and pans and marched toward the Square.

———◈———

Outside the shops, Brisa hopped off her bike and waited for the crowd to form around her. She reveled in her ability to give impromptu speeches that jazzed everyone up. She would make their cause sound clear and the change, inevitable. She planned to recall the residents' collective sacrifices, the high regard to which they held the proprietors, and the way they labored without complaint. She needed to demonstrate how far things had fallen and how little their leaders now cared for their wellbeing.

Before Brisa even turned toward the crowd, a voice boomed from behind her. It was Jeannine. She stood on a small box and addressed the protesters. Brisa felt a small jab to her ego—she had been the one to organize this event, after all. A few years ago, she might have allowed this perceived insult to build into a seething rivalry. While Jeannine began to speak, however, her annoyance slipped away. Brisa didn't need to be the one on the soapbox. As she listened, she even felt pride in seeing Jeannine rise to the occasion.

"Thank you for joining me today," shouted Jeannine. The sun shone brightly, and she shielded her eyes. "I'm new to this, so bear with me." A few voices called out to encourage her, and others clapped to approve of each new sentence. "The last week has been unbearable. The quakes are ruining almost everything we've built. Look around us at the deplorable state of the Square. The buildings are up, but the butcher's front door won't close, there's shattered glass all over the sidewalk, and at night most of the lampposts are busted, throwing the entire area into darkness. Not to mention how unsafe it feels to walk anywhere for fear that a tree will come down on us at any minute. Our valley was so beautiful a mere eight days ago, a true oasis that we built and maintained, based on our environmental practices. We're actually doing things right here. We mostly tried on the outside as well. That's why we're here now."

Most of Jeannine's plan aligned with what Brisa would have said. The valley had fallen into disrepair and not for lack of trying. The residents had been quick to fix as much of the area as possible, but the destruction from the multiple quakes each day outpaced their efforts.

However, Jeannine soon veered off topic, promoting the vision of Sediment Valley as a solarpunk alternative to a world in ecological crisis, as if the people living here were somehow better than everyone else. As if they had earned their right to live in isolation from the outside world. As if half the products they relied on to maintain their level of comfort weren't harvested, extracted, and manufactured somewhere beyond the security perimeter that, curiously, had not been affected in the least by the earthquakes.

Jeannine, unwittingly, was repeating SustainAble's propaganda. She refused to see that this exclusionary refuge relied on the same destructive practices that created the climate crisis in the first place. Sediment Valley was a greenwashed ploy to grab money and power, nothing more.

Brisa wanted desperately to intervene. She needed to lecture the crowd, to point out their complacency and cooperation with the same entities they now protested. They could not have it both ways, she argued in her head.

But the crowd ate it all up. Their cheers drowned out Brisa's internal monologue, and Jeannine gained confidence from the applause.

"We deserved this refuge," she continued, driven by a burgeoning righteousness. "We do not deserve this torturous shaking. It's unnatural. We can all feel it. These are no mere earthquakes. We demand answers."

The crowd shouted their approval over their own roaring applause. Jeannine's charisma swayed even Brisa. Maybe it was better to let the crowd do the right thing, even if it was for the wrong reasons. That conversation could be had at a later date, when Sediment Valley was free and the missing were back safely in their homes.

Also, Brisa was desperate to join the cheering crowd and feel like she, too, belonged. The build-up of anxiety from restless nights required an escape hatch. Reflexively, she shouted an emphatic, "Yes!"

"We especially need answers about the people who have gone—" Jeannine's voice broke under the emotional turmoil she must be experiencing.

Brisa's heart broke for her, and tears welled up in her eyes. She missed Val. Even though Val was safely at home, Brisa felt like her own wife had gone missing since the comms blackout. And in a sense, she had. Dixon and Lady Duggery had taken Val from Brisa just like they had taken Hiroshi from Jeannine.

"It's ok, Jeannine. We're here for you," said Brady, standing by her side.

Jeannine wiped the tear from her eye and tried to go on, shouting at first just to get the words to come out. "We need answers about the people who have gone missing!" She paused again, but having said the hard part out loud, she quickly gathered the strength to push through the rest. "We demand to know what happened to our loved ones. By our estimation, more than twenty-five of us have gone missing. After the Militia kidnapped Calla in broad daylight, they turned to clandestine tactics. The others simply did not show up for work one morning or they never returned home at night. We have no witnesses, no trace, nothing to go on. We need to know if they are alright. We need to find them, and get them back, and hold whoever is responsible for these crimes accountable!"

The crowd banged on their pots and pans. They shouted and yelled their support for their new leader's speech. One young man boosted another on his shoulders to rip the Militia banner from a nearby light post. As the young men shredded it, their neighbors clapped and cheered and broke out into a chant. "Stop the quakes! Bring them back alive!"

And the whole time Brisa had become one with the crowd.

Jeannine instructed them to march toward the mansion. Brisa grabbed her bike, and more residents joined during the speech.

As the march left the Square, following the pothole-riddled road toward the mansion, Brisa caught sight of Henry through the window of the bakeshop. She waved at him, urging him to come out and join the march. He was speaking on the phone. He looked right in her direction before quickly turning around and walking into the back of the bakery.

Henry was skittish and introverted. She was used to that part, and getting him to join the protest always felt like a long shot. But one question ate at the back of her mind. Had he delivered her messages over the past few days? Or had he backed down?

The march continued. No point in letting him sour her mood. She turned her back on the bakery and fell into the rhythm of the crowd, ready to burn this place to the ground.

———◦◦◦———

By the time the protesters arrived at the gates outside Lady Duggery's mansion, the crowd had almost doubled in size from the group standing outside the Square. They exceeded one hundred people. No one knew how many had been brought into Sediment Valley, but Brisa estimated the total population to be between three and four hundred, including children. More than one quarter of the population was rising up. Under most regimes, such a stunning show of force would lead to a quick toppling of its leadership. Things were looking good.

Unfortunately, there was no space that could be readily occupied by such a large group to make their demands known. Lady Duggery would not have designed a kingdom with a town square that the peasants could occupy. The Square was basically a strip mall. The security gate abutted the road, and on the other side, the ground sloped precipitously toward the river as it rushed along.

The protesters spread out on the cracked pavement like a serpent, making it more difficult to communicate directions from the head to the tail. From this vantage point, the mansion was all but indiscernible. Only the peak of the pitched roof could be seen by backing up to the river's edge. Still, the protesters chanted at the trees and the handful of guards who manned the station.

In her attempt to corral more residents into the march, Brisa fell into the middle of the pack. How many of them knew someone who had been abducted? The odds were high.

As they approached the hour mark with no response from Dixon or Lady Duggery, Brisa's stomach began to growl. "Silence was such a powerful tool," Brisa said to the parent of two teenagers and the young couple standing next to her. "We tend to think of silence as a retreat from politics. We equate it with complacency, and it's often a mark of approval of the status quo. But the refusal to participate in a broken system can be a form of action." The people beside her nodded along. She did not know if they agreed or were just humoring her to be pleasant in the moment. Besides, there wasn't much else to do. "Of course, when your leaders are silent, that's another flex of their political muscle. It's them saying we don't owe you anything, and we don't think you're important enough to threaten our grip on the levers of control." Her fellow protesters ignored her at this point.

She read the room and changed topics. She asked if others were getting hungry or thirsty as well, and she organized a small group to restock water and snacks from the bakery. Those with bikes would form a supply chain.

As Brisa and the supply runners approached the tail of the crowd, they heard an uproar from the head. She figured either

Dixon or a group of guards must have appeared. Lady Duggery would never clean up a mess in person. She'd send her goons.

Brisa was torn. Getting food and water to the crowd was vital to sustain them, but something big was happening. She couldn't miss the chance to hear the heated debate between Dixon and the crowd, and if she could heckle Dixon, that would make it all the better. Brisa tapped one of the supply runners on the shoulder. "Go on ahead. Tell Henry I sent you and that we'll help him restock later on. I'll catch up." The runner nodded, though Brisa could tell he, too, considered rushing back.

Brisa had to abandon her bike as she nudged her way through the crowd. "Excuse me. Thank you. Behind you," she said in her polite voice, the one her mother trained her to deploy when she was the only Latina in the room. She made some progress, but by the sound of things, the exchange was heating up. At this point, most of the people in front of her were also trying to work their way forward. She stood on her tiptoes, but all she could see were the tops of people's heads.

The shouting grew so loud it began to echo off the surrounding ridges, and Brisa felt herself pulled forward with the crowd. They had forced their way past the guards at the gate and onto the mansion grounds at the base of the mountain. The crowd had grown jubilant as their anger gave way through their collective action. They glimpsed answers on the horizon.

Until they heard the first gunshot.

A flock of sparrows fled a tree, and the protesting crowd, shocked into a momentary silence, began to scream. The panicked mass shuffled backward, each body out of sync with the others around it, and Brisa feared she would fall under so many legs and feet.

Another gunshot resounded, followed by three more. Various voices cried out.

"They shot him!"

"It's Brady!"

"They shot Brady!"

As the news rippled backward through the retreating crowd, the message countered their retreat. Brady's injury, and the possibility of his death, galvanized them for the fight. They reversed course again and stormed the gate with an even greater force. By the time Brisa approached them, she could see a small group, including Jeannine, tending to Brady's wounds near the guard station. He was alive, and the bullet had only grazed his arm. Some of the people were pushing their way toward the armed guards who were backing up the winding trail.

Brisa felt a rumbling beneath her feet, and she braced herself. *Another quake is the last thing we need right now*, she thought. But the vibrations had a different cadence to them. They did not create a steady wave that grew in intensity. Short, intense shocks, one after another. Like the pulse of a bass. Along the mountain path, something rustled the trees. An unseen force, heavy and leaden, came running down the trail, gathering speed and shaking the ground with each and every step. Brisa braced herself in anticipation.

Chapter 23

Lady Duggery

THE SURFACE OF LADY Duggery's afternoon tea rippled, but she paid it no attention.

"Did you feel that?" asked Colson. He seemed distracted today, his gaze darting to different corners of the formal sitting room, while he served her. She did not particularly appreciate being peripheral to his attention.

"No. What's going on with you?"

"Hmm?"

"Are you unhappy with some aspect of our work together?" Perhaps it was the new powers, but she felt light as air in recent days. The crypto mines were up and running, and profits were flowing in as she sold the excess electricity to the Pennsylvania grid. At this rate, she would be able to power half of the state within two years and earn twice its GDP in crypto. Or so she had been told.

She expected Colson to revel in her success, because it meant his own station in life would soon be elevated as well. Her operation was not subject to the Militia's not-so-unspoken white supremacy. She never cared much for those policies. They seemed wasteful, and anyway, Colson was one of the good ones. He just had to be a bit more patient. His star was on the rise, right behind her own.

"Unhappy isn't the right word. Not with our work, no."

"Then what is it? Do you desire more clothes? More authority with the servants?"

"No, Lady Duggery, nothing like that. It's the earthquakes, I suppose. I'm not sleeping."

"I can understand all too well," she said with a sympathetic tilt of her head. "It's rattling my own nerves, to be sure." Still, she suspected a subtle shift in his overall demeanor. "How are things with the baker?"

Colson's eyes about bugged out of his head. He knew of her extensive surveillance network, but he might have fancied himself immune to her spying. He seemed slightly embarrassed. Better not to admit that she had even replayed some of the spicier moments of their date in the park.

"It's complicated."

She was about to pry for details when her teacup audibly rattled on its ceramic saucer.

"There it is again," said Colson.

"Yes, I couldn't miss it that time."

The tremor was brief but followed by another that rattled the windowpanes. Lady Duggery did not appreciate this intrusion upon her much needed quiet hour.

"What is that?" She hurried to the window, allowing the points of her toes to glide just above the oak floors, hidden under the folds of her silk chiffon dress. The pounding sensation continued, growing in its power and frequency, but she couldn't see anything from this side of the mansion. "I bet Dixon is up to no good," she said, gesturing for Colson to follow her to the front porch.

The lawn outside the mansion was one of the remaining pristine areas of the entire valley. It too had been subjected to the constant quakes, but the staff focused daily on picking up fallen branches, replacing quadrants of the lawn with fresh sod, and replacing loose stones in the fence.

From this distance, the valley below appeared mostly unchanged. As far as Lady Duggery was concerned, the only damage to her domain was the temporary mental duress, and it would fade as soon as stability returned. Most of the temporary residents would be underground before long, and the true residents would replace them, having never experienced the damned quaking. She'd survive a few bad days, a week tops, a small dip of an initial investment that would soon skyrocket beyond her wildest dreams.

But on this particular day, the rhythmic chant of a large crowd echoed through the forest. Thunderous stomping picked up its pace while moving farther away. The tree line impeded her view of the gates, by design, so as to hide any view of the mansion grounds from below.

"I need eyes on the security fence," she said to Colson.

He ducked inside to retrieve a tablet, but he returned shaking his head. "They're all blacked out."

"Give me that." She snatched the tablet from Colson's hands and tapped furiously on the screen, opening hidden menus with her fingerprints and trying to force the cameras to resume operations. To no avail. The tablet produced multiple deadpanned notifications claiming she'd been locked out of her own systems. "You've got to be kidding me!"

"Dixon lock you out?" asked Colson. He always kept pace with her. It's why she liked to keep him nearby. Whatever her needs, he could be counted on to anticipate her thoughts and smooth out the wrinkles.

She swiped and reviewed a series of documents, pausing to verify what they both assumed to be true. "By the look of things, yes."

"I'll grab the walkies, run down, and get some eyes on the front gate," said Colson.

"No, you stay here. I don't need you getting caught in the middle of whatever he's got planned right now. I'm going to do something that might surprise you. Don't panic."

He shot her another quizzical look. He might be quick, but he could not possibly anticipate what happened next.

Lady Duggery glided down the porch steps, but before she landed on the stone pathway, she raised her arms in elegant curves, arched her back, and straightened her neck as she soared above the lawn. This pose was not necessary to take flight, but she did want to impress Colson. She needed to awe him not only with her power, but with her grace, lest he be swayed in the near future to join the ranks of Dixon. This moment marked a turning point in the history of Sediment Valley. Though she was prepared to suffer some losses in the battle, she could not forfeit her most loyal servant.

She shook her head as she soared. That word, "servant," it was not incorrect, but she felt it somehow indignant of his station and importance. "Friend" was too intimate, "confidant" as well. Colson was her lieutenant. Yes, she thought, *a fitting title on a path toward promotion.* She spun in the air as her head crested the tree line.

Colson's mouth was agape. His eyes locked on her floating body. She delighted in her ability to stay at least one small step ahead of him. She did a little, mid-air curtsey before rising above the canopy and swooping halfway down the mountainside.

Lady Duggery kept her distance from the raucous crowd that snaked its way down the road and breached the security perimeter. There were more protesters than she had expected. This did not bode well.

She remained high in the air where the wind whipped her dress with such fervor that she had to position herself against the currents to prevent the folds from blowing upward.

The crowd shouted, but suddenly their chants slid into desperate screams of pure terror. She squinted to locate Dixon among the mass of bodies. She found some bloated, misshapen version of him barreling down the wooded trail.

Of course he would use the amulet to inflate the physical size of his body. No one spent more time fixating on his stature than he did. In his circles, size was equated with power. She could only imagine the literal dick-measuring contests that must take place in windowless barracks. The men daring each other to drop their standard-issue briefs. Someone retrieving a tape measurer from the tool shed. The mental gymnastics they would perform to explain away the ease with which they became erect.

Lady Duggery had grown up around men like Dixon, obsessed with perpetuating standards of masculine beauty—though they would never call it that. They took great pride in affirming impossible gender norms none of them could ever fully attain.

Even with an amulet like the one clasped around Dixon's veiny, leaden neck, he failed to achieve that beauty. His body was distorted and overblown. His arms bulged with cancerous growths. She always assumed his true form would be this monstrous.

At this point, she feared the worst. If Dixon cut the security feed, it was not because he didn't want a record of the protests. He cut the feed because he did not want evidence of the violence he planned to unleash.

She could not watch. Her stomach tied itself in knots she might never undo, but she could not remain here. Such rubbernecking was unbecoming of a woman of her stature.

As Lady Duggery turned her back on the crowds, some part of her appreciated Dixon's foresight to purge this scene from the official record. She told herself it was not necessary to witness the coming events. Her primary concern was to prepare for the moment after Dixon's victory over the rebellion.

Chapter 24

Brisa

Brisa had seen it all. The hidden levers moving society. The psychological acrobatics humans could perform to justify cruelty in exchange for comfort. Even magical amulets that granted the gift of flight.

But nothing could have prepared her for the sight of Dixon emerging from the tree line.

His skin had traded its orangey, fake tan hue in favor of a matted, copper finish. His head remained its normal size, but his chest and legs had swollen, as if inflated. Yet he did not appear to be filled with air. Instead, molten lumps bubbled up from beneath his muscles. As each malignant growth hardened like iron, thick purple veins crawled across the surface of his skin.

Brisa shuddered at the inhuman figure who made the earth quake with each approaching step.

"Disperse now!" Dixon shouted as if using a loudspeaker, even though his hands remained empty. Two guards parted, but he knocked one of them over as he stomped toward the seething crowd still holding the line.

The crowd's determination impressed Brisa. Apparently wounding Brady in the light of day had been their tipping point. Yet she was not certain they could win this fight.

A silk-wrapped woman hovered high above them. Brisa had no doubts. That was Lady Duggery. For a fleeting moment, Brisa hoped her adversary was here to muzzle her attack dog, but the thought soon perished. As Dixon broadcast his final warning, Lady Duggery turned and sped away. She had come to oversee the work of her minions. Brisa felt foolish for giving that woman the benefit of the doubt. She would not make that mistake again.

"Disperse, or there will be deadly consequences," Dixon repeated. He stamped his feet to punctuate his sentences, and everyone felt the full force of his empowered limbs rattling through their bones.

Despite the threat, a clear voice rang out. "For Brady!"

Followed by another. "Justice for the missing!"

"Get them!"

The raging masses had committed to this fight, come what may, and once more they rushed forward, dragging a reluctant Brisa with them.

The guards raised their guns, but Dixon ordered them to lower their weapons. He swung his arms to the side, and as he flexed, his molten fists reshaped into cannon balls.

Brisa heard the thud as Dixon landed a blow into the nearest man's chest. Before the protester fell to the ground, breathless, Dixon's other hand swung at a woman. Blood and teeth sprayed from her mangled face. Two others rushed Dixon without a clear plan, without a defensive posture or weapon. Dixon did not flinch. They bounced off his chest, sturdy as a stone cliff, and fell to the ground. He raised his glowing fists, which shifted from ball to hammer, and brought them down on each of their heads simultaneously. The gore blew back onto him, and he licked his lips with murderous intent.

Brisa retched. Their blood was on her hands. She had convinced these people to leave their homes and encouraged their rage. Had it not been for her, they would still be alive. She froze in place. She could not force her mind to make a single further decision for fear of the consequences.

To her relief, the next wave of protesters turned to run having seen the ease with which Dixon crushed their comrades, stamping them out like ants. It had not mattered. He lunged toward the runaways. He jumped in the air, tucked his knees to his chest, and slammed his boots onto the ground. The resulting shockwave knocked those closest to him to the ground.

At least ten people landed with their backs exposed to the crushing weight of his hammer fists. He cracked one spine, then another, and a third, amplifying the snap of their vertebrae so all could hear the relentless destruction he would unleash without remorse.

Dixon stood over their bodies as blood pooled into the soil, and he ordered his guards to arrest the others who had fallen and anyone else they could catch.

Brisa's flight instinct shook her. Her hands trembled, and her rib cage tightened around her lungs. She had to run. She grabbed the hand of the person standing next to her and pulled them toward the gate.

The rest of the crowd ran as well, and Dixon amplified his laughter over their collective screams. "Return to your homes," he instructed them. "Let this be a lesson to you all."

As far as Brisa could tell, he no longer pursued the crowd. She kept her eyes fixed on the damaged pavement beneath her running feet, because she did not want to risk tripping. The stranger pulled away and outpaced her.

Brisa ran all the way to the Square where she collapsed on the sidewalk, right against the bakery's door. She banged on the glass, shouting for Henry to open up in between deep gasps.

Slumped against the door, she caught her breath. She knocked again, less frantic this time, but still Henry did not answer.

She peered through the glass. The lights were off, except for the glowing register and the display case. In the back of the shop, something moved. She shouted. "Henry, I know you're in there." Another shadow darted past the shelving, and a metal bowl hit the floor, confirming her suspicion. "Open up!" She shouted and banged again, but Henry ignored her.

This asshole, she thought. He had been so close to helping her out, and now, he was hiding in his shop in her time of need. *Pathetic.*

Brisa had made too many excuses for Henry. No more. If he was going to bury his head in the sand when his friend needed him the most, then she was done with him. She would direct her rage at him long enough to drag herself home.

Chapter 25

Lady Duggery

Lady Duggery crashed to the ground like a falling star.

"What did that asshole do?" Colson shouted the words as he rushed from the deck to aid her. The anguish was plain as day, but he seemed uninterested in her ability to fly through the air. He must have been worrying about his friends.

"He . . ." her voice trailed off. She struggled to say the words. To speak them would make the events real, would condemn those people to death. Such brutality had never been her plan.

"Tell me!"

"He's attacking the protesters." The color drained from her cheeks, and horrific screams echoed up the mountainside.

"Is Henry there? How about Brisa?"

"I didn't see Henry. And Brisa—I don't know her."

"I've got to check on them," he said. He withdrew his hand from the small of her back.

"No." She fought against her cramping gut to stand. She had to demonstrate that she could regain control of the situation, and she needed Colson to back her up. Without him, all would be lost. "You can check on your friends later. This is more important. We cannot let Dixon assert authority over the entire project."

Colson opened his mouth to protest, but Lady Duggery cut him off.

"Look, there are details I have kept hidden from you. Details I'm not terribly proud of. But they lead toward a better life for us in the end. All that goes away if Dixon continues on this rampage. He will destroy everything we've worked so diligently to create. Then he'll take what remains for himself."

She exaggerated for effect. The Militia would never allow Dixon to destroy Sediment Valley. This operation was the keystone in the Militia's plan to secure their hegemony over the entire Commonwealth before expanding their reach. The undesirables were needed as a servant class to keep this place running, both above and below ground. To annihilate them would be counterproductive.

Lady Duggery's true concern was her own prosperity. Dixon was hell bent on sidelining her, but this place would fall to ruins in her absence. She was the charismatic authoritarian who evaded suspicion by casting a spell of reasonable doubt over the minds of her followers. A beautiful, wealthy white woman like herself could not possibly be the architect of anything terrible, or so the inhabitants of Sediment Valley believed. When they looked at Lady Duggery, they saw the mother they never had, the sister or cousin they always wanted, the woman with the hot mouth they desired.

She knew all this. A part of her despised this reaction, but she wielded their fantasy to secure her power over them.

Even as so many people had been abducted, she heard their complaints over her surveillance network. They all assumed Dixon and the Militia were the sole perpetrators. No one even mentioned her name, except as a mother figure to soothe their aching stomachs and make the monsters go away.

Once they were strapped to the machines underground, Lady Duggery might become more of a liability than an asset to the Militia. To make matters worse, she had humiliated Dixon on more than one occasion, and he would not rest until he stripped her of her power.

But Lady Duggery still had a few cards to play. "Colson, I need you."

Colson sighed heavily. "What can I do?"

He was more clear-eyed than the rest. She was grateful for the little win. "For now, fetch my satphone."

"The one locked in your chambers?" asked Colson. He appeared even more panicked at the mention of her break-in-case-of-emergency phone.

"Yes," she said, confirming both of their fears. Calling in Ember was a last resort. "And for you to fix my make-up. I can't let Dixon see me like this."

"I know just the thing."

After Colson handed over her satphone, touched up her eye-liner, and splashed a bit of rouge on her cheeks, she sent him on his way with an unlocked tablet that contained her security codes. She instructed him to compile evidence of wrongdoing from the surveillance feeds. Once Dixon's superior arrived, she would present her case and work her charms. In the meantime, if she ended up under house arrest, Colson could be her ally on the outside.

With Colson disappearing into the tree line, she tapped her wristwatch to the satphone and entered a code to temporarily override the comms blackout. Her heart fluttered as she waited for a voice from the other side.

She recalled the moment the tunnel to Sediment Valley was completed. The Militia provided the engineers and the equipment, but Dixon had not been part of the picture just yet. Those were the good old days.

When the dust settled, the machines pulled away to reveal the pathway into her new world. It was a sprawling green valley, filled with wildflowers and birdsong that distracted from the dilapidated cabins and campers abandoned decades prior.

She had also been distracted by her companion at the time. He had a boyish appearance despite the battle-hardened weariness behind his eyes. The two leaders of this new venture had celebrated with a bottle of champagne, followed by another, and only after he climaxed did she learn he had risen through the ranks more quickly than he finished in the bedroom.

She appreciated that about him—the *quickly rising through the ranks* part, of course. It was reminiscent of herself. In due time, she would teach him the pleasure of satisfying her as well. The next morning, when she woke in his quarters, she found a "thanks, babe" scrawled on a note pad and her clothes piled neatly on a chair.

Only occasionally did she hear from him. At times, he sent her people he wanted saved from the chaos of the outside world, but at others, he sent her those who had wronged him, happy to see them disappear into the underground machines powering his rise. Ember had hand-selected Dixon, as well, suggesting it was better to keep his competition happy than to risk a rebellion from within his own ranks.

He also wanted her to talk dirty to him, and she obliged, keen to keep her options open.

"Go for Ember."

"I need you," said Lady Duggery in a sensuous, low voice to mask her apprehension. She preferred to lure him to her chambers with ulterior motives than to risk his refusal.

"Be there in a few hours," he said without missing a beat.

The line disconnected immediately, but her ploy had worked. Ember would set Dixon in line once she had her way with him.

She restored the comms blackout and changed the security code used to access those particular systems. Colson could get by without radioing for outside help. He had access to everything else. Meanwhile, she would stay up all night to persuade Ember to remove Dixon by any means necessary. She could still come out on top.

As she waited on the sprawling front porch, the sun set over Sediment Valley, shrouding everything in darkness except for the faintest light beyond the western ridge. She took deep, slow breaths to calm herself so that she might remain graceful yet stalwart when confronting a debased and depraved Agent Dixon. She just had to hold him off for a short while until her backup arrived.

But as his grotesque figure lumbered across the lawn, she shouted at him. "You stupid asshole!" So much for keeping her cool.

"No need to get your panties in a twist," Dixon shouted back, as if that image would settle her into submission. His boots still produced minor tremors, but he had mostly returned to his normal size.

She stood at the top of the stairs to the deck to make him speak up to her, but the treads groaned under his heavy feet. Five guards, in full armor, waited near the gate.

"I had no intention of subjecting you to that unfortunate scene below," he said. "I even cut the security feeds to shield you."

"I do not need protection from the likes of you." She eyed him up and down to underscore the point, but his newfound stature threw her off. Even though his body was deflating, he was as tall as her. His hands, returned to a human form, remained oversized, and purplish veins rippled across his eyelids and down his engorged neck.

"I seem to recall you asking me to keep the—how shall we put it—less desirable tasks behind a veil of secrecy. I followed your orders."

She wanted to slap the sly grin off his face. "I never ordered you to massacre the good people of this valley."

"Now her majesty has developed a moral compass, I see." He chuckled, and his entourage followed suit. He summoned them. "What would you have had me do instead?"

"For starters, not use the amulet to murder people."

"That's curious. I'm not sure if you're more upset about the lives lost or that I revealed our magical secret."

"Don't twist my words, Dixon."

"I'm simply attempting to understand your sudden contempt. I thought we had an agreement."

"We agreed you would keep this valley operational. Not use the amulet to roid out so you could feel like a big, strong man."

He flashed her a closed lip smile and took a breath, deflecting her attempted emasculation. "I promised I would keep order. That's exactly what I did. Perhaps you did not realize, but there was a mob storming your castle. Thanks to me, we are standing here having this conversation instead of sheltering in some panic room or fleeing through the woods. I believe you owe me a bit of gratitude." He threw up his hands in exasperation and said, "I practically saved your life, dearie."

"You're way out of line, Dixon. You jumped past any possible attempt at a peaceful solution. The people are rightfully scared and under duress. The machines are rattling their nerves raw. They needed reassurance, not a show of force."

"No, that's where you're wrong. The quakes are not the problem. They were down there demanding to see the missing people who, I might remind you, are spinning in circles to make you the wealthiest woman in the Federation. You might have skimmed this part of the plans, but we were prepared for an upheaval once the population became aware of the disappearances. This little revolt was always going to happen. Our simulations estimated upwards of fifty deaths, but thanks to my restraint, the body count remained well below that threshold."

"Give me a break." Lady Duggery practically spit as she spoke. "You didn't keep the rabble under wraps. You drove them to revolt with your pathetic need to create a spectacle of your power. You have been nothing but a failure."

"I admit I may have taken a slight misstep when we removed that young woman in broad daylight."

"Let me guess, she wouldn't suck your dick, so you had her thrown into the machines."

Dixon turned halfway toward his guards, who now awaited his orders at the base of the steps, and winked. "She didn't refuse me anything, that's for sure." A few of the guards laughed like boys who spread rumors about the girls in school. "Quite the opposite. She was too clingy. I had to get rid of her."

Lady Duggery had not known that detail. In fact, she had chosen not to investigate the incident at the lake, even though a different person had been slated for the grotto that day. The knots tightened in her stomach. Dixon treated her valley like a despot's playground. "You're a monster."

"I may be, my dear, but your claws are no less sharp."

She scoffed at his rebuttal, unable to think of a comeback. They had arrived at an impasse. She stood on the precipice of defeat. Her moral outrage was no match for his apathy. He did not care what harm came to those people. He did not care if they hated him or the Militia. They were a means to an end, whereas she took solace knowing they would live out their last days in relative bliss, surrounded by their loved ones, eating well, enjoying the sunshine and the rain, until they were invited into the grotto, put gently to sleep, and merged with the ebb and flow of the Earth. In her mind, the valley provided these people with a gentler end than whatever would have befallen them on the outside.

Dixon, in contrast, had declared them dead from the second they walked through the tunnel. How they were treated in the interim was of little consequence.

He was on the wrong side of history, but only now did she doubt the rationale she had concocted to explain away the inherent violence of Sediment Valley.

With his back to her, Dixon asked into his comms, "What's that? Interesting. Don't let him pass."

"Who are you talking about?" The lilt in her voice belied her stoic exterior because she knew the answer to her own question. It took all her strength, magical and physical, to restrain the chill gathering at the nape of her neck.

"Would you like to explain why your little lap dog is running away from the mansion at this very hour?" Dixon had answered her question with another question. He could take Colson hostage. He had regained the upper hand.

"I assume he wants make sure you didn't just murder his friends," she replied.

"Who exactly would Colson consider his friends?" asked Dixon.

Dixon had been gathering intel and would likely target whoever she named in this moment, but she had one final ace up her sleeves. She could offer a half-truth without putting anyone else directly in Dixon's sights. "Henry comes to mind first."

"*Henry*?" asked Dixon, perplexed.

"Yes, *that* Henry," said Lady Duggery.

"Why him?"

"Don't tell me with all of your spies you don't know about the two of them."

"You mean—" Dixon tapped his pointer fingers together, as if saying the words were too repugnant.

"Boyfriends? Yes. Leading in that direction, it seems."

"Colson . . . and the baker? Now that is rather interesting, yes." Dixon stroked his chin, weighing his options.

As far as Lady Duggery could tell, she had outsmarted Dixon just now. There is no world in which he would risk angering his superior by bringing harm to poor, little Henry. The baker was in a protected class of his own. And if Dixon had even an ounce of intelligence, he would expect Ember's imminent arrival.

Colson would slip through Dixon's fingers. She had won—for now.

Still, a snide smile widened across Dixon's face. "Release him," he said into his comms, with a childish glee. He was all too *happy* about this decision, and Lady Duggery had no idea why.

The game was not over.

Ember would fix this, she told herself. She only had to buy herself some time. Dixon could have her arrested. She needed to back down before he locked her in a spinning tomb.

"I suppose you did manage to quell their anger." The words stuck to her tongue, but she managed to release them.

Dixon flicked his wrists toward the guards, and they retreated to the gates. Lady Duggery's shoulders relaxed. She had made the right move.

"Are the gates secured now?" she asked.

"Perfectly," he said, beaming with glee. "The mob has retreated. They've blown off some steam, and they will be adequately terrified into submission by our show of strength. They won't try anything else for a few more days at least. That's all the time we need."

"Thank you, Dixon," she said gracefully. "But please do try to deploy subtler methods. I'd appreciate it if we could prevent any further deaths."

"I'll do my best," he replied. He took leave of her without waiting to be dismissed.

She held her position and her breath until Dixon and his guards left the grounds. She did not believe him in the least, but that was not the point. She had survived to fight another day.

Chapter 26

Colson

Dixon said to let *me go*. Colson had heard the man's voice over the comms in the guard station. The order had been unequivocal. The guards acknowledged without hesitation. And yet he could still feel their murderous gaze.

This had to be a trick. His legs resisted each step between the guard station and the gate. His back anticipated the bullets that would shatter his spine like the glass in the station's windows. It would be too easy to say he tried to escape.

Shoes littered the ground and tattered pieces of blue cloth were stuck in the bushes. For a brief moment, Colson was in awe of the people who gathered here to shake the foundations of such a powerful institution. But that reverence snapped into horror as his foot squished into a dark, wet stain in the gravel. Dixon's heavy footsteps had pockmarked the earth. The bodies of the victims were nowhere to be seen. Dixon's men had moved fast to hide them, but the trace of their deaths leeched into the soil as a reminder.

Colson held his breath as he crossed the gate and stepped onto the crumbling roadway, questioning his own continued existence at every passing second. No boots approached from behind. He might be in the clear. Still, he dared not look back at the guard station.

Once he was out of view, he exhaled and broke into a headlong run to find Brisa. He had to know if she was alright, since she had led the march, and he could use her help with the tech now in his possession.

He ran out of steam just beyond the Square and slowed to catch his breath as the sun set over Sediment Valley.

"You know," said Colson to Gaia between gasps, "now . . . would be a good time . . . to check in." Gaia, of course, did not respond. Their silence remained as their only constant characteristic of late. The difference being, Colson now understood the failure to communicate had little to do with his own shortcomings. It must be related to the way Dixon and Lady Duggery harnessed Gaia's powers.

He found Brisa pacing around her front yard. "I'm so glad you're ok!"

"Colson?" Brisa snapped out of her inner monologue. "What are you doing here?"

"I need your help."

"With what?"

"Lady Duggery sent me—" he began to say.

Brisa interrupted him at the mention of her name. "She can fuck right off. And you can, too, if you're still working for her after what they just did." Brisa turned to walk away from Colson.

"It's not like that. I promise," said Colson. He ran around to cut her off. He would need to explain himself better if he was going to keep Brisa on his side. "She didn't order the attack." He placed his hand on her shoulder, and she quickly shook him off. But she stopped walking away. He took that as a good sign.

"She did nothing to prevent it either. I saw her floating above us all as Dixon—" Brisa gasped for air, as if trying to swallow back the horrid memories of a fate she had just barely escaped.

"I know. You're completely correct. She's to blame, too. But Lady Duggery and Dixon are at odds with one another right now. Dixon is trying to depose her."

"I'm listening," said Brisa half-heartedly. She chewed her lower lip as he spoke.

"I'm not asking you to take her side. I know she's not great."

"That's the understatement of the century."

Colson nodded. "She was really shaken by what he just did."

"It was horrible!" Brisa shouted. Her voice cracked, and her attention went elsewhere for a moment. She shook her head and returned to the conversation. "We've got to make that bastard pay."

"Exactly. Dixon is the major threat right now, and Lady Duggery is hoping I'll work with her to get rid of him. She doesn't suspect we have our own agenda. Trust me, I am well aware that she could turn on us as soon as Dixon is out of the picture, but for right now, she's given us exactly what we need. Here, look at this." Colson handed the tablet from Lady Duggery over to Brisa.

Brisa's glower faded as she read through the contents of the document inside. "Are these her security codes?"

"Yeah! But we have to act now. Before Dixon gets around to locking us out of the systems. He's already put a few blocks on her surveillance cameras. I was hoping you knew where we might access the . . . whatever you need to access to shut things down so we can infiltrate the grotto?"

Brisa stifled a laugh at his admission of ignorance. "A security console. Ok, I'll help you gain access to the grotto, but I've got my own reconnaissance to do in the meantime."

"The crypto servers."

She nodded, always careful not to reveal too much, but a spark of ambition flickered across Brisa's face. She gave him a friendly punch on the shoulder.

"Finally, something is going our way. I have a good feeling about this," said Colson.

"And what little conspiracy is forming here?" asked a voice from the shadows.

Colson and Brisa both jumped at the sudden intrusion. They had come too far to get caught right now, but in their rush, they had become careless, blurting out their plans in the open like this.

"For fuck's sake, Henry," said Brisa, shaking her head, as he stepped into the light from her front porch. "So now you show up?"

"What do you—" he started to say, but Colson interrupted them.

"You're safe!" Colson went in for a hug, grateful to see Henry had not been harmed during the protest, but Henry reached out his arm for a handshake that got squished between them. Colson backed away awkwardly.

"Do you have new information?" asked Henry. He balled his hands into fists at his side.

"We got Lady Duggery's security codes," whispered Colson. He did not want anyone else overhearing any more of this conversation.

Before he could fill Henry in on the details, Brisa punched him in the shoulder again as if to tell him to shut up. He didn't understand why and gestured for her to relax. It was Henry after all.

"That's big," said Henry. "So you're going into the grotto tonight?"

"Yeah, that's the plan. Once we find a security console," said Colson.

"It's none of your business," said Brisa with rage on her lips.

Obviously, something had happened between the two of them, reasoned Colson.

"Sorry, I didn't mean to intrude," replied Henry. He took a half-step backward.

"You don't mean to do a lot of things, do you?" She practically shouted this time.

"Brisa, what's going on?" asked Colson. He hoped they resolved this quickly or put it behind them. Tonight was not a good time for in-fighting.

"You want to know what's going on? Your friend here left me outside of the bakery to rot as we were running away from the mansion. He's a—"

"A coward," said Henry before she could finish.

"That's one word for it." Brisa spat her words, but she uncrossed her arms. Henry's admission softened the defensive wall she had thrown up.

"I freaked out, okay?"

"No, you don't do that to your friends," she said and walked away.

Henry was holding back tears, but Colson went after Brisa. "Hey, wait up." Brisa swatted him away, but he followed her. "Please don't give up right now."

"No one's giving up," she said. "I'm going to look for a security console."

Colson was relieved that, despite the current mess, Brisa remained focused on the bigger issue. He did not know if he could patch things up between Brisa and Henry, but for now, he just needed them all to keep their emotions under wraps.

"There's a console right behind the bakery," offered Henry. He ran to catch up with them. "It might be offline. Weeds had overtaken it a while back, but it's worth a try."

"Let's go there," said Colson. He was eager to move into the next phase. He hoped Brisa would be, too. She glared suspiciously at Henry, willing to accept a truce, but only for the time being. Colson intended to encourage her as well. "And maybe we can find the—"

"The secrets hidden in the grotto," said Brisa, cutting off Colson before he could mention that she was going to look for the server farm tonight, too. Her caution seemed excessive. Henry knew about her general mission and could surely piece it together, but if that's what Brisa needed to get back to work, he wasn't going to interfere. She was the professional spy, after all, and they had shown a lack of caution tonight. The three of them walked in silence toward the Square.

———◈———

Brisa held a slender flashlight in her teeth to illuminate the dense vines she and Henry were ripping from a metal box behind the bakery.

While they worked, Colson wondered what had stirred Henry in the middle of the night. Perhaps a bit of insomnia, given recent events. Colson could understand the need to walk around rather than lie in bed feeling powerless.

He would sleep soundly next to Henry if he ever had the chance. How stupid to have made it this far in life, this far in a world beyond the brink, and still hesitate to find happiness, love, or even just a quick fun fuck. Once they got out of this mess, assuming they survived the next few hours, Colson promised to live more in the moment.

"Are you just going to stand there or are you going to help me?" said Brisa, pointing the pen light at him.

"Alright, alright," he said and wiggled the rusting cover free.

Bu doop. A green light greeted them with a delicate chime. The monitor inside the box prompted them to enter a security code. Colson hoped it was the kind of security device that didn't require biometric data. He was not prepared to sever a finger or pluck an eyeball from a corpse—unless they belonged to Dixon.

"Snap out of it, bro." Brisa might have agreed to let bygones be bygones but her impatience only grew as they worked. "I need the security code on your tablet."

"Right," he said. He slowly read the string of random letters and symbols while Brisa typed.

Dum dummm. The screen flashed red. Either the codes were incorrect, or Colson had misread it to her.

"Let me see that," said Brisa as she dug a pair of black glasses out of her backpack. She looked at the screen and tapped the side of her frames, obviously taking a photograph of the long code, and handed the tablet back to Colson. She entered the code directly without his help this time.

Bu doop. A brighter blue light welcomed them inside the operating systems for the entire valley. Or so Colson hoped. He was rather clueless with this sort of thing.

"So what do we—"

"*We* don't do anything," Brisa interrupted him. "Keep an eye out as I work."

Henry peered into the darkness to search for guards, but Colson fell under Brisa's spell as she typed and clicked and swiped. Screens lit up, pages of code whooshed past, and all the while Brisa spoke to the console.

"Clever," she said. Her mood shifted as the security system tested her abilities. "Come out, come out," she said, taunting the Militia's coders.

Dum dummm, it responded. It would not give up the goods that easily.

"Not so fast, you little bugger," she said, before the whole system went dark.

"What happened?" asked Henry.

Brisa froze while Colson held his breath, following her lead.

"Should we—" said Henry.

Brisa shushed him, and they waited for an eternity during which, at any moment, Dixon might pop out from the shadows.

Finally, a particle effect swirled onto the screen. Tiny blue dots took the shape of Sediment Valley's terrain, and then it populated with markers for the drone security perimeter, the mansion, and each of the cabins and shops. Every security camera had its own yellow symbol. There were easily three times the number of such cameras than what Colson imagined, likely hidden in every lamp post, doorway, and even tucked away in trees or bushes. Goosebumps prickled his forearms.

Brisa zoomed in and instinctively shifted the map to show the shapes of tunnels and secret rooms.

"Go to the grotto," Colson suggested, but she was already scrolling in that direction.

"The passageway leads deep underground, down a long corridor, and turns toward some seriously massive chambers. Like a cavern almost. But the corridor continues toward the Square. Look here. This shows an entrance almost right under our feet."

"That's odd," said Henry. "I've never noticed anything like that back here."

Colson couldn't see much. "The light, please." Brisa lent him the pen light and he scoured the ground. There were no signs of a hatch, a doorway, or anything other than the walled-off dumpster and the concrete sidewalk wrapping around the strip of stores.

"Look at this," said Brisa, calling him back to the tablet. "It's the charter for Sediment Valley." Brisa skimmed the text. "It's mostly corporate lingo, machine-written drivel for marketing purposes. Until this part." She paused to read in more detail. "Oh fuck."

"What is it?" asked Henry. He nudged Colson as he sidled up to the monitor.

"It's about the final phase of Sediment Valley. Everyone currently living here is holding a place for one of the actual donors. They're mostly corporate types from SustainAble. I'm guessing these others are the Militia and their families."

"Where are we supposed to go?" asked Henry.

"No," said Colson, putting together all the pieces. "They plan to take *everyone*?" This was worse than he had imagined.

"Yes, everyone is going to end up in the grotto, sooner or later," confirmed Brisa. "I always thought it suspicious that the Militia would populate this valley with so many people of color, interracial couples, and queer people. It was a bait and switch. Lure us in with the promises of a happy little valley, and then chain us up in their lair."

"But what are they using us for down there?" asked Colson.

"Henry," said Brisa. "You wouldn't happen to have any snacks, would you? Some bear claws? I'm suddenly famished, after everything that happened today."

"Uhhh, yeah. I'll grab some of yesterday's pastries if you don't mind them being a bit stale."

"Anything would be great." She waited for the back door to the bakery to close firmly. Then she turned back to Colson. "I think, somehow, they're using people to power the crypto mines. Or the amulets."

"Or both," said Colson.

"Look at this," said Brisa. She pointed to the lake on the monitor and scrolled beneath the surface. "It's the crypto server farm. Of course it's under the lake. I knew the technology existed to submerge entire server farms under bodies of water. It provides a natural supply of cold water to counter the intense heat generated by all of that computing power. But none of our research suggested SustainAble had adopted that practice. The other crypto valleys were much more traditional."

"Nothing here is what we expected."

"You can say that again. I need to find the access point to the server farm. If I can shut that down, we can really fuck this place up."

"I don't see anything around here."

"The map shows a tunnel leading from the lake to the base of the ridge far behind Henry's cabin. I'm going to head over there. No use wasting our time back here. You need to find out what's going on in the cavern under the grotto. Here," said Brisa as she tapped away at the tablet. "Place your watch here. I'm giving you full access. Or at least as much as Lady Duggery had. You should be able to unlock any door by tapping your watch."

Bu doop. The tablet and watch confirmed Colson's new access. Then Brisa tapped her own watch as well. *Bu doop.* "But be careful. There might be guards anywhere along the way."

"You too," said Colson. "Aren't we going to wait for Henry?"

"I'd rather you not tell him where I'm headed."

"Are you for real right now? He helped us find this console."

"I'm sorry, Colson, but I just don't trust him."

"That's not fair," said Colson.

The door to the bakery opened. Henry popped out with two brown paper bags.

"Meet back here at dawn?" asked Brisa, changing the subject abruptly. "We'll come for breakfast if anyone asks."

Colson glowered at her but would not make a big scene. They were on the cusp of something more important.

Brisa darted into the shadows.

"You forgot your bear claws," said Henry, but she did not return. "Where's she off to?"

Colson did not know how to answer that question. What harm could there be in telling him? But something about what Brisa said stuck in his mind. "She's headed back to her cabin to see if she can get the comms system up and running again," said Colson. The lie rolled off his tongue all too easily.

"She must be desperate to speak with her wife," said Henry. "More pastries for you, I guess."

"I'm not really hungry right now," said Colson.

"Oh, alright," said Henry. "Is this it? You're really gonna go down there?"

"I am."

Henry moved his lips as if rehearsing what to say next.

Brisa had gotten into Colson's head. He couldn't help but wonder if Henry was keeping his own secrets. Colson resented how difficult it had become to trust anyone around him in this forsaken valley.

"What is it?" he asked.

"Nothing. Just be careful, ok?" said Henry.

"I will."

"Do you want me to come with you?"

"No," he said without hesitation. "It's better to have someone on the outside in case things take a turn."

"Makes sense," said Henry, sounding relieved that he could wait out the storm in his bakery. He leaned in to hug Colson, and the two patted each other on the back. "Good luck, Colson."

Colson squeezed Henry extra tight, and then he too slipped into the shadows.

Chapter 27

Lady Duggery

Inside her chambers, Lady Duggery found a dozen new candles placed around the room and her emerald nightgown and organza robe draped carefully across the bed. She stepped behind her folding screen to slip into the seductive lingerie. The nightgown hugged her modest curves and draped gracefully down to her mid-thigh. The low-cut neckline framed the amulet that hung just below her clavicle. The robe's billowing sleeves and ample skirt were hemmed with ostrich feathers that transported her to Old Hollywood. The look was befitting of the grande dame of Sediment Valley. Colson had chosen well.

When she stepped out from the screen, Ember would find Lady Duggery's demands irresistible. Dixon never stood a chance.

She waited almost two hours, running through the script in her mind. She would convince Ember that Dixon had overstepped. She knew better than to criticize any of the Militia's tactics, so she would appeal to his sense of honor.

In their prior negotiations, Ember had always framed the Militia's conquests as a battle for the fate of the planet and the wellbeing of his people. Moreover, he treated her as an equal. Dixon was never supposed to be more than the head of security. Of *her* security. Tonight, she would remind Ember of his commitment, but she was willing to sweeten the deal.

By the time one of the guards rapped at her door, her leg had fallen asleep.

"One moment," she said with a wily charm as she stamped and shook out the prickling numbness in her leg. She swallowed any audible reactions. Then she slipped on heels, dimmed the lights, and posed behind the screen. The show had begun. "Come in."

"Where is my favorite girl?" asked Ember. He spoke like a southern gentleman emerging from a distillery, but behind his words, she could pick up a hint of that South Central Pennsylvanian charm. She understood the need to adopt a new accent and a new name in pursuit of a life that exceeded all expectations.

Lady Duggery stepped out from behind the screen. She arched her back and pursed her lips. She might have been overdoing it, but she wanted to leave no room for doubt about her intentions. "Well, what do you think?" She floated ever so slightly off the ground and gave him a little twirl. The ostrich feathers flared out, twisting the skirt around her waist, as she came to a halt mid-air.

"Aren't you just a sight for sore eyes," replied Ember. His pupils twinkled, deep orange and red. "To what do I owe the pleasure?"

"I haven't seen you in a while, and I thought with the systems nearing completion, we could take a night to enjoy one another's company. What do you say?"

Ember nodded in silence. He never took his eyes off her as she glided toward the bar cart and poured them each a large glass of whiskey. He ran hot, but she knew better than to ask if he wanted an ice cube.

"Careful now, or you'll get me all hogged up."

She poured a tad more, despite his protestations. He flashed a big cheeked smile and drank the entire glass in one go. He arched his eyebrows, challenging her to keep up with him. She, too, downed the entire glass. The night was off to a good start.

They stood face to face. Lady Duggery brushed the back of her hand against Ember's beard that now hid his scar. "This is new."

"I thought it was time for a little change," he said cryptically.

"I like it." As she leaned to whisper into his ear, her breath caught the ashen cinders beneath his beard.

He snapped his fingers, and the candles all around the room lit instantaneously. He sat on her bed in anticipation, his cheeks glowing brighter than the bedside flames.

Lady Duggery untied her robe and let it slip from her shoulders. She maneuvered the hems away from any open flame. Then she rose up in the air and flew toward him, alighting on his lap. Though she let her thighs make contact with him, she remained airborne.

Ember closed his lustrous eyes and leaned in for a kiss, but she met his lips with her pointer finger. The long, manicured nail grazed the bottom of his nose.

"Is something the matter?" he asked. The light faded from his pupils, and his expression hardened for negotiations.

"Not exactly," she said. "There's just a small matter I'd like to address."

"Dixon giving you troubles?"

"How did you ever guess?" She laughed in imitation of a schoolgirl to mask her concerns that Dixon had anticipated her move and already swayed Ember to his side.

"He always manages to stir up a ruckus wherever he goes. What has he done now?"

"Nothing I can't manage," she lied, somewhat relieved he did not know the details. "It's just that he takes his role seriously. I fear he's overexerting his influence."

"The guards tell me he was successful at clearing up the little show of force your volunteers put on today."

So he had been clued in, at least by the guards. Lady Duggery had to choose her words carefully now. Directly criticizing his forces would be a surefire way to lose. "Yes, he allowed them to vent some steam before quelling their rage. I worry—"

"Now there's no need to worry," said Ember. He wrapped his arms around the small of her back, signaling that her time was running short.

"We're going to do so much good here, providing a safe home for our loved ones. And the profits won't be half bad either. We're so close to the finish line. I don't want to see anything upset the delicate balance we've established."

He squinted, as if uncertain about what she was asking. She had to pierce the heart of the matter. Dixon wanted her removed from her position, and she needed Ember to intervene on her behalf. But she could not just come out and say that. Not yet. She would work him a little longer. All night if need be.

"I have full faith that Sediment Valley will be a resounding success. Once things settle down, surely you and Dixon can work out any minor differences between you. What do you say?"

He had other things on his mind besides a workplace spat. She relented for now.

"You're so right," she said. "I was being silly. Now. Where were we?"

Lady Duggery slipped the strap of her nightgown off her left shoulder as Ember placed his rough hand on the back of neck and leaned in for a deep kiss.

Once she wore him out with all manner of aerial stunts, she could take advantage of the afterglow. She'd have him wrapped around her little finger by the first rays of dawn.

Chapter 28

Brisa

THE HALF-MOON GLINTED OFF the lake. In the dead of night, the waters were otherworldly. Brisa forced herself to contemplate the body from its northern shore. Only now did she realize she'd made a habit of averting her gaze after dusk. Something eerie emanated from within. The lake never felt like it belonged in this valley. The longer she stared, the more unnatural it appeared. It was almost too symmetrical, too evenly rimmed by a sandy beach and a fleet of paddle boats.

If asked on any prior day, Brisa would have chalked it up to the improvements provided by Lady Duggery's team. Of course the shores had been reshaped and the sand imported. But Brisa never questioned the lake itself. No one did. That must have been part of Lady Duggery's plan all along. To hide everything in plain sight.

It had worked, until people started to disappear.

Under moonlight, the waves rippled outward from the two focal points of the elliptical lake. They were likely the hearts of the underwater chambers where the coolant systems took in chilly water to prevent the servers from overheating.

The stylized map on the monitor behind the bakery indicated an entrance closer to the base of the ridge, not far behind Henry's house. Much in the same way the Square and the grotto disguised entrances to underground tunnels and chambers, saplings and cabins obstructed her vision, designed to prevent anyone from stumbling into the server farm's entrance.

Brisa buzzed with an excitement that made her forget all about Henry's behavior. She was back to her old self again, sneaking around in the night, hacking into protected systems, discovering schematics for SustainAble's environmentally destructive projects. For a moment, she even tucked the scenes of horror she had witnessed only hours ago into the recesses of her mind. She couldn't do anything about them now, and if she let them surface, they just might drown her. Better to focus on the mission.

The brush was thickest near the base of the mountain. The red light of the perimeter drones blinked almost directly above her head at the top of the ridge. The mountains were deceptively large. From a distance, especially when compared to photos of the Rockies or the Andes, the Appalachian Mountains looked like mere hills. Their peaks had been smoothed out into rolling curves. No rocky formations jutted into the sky, but up close, knee-deep in vines and prickly bushes at the edge of the pine and oak canopy, the ridge dwarfed Brisa. Nature made her feel small in a way that only massive technological breakthroughs or marvels of engineering usually could.

She breathed the chilly night air to calm her nerves. Amidst all the overgrowth, she would never be able to locate a camouflaged hatch or a button disguised as a broken branch. This area was too large and overgrown. She sat on a fallen tree, rested her hands against the mossy bark, and closed her eyes, hoping to accidentally pull on a secret lever.

Her hands buzzed with a faint electrical current. An image of the sunken server farm flashed in her mind clear as day. A rectangular warehouse of thick, one-way glass that allowed her to see the fish swimming by as if in an aquarium. Inside, there were enough servers to power a small city entwined by millions of smaller tubes through which the cold lake water siphoned off immense amounts of heat. The vibrations of the underwater data center rattled her mind and sent her back to the real world. She shook out the tingly feeling in her fingers.

When she opened her eyes, three squirrels—two grey and one red—perched on the log beside her.

"Hello, friends," she said.

The lead squirrel batted its tiny nose with its forepaw and squeaked. The other two responded by bouncing on their hind legs and repeating the lead squirrel's squeaks. Then all three ran in opposite directions around the log, ducking underneath it before returning to their triangular formation on top.

Brisa had always been fond of animals, but she'd never seen such behavior in the wild. Though now that she thought about it, the little critters in this valley had been awfully interested in her. There was the field mouse in the mansion, the squirrel just before Calla got struck by Dixon, and even the two chipmunks in her window first thing this morning.

They couldn't be trying to tell her something, could they?

The three squirrels began squeaking again, as if responding. All three turned their backs to her and waved their bushy tails. The lead squirrel pushed past the other two, but before they proceeded, all three looked back at Brisa. The lead then beckoned her with its forepaw, as if to say, "Follow us. We know the way."

Brisa looked around, half expecting someone to jump out of the brush and reveal she was being pranked. But it was just her and her new squirrel friends. She had seen all sorts of unexpected things in Sediment Valley, so why not be led through the forest by a merry band of furry creatures?

"Alright, after you then," she said.

The trio nodded at each other and made excited little squeaky growls. Then, they marched forward, not with the regularity of an army but with the delightful antics of their species. They hopped from branch to branch and ran circles around tree trunks while Brisa pushed through the brush. Every so often they stopped to make sure she was still following. While waiting for Brisa to free herself from a particularly thorny bush, the two subordinate squirrels chased each other into the canopy and back down to the ground. The red one tackled the grey one, and they tumbled through the dirt until the lead squirrel chastised them both. Fortunately, they halted their play and ran toward Brisa, gnawing through the thorns ensnaring her.

She followed them for a few minutes, deeper under the tree line than she would have wandered on her own, until suddenly the squirrel trio stopped. They spaced themselves out a few feet and faced a common center. They were telling her where to search.

In the center of their formation, her boot clanged against something metal, and she reached down, brushing away fallen leaves and branches. She pulled at an olive-green tarp encrusted with moss and soil and threw it aside. There it was—an entrance hatch. She tugged at the metal ring, but it was locked. The red squirrel squeaked and ran in little circles, drawing her attention to the box on which it stood. She tapped her updated watch to the security console. *Bu doop.*

The squirrels cheered and did a little dance at the sound of the hatch as it unlocked.

"You guys are the best!" she said to them. She knelt down and held out her arms, welcoming them to join her. The leader approached first, but the other two wasted no time. Their warm, fuzzy bodies leapt onto her. The leader climbed into her right hand, and the other two each perched on her thighs, careful not to scratch her with their tiny claws. They nuzzled her, and she pet each one of them on their heads, scratching the space just above their eyes. But this was not the end of Brisa's mission. They accepted her gratitude and hopped down.

Sterile air with a hint of plastic rose from the opened hatch. Brisa waved goodbye to the squirrels, and they disappeared into the brush.

Motion-sensing lights illuminated the path down, a solid fifteen-foot drop leading to a concrete tunnel limned in blue light. Brisa started recording on her glasses as soon as her boots hit the ground and waited for her eyes to adjust.

The structure was disorienting. The ceiling sat just a few inches above her head, and it was only wide enough for two people to stand shoulder-to-shoulder. Though the walls were perfectly straight and plumb, the slope of the tunnel played tricks with Brisa's mind. She reached for a handrail to steady herself in the dizzying architecture, but there was no support to be found.

Brisa guessed when she was underneath a cabin—maybe Henry's, maybe his neighbor's—and when she had reached the sandy shore with the dragon paddle boat. As the pressure built in her ears, she walked onward, drawn to the droning vibrations beneath her feet.

At the end of the tunnel, a massive, round metal door blocked her path. Another terminal, identical to the one at the hatch and behind the bakery, was skeptical of her presence here. The blue lights turned red as a warning to intruders. She was not dismayed. She tapped her watch.

Bu doop.

Seconds later, circular segments of the door spun, some clockwise, others counter. Metal screeched and clanked as the locking mechanisms parted in the presence of Lady Duggery's codes, unaware they were granting passage to Brisa.

She stepped inside the mantrap, and the massive door slammed shut behind her. A frosted glass wall still blocked her way, but a panel opened in the side wall to reveal another terminal. This terminal did not allow for a simple tap. Rather, it required the painstaking manual entry of a string of letters, numbers, and symbols. Brisa typed furiously from the codes displayed in her glasses. One after another the terminal rejected her attempted break-in. If she failed now, she might suffocate inside this narrow prison before anyone found her. She kept typing until, finally, she found the right one.

The frosted glass turned clear and slid into the wall to grant her passage.

"This is it," she said in awe as she stepped on a sticky, blue pad that removed particulates from her boots. She had almost forgotten how loud these data centers could be. She plugged her ears to adjust, while she scanned the sprawling underwater chamber. Slowly, for her recordings.

Stacks of servers stretched some twenty feet toward the glass ceiling. Walkway grating led straight through the center of the chamber. It appeared to float a foot above the glass flooring. She must have been deep underwater, for only the faintest hint of moonlight rippled through the dark.

While the rest of Sediment Valley's infrastructure had fallen into disrepair due to the constant shaking, the server farm could not be in more pristine condition. The underwater location, in addition to offering advanced cooling, must have buffered it against the shaking earth. Still, Brisa tried not to think too hard about the water surrounding her on all sides.

When Brisa reached the far end of the chamber, she looked left and right, discovering some thirty other rows of servers lined up in each direction. The scale of this operation overwhelmed her. Each caged tower was identical to the next. Stacks of blinking servers. Bundles of meticulously bound cables snaking from floor to ceiling in symmetrical patterns. Nothing to suggest the presence of human activity. Brisa could easily get lost inside these sterile, self-same hallways.

The farm stretched under half the lake, at minimum. The sheer amount of electricity needed to power such a facility would exceed that of most small towns. At the western end, generators purred effortlessly, presumably attached to a hydroelectric system hidden upstream from the lake. They must be a back-up power source in case of catastrophic failure—an easy target for ChainBlock's team. But she doubted these alone could power a server farm of this scale.

Brisa wanted to yank each and every server from its rack and smash them onto the ground. She would fry every circuit in this facility if she could. But that was the old Brisa, the one who first showed up in Sediment Valley with a one-track plan. The new Brisa had to think strategically. The server farm formed only one part of a much larger enterprise. Answers would be hidden in here.

If not for the recording in her glasses, Brisa would have lost track of the time. Two hours breezed by as she scoured every aisle and every rack, creating a perfect digital map of the server farm to send back to ChainBlock.

Once she felt certain she had documented it all, she pulled out one of the many consoles at the end of an aisle and began trawling their systems. She skimmed countless files detailing the waivers for permits and the back-door dealings Lady Duggery had negotiated between SustainAble and the Militia. She uncovered sketches that at first looked like jewelry designs, but in fact, they were the R&D behind Lady Duggery and Dixon's amulets, in addition to another singular, much more powerful amulet. They relied on locally sourced Eastonite and delicate strands of gold. She clicked through further designs for large golden rings that appeared to hover above the ground as they spun. Singular parts were forming a clearer picture.

This third amulet, in particular, worried her. She had yet to see any signs of a third person with powers, but she did know one more person playing his cards closely to his chest—Henry. Now that she thought about it, there should at least be a few technicians working here around the clock. A chill ran up her spine, and she turned around quickly, half expecting to find Henry flanked by guards waiting to immobilize her.

The shadows remained still and silent. The Militia must not yet trust anyone to work down here unsupervised. Not her problem. She was alone, so she went back to work despite the tremor in her hands.

Eventually, she found it. One simple document detailing the basic operations of the final design. The rings held actual human beings, and as they spun, they harnessed the Earth and siphoned its energies, the same energies it used to grant magical powers to the Awakened. Those powers would then flow into the amulets, allowing the Earth's enemies to access the magic reserved for the Awakened. This explained how Dixon and Lady Duggery now wielded the very powers that Colson had lost. He would be relieved it had not been his fault after all.

The more rings the Militia activated—each requiring its own imprisoned human—the tighter the Militia's harness restrained the Earth. A fully operation system meant thirty-six rings and thirty-six victims. Countless others would be placed on standby as back-up human batteries. The obedient ones would continue to work as servants in the valley, while anyone who caused problems would be held in suspension chambers.

Once the final ring was activated, the Earth would be blocked from granting powers to its human allies within a three-hundred-mile radius centered on Sediment Valley. The Militia would be freed from concerns about the Awakened in almost all corners of the state of Pennsylvania. Their power would be limitless and uncontested by anyone with enough might to overthrow them. They could take back Philadelphia and, if they built more systems, they could march on the Midwestern Federation within a few years. Sediment Valley was only the beginning.

At the same time, their machines provided a near limitless source of so-called "renewable" energy that SustainAble could promote as a breakthrough in green engineering. They would use it to power all of their server farms, like the one in which Brisa now stood, and mine fortunes that would dwarf even the largest global corporations. They could sell off the excess energy, or give it away for free, to distract their future subjects as they built up their war machine. SustainAble would be celebrated as global heroes while staging a fascist renaissance.

Brisa's head spun. This was the biggest discovery of her lifetime. She struggled to keep her hands steady as she hacked deeper into the systems.

Before she could rendezvous with Colson, she needed to lift the comms blackout in the valley. She did not know what would happen to her in the coming days. The odds for her escape were not looking great, especially now that she felt indebted to the people who had fallen into this trap. But she could not let this information die with her. Her best bet was to send everything to ChainBlock as quickly as possible. At least if she never returned, her wife would know her sacrifice had been worthy.

Among the codes, she found a small series that were labeled "Comms." She entered them into the console, double- and triple-checking each and every one. No matter how many times she tried, the system denied her entry. She even tried all of the others on the sprawling list, but nothing could lift the blackout.

She banged her fists on the keyboard in frustration. She had come so far. These files would condemn both SustainAble and the Militia, or at the very least alert others to the existential threat they posed to the Midwestern Federation and the world. If only she could figure out why all of the other codes worked except for these.

Brisa closed her weary eyes for a brief moment to prepare herself to for an all-night hack-a-thon if need be.

Chapter 29

Colson

The grotto no longer smelled of soothing, damp clay. Instead, the scent of burnt hair and ozone lingered in the air. The guards had built a staircase to the secret entrance, and alongside it now sloped a metal chute, presumably to slide unconscious bodies easily underground.

Colson reached out for the uneven stones as he tiptoed down the stairs. Images of his hometown, the buildings charred and smoking, resurfaced in his mind. The moldy planks creaked under his weight, and with each crack, he reheard pops of gun fire. His rage threatened to burst through his determination to set things right and instead light the world on fire. All the while, Gaia collapsed into a blackhole behind his heart. His emotions yanked him in opposite directions with no guide and no restraints.

As he stepped out of the moonlight and into the natural darkness of the grotto, he reached for a handrail but found nothing to provide balance. Fumbling around, his foot kicked something lumpy wrapped in plastic. He leaned closer, and as his eyes adjusted, three body bags came into view.

Colson clapped his hand over his mouth to stop himself from screaming, shocked and distressed, as the deaths from earlier that day materialized before him. He backed himself against the stone outcropping in the center of the grotto and allowed the cold rock to absorb some of the horror. He steadied himself, cleared his head, and recalled the importance of moving forward to prevent Dixon from enacting yet another massive tragedy here or elsewhere.

Colson was desperate to speak with Gaia, to know he was on the right path, that even if he was no longer acting solely for revenge, all would be well. His confidence up until a few days ago had been based entirely on his sense of superiority. He had been backed by powers granted to him by Gaia, the Earth itself. What better proof of his moral righteousness? What better shield and sword than those offered by the planet? Humankind had spent its entire existence trying to dominate the forces of nature by one means or another, and they failed at every turn. When the power of nature flowed though Colson, he had felt invincible.

Now, however, Colson was reminded of his mere humanity. He was a small squishy sack of meat and blood. He had no armature, no sword or gun, not even a hat or a pen knife. Yet here he was sneaking into the secret lair of the most violent man he had encountered in a world full of hatred, fear, and betrayal. He had to shut it all out of his mind if he was to take another step.

He carried on, descending the winding stairs that led underground, not because he was buffeted by Gaia's strength, but because he had a small part to play alongside Brisa and Henry, maybe Lady Duggery, too. He had to prevent this terrible experiment from succeeding. Once he saw with his own eyes what was going on with all the missing people, he would find a way to free them.

A digital humming pierced his ears as he stepped into the underground corridor. There was an entirely other world beneath the surface of Sediment Valley, a world that merged the natural beauty of ancient caverns with the sleek futurism of earthshattering technologies. The main corridor arced in neo-Brutalist splendor. The geometrically precise patterns of the concrete were still fresh and smooth, unlike the oppressive facades of the original buildings from a century ago.

In this century, the style no longer represented equality, a blank slate to be filled with the energy of a thriving community. Under the auspices of the Militia, Brutalism had been revived for its stark, emotionless, and rigid forms. Its harsh exteriors would only house the blue and black banners of the regime or, in the case of this corridor, be backlit in cobalt LEDs. The lighting cast an early-twenty-first century glow on the space, out of touch with the mid-century modern style Lady Duggery had revived in the mansion. Then again, the clashing aesthetics were really two sides of the same rusted coin. They featured clean lines and symmetry to ensure that fascism returned with a spectacular yet orderly beauty.

Colson was surprised; not a single guard had confronted him so far. Dixon must have felt secure in his power after the display earlier today. He would allow his men to retreat to their bunks after a day of fighting and cleaning up gore. They would need to rest before engaging in whatever phase two of his assault would be in the days to come. Still, something was off.

Colson arrived at the entrance to the lab. He recognized this metal door. He had seen it in Lady Duggery's mirror feed days ago. She had warned him that he was not prepared to witness what took place in this lab, but he pressed onward.

Before he could even tap his wristwatch, the console's lights turned blue, and the hydraulics in the thick door hissed as steel locks retreated into the bedrock.

"Here goes nothing," he said.

He passed through the empty lab, where control panels blinked and beeped. Through the windows, he caught sight of spinning lights stretching deep inside a vast chamber. That's where they would be keeping everyone. He had to investigate. He threw open the lab door and cautiously ran down the rickety metal steps until his feet smacked the stone base of the cavern.

Silky threads of gold whirled in graceful circles around beams of light connecting the cavernous ceiling to the ground beneath. They reflected the greenish lights back into the deep recesses of the chamber. To Colson's estimation, spinning rings formed concentric circles before him.

Time almost stopped as he peered inside the rings. He steeled himself before looking inside one and then another, catching blurred glimpses of those who Dixon had abducted. He tried to grab the rings as they whipped around, but a force field prevented him. When he pressed against the field, green tendrils of light snapped out of place and whipped at his wrists like a cantankerous schoolteacher wielding a ruler. He backed off, shaking off the sting. This was not the way.

He explored further into the dark recesses of the cavern, beyond the activated lights, where another force attracted his attention. He knew this sensation. This staticky buzzing around his temples and under his fingernails. It felt like home.

"Gaia, is that you?" he whispered into the dark.

There was no answer.

Colson reached out to get a feel for the terrain that only lit up as faint flickers of light bounced around the cave from the golden rings far behind him. He stubbed his toe more than once but managed not to fall.

As he turned another corner, a wispy figure moved in the distance.

Colson bumped into another force field that prevented him from getting any closer. He knew it was Gaia from their presence and the way they constantly receded, just like during his vision in the grotto.

Despite the near total darkness, visions burst in his mind. It was as if Gaia's power, or some representation of it, had assumed an almost-human form. Perhaps not of an entire body. It was hard to tell. What at one moment took the shape of an arm then shifted into a torso before transforming into a rocky ledge that melted into volcanic activity and hardened back into a headless bust harnessed by golden chains.

Whatever mixture of technological innovation and stolen magic he was witnessing, Colson now understood the reason he had been unable to communicate with Gaia. They had been the first disappearance in this valley. Another of Dixon's victims. He had intuited this much, but it had been just that—an intuition, a comforting guess. Now he had proof. Gaia had not abandoned him after all. They had been right here, underground, practically under his feet, struggling for liberation. The earthquakes, as disorienting and dangerous as they had been, were Gaia's cries for help.

How could he have not known? How could he not have felt their pain? He may not have imprisoned Gaia, but he had accused them of leaving him, when all this time, Gaia had been in need of saving. He did not know if they would ever forgive him.

A heavy hand fell on his shoulder. Behind him, a hot breath that reeked of cooked onions and corned beef forced its way down his throat. It was enough to make him gag.

"Colson, my boy," said Dixon. "Funny finding you here. I have to admit you had me fooled. I never believed you were much more than Lady D's lackey. Her lap dog who kept everything neat and tidy. I might have underestimated you."

"And how is that?" asked Colson. He kept his back to his nemesis. All guilt melted in the fire that grew in his belly.

Dixon probably realized by now that he had been the one to try to sabotage the Founder's Day party, but Colson wasn't going to come out and admit it. He kept his gazed fixed on Gaia's chains, while the footsteps of at least two other armed guards saddled up behind him and Dixon.

"You're not going to take credit as one of the Awakened? As the one who tried to suffocate us all? I suppose I might be a bit embarrassed, too, if I couldn't get it up in the moment. Not that I ever had to worry about that."

"Yeah, the people who say that the loudest usually have absolutely zero problems in the bedroom," replied Colson. That may have been testing his luck a bit much given his circumstances, but he couldn't stop himself. Dixon's every breath, his every word and gesture, made Colson seethe with hatred.

Dixon's hand gripped Colson's shoulders even tighter. "You, cuff him and take him to the tunnel where he will await trial. Lady Duggery will be interested to learn her most trusted advisor has been stabbing her in the back all this time. The rest of you, keep installing our volunteers in the rings. We need to finish this today."

Interesting, thought Colson. Dixon still believed Lady Duggery was fully committed to the Militia's cause and that Colson was a traitor to her. He refused to say another word. It was futile to try to talk his way out of this situation. His hands were literally being tied, he still had no powers, and he was outnumbered.

He had walked right into their trap. No guards had been standing watch. The metal door had not even required security clearances. He had been so reckless. But how did they know to catch him tonight of all nights? Only Brisa and Henry knew of his plans. Henry had appeared uneasy when Colson said he was going into the grotto, but Henry couldn't possibly have known Dixon would be waiting for him, could he? Even if he wasn't as committed to the cause as Colson had hoped, there was no way Henry was working with the enemy. Not after having shared so much about Levittown and his family. Colson had never opened up like that to anyone other than Gaia. If it had all been a ploy, he might never recover.

No, best not to consider that possibility at all.

Despite his protestations, as Dixon's men dragged him up and out of the grotto, Colson could not help but think of Henry's silences. His refusal to get involved. His obsession with pleasing Lady Duggery. And that vision of a threatening face that crept up from the deepest recesses of Colson's memory whenever Henry got too close. Something had been warning him about Henry, but he hadn't listened.

Doubt sunk its claws deep into Colson's psyche. All the signs had been there, but he still wanted to doubt that Henry had been a honeypot.

Colson admitted his defeat. He no longer resisted the guards. They would not need to drag him across the valley to stand trial. Instead, he walked upright toward his own sentencing as the light of dawn slowly rose behind the eastern ridge.

CHAPTER 30

LADY DUGGERY

LADY DUGGERY AWOKE UNDER her silk sheets. She rolled over to wrap her arm around Ember's naked torso and tease him as she made her final appeal. But her bed was empty. The space next to her remained warm with the heat from his drained body.

She found him whispering to a guard through a crack in the door. Three glowing scars similar to the one under his beard slashed across his shoulder blades. For a brief moment, she was distracted by the sight of his buttocks, rounder than his cheeks, in the early morning light. He, too, had learned a few new tricks since the last time they slept together.

Snap out of it, she thought. She had yet to win him over. This would be her last chance. She struggled to hear what they were saying.

When he closed the door, she pretended to be asleep. He leaned in to kiss her on the forehead, and she stirred. She grabbed his arm to lure him back to bed, but he pulled away.

"You were amazing," he said as he looked for his underwear.

"Don't go. There's more where that came from."

"Duty calls, I'm afraid. And a small family matter to attend to. You understand, don't you?"

She had to ask. It was now or never. "I just—"

"Shhhhhh," he said as he leaned in to silence her with a final kiss. "There will be plenty more where that came from." He grabbed the rest of his clothes and shuffled out of the room.

Lady Duggery beat her fists against the downy mattress and threw a silent fit. After everything she had done, he still slipped right through her fingers. Once the self-pity subsided, she better understood her predicament.

All this time, she had consider herself the queen to Ember's king.

That had been her mistake.

In the light of a new day, this arrangement took a different shape. It was not Ember and her against the world. No, Ember would accept no equal, no partner. He only recognized subordinates and the ranks distinguishing them from one another. In Ember's eyes, she was *Dixon's* equal. The two of them were second in command of distinct operations. Ember had pitted them against one another. In the event either grew dissatisfied with their rank, they would be more likely to turn against each other than to turn on Ember.

Lady Duggery was furious with herself for being so short-sighted. She had played right into Ember's hands all along.

"So be it," she said to the empty room. At least she now saw the world clearly. She would have to defeat Dixon all on her own.

Before she could even formulate her next step, a guard rapped at her chamber door.

"Go away!" she shouted from her bed.

The guard knocked again. Then he cracked open the door and, without sticking his head inside, explained his orders. "Ma'am, I'm sorry to intrude, but Agent Dixon requires your presence in the tunnel." He then closed the door as quickly as possible.

Now she was pissed. Who did Dixon think he was? To summon her—her!—to meet him all the way out at the tunnel. He had to drag her down past the rabble, all the way out at the farthest reaches of her domain. This was a power trip if she had ever seen one.

She would play along. With her new insights, she could beat Dixon at his own game.

"Give me a minute!" she commanded, reaching for a dress. She had no time to put on her face, so she grabbed a moisturizing cream and tied her long hair in a rushed ponytail. The fly-aways would bother her all morning, but not nearly as much as realizing she had mismatched her pumps to her dress in the frenzy.

It was too late for that now. She checked the security cameras to figure out what Dixon plotted. "Screen on," she said to the mirror display on her vanity. "Locate Dixon."

The display faded to black, while a loading icon spun in circles on the screen. Dixon might still have her blocked from the surveillance feeds.

The guard banged on the door again.

"Do you want me to arrive in the nude?" she shouted at the impatient guard.

The banging stopped, so she had a few seconds to assess the situation. Anything would be better than leaving home unprepared to rendezvous with that deranged man.

Multiple camera feeds lit up with different time stamps from the previous hour. Dixon had let her back in. The facial recognition software was buggy, so the first several images focused on a few of the men who had similar features. She swiped them away until she caught his rat-like eyes peering into her screen.

The image was from three minutes ago. The camera had zoomed in to frame his upper body. He was backlit by a dank, yellow glow. Usually, his expression contorted in some sort of grimace or wrathful lust, but at the moment, the giddiness was so apparent, Lady Duggery could almost imagine what Dixon had looked like as a child.

His glee sent a shudder down her spine. He was winning. He had crossed a threshold from which no one else could pull him back. He must know by now that she had summoned Ember.

She instructed the camera to zoom out, and as it did, it revealed the source of his joy. Colson knelt beside him with a spotlight illuminating the stalwart expression of a prisoner who intended to maintain his dignity right up until the end. His hands were tied behind his back, and he had been gagged with a floral necktie. The two of them were inside the tunnel, standing on the threshold where the laws of Sediment Valley faded into the chaos of the outside world.

She went to the live feed, and Dixon waved directly into the camera. He had staged this preview of their meeting.

"Cameras off!" She shouted so loud the guard burst into the door, in part to check on her, in part to drag her out before Dixon blamed him for their tardiness.

Her mind had gone blank from the shock of seeing Colson, poor Colson, caught up in the middle of her dispute with Dixon and the Militia. Linking him to Henry should have protected him at least through the night, unless he got caught snooping through the security feeds. *Oh Colson, I told you to be careful.*

Lady Duggery steeled herself for the possibility that she would have to say goodbye to the one person she most trusted in this world. If it came to that, Colson would see the bigger picture. He would understand his sacrifice had been necessary for the greater good. *Yes, Colson will understand.*

The guard coughed, and she swore if he didn't calm down, she would suck the living life out of him right then and there. "Let's go," she said in a low tone. She pushed past him, and she drew the air with her to slam the door as she glided out of the house, unbothered by the guard's inability to keep pace.

⸺⬧⸺

Lady Duggery soared headfirst toward the tunnel, barely passing above the residents who were up and moving at this early hour. One woman jumped into a ditch as the usually unseen and unheard leader of the valley rocketed past. A horde of unsupervised children ran in her wake, giggling and shouting for her to slow down. The winds she whipped up ripped desiccated leaves from dying trees, blew clothes from the drying line, and toppled the remains of a cabin previously damaged by the tremors. She did not slow down.

The road approaching the tunnel entrance dipped then rose, as if directing all travelers' attention toward the engineering marvel that bored through the mountain. Morning fog hovered in the canopy, casting the ridge in a haze that threatened any trespassers with the unknown consequences that awaited them on the other side. *Think twice before taking another step.* The message read loud and clear as Lady Duggery slowed her approach, blasting the guards standing outside the gated entrance with a gale. It sent the three of them reeling as she penetrated deep inside the mountain tunnel.

She came to a blustery halt just behind Dixon. A bound and gagged Colson knelt before him. As her feet alighted on the pavement, her dress fluttered in the wind of her own creation.

"I'm so glad you could join us, Lady Duggery." Dixon kept his back to her as if to highlight how little concern he had for her powers. "It seems a little snake has been slithering his way into your inner circle for quite some time now."

Colson tried to speak through the gag, but his words were incomprehensible.

"Hush now," said Dixon. "You'll get your moment to defend yourself before the Court." As an aside to Lady Duggery, he said, "Not that it'll do him any good."

"What is the meaning of all this?" demanded Lady Duggery. The breeze in the tunnel fell to a standstill, and her heart thumped behind her ears. She could not bear to even look at Colson, so she stepped beside Dixon. He held a thick folder overflowing with documents. The three of them formed an uneven triangle, from the height of Lady Duggery's head, down to Dixon, and Colson even further below.

"Patience, my dear. I hope you're ready to give the people a little show."

She took a deep breath through her nose, but instead of soothing her nerves, the stagnant air inside the tunnel irritated her throat and lungs.

"Honored members of the Militia," said Dixon. He spoke directly at the camera mounted on the tunnel wall. He must be broadcasting this stunt on a channel under his control. "It brings me no joy to share this news, but I have discovered a traitor in our midst."

"Don't do this," whispered Lady Duggery. The presence of cameras unnerved her. One false move and her entire reputation among the Militia could be ruined.

Dixon ignored her plea and waved his arm. The camera stand creaked as it panned toward Colson.

"The Court calls to order the case of *Sediment Valley v. Colson Dagwood.*" Dixon summoned a steel beam from the rafters. Bits of concrete and dust littered the roadway.

Lady Duggery ducked reflexively as the beam flew through the air toward her. She prepared to shield herself, but it stopped in front of Dixon and, with a flick of the wrist, he molded it into a judge's bench with a step at the base. He leered over the edge at the defendant below and slammed the file folder on the podium.

With the wave of his hands, the screeching of metal against concrete echoed through the tunnel. Lady Duggery plugged her ears. Then, he formed a smaller podium and chair from the second beam conjured from the ceiling. She obeyed his indirect command and took a seat.

Dixon's grasp of his powers genuinely scared Lady Duggery. She had known of his ability to reshape his physical form into leaden objects, but his ability to command any metal object was alarming. Especially because she had barely considered all the possible ways her ability to manipulate the air could be put to use. She had spent the previous days mostly hiding her abilities from her servants, whereas Dixon had been testing the limits of his powers. She had miscalculated on every front.

A thick, black line crossed the pavement, bisecting the tunnel at its midpoint. On one side sat Dixon and Lady Duggery, and on the other, Colson. Behind him, the tunnel, straight as an arrow, narrowed into a small circle of light that led to the world beyond. Normally the opening was barricaded with a steel door, but today it stood wide open as if sentencing Colson to exile.

"The defendant may now rise."

Colson struggled. His arms were bound behind his back, and his feet shackled. Before Lady Duggery could offer her assistance, Dixon yanked at the metal chains through invisible strings in the air, pulling Colson to his feet like a marionette. He staggered, his legs obviously cramped from the distorted posture.

"Three charges have been brought against the defendant. First, the Court charges Mr. Dagwood with forty-eight counts of attempted homicide."

"This is preposterous!" cried Lady Duggery.

"Is it? Colson, why don't you tell your master how you've duped her all these years as a part of your plans to infiltrate Sediment Valley?"

Colson avoided Lady Duggery's gaze. She wanted to believe he was in shock, but she saw only a guilty criminal caught in the act.

"Nothing to say for yourself? In that case, let's lay out the evidence. It is known that you disappeared from the Founder's Day party moments before Lady Duggery entered the grand foyer. Wait staff recall a shouting match between you and your little girlfriend, Henry, and then seeing you dart into the basement. And everyone confirms that the menu, suspiciously replete with seeds of all varieties, was your own invention."

"What does this have to do with anything? Colson was never to be in attendance at the party," said Lady Duggery. "Only the servants circulated with food."

Dixon produced a photograph from the file folder. A withered stalk rested inside a hole in the concrete floor of the basement. Seeds were scattered across the floor, and a wet stain spread from a water jug knocked on its side. "Colson's muddy fingerprints are all over the water jug and around the opening in the floor. The Court charges Mr. Dagwood of having attempted to deploy his clandestine powers to suffocate all forty-eight attendees at the event."

Lady Duggery's mouth dropped wide open in shock. She could almost hear the collective gasp of the Militia members watching the live feed. "Colson, you're not one of the—" she paused, and then whispered the prohibited word. "The *Awakened*, are you?"

Colson nodded, admitting his true identity.

Lady Duggery could have collapsed in disbelief. She sunk back in her chair, unable to maintain her regal posturing for the cameras.

"Lucky for us," said Dixon as he turned to speak directly to the camera, "our assassin was unsuccessful. Colson had begun the outlawed ritual, coaxing the seeds we had all consumed that evening to sprout in our stomachs and throats. However, our second volunteer had just been connected to the devices earlier that afternoon. You'll recall the first quake that happened as the Earth realized we had begun to harness it. Colson's powers—*illegal* powers, I should add—were the first to be blocked. Since only two volunteers had been connected, Colson had been able to siphon a bit of power, which is when we all felt queasy from the sprouting seeds. Ultimately, our machines stopped him from committing mass murder."

Colson shouted through his gag, presumably cursing at Dixon and everyone in the Militia who had tuned in to his execution. Lady Duggery feared she was also a part of his muffled screed, but his eyes shot between Dixon and the camera.

When Colson finally shifted his gaze toward her, his rage melted, his shoulders sagged, and his mouth mumbled a garbled apology. "I never meant to harm you." Those are the words she hoped he had said. She never consumed food at social gatherings, so it was possible his plans had been arranged to only attack the other guests. Even if that were true, she did not understand his motives.

"Regardless of the fluke that caused him to fail, the Court finds Mr. Dagwood guilty of attempted homicide on all accounts." Dixon banged his gavel-shaped fist against the steel podium with a surfacing smirk.

Lady Duggery could forgive Colson if he had meant her no harm. She could understand his rage against someone like Dixon without knowing the specifics. She felt the same on many occasions, including now. In fact, she considered blasting his docket with the stifling air and siphoning the breath from Dixon's lungs in that very moment, but something ate at her subconscious. Colson had obviously hidden his true identity and, for now, Lady Duggery was curious what else Dixon had discovered that she had not.

"Second," continued Dixon, "the Court charges the defendant with hacking classified systems, breaking and entering into restricted military areas, and conspiring to destroy state-owned infrastructure."

Dixon produced a series of files and screengrabs of Colson inside the underground lab.

Lady Duggery suddenly felt hot. She was no longer as concerned for Colson's murderous intent. She was ashamed, almost, embarrassed even, to admit to Colson that she too had hidden most of the unseemly aspects of the valley from him. To have him discover that grotesque laboratory, to know that he would see her as someone willing to abduct these people in pursuit of her own power. All of it forced Lady Duggery to confront the harm she allowed to happen, the harm she had caused. Even though she had given him the codes that would allow him access to the grotto, only now did she realize just what she was revealing to him.

Both she and Colson had been hiding secrets from one another, and now his trial had become a mirror held up to her own horrific acts.

"If there are no objections from Lady Duggery, then the Court finds Mr. Dagwood guilty. Finally," continued Dixon without waiting for a response from her, "the Court charges the defendant with evading a former sentencing for twenty years."

"Twenty years ago? He was ten at the time, Dixon! That would have been before Pennsylvania joined the Midwestern Federation."

"Precisely. The defendant, who did not even bother to change his name, had been a member of an eco-terrorist cell in Levittown. The Militia, newly tasked with controlling the chaotic populations in order to restore peace to the Commonwealth as we entered a new era, entrusted both Ember and myself, in our early days, to lead an elite strike team to destroy the cell to which Colson and his extended family belonged. He was the sole perpetrator, though long presumed dead, who was never brought to justice. Do you deny the charges?"

Colson shook his head.

"I insist Colson be allowed to speak."

"Fine," said Dixon. He hopped off his stool and untied the gag.

"Well, what do you have to say for yourself?" asked Lady Duggery. In part, she wanted to let him defend himself, to clear the air, maybe even to apologize or convince her it had not all been a lie to swindle her out of everything she had worked so long to achieve. In part, she needed to vamp so she could figure out her next move. Until Colson was untied, it was going to be very difficult to work with him against Dixon.

"It's true." Colson coughed, his mouth parched from the gag. He struggled to eke out the next few words. "Dixon burned down my hometown. The Militia killed everyone in my family. All my friends. They hunted us through the streets in order to purge our lovely neighborhood of its Black residents and restore it to its former lily-white glory."

Lady Duggery turned to Dixon aghast. She knew of the horrors of the Militia, especially in the early days, but she and her family, like so many white wealthy families, had been insulated from such shows of force. She understood all of that, in theory, even if she went about the world as if it were all a fairy tale.

Dixon started to respond, but Colson continued, his voice growing stronger. "They destroyed the most prosperous, majority Black neighborhood in the state of Pennsylvania, burned it to the ground, and seized the assets of the dead to finance their militant overthrow of the civilian government."

"I didn't realize—" Lady Duggery started to say, excusing herself behind a cloud of guilt that only manifested as she confronted the origins of her own wealth.

"You were not my original target," said Colson. "But it's true, for a while, I considered you as potential collateral damage on my path toward retribution. He can call me a 'terrorist,' a 'traitor,' a 'radical,' whatever. It doesn't matter. My plans were to do as much damage as possible to Dixon, the Militia, and the rest of those fascists hiding behind a greenwashed ideology to justify their white supremacist reign of terror."

"Oh boo hoo," said Dixon. He wrung his fists near his eyes to mock Colson for being a little crybaby. "We did what we had to do to take Pennsylvania back. Everything had been ruined by your whiny-commie-hold-hands-and-change-your-gender-every-day bullshit. That's the real reason we're in this mess in the first place. We did you"—and now Dixon spoke directly to Lady Duggery—"and people like us a favor. It was too late to fix the country, but we fixed our part of it. And to be honest, Lady Duggery, once we deal with the matter at hand, you and I will need to have a talk about your failed leadership."

"Colson, I—" Lady Duggery choked on her words. This had all become too raw, too real. Despite some reservations, at the end of the day, she had aligned herself with the Militia. The frame that supported her sense of justice cracked, and Dixon was streaming it for the entire Militia. At the same time, she worried deeply about everything she might lose.

"You're next, Lady Duggery," said Colson, as if he could read her mind. "I've tried to warn you. The Militia would never allow a woman to acquire more power than necessary to help them achieve their own ends."

"Enough!" shouted Dixon. His voice echoed through the tunnel. Its high pitch sounded like the side of a knife being sharpened against a steel pole. "The defendant has admitted his guilt. In the name of God, the Midwestern Federation, the great Commonwealth of Pennsylvania, and the Militia, I, representative and Supreme Authority of the Court and Administrator of Nature, hereby sentence you, Colson Dagwood, to *death*."

Dixon banged his gavel-fist three times, and on the third, his hand glowed hot yellow-orange as if it had just been removed from a kiln.

Lady Duggery backed away from her podium as it began to warm, steam, and glow as brightly as all the other steel Dixon manipulated.

Colson shouted as the chains around his wrists seared into his skin. The intense pain in his voice pierced Lady Duggery's subconscious. Though she still struggled to comprehend Colson's true intentions, though she felt betrayed by his lies, she could not simply stand back and allow Dixon to execute Colson. She now fully regretted ever allying herself with the man. The only path back to power was to destroy him here and now.

And, in the process, she would save Colson.

Dixon's body began to swell as he absorbed the molten steel from the gavel and the two podiums. He was insatiable, absorbing even the chains bounding Colson's hands and feet.

Once freed, Colson collapsed to the ground as his open wounds hit the dry air. Dixon likely did not doubt his ability to contain an unbound Colson. He had him trapped, and he could even slam shut the massive door at the far end of the tunnel well before Colson reached the exit.

Lady Duggery levitated just behind Dixon's line of sight. She had an idea. She lifted herself off the ground and hovered in the exact center of the tunnel. She extended her arms to the side in graceful curves, and her stark white skin began to shimmer despite the subdued, yellow lighting reflecting off the tiled walls. Her limbs felt like a mirage in the desert. They became incorporeal and translucent. The light wavered as it passed through the space where her physical body barely existed. She no longer floated or conducted the breeze; she had become the air.

Meanwhile, Dixon stood larger than ever without a care in the world. Streaks of molten steel swirled around his bulked-up limbs and torso like the currents on a distant planet. He commanded more and more beams from the tunnel walls. Some he melted from a distance, and glowing tendrils shot into his chest, swelling his proportions. Others flew toward him as solid blocks that stuck to his forearms, back, head, and crotch, forming protective armor and an exaggerated cod piece. Between the sizzling and the clanking, Dixon ignored Lady Duggery and roared over Colson's trembling, unprotected body.

Colson, wincing in agony, shuffled backwards to put some distance between himself and Dixon. He looked around, as if searching for her. The signals she sent him were not being communicated given her ethereal form. She rematerialized her arms, swooped a bit to the side of Dixon without entering his line of sight, and gestured for Colson to run as fast as he could toward the outside door.

The fantastical forms that she and Dixon had inhabited did not surprise him. Then again, he had been one of the Awakened long before she believed in these powers. Transfiguration would be nothing new to him, nor were the horrors perpetrated by Dixon and the Militia.

Colson clambered toward the tunnel walls and managed to stand. He used the walls to maintain his balance and run while Lady Duggery distracted his executioner.

"Hey, motherfucker!" she shouted to grab Dixon's attention.

The metal beast lurched, and his thick neck grated. His pupils rippled with fire. "Your insolence is futile," he said calmly in a voice that reverberated as if passing through a stone wall. He was still showing off for the cameras. "You think you can stop me now?" He stepped toward her, heavy and unhurried. He pulled back his fist and swung toward her. The slow movement belied the sheer force with which his body could damage another.

Lady Duggery faded as his bulging arm connected with nothing but air. He swung again, and again, missing each time. She countered by swirling behind him and pushing the stale air against him to knock him off balance. He stumbled the first time, before he had considered the force with which she could generate a gust, but once he learned her trick, he braced himself easily against her gales. Still, as long as she remained in this ethereal state, he could not touch her.

She amped up the air flow, drawing from the far side of the mountain to generate a mighty force inside this wind tunnel. The currents sped along so fast they became visible as they hit the blunt facades and bent around the sharp edges of Dixon's blocky body.

He pushed against the current, but this time, she managed to get some leverage. His feet dug into the pavement but could not root him to the ground. Sparks burst as his metallic heels dragged across the concrete. She had turned the tide. She had a chance now. She just had to see this through.

The hope, however, was short-lived when Dixon turned another trick. He reignited the steel forming his body, slowly at first as the rushing winds cooled and cracked his outer layers. Outraged by this persistent woman, he heated his body to extremes. Once flowing, his head reformed into the aerodynamic shape of a bullet train, and the chunky figure of his arms and chest rounded out to reduce the drag against his steely skin.

Lady Duggery increased the speed of the winds, but she had her physical limits. The tunnel stretched over a half-mile long, and the opening was too small to accommodate any more air. Plus, Colson was still inside the tunnel, far from freedom. She had to divert some of the winds to form a protective air pocket around him. The last thing she needed was to send his all-too-human body flying into the arms of Dixon.

Little by little, Dixon resisted and regained his ability to step forward against the whistling current. He pulled more rafters and beams from the tunnel walls. Many caught in the wind and whipped past him, sparking as they hit the pavement. Some flew so far as to slam into the folding gate on the valley side of the tunnel. Concrete slabs cracked and fell to the ground as Dixon yanked at any beam before him, load-bearing or not, until he had acquired as much raw material as he needed for his own ends.

Lady Duggery continued to power her assault, as Dixon formed a steel shield, anchored deep underground, to redirect the current around him. She altered the flow, but his design was airtight. Any major shift in the currents slowed their speed to the point of becoming ineffectual against this hulking monster, a grotesque creature she had tolerated for far too long.

Dixon hunkered down in the relative calm and, before Lady Duggery could predict his next move, the thick metal door leading to the outside world slammed shut. Her current was cut off. The winds died almost immediately.

Lady Duggery rematerialized, breathless, and flew into the floor headfirst with a deafening thud.

Chapter 31

Colson

For a second, Colson worried Lady Duggery had died. Her body did not so much as twitch after it slammed into the pavement.

After a moment, she pulled herself to her feet, fazed but undefeated.

Colson considered running to her defense, but he stood no chance against Dixon's molten steel. Not without his powers. He stayed put.

Lady Duggery faded into the air just as Dixon peeked out from behind his shield. They had reached a stalemate. Colson racked his brain for a solution.

"The mist!" he shouted. The words echoed down the tunnel, and her shimmery figure turned in his direction, as if to ask for clarity. "He's made of steel. Exposing him to water could turn him to rust."

Lady Duggery wasted no time. Within seconds, the mist lifting off the dewy mountainside came pouring into the tunnel through the valley-side gates. Wispy, damp tendrils lashed at Dixon, first cooling his outer layers, and eventually leaving him wet and steamy. Lady Duggery then conjured a swirling gale to continuously dry and rewet the steel, amplifying its corroding effects.

The surface of Dixon's sleek, metal body began to oxidize. Orange-brown splotches formed like an aggressive bout of eczema, and he let out a ghastly scream as Lady Duggery's forces ate away at his skin. Dixon ripped at the corroding areas to slow the damage, and shards of rust flew into the air. He could not outpace her, however, so he shifted tactics once more.

The uneven sputtering of a prop plane resounded above Colson's head. Industrial exhaust fans lined the tunnel's ceiling.

Colson shouted to Lady Duggery. "The fans! Brace yourself!" But his warning came too late.

Dixon powered the massive steel blades to draw both the mist and the shimmering cloud that was Lady Duggery away from him. The fans sucked her from one to another at the top of the tunnel, and Colson feared all had been lost. Dixon could form a loop with the fans and trap her here indefinitely.

But Lady Duggery surprised them both. She waited until her particles passed through one of the fans before suddenly materializing. She plummeted again to the ground beside Colson, though with a bit more control than before.

If there was one thing he had appreciated about Lady Duggery, it was that she always had one more trick up her sleeve.

She struggled to sit up before collapsing back onto the pavement. She could barely move, let alone continue in this battle. She reached for the chain around her neck, yanked it loose, and tossed the amulet to Colson. He snatched it mid-air.

Time came to halt.

The physical world melted away, and Colson found himself inside a cavernous void. A drip of water echoed into a puddle, and he reached out with long, verdant tendrils toward the space that had once been occupied by Gaia. Leaves sprouted while pink and purple wildflowers bloomed. He sensed Gaia, unlike when they had disappeared into the void, but something was still off. Gaia's powers did not flow through him unbounded, as it had since childhood. Rather, they writhed in agony from deep underground. The more they resisted him, the harder he clutched the amulet to harness those powers and direct them into his own body against Gaia's will.

Harnessing Gaia's power through the amulet was a violation, but he did not know another way to survive the present. He asked for forgiveness. He promised to drain as little power as possible to stop Dixon and free Gaia and all the others from the clutches of the Militia.

But Gaia did not respond with the words that used to guide him; they did not grant him permission. They only wailed out of dejection and distress. Colson wondered if Gaia even recognized him. He did not know if he could ever recover the lost bond that had formed the basis of his identity after this, but he pressed on.

Colson opened his eyes.

Dixon reformed his steely armor. He laughed with the roar of a demented lion as he pounced toward his prey lying on the ground. "You had me there for a minute," he said to Lady Duggery. He winked at the camera as he ran past it. "But look at you two. A frail woman and her little fag. A shining example of the multi-culti modern life that dragged us all into this global crisis. I will not pay for your sins any longer."

The pavement before Colson cracked. New life pushed up from underneath, forming a mound of crumbling asphalt. A sprout, Colson's sprout, surfaced through the built environment. Beside it, other little mounds grew, burst open, and revealed their own sprouting vines.

Dixon lunged toward them, still fifty feet away, but with each step, tens of flowering vines erupted from the roadway at Colson's command. They writhed like garden eels undulating in the currents. Dixon tried to stop, but his momentum carried him two steps too many into the sea of vines.

Colson commanded a small tendril to wrap itself around his ankle, testing Dixon's reaction. He directed the molten steel to sear the tendril and free himself. In response, the vines stretched as if in a time-lapsed recording to the ceiling of the tunnel, all the while growing thick and covering themselves with bark. Dixon turned to run away, and he sent hot steel rods flying into the branches in a desperate attempt to sever them.

For as much as Dixon may have mastered Gaia's powers, Colson had developed a lifetime bond with them. He blinked, or rather, his eyes were closed for him, and in that flash, Gaia spoke to him with a meek voice unbecoming of their nature.

Colson. I feel you. I will aid you through these forsaken chains.

Before Colson could share his gratitude, he was back in the tunnel, rising to his feet both of his own volition and without exerting any of his own energy. Thick vines lifted him off the ground. He reached out to the field before him, and his arms conducted a symphony of sprouts and tendrils, of vines and bramble and underbrush. The tunnel erupted in vegetation from all sides. It closed in on Dixon as it grew and bloomed in the fading light. Colson and Gaia, rejoined in this painful, shackled embrace, inhaled. The growth withdrew from Dixon in all directions, responding to their collective breath, and as they exhaled, the vegetation swarmed the metallic fascist intruding on their forest.

They overpowered him with the might of nature that would always outlast every human attempt to control its raw force.

While Dixon struggled, the new growth formed a small clearing around the camera to broadcast a message to his collaborators. He screamed, and in one last outrageous fit, tried to light the flash forest on fire, but the dense growth snuffed out any nascent flame. They squeezed his inflated body, twisting around each limb to restrain him in imitation of the way he had harnessed Gaia.

Colson closed his eyes to see, with his mind, what the vines touched. He followed their twisted, fibrous shapes, up and down, spiraling into corkscrews, and entwining themselves to reinforce their collective might, until he found the tendril snaking around Dixon's steely neck. Colson felt around with the tip of the vine until he located the delicate chain holding Dixon's amulet. He unclasped it. The vines raced to place the amulet in Colson's open palm, while Dixon's body shriveled back to its natural frailty.

Colson pocketed the second amulet.

He closed his eyes and inhaled deeply, as if to grant Gaia one moment of respite before he called on this torturous device once more. They let out a combined shout that sent vines burrowing into Dixon's every orifice. Dixon could not scream as the bark hardened inside his esophagus and nasal passages, coursed through his urethra and anal cavity, and even pushed past his eye sockets to crack his fragile skull. Where there was no opening, thorns perforated his skin and dove inside his veins.

The hateful rhythm of Dixon's heart pulsated through the vines. First at an accelerated rate, as the fear overtook him, before slowing to a crawl.

Dixon's heart beat once, then twice, then again, before it could no longer drive the violent monster of a man to destroy another life. He was dead.

Colson dropped both amulets to the ground, and he sobbed with a relief at having gotten revenge. A feeling immediately tampered by deep remorse. He had just killed another human being. A terrible one who terrorized until his dying breath, but a human being nonetheless. Colson collapsed on the vines as they wilted throughout the tunnel until he laid on the pavement beside Lady Duggery.

For a second, he let himself believe it was all over. He smiled while catching his breath. Lady Duggery reached out to hold his hand. He could have stayed right there, desperate for sleep to grant him a respite from the real world.

He rested his eyes and wiped the sweat from his brow.

Once his pulse steadied, his false sense of security wilted like the vegetation in the tunnel. He still had to unharness Gaia writhing in agony deep underground. He pulled Lady Duggery to her feet and returned her amulet. Then, they headed for the bakery to rendezvous with Brisa—and confront the truth about Henry.

PART FOUR

In Harness

CHAPTER 32

HENRY

HIS TUNNEL VISION COMPLETELY ignored the gust of white silk blasting past the Square early that morning. Henry had stayed up all night. He was concerned for Brisa and Colson, yet relieved to not have been invited on either of their excursions. Instead, he busied his hands with another special order from Lady Duggery.

When she phoned last night, she seemed completely out of the loop. She spoke deliriously of the imminent arrival of a special guest. A man she would ravage all through the night, draining him until nothing but a withered husk remained.

From what Henry could surmise, Lady Duggery maintained a romantic relationship with some higher-up in the Militia. That did not bode well. Agent Dixon's pathological need to be the big dog in the room would shoot into overdrive if his superior showed up and bedded Lady Duggery before he quelled the chaos of Sediment Valley. Henry only hoped that wouldn't become his problem. He had enough contact with Dixon already.

In particular, Lady Duggery required entremets that would dazzle in both appearance and taste. He had never made an entremet before, let alone thirty-six of them on such short notice. There were so many components: a cookie base, a white chocolate truffle center, and a mousse that had to set properly or else it would all melt into a gloopy puddle. Each had to cool before they could be layered and decorated with the shimmery mirror glaze. The blast chiller had been on the fritz in recent days, and he had just enough gelatin to complete the order. A single failed layer and all would be lost.

He had tried to express the difficulty of the situation to her, but she dismissed his concerns with praise for his mastery of the culinary arts.

The explosive banging of metal echoed across the lake and into the Square that morning, but Henry only had ears for the hum of his stand mixers running at max speed. Meanwhile, he weighed his dry ingredients to the one hundredth of a gram. He would not let good enough be the enemy of perfection.

As Henry rolled out the cookie dough, he imagined Colson standing behind him, his warm hands snaking around his sides like snapdragons to loosen the buckle in the center of his chest. Colson's scruff would brush his cheeks, sending butterflies down his spine. Henry would bite his lower lip and let his head fall backward, exposing his neck to Colson's tongue and teeth. He wanted nothing more than for Colson to clear the island of pastry bags and dirty bowls and lift him with his magical powers onto the cold, stainless steel.

The early morning fantasy almost swept Henry away. He overpoured the flour and it exploded into a white cloud. As he stooped down to clean the mess, the memory of Dixon, his halitosis pushing its way deep into Henry's lungs, flashed across his mind.

He shuddered and stared at the ceiling. He needed to block his imagination from running wild, because in his current state, he could not reliably direct his thoughts toward happy fantasies without this nightmarish reality creeping in.

Ever since Dixon's unannounced visit, the officer had pestered Henry nonstop with questions about anyone who even glanced in the direction of the bakery. Henry demurred and deflected, even when he had been in possession of damning evidence, like Brisa's secret notes. During the protest, Dixon demanded to know who was responsible for leading the crowds. Henry pretended not to have locked eyes with Brisa through the bakery window and stretched the landline's cord into the back of the kitchen. He played the fool, stammering his way through claims of ignorance and incompetence, until Dixon hung up in frustration. Henry's acting skills left for wanting, but his genuine terror in the face of the Militia leader masked the flimsy veil of his lies.

Still, Henry could not withstand sustained interrogation. For that reason, over the previous days he kept his friends—if he could still call them friends—at arm's length.

He hated disappointing Brisa. It took all his courage to approach her last night after burning her notes in the oven and ignoring her pleas for help. Dixon had been watching him too closely. The last thing Henry wanted was to give the officer a reason to target Brisa, especially in the immediate aftermath of the riot. Or at least that's what he told himself to cover up his cowardice. If only he could explain, but every time he opened his mouth to speak, his excuses rang hollow.

He also failed to understand what he had done to make Colson uneasy on their date. He must have said something untoward or given Colson some inadvertent sign that he was no longer interested. Maybe his breath had been rancid or his kissing technique somehow not up to par. The possibilities for how he had fucked it all up were endless.

He was trying to do right by them. But he kept getting in his own way, letting the dangers deter him from becoming attached.

In the end, he hoped they could forgive him.

Regardless of how Henry felt about the future, right now, he had a task he could sink all his energy into. He preferred to stay up all night baking, anything to distract himself while Colson crept through Sediment Valley's secret lairs.

Dark shadows fell across the valley, and a fierce wind whipped up the trees in the park across the Square.

Since his last pastry had been a sophisticated classic, he prepared something more whimsical. Given the romantic undertones of Lady Duggery's event, he had considered shiny red hearts filled with layers of chocolate, caramel, and red velvet cake, but anything reminiscent of blood felt déclassé in the current climate. Another option had been gold-sprayed chocolate spheres; a warm raspberry sauce poured tableside would melt the outer shell to reveal an assortment of truffles and candies tucked inside. With the recent abductions and popular unrest, he did not know if anyone would be working at the mansion who could execute his plan.

He finally settled on galaxy entremets. He had never tasted them, but he remembered the profile of a pastry chef in the *SustainAble Times* who had perfected the recipe. Half-dome cakes coated in stunning, reflective streaks of cerulean, purple, and just a hint of pink, all flecked with white to imitate twinkling stars in the vast expanse of space. Lady Duggery's gentleman caller would be instructed to slice each entremet in half to reveal a vibrant truffle floating inside inky black mousse. Each white chocolate sphere would be dyed a different swirling color combination for him to identify. Blue and green for Earth, red and brown for Mars, red and white stripes for Jupiter, and a blazing yellow-orange ball for the sun. He hoped the added mental stimulation could restore the man's mind after Lady Duggery was finished with his body.

Henry had a million little parts to make, each a delicate operation, delicious in its own right, but once assembled, the flavors would meld into a complex symphony. His arms rose and fell like a conductor as he gathered ingredients and specialty tools from their protected enclaves in all corners of his kitchen—oblivious to the roiling weather outside. Tangy berry notes would sing at first before taking a back seat to the richer cacao beans and espresso. When the primary flavors faded, unnoticed mint would refresh the palate in an unexpected encore.

The shop bell tinkled behind his back at the worst possible time. A gust of wind whipped through the back of the kitchen. He swore he had locked the door. "We're closed this morning," Henry shouted in his sweetest voice, as he slid the activated charcoal chocolate cookie bases into the oven.

The kitchen was a total disaster scene. Melted chocolate in every color of the rainbow smudged the sides of one container after another. Jam simmered on the stove. The mousse, if left unattended, could seize. Henry could not afford any mistakes right now by tending to a customer. He could not even imagine who would be out and about this early in the morning.

"Long time, no see, *Henrietta*," called out a distant yet familiar voice.

"Do *not* call me that," shouted Henry reflexively. A deep-seated anger slipped through a poorly locked door in the back of his mind. He turned around to expel this asshole from his bakery, realizing he had not been called that name in years, not since his brother—

"You're not still upset about that, are you, little bro?"

The spatula slipped from his hand as he turned around. Runny mousse spurted across his work shoes. He never expected to see his older brother again. Not after he ran off. Not here.

Kenneth looked mostly the same. The fresh buzzcut and head-to-toe camouflage. The boyish smile that charmed everyone. Even the round cheeks they both hated. The only differences now being his crow's feet, his dry, flaky skin, and his thin beard, which appeared to be hiding a scar.

"Come give your brother a hug! What's it been, twenty years?"

Kenneth outstretched his muscled arms and beckoned Henry to bring it in. When Henry refused to budge, Kenneth made up the distance between them and wrapped himself around Henry. He returned his long-lost brother's embrace with a lackluster pat on the back.

When Kenneth stepped back, Henry's disbelief crashed into the mental image he had carried around of his brother as a man twice his size. Henry had just turned thirteen when he bid Kenneth goodbye. He recalled Kenneth as a giant towering over him and mussing his hair before closing the door to their childhood home. Only after did Henry get a final growth spurt. They were now the same height. Even though Kenneth had built his body into a knot of muscles tugging at the seams of his Militia Officer's uniform, Henry's self-image suddenly stood much taller.

"What's so funny?" Kenneth's good humor wilted before Henry's condescending smirk.

"Nothing," he said, backing down, as a two-decade old pattern emerged before they could exchange any meaningful dialogue. Neither Henry nor Kenneth had been shining examples of healthy self-esteem, but as a kid, the only parry available to the much smaller Henry had been to demonstrate indifference toward his brother's minor achievements. Henry recalled the day Kenneth strutted into the kitchen holding a dead squirrel he had killed with a BB gun. He beamed with pride—until Henry shot the puny critter a devastatingly unimpressed glance that decimated his brother's mood. Kenneth slammed the bloodied squirrel onto the counter and stomped off to his bedroom to punch a hole in the wall. Henry could bore through his brother's heart with a single look that caused more damage than any of his brother's high-powered assault rifles ever could.

"I'm famished," said Kenneth. He glowered as his interest in catching up with his little brother appeared to have evaporated. "You'll never believe the night I just had up at Lady D's."

Henry felt a bit queasy. "You're the special guest?" The fact that both he and his brother admired Lady Duggery, though each in distinct ways, unsettled him. He preferred to think of his brother as his polar opposite.

"Is that what she called me?" asked Kenneth, bemused by Henry's astonishment. He strutted around the kitchen. "I mean, if you could hear the way I make her moan, you'd get it."

"Please spare me the details," said Henry, realizing he had been baking to replenish his own brother's stamina after bedding Lady Duggery. "That's disgusting."

"You're not one to talk about disgusting behaviors," said Kenneth.

The accusation slapped Henry across the face.

"You've got a decent set-up here," Kenneth said, ready to move on now that he had regained control of the conversation. He popped an Earth-dyed truffle into his mouth, and his eyes rolled back in his head. He slurped on the chocolate ball as he spoke. "These are fucking fantastic, bro."

"Thanks," he said, embarrassed at how much a compliment from his older brother meant to him. He let out a deep sigh, shutting off the near-constant drip of dread that had characterized his life in Sediment Valley ever since that first earthquake.

He felt so lonely. Not just since arriving in Sediment Valley, but for most of his adult life. Jonny's departure had wrecked him, and he spent the following years in isolation, refusing to make friends. Even recently, as much as he was falling for Colson, as kind as Brisa had been to him, he caught himself pulling away when their relationship threatened to develop. If he was being honest with himself, it was not just because of Dixon's looming threats. Deep down, Henry believed he was unlovable.

Regardless of how fraught their relationship had been, Kenneth had been in Henry's life from the moment he was born. After all these years of believing everyone in his family was long gone, Kenneth's sudden reappearance anchored Henry to the world in a way his harness never could.

Henry had to shut off that train of thought or else he just might burst into tears. After so much time, he wanted to give his brother a great first impression. Not reinforce his idea of Henry as a fragile crybaby. He pulled himself together. "I'm definitely lucky I get to work here, you know? It was pretty bleak on the outside."

"Well," said Kenneth, bobbing his head back and forth, "I wouldn't call it luck."

"You're just saying that," said Henry. Had his brother just admitted that Henry was skilled enough to earn such a coveted job? It seemed uncharacteristic, but maybe he had changed. To be fair, they weren't kids anymore.

"No, I mean, there was literally no luck involved. I got you this job." Kenneth dipped a spoon into the simmering jam, blew on it to cool it off, and sucked the spoon dry. "Could use a bit more acid."

Henry's fuzzy feelings toward his brother shed like a dying dandelion in a hot summer breeze. "No you didn't," he whined. "I went to school. I applied for this job after years in the SustainAble kitchens. My boss recommended me."

"Yeah, but you were basically a glorified cafeteria worker. Did you think you earned all this?" Kenneth took another spoonful of the blackberry jam. "You're talented, kid, no doubt. But I pulled some strings. This"—Kenneth spun his pointer finger in a circle—"is all because of me."

Henry shook his head in silence. It didn't make any sense. He hadn't heard a peep from Kenneth this whole time.

"I could give you a million excuses why I never called, but it doesn't matter now. It's not like you were that upset when I left anyway. This whole time I've been working my way up the ranks of the Militia, restoring Pennsylvania to some semblance of a decent, civil society. We live in crazy times. But let's get one thing straight. I've always kept tabs on you."

"I find that hard to believe."

"Someone had to look out for you after Mom died."

"Don't bring her into this," said Henry. He was upset, but he reconsidered. If Kenneth had information, he had to ask. "What do you know about her?"

"Same as you. She took her own life."

"She wouldn't do that."

"You mean she wouldn't do that to *you*." Kenneth spat the words with resentment. "You would think that. She always preferred you to me."

"She protected me from your bullying."

"Let it go, kid. That's ancient history. Who do you think bailed you out when you got arrested for *indecency*?"

Henry scoffed, but the contours of his harness dug into his shoulder blades. His brother must have been waiting for ages to lord something like that over him. Henry had always been the well-behaved child, the one who could never do any wrong, while Kenneth was constantly berated for infractions, minor and major. "I don't believe you," said Henry, despite his doubts.

"I'm not here to judge your lifestyle. I mean, I don't get it. Did you ever even try sleeping with a girl?"

"Did you ever try sucking a dick?"

"Hell, no."

"Alright then," said Henry, impressed with how he handled the question. Maybe he had not fully fallen back into old patterns. In his family's absence, he had been able to cast off some of the self-loathing.

"Point is, I got you and Jonny out of jail. My superiors were not thrilled. We worked very hard to pass the Two Gender Act. Luckily, I wasn't the only officer with an errant sibling or cousin. I'm just glad you didn't get caught again, because they only let you pull a get out of jail free card once before they start to question your loyalty to the cause."

Henry was speechless. These revelations shifted everything he thought he knew about the world, both inside and outside the valley.

"I couldn't believe you didn't follow Jonny out west. I mean, I had it all planned out, paid for your tickets and everything. I tried to get you out before it was too late. If I had intervened directly, you wouldn't have gone out of spite. You had to make the choice for yourself. But then what did you do? You just holed up in that cracker box you called a home."

Kenneth had prompted Jonny to leave. Henry let his harness drag him toward the wall while his brother carried on talking. Otherwise, he might not be able to stand.

"Maybe it was for the best though. Jonny never made it to his intended destination."

"You're lying," he mumbled.

"Sorry bud. It's dangerous out there."

Henry balled up his fists. Jonny was dead. Gone. He would never get the chance to make amends. And it was all Kenneth's fault.

"When we were brought in to oversee Sediment Valley, I thought, what better way to rehabilitate my little brother? Get him out of the factories, away from the smog and bad influences, let him do what he always dreamed of doing. This here is the proof." Kenneth pointed to the half-finished confections sprawled across the countertops. "I always wanted the best for you, little bro. Even if I didn't show it when we were kids. But that was then, right? This is the start of a new day."

The longer Kenneth spoke, the more his cadence reminded Henry of Agent Dixon. He hadn't spoken in that accent when they were little. He must have adopted it to fit in. They even wore the same enormous belt buckle, a bald eagle clutching five arrows. The only difference? Kenneth did not carry a nightstick. He was playing the good cop to Dixon's bad.

Henry felt ridiculous in his harness. He struggled to unclip himself from the wall and slip the faux leather straps off his shoulders.

"Let me help," said Kenneth. He grabbed the straps wrapped around Henry's shoulders, restraining him while he spoke.

Henry smelled the whiskey on his brother's morning breath. Had he even showered since climbing out of Lady Duggery's bed?

"You've done good so far, little bro. Dixon's taking care of the saboteur as we speak."

"What saboteur?" asked Henry in a panic. He thought of Brisa, running into the woods only to be snagged by one of the guards.

"I hate to break even more bad news to you, but seems your little *friend*, Colson, is not who he claimed to be."

"No! It can't be," shouted Henry. He wanted to jump out of his skin and run to Colson's protection, but Kenneth was still holding him by the harness.

"We caught him sneaking into a military facility and have tied him to an assassination attempt during the Founder's Day party."

He struggled to free himself from Kenneth's grip, but his brother just pulled him closer.

"Don't worry," said Kenneth. "No one is going to blame you for getting hoodwinked. Though I had hoped you'd have learned your lesson about flaunting your . . . choices. Colson fooled the best of us. But that'll all be over soon. I need your help with something else."

All of this talk of his friends, one dead and the other facing the Militia's wrath, burst any lingering belief that Henry could get the upper hand. The man before him was not just his brother. He was a high-ranking officer in the Militia who could not be manipulated as easily as when they were little kids.

Henry had learned to never refuse a direct order from an officer in the Militia. He stammered out an uneasy "Wh-what do you need me to do?"

Only after acceding did the officer release his grip and remove the harness. It hung sadly from the retractable cord anchored to the wall. "Let's go for a little walk. It's easier to show you."

"I just need to—"

"Lady Duggery has been informed that your services are needed elsewhere. She wanted to butter me up so I'd take her side in a little spat with Dixon, but what she doesn't realize is that she's already lost." Kenneth took Henry's letterman jacket from the coatrack and handed it to him. "I probably won't be seeing the undersides of her sheets again. Pity."

His brother guided Henry toward the bake shop door without bothering to lock it behind them. One of the guards helped Henry climb into a rickshaw, and another one invited his commanding officer to step inside his own. Henry sat down, but as the guards hopped onto the bikes, a foreboding metallic bang echoed off the ridge. He assumed the worst and slumped into the seat. This was the end of the line.

"Pay that no attention," said Kenneth. "It'll all be over soon. We've got big plans for you, bro. To the grotto," he ordered the guards.

CHAPTER 33

BRISA

AS THE WATERS SURROUNDING the glass-encased server farm brightened with the morning sun, Brisa banged her fists on the console keyboard. She had spent the entire night hacking into the terminal to lift the comms blackout yet found no success. Somewhere, lurking in the systems, a hidden door waited.

She had to get this dossier out of Sediment Valley. More importantly, she needed Val to tell her she would make it out of this hellhole.

But she had run out of time.

Brisa promised to rendezvous with Colson at the bakery at dawn. She locked up the console and reprogrammed the server farm's steel door to grant entry only to her in the future. If she couldn't send her detailed report on the schematics of this crypto farm to ChainBlock, simple sabotage would have to suffice for now.

Once outside, her squirrel friends greeted her with frantic squeaks. She tried to cover up the hatch with fallen leaves just in case anyone walked by, but the fuzzy critters pulled at her pants legs to hurry her along. She chased after them. Branches scratched her arms and neck, but she kept running. When she emerged near the lake, the squirrels disappeared into the tree line, as she'd been safely delivered from their territory.

A chilling breeze blew across the lake. Something felt wrong, as if the valley had been suddenly abandoned by everyone except her. But there was no time to investigate. She caught her breath and ran toward the Square.

As she approached the shops, a smoke detector pierced the air. The roof of the clothing exchange had caved in, and the front window on the now-defunct fruit and veggie store was shattered. Inside the bakery, a haze of burnt sugar lingered.

"Henry! Where are you?" she shouted as she ran past the counter. The bakery was empty. Despite her suspicions, she still cared for his wellbeing. Even if he was working with the Militia, he would only remain alive for as long as he could provide them with something they needed. She had no doubts about that. A small part of her almost understood how he could be cowed into collaborating in this environment. But only a very small part.

Brisa opened the wide commercial oven doors, and smoke poured into the kitchen. She coughed and waved away the fumes. With a mitt, she retrieved the charred cookies.

The smoke alarm suddenly shut off, despite the dense black cloud. Someone had arrived. Brisa wielded a smoldering pan in self-defense.

"Don't make a move!" she shouted to the intruder.

"What are you going to do? Smack me with a cookie sheet?" asked Lady Duggery. She hovered near the ceiling, having ripped the alarm from its socket, and waved her arms to clear the air. Her dress was in tatters, and bruises were forming around her eye sockets and nose.

Colson entered the kitchen behind her, his face contorted and streaked with blood.

Brisa tossed the pan into the sink. "What the fuck happened?" she shouted. She sounded more angry than concerned, despite her intentions.

"I'm ok," replied Colson. He wrapped his arms around her like vines encasing a majestic oak. "Dixon is gone."

"What do you mean gone?"

Lady Duggery mimed a slit throat with her pointer finger after placing both feet not so firmly on the ground. The gesture appeared to cause her shoulder pain.

"Wait, is he really dead?"

"I saw to it myself," said Colson. He cleaned his face on a dishtowel. "And let's just say, it was not quick or painless."

While Colson described the rigged trial and the ensuing battle, Brisa failed to suppress her satisfaction. She never gloated about the misfortune of others, but she made an exception for those who made it their life mission to harm actual people, animals, or the environment. Dixon had destroyed anything and anyone who stood in the path of his white supremacist ecofascist ego trip. His death deserved to be commemorated with a rapturous parade. Today, the world held one less man who would crush thousands of lives if left to his own devices. There was no moral ambiguity in feeling happy at the news. But she did not want to get too far ahead of herself.

Colson circled the prep station in the center of the kitchen, studying the assorted half-baked goods. Dirty cake batter bowls, full pastry bags in every color of the rainbow, a pot of berry jam still slightly warm. He looked rattled. "Dixon is gone, but it's not over yet."

"I'm relieved you're ok—"

"Henry's been taken," he said, interrupting Brisa's train of thought.

"How can you be sure?"

"How else do you explain the state of the kitchen?"

Brisa considered that Henry might have left willingly, but she knew how to read the room. Colson had just survived in a battle against Dixon, and now Henry was missing. This was no time to lob accusations. Not in front of Lady Duggery. "We'll find him. We'll figure this out. With Dixon out of the way, our job will be much easier."

Meanwhile, Lady Duggery sampled the truffles, as if she were alone in a boutique shop on a regular day. "I'm so glad his brother made me hire him," she said. "Who knew he'd be so talented? Kenneth could learn a thing or two from Henry about paying attention to details, if you know what I mean." She raised her swollen eyebrow, suggesting a sordid relationship with this Kenneth figure that Brisa did not want to know anything else about. Lady Duggery licked her lips. "I needed that."

"What is she even doing here?"

"She helped me take down Dixon. If it weren't for her, I'd be a ruddy smear on the pavement by now." He turned to Lady Duggery. "I'm sorry. Did you say *brother*?"

The story confused Brisa. There were too many revelations taking place in this tiny kitchen.

"That's right. Henry and Kenneth Townsend. Kenneth goes by Ember now. It's a bit silly, if you ask me, but you know how seriously these boys take their code names. Kenneth and I go way back," she said, pausing as if memories of the good ole days flitted through her mind. "Before he made General in the Militia, he led a security team at my family's fracking sites a good ten, maybe twelve years ago. We were always under threat of some terrorist group trying to blow up our operations. Kenneth's men kept us safe." She fingered a number of the half-finished desserts on the table. "When we opened Sediment Valley and Kenneth asked us to find room for his little brother, I felt obliged. It's not every day that nepotism and talent overlap. You should try one of these." She offered a truffle to Colson, who shook his head.

"Are you kidding me with this?" asked Brisa. "Henry's brother, who is here now, is Dixon's boss?"

"*Was* Dixon's boss," replied Lady Duggery with a sly grin.

A million thoughts clogged Brisa's capacity to logically examine the situation. Henry's dubious actions replayed one after another. How he left her unconscious at the top of the mountain. How reluctant he had been to deliver her secret messages. How he had hid in the back of the bakery during the protest. He even knew their plans to infiltrate the grotto. Brisa was relieved her instincts had led her to keep last night's trip to the server farm a secret from him. "Is Henry working for his brother?" Brisa, no longer able to contain her suspicions, blurted out the accusation.

"No way," said Colson reflexively. He looked to Lady Duggery to confirm.

"Who's to say? All I know is, they haven't spoken since Kenneth turned eighteen, moved out, and got involved with those rag-tag 'good guys with guns' groups, before the Militia had fully formed. I doubt they had a strong relationship. Then again, Dixon did have his informants. I'd have to review all the security feeds to confirm whether or not Henry had been working for him."

"There's just no way," Colson denied. "He wouldn't betray me—us—like that, would he?" Colson pleaded with Brisa to find another explanation.

Brisa placed her arm around Colson, and he turned in for another tight hug. "Look, I'm not gonna lie. I have my doubts. Henry has been inconsistent at best. He's so stand-offish, so quiet. It's hard to get a read." Colson pulled away as she spoke. "I tried to give him the benefit of the doubt. You never know what someone has gone through, especially in recent years.

I don't know his life story, but he had probably come out a few years before the Two Gender Act became law. That alone would fuck you up. It's bad enough being born into a world where homophobia is law, but to have that sense of security and freedom stripped away as an adult? I don't have to tell you that," she reached out and squeezed Colson's hand. He was no substitute for Val, the way they held each other in bed and cried, unable to sleep, the night their love became a crime. The recurrence of grief almost consumed her, but she shook it off. It would not help her to relive that pain right now. "I thought Henry had turned a page after he saw Calla being carted off by Dixon. That shook him to his core. But when I asked for his help to organize the march, he was back to his old, secretive self."

"So that was *your* idea," said Lady Duggery. Colson and Brisa continued talking as if she were not in the room.

"He helped us last night." Colson's voice cracked. He was desperate to find evidence that his hot-and-cold thing with Henry had been more than an attempt to spy on them.

"Hold on. When did you run into Dixon?" she asked, having already guessed at the answer.

Colson paused, defeated, before admitting: "He was waiting for me in the grotto."

"I hate to say this, but you know what I'm thinking. Henry was the only one who knew your plan."

"No," said Colson. He stepped even further away from Brisa, backing into a metal rack while shaking his head. "I'm sorry. I know it looks bad. I admit that. But I refuse to believe that is the entire story. Dixon himself said he had laid a trap to catch whoever was responsible."

Brisa didn't know what to say. She couldn't imagine being in Colson's shoes right now. The one person he let into his life, the one person he showed a bit of vulnerability, might have been a spy for the man who murdered his family and friends, who destroyed his hometown and took everything from him, who an hour ago tried to execute him. She would refuse to believe it, too, if only for her own sanity.

"For what it's worth," said Lady Duggery, "Dixon was bad at keeping secrets. I agree. He was shocked to find Colson in the grotto last night. The way he gloated when he finally had something on me. My trusted confidant, the enemy on the inside. There's no way he could keep that discovery to himself. He definitely only found out about Colson's true identity within the last twelve hours at most, and as far as I know, he still has no idea who you are, Brisa."

"You really think so?" pleaded Colson.

"I do," said Lady Duggery, reassuring him with a warm smile that felt out of place.

Brisa struggled to read Colson's expression as he listened to Lady Duggery. He appeared to feel guilty for having deceived her all this time. Had the two of them become friends? Had he not seen how Lady Duggery collaborated with the same people responsible for the massacre in his hometown? This valley had become a tangled web of frail and unlikely alliances. People make all sorts of deals in order to survive, but Brisa was unwilling to join forces with Lady Duggery of all people.

"All I know," said Colson, "is that the man I'm falling in love with has either deceived me or is in grave danger. He never leaves a single unwashed dish in the sink or the tiniest crumb on his counters and floors. He's meticulous to a fault. For him to leave the bakery in this state, with cookies burning in the oven, no less, means he left in a hurry or he was abducted. He may not even know how dangerous his estranged brother truly is. I owe it to him to make sure he's safe, and I owe it to myself to know whether it was all a lie."

"You're right," said Brisa, despite her doubts. She could not believe Colson had just used the L word. Poor thing was smitten. He deserved answers, and she was partially responsible for encouraging this relationship after all. The only way forward was to search for Henry and his brother. For Colson's sake, she hoped she was wrong about Henry.

"Follow me," said Lady Duggery. "I think I know where Kenneth would take his brother." She beckoned them with a gesture worthy of a princess in a parade and glided out the back door, dragging the smoky air with her. It slammed shut behind her.

"I don't trust her," said Brisa. She rested her hand on the door, waiting for Colson's response before she walked outside.

"And I'm not asking you to," replied Colson.

"What's the deal with you two anyway?"

"It's messy. We became . . . friendly over the past two years, I guess. I was only ever after Dixon and his men. She was a way to get to them. She's promised me so many things, and I never really believed her. I'm not that naïve. I know she comes from the same world that backed the Militia's rise to power." He paused to collect his thoughts. "The trial was fucked up. I thought she was going to sit back and watch me die for a minute. But she didn't. She literally just saved my life. Some part of her, small as it may be, is different. I don't know how to explain it."

"That may be, but she's not coming with us," said Brisa.

"Okay," he said to her relief. The two of them joined her out back.

Lady Duggery swiped her wristwatch at the terminal behind the bakery and began typing on the touchscreen Brisa, Henry and Colson had uncovered last night.

Brisa wanted to slam Lady Duggery's head against the console and make her pay for the damage she had caused over the course of her life. But she restrained herself. She needed Lady Duggery in this moment. Brisa hated always having to make these sorts of compromises. What she would give to be petty, just this one time, and do the loud, angry, immature thing that would feel so good. Even if it doomed their bigger plans. She was so close to giving in to those impulses.

Then the ground began to rumble. Lady Duggery stepped away from the terminal with only the bruises she received in the fight against Dixon.

"Another earthquake? Right now?" asked Brisa before she saw the source of the vibrations.

"Just watch and see," replied Lady Duggery.

Brisa would have called out her tone if she hadn't been mesmerized by the sight before her. The concrete slab housing the large trash and recycling dumpsters for the Square slid backwards as if sat on two large rollers. A warning siren sounded, and hydraulic pumps hissed as they revealed a deep, circular pit where no one would think to look.

A metal banister rose from underground to form a gate around the pit. Brisa leaned over the railing to see just how far down it went. A spiral of white dots traced the outlines of the cylindrical shaft all the way to the bottom. Echoing from the depths of the pit came a rhythmic clunking of metal. Something banged along the walls, and it became louder and more frequent as the source of the sound approached the surface. The treads of a stairwell popped out of the walls, one by one, starting at the bottom. A modular handrail, attached to each tread, snapped into place, forming a tight spiral staircase. When the last step locked, the sirens died out, and a door opened in the perimeter gate, inviting them to climb down. Brisa feared they were too flimsy.

"This is probably not the best time to bring up my slight fear of heights," said Colson. He took tiny baby steps toward the gate, but he maintained his distance.

"Maybe Brisa and I should go," suggested Lady Duggery.

"Absolutely not," said Brisa. "Colson, you'll be fine. Just don't look down, except for keeping your eyes on the step. So I guess look down but not too far down, ok?"

"Yeah, the whole 'don't look down' thing is something only people without a fear of heights say."

"I'll go first. You'll be fine. Focus on me."

"Oh you're definitely going first."

"And I'll stay behind you," added Lady Duggery.

"She is not coming," said Brisa.

Colson reasoned with Lady Duggery. "We need you to stay above ground. This could get nasty. And dangerous. Someone has to help the hundreds of people hiding out in their crumbling homes either into some sort of shelter or to escape when shit hits the fan."

Brisa offered no sympathy. Instead she glowered at Lady Duggery, daring her to push back.

"Fine. I can be your person on the outside. And maybe I can make up for some of the . . . misfortune I've caused the little people of this valley."

"Misfortune?" Brisa's head almost exploded. "You've ruined their lives!"

"I've done no such thing!" snapped Lady Duggery. Her voice adopted an almost British cadence.

"Tell me then. What is the source of your wealth?"

Lady Duggery started to speak but Brisa cut her off.

"Mining and burning fossil fuels for profit! Your family is literally responsible for a great deal of the climate crisis. Your father bankrolled both the movement to fracture the United States and, after that was successful, the overthrow of representative government in the Commonwealth by the Militia."

"I am *not* my father."

"Then tell me, what have you done ever since taking over his blood-soaked corporate portfolio? Nothing to undo the legacy of your riches, that's for sure."

"I built this valley to give some people, at least, a better life."

"Some people?" Brisa threw her hands up over her head and spittle flew from her mouth as she unleashed on Lady Duggery. "You mean the wealthy white people waiting to replace us? In a valley built on a crypto farm that will keep draining the Earth to grow your coffers? A green-washed utopia that will keep the lights on at SustainAble and fund its push toward hemispheric dominance? A place that is literally abducting the 'little people' you pretend to care for but actually despise and ridicule to turn them into human batteries? Not to mention the past few days of constant agitation and fear caused by the earthquakes." With each accusation she took a step toward Lady Duggery and cut off any attempt for her to respond. "You are no savior. You are no white knight riding in on a horse to free the peasants. You're the evil queen cackling from the top of her tower and the privileged princess with her head buried in the sand, depending on whichever state of mind better quiets whatever tiny speck of a conscience you still might have."

Lady Duggery narrowed her eyes in defiance, but she did not contest Brisa's claims even as she began to rise off the ground.

"And one more thing. You do not get to wash your hands of the blood spilled by Dixon. You invited him here. You handed him power. You sat back and did nothing while he bashed those people at the foot of your mansion. I saw you hovering above us all. How you turned your back on us just as he—" Brisa choked up as the memories from just yesterday burst through the flimsy barrier she had erected to keep herself from falling apart. Her entire body trembled with pain and rage. "This is your fault."

Brisa expected Lady Duggery to fly off or attack her. She braced herself against the winds she was sure were about to blow.

But Lady Duggery did no such thing. She returned to the earth. She reached behind her neck and unclasped the amulet. She stumbled, presumably at the loss of her aerial powers, before regaining her composure. Then she offered the amulet to Brisa.

"Be careful when you first put it on. It takes some getting used to," said Lady Duggery.

"I don't need your advice," said Brisa.

"Brisa," said Colson quietly. "You made your point."

"No one asked you!"

She could not possibly understand how Colson could be ready to forgive Lady Duggery, because she was not prepared to let things go. But she could see that Colson, however he actually felt in the moment, had chosen to take the help where he could get it. None of them knew how long they had, or if it was in fact too late, to rescue Henry. If he even needed rescuing. Or if he and his brother were about to unleash some unstoppable force on the valley that would crush them all.

Brisa snatched the chain from Lady Duggery's hand, hesitant to touch the amulet just yet, and decided to get on with it all. "Keep the people you brought into this nightmare out of harm's way while we clean up your mess. Do you think you can handle that?"

Lady Duggery nodded and turned her back on them. It looked as if she tried to fly away before realizing she now had to walk like the rest of the plebes in her domain.

"Are you ready for this?" asked Brisa as she opened the gate and peered into the depths.

"Are you?"

"Not one bit."

"Me neither, friend." Colson took a deep breath. "Me neither."

CHAPTER 34

COLSON

EVERY STEP FELT LIKE it would be Colson's last. The treads of the spiraling staircase wobbled as he and Brisa descended. He gripped the railing with his left hand and clung to the chilly concrete wall with the creeping vines that sprouted from his right. He leaned over the railing to get a final glimpse of the blue sky. A wave of dizziness knocked him into the wall.

"You ok back there?" asked Brisa.

"Mmhmm," he replied unconvincingly through pursed lips.

"Keep your eyes on me, Colson. We're over halfway."

Colson refocused on the sound of the floating stairs creaking under his and Brisa's feet. They worked together to keep a steady rhythm, which helped Colson feel the groaning metal less as an effect of their corporeal presence bearing down on the structure and more as a musical cadence planned by the architect. It didn't work, but he kept at it.

"I didn't mean to snap at you back there," said Brisa.

"I know."

"She's fucking unbelievable. To think that now, all of a sudden, she's a good person? She doesn't get to play the hero just because she cleaned up a bit of the mess she made in the first place. Right?"

"For all the complicated feelings I have, I know she mostly turned against Dixon because she had already lost to the Militia. They played the long game, letting her do most of the work for them, and then swooped in at the last second to push her out. She was always astute and levelheaded. I don't understand why she thought she would be the one woman they allowed to accrue real power."

"It's narcissism. Pure and simple. These anti-feminist women who side with obvious misogynists as a way to climb to the top. I fundamentally cannot understand them."

"Right? They rail against the decades of feminists who shattered the glass ceiling as they climb through that hole, only to pull up the ladder from the top. The same goes for the gays and people of color who pull that shit. Save themselves by throwing their own communities under the bus."

"The only good thing to come out of the fracturing of the United States," said Brisa, "was watching all those conservative women lose their jobs as judges, governors, and senators. Anything other than secretary, nurse, or elementary school teacher. I still don't know what they were thinking. They spent their lives rolling back rights for women and minorities and then they're shocked when their own laws are used against them."

"It's all too easy to convince yourself you're an exception. That they won't come for you. You're one of the good minorities. The normal ones. Not the lazy or the genderbending or the uppity types."

"Until it's too late."

"Until it's too late." Colson paused. Hadn't Henry done exactly that? Bury his head in the bakery and hope for the best? Brisa was not one to keep her mouth shut, in Colson's experience, but he suspected she didn't want to upset him further for the time being. Still, he needed to confront the obvious. They could be walking into a battle against Henry and his brother. "Do you"—he swallowed so hard he thought it echoed—"think Henry's one of them?"

Brisa kept quiet for the longest three seconds of his life. Then she said, "I don't know, but we should prepare for the possibility."

Colson only nodded before realizing Brisa couldn't see his reaction. "I know," he admitted with reluctance.

"The family thing can get in people's heads. It's his brother. I didn't even know he had a brother. Did you?"

"He mentioned him once, but they were estranged. Same with an ex-best friend. His parents died a while back. He seemed resigned to being alone."

"We're all a little broken these days."

"Or a lot," Colson added.

"And even toxic family can feel like a way to be grounded in times of crisis."

"I wouldn't really know," said Colson.

Brisa stopped, even though they could see the final step, and hugged Colson. He retracted the stabilizing vines sprouting from his hand as he embraced her. She whispered, "We're going to make this right, one way or another."

"Or die trying," he said. Her warmth wrapped him like a heavy, woven blanket on a snowy night. He soaked in her generosity, her care, and he hoped she felt some fraction of their bond bracing her for the fight ahead as well.

"This is it," she said, and they hopped off the final wobbly stair.

With both feet solidly on the ground, Colson leaned against the cold wall. Then he squatted down, recentering his ties to the earth, and stood again. "We need to get into the lab to free the people who were abducted and unleash Gaia from their bonds. But I have a feeling that's where we'll find Henry and Kenneth, too."

"I've got your back."

CHAPTER 35

HENRY

HENRY SAT AGAINST A large ring on the damp cavern floor as his brother prepared him for the machine. He unbuttoned his letterman jacket and lifted his shirt. Ember placed a gold-plated socket on his abdominal wall that sparked upon contact. He gritted his teeth as glowing green tendrils burrowed through skin and muscle toward his stomach. He tried not to flinch.

For some reason, Henry still felt he had something to prove. He would not let his brother see him writhing in pain. He would hold strong, choke back his tears, and take it like a man.

He hated that expression. It had been Kenneth's go-to line as kids whenever he took Henry's toy, smashed his block tower, or held a pillow to his face. He expected Henry to sit back and let it happen without complaint. Telling his parents only led to more intricate forms of revenge down the line. If he showed any emotional reaction or dared to shed a tear, Kenneth and his friends would dance around him in mockery and sing:

Crying boy.
Lost his toy.
Like a little girl!
Let's forget her.
Even better.
Call her Henrietta!

Even after all those years, the shrill notes of their unrelenting chant played clearly in his mind.

This time he would not give Kenneth—or Ember as he was instructed to call him—he would not give Ember the satisfaction of seeing him cry. *What a dumb name*, Henry thought, *definitely not overcompensating at all.* He wanted to leave this world with a shred of dignity, however wrapped in self-loathing it might be. Whatever it took not to be called *Henrietta* one more time.

When the tendrils finally reached his stomach, Ember ran his smoldering finger around the socket, cauterizing the open wound on Henry's belly. Then, he unwound a fibrous feeding tube that appeared to have a mind of its own. Henry groaned quietly as it snaked its way inside his guts.

All the while, Ember ranted about the engineering marvel these machines constituted. How he would wield this new power from outside. How Henry would serve as the keystone inside the central ring. How he had saved this special honor for his little brother. Henry's sacrifice would be celebrated the world over. The two of them, reunited, rebuilding the world. Together, they would be unstoppable.

Henry paid little attention to Ember's grandstanding. There was no glory in being locked unconscious inside a machine to power the Militia's final assault. Men like Ember always framed their unbridled pursuit of raw power as a service for the good of mankind, for all those poor souls trampled along the way. In reality, only Ember would be unstoppable.

In the end, though, who was Henry to judge? His hands were not clean. He had sat back too many times and baked as the Militia plowed forward with their plans. It had been all too easy to do nothing. To let others throw themselves in harm's way while he withdrew into the shadows. His acts of sabotage, his attempts to withhold information, seemed so insignificant now.

While being strapped inside this machine was not the ending Henry had imagined for himself in Sediment Valley, it was the ending he deserved.

Ember placed a second socket on his side, and more tendrils opened a connection for a waste tube. Henry dug his hands into the cavern floor and thought of Colson to distract from the pain.

In recent days, as he tossed and turned on his mattress in the bakery, he fantasized about Colson. Tangled in each other's arms, they would lean into the rhythm of the quakes. The violent shaking would transform into the tranquil rocking of a paddle boat on a breezy summer's day. By holding onto this dream, he had managed to quiet his mind and fall asleep for a few hours.

Now he dreamed of being rescued. Colson would storm the cavern and, with his powers magically restored, punch Ember in the throat. Ember would repent and run away. Then, Colson would pick him up and fly him out of this cavern to a safe haven far—

Ember's cauterizing touch snapped him back to reality. He opened his eyes and found himself staring at a belt buckle. The bald eagle clutching five arrows glowed as if it were molten gold. The eagle's talons gripped around his own throat. He took short, shallow breaths as Ember inserted the waste tube.

Henry felt powerless. There would be no escaping from Ember.

Henry had lost the day he set foot in Sediment Valley, even if he only realized it now. It was not fair to wish for Colson to rescue him. In reality, Colson could no longer count on his magical abilities. What chance did he have of taking on jacked up Militia officers without them? If Dixon did not crush him, Ember would set him on fire while Lady Duggery stoked the flames. Together they would watch him burn.

Henry had to do something, but right now, the best he could hope for was to slip into a deep dream inside the machine while Colson got as far from Sediment Valley as possible. And Brisa, too. Not to mention all the others trapped in this slaughterhouse.

But that was another fantasy. Deep down he knew they would all suffer. The Militia had won, and before long, they would expand their reign of terror beyond the valley.

Henry's legs trembled when he stood, but he refused Ember's assistance. The large golden ring chilled his spine even through his jacket. He placed his arms above his head and crossed his ankles.

Ember tightened rubber cords around his body to hold him in place until the centrifugal and magical forces took over. "You must be freezing," said Ember. He ran his hands along the inner rim of the ring to warm it. "I want you to be comfortable. We're about to change the world."

This is it, thought Henry. He rested his eyes, waiting for the end.

Ember tipped the upright ring on its side. As it lifted off the ground and spun, the rubber straps barely held him in place.

His toes and fingertips prickled with static. It reminded him of the weird feeling he got while holding the cake just before the first earthquake. Then that familiar voice, grave and volcanic, erupted within his mind.

Hen–

–ry

you

came

let

me

in

Henry opened his mind to the electricity coursing through his veins. It quieted the rambling thoughts rattling around his brain. For the first time in his life, he felt truly awake.

Chapter 36

Colson

"In here!" shouted Colson. Brisa had been staring in awe at the vaulted, pulsing ceiling of the underground passageway. He understood that reaction.

"Sorry," said Brisa. "I feel small. Like we're scurrying through massive tunnels that have no right to exist."

"Then you'll want to brace yourself for what's on the other side of this door."

Colson tapped his wristwatch at the terminal, and the hydraulics granted the two of them passage into the laboratory. His skin prickled in anticipation. He knew Dixon was dead. He had felt the blood drain from his body not long ago, but he could not shake the sensation that the man who had tormented him for over two decades might somehow still pop out from the shadows. It did not help that Dixon's commanding officer—*Henry's brother*—had arrived on the scene.

New growth sprouted through the tiled floor of the lab, as if to comfort him, to ground him in these final moments before he learned the truth about Henry.

Brisa fiddled with various control panels overlooking the cavern. The spinning rings tethered to the ground and the ceiling oscillated in tandem with one another. The twisting, curling cavern surfaces were slick with moisture. Light bounced off crystals and shimmering pools of water.

"Down there," said Brisa. She pointed into the cavern. "See the steam rising from the ring near the center? It has to be them."

A chill appeared to ripple across her body as she stared at the glittering machines. She fished the amulet from her pocket and pressed another button on the panel. A door opened onto a rickety staircase that descended from the heights of the observation lab to the cavern floor.

"Let's go!" shouted Colson as he ran down, no longer bothered by his vertigo. "Henry," he called out, sidestepping rings that spun at breakneck speed. "I know you're down here!"

From the depths, a small voice cried out. "Go away!"

It was Henry, but Colson couldn't locate the origin of his words as it echoed across the cavern.

"Don't do this, Henry," implored Brisa.

The electric whir of the devices muffled her speech as well. It sounded like she was speaking down from above. The flickering cavern played tricks on Colson's perception of the world.

"Further back, to the left," said Brisa. "I see him."

The lights grew brighter as Colson approached a flatter area. Five rings rimmed an unnatural circular clearing in the cavern. Stalactites hung from the ceiling, but any corresponding stalagmites had been removed. In the exact center, another golden ring floated. It rotated slowly as green tendrils stretched from the ceiling and the floor. Henry, shrouded in vapor, stood vigilant over the body spinning in the ring.

"Henry, please!" Colson ran over and grabbed him by the shoulder. He was feverish to the touch. "Henry, you're burning up—"

Colson fell silent as the man turned around. It was not Henry's face staring back at him. No, it was the face he had hallucinated, the one he had seen replace Henry's during his vision in the grotto and their failed date in the park. The two men looked so much alike. Except this man had a beard that glowed like hot ash.

Colson staggered backward, finally realizing why Henry triggered such flashbacks. Henry's brother had been the only man who gave orders to Dixon in Levittown. Ember had led the massacre of his home. And now he was standing directly in front of him.

Colson bumped into one of the surrounding rings, and its forcefield almost knocked him to the ground.

"You're a bit too late," said Ember, pointing to the ring. His voice crackled like a dry branch in a bonfire.

Henry was strapped to the inside of the slowly spinning ring. Colson's doubts fell away. Henry had not been working for the Militia all along. That explanation, despite the circumstantial evidence, had never been convincing to Colson. He firmly believed Henry was yet another of his brother's victims. Whether he had been guilted into this or forced made little difference to Colson now. He gathered himself and stood tall.

"Let him go," he said in an even, deep tone. He matched Ember's burning stare. His skin adopted the hue of an evergreen forest witnessed in the flash of a lightning bolt.

From inside the ring, Henry pleaded with Colson. "You need to get the fuck out of here or else!" His voice was strained and fading.

Henry's sudden outburst puzzled Colson. Those words, remarkably harsh, bounced off a faint memory in Colson's mind. Shrouded by the chaos of the moment, he couldn't place it.

"Henry, it's me. Colson. We came for you," he replied, desperate for Henry to understand. But he kept his distance for the moment.

"You heard him," said Ember calmly. "Your best bet is to run away. That's what you do, isn't it? Run away while I watch your family burn."

"What did you say?" Colson intended his words as a warning to Ember.

"You're too late." Ember's beard glowed white hot as he spoke with a cool patience that underscored his confidence. "Look around, boy. It's over. I won. The final machine is coming online. Gaia's powers are mine to wield as I see fit. To purge the world of your kind and restore us to the glory days of old."

"I'll stop you just like I stopped Dixon." Thorned bark surfaced like protective armor across his body.

Ember laughed at him. "That grating little man always did get on my nerves. You could never trust him. I was going to hang onto him a little longer, but I suppose I should thank you for disposing of him for me. You should listen to lover boy over here and make yourself scarce. I tell you what. In recognition of your service to Lady Duggery and me, I won't even pursue you. You're free to run away. Go on now." Ember flicked his wrist dismissively.

Colson's thorns sharpened. "I *never* served either of you!" His arms whipped like sentient vines.

Before he lunged toward Ember, Henry's dry voice tried once more to stop him from taking the bait. "I said, you need to get the *fuck* out of here or else!"

Colson held back in confusion. Was this retribution? Payback? No, it could not be that simple. Henry was still on their side. He had to be because otherwise Colson was all alone in the world. He refused to let that be true. This was such an uncharacteristic thing for Henry to say. It had to be a sign or a coded message. Something. Anything.

Colson let Henry's words settle in, much like he let Gaia blend with his own psyche to conjure verdant powers.

Another scene replayed in his mind. That first night at the mansion, when Henry returned unexpectedly with a platter of cookies to replace the destroyed cake and Colson snapped at him. He needed Henry to get the *fuck* out of there. Not because he was angry at him. But only so Henry did not get caught up in the violence that was about to unfold. Henry had even accepted his apology.

Now it made sense. Henry hoped to protect Colson from his brother's rage.

Colson smiled as the realization washed over him. But there was no way he would leave Henry down here to rot. Or let Ember live to see another day. He had come to Sediment Valley for one reason. To get revenge on those responsible for Levittown. He had already crushed Dixon. But now his efforts exceeded any personal need for retribution. With Gaia's harnessed powers, he and Brisa would take down Ember and destroy these machines once and for all.

Or they would die trying.

"I'm not going anywhere." He aimed his dagger-sharp words at Ember's heart.

The surrounding rings crackled like power lines. Henry's ring spun faster as the light beams connected.

Colson and Brisa were too late. He had no idea what happened to the people once their machine was fully powered. If only they had run faster, barreled down the spiraling stairwell, or not spent so long lingering in the bakery, maybe they would have made it in time.

Colson could have told him how he felt. How Henry's presence soothed the pain always pulsing under his skin and behind his teeth. How he was sorry he had been too blinded by the need for revenge. How he wished he had been there to pull Henry out of his self-imposed isolation, to strip him of his harness and throw his arms around Henry's shoulders instead. Colson was finally ready to open up about his feelings, to let another person into his life, and yet again, that person had been taken from him.

But Colson was no longer the scared, little boy caught off guard by the sudden violence of the world. He was ready to fight for his loved ones.

Colson commanded a vine to lash out at Ember. It slung around his wrist, but before he could tug him off balance, Ember's entire body faded into ashen grey. He looked like death, charred and smoky. Flames flickered across his body, and his eyes glowed with destructive potential. Colson's vine retracted, singed by the cinders.

Ember's laughter erupted within the ancient chamber. "You stand no chance against me, boy. You'll go up in smoke faster than your childhood home."

Colson stood firm against the memory of the heat rolling off every building on his block. He needed a new plan. The tricks he used to counter Dixon's molten iron would not work. Ember had a tremendous advantage in a battle of plant life versus searing cinders.

Where is Brisa? He could use her help.

Colson plunged vines into the earth where fire could not reach. The ground bulged and cracked as they burrowed swiftly toward the enemy. Ember, glowing white hot, braced himself to fend off the vines, but they never surfaced. Instead, Colson routed them deep underground and pumped them full of energy until they swelled, exploding directly beneath Ember's feet. The blast from below knocked him backwards. Ash streaked across the cavern floor, and he smashed into one of the spinning golden rings. The crash of a cymbal rang out as it wobbled, its light flickering before its forcefield restabilized.

A figure scampered through the dark recesses above. Colson followed the flitting shadows to his left, then his right, when suddenly a furry, red-brown creature soared through the air, arms and legs outstretched, gliding through the cavern. Before Ember could stand, a transfigured Brisa landed on the enemy general's chest. Her body appeared lithe, but her movements were erratic, almost frantic. Yet, intentional. Her feet seemed unbothered by the hot coals that pulsed with the flow of air, and incisive claws protruded from her fingers and toes.

Brisa dug her padded feet into Ember's thighs to anchor herself while swatting at his face with her paws. Ember tried to protect his eyes, and as he grew more desperate, the scent of sulfur and burnt fur permeated the damp cavern.

"Colson, help me tie him down," commanded Brisa. Her voice was high-pitched, as if someone had hit fast-forward on a recording of her normal speech.

"I've got you," he said. Colson's vines snapped stalactites from the ceiling and impaled them, one after another, in a circle around Brisa and Ember. He commanded hundreds of brambly, spike-laden shoots to weave around the newly planted stakes and build an inverted bird's nest to cage him. On Colson's mark—"Now, Brisa!"—she leapt into the air with outstretched limbs and glided over to Colson while dense bramble enclosed a wounded, weakened Ember. They had him trapped.

"We have to free Henry," said Colson.

"Yes, he can decide his brother's fate," added Brisa.

Ember roared from within his makeshift cage. Colson wanted Ember dead, but Brisa was right. This wasn't the same as with Dixon. There were too many entangled emotions and histories, even though Ember's destructive ambitions far outpaced Dixon's.

They grabbed at the golden ring in which Henry spun faster, but their efforts were futile as long as the forcefield remained in place. Brisa clawed at the node on the ground to no effect. Then she scampered away, leaping from one stalactite to another, climbing higher and higher until she reached the node in the ceiling. It, too, resisted her attempts to rip it from the surrounding rock.

Meanwhile, Colson's vines reached over and into the ring, dodging the tendrils from the beam of light that snapped at his own, but he found no way to latch on and force it to stop. Once, he managed to wrap a vine around the ring, hovering just beyond the edges of its defenses, but when he closed the noose, the ring ripped the vine in half, as if weeding a garden. His fibrous skin tore apart.

"It's not slowing down," said Colson, growing concerned.

"Quite the opposite," shouted Brisa from above. "It's going faster than ever."

"I don't know how to stop it."

"Oh fuck!" shouted Brisa. "Colson, get away from there. Now!"

In the distance, the other glowing nodes grew in brightness, illuminating the entire cavern until not a shadow remained. Colson turned his back on Henry and ran. As he passed the other rings rimming the central node, the lights blinded him. He dove forward, hoping to land somewhere outside the circle, for whatever was happening, Henry's ring would be the epicenter. A freshly sprouted pile of tall grasses cushioned his fall. He shielded his eyes.

The ground rippled beneath him as minor shocks radiated outward. The tremors intensified, and the cavern rocked back and forth, tossing him like a rag doll accidentally locked in the dryer. He struggled to predict where he would land, where he needed to grow sudden cushions of greenery to avoid severe injury. The earth bounced around as Gaia struggled to free themself in one final, desperate, and undiscerning act of rage against the chains that harnessed them in this forsaken cavern.

But it was not Gaia who broke free.

The lights dimmed, and the earthquake faded into a low, constant hum. "Brisa, where are you?" Colson shouted, blinking aggressively to make the flash of white still imprinted on his sight disappear.

She leapt down beside him and pulled him to his feet. "I'm right here—"

But her words were cut short by Ember's maniacal roar.

The cage surrounding the enemy cracked apart, and he emerged like a demonic phoenix from a charred nest.

Before Colson and Brisa could even launch into action, another tremor shook the cavern. Ember's body glowed with a white light, no longer from the cinders but from the power visibly emanating from the rings. He lifted off the ground and levitated near the center of the vaulted cavern. The green beam of light connecting Henry's ring to the upper and lower nodes pulsed directly behind Ember's glowing body. He lifted his arms over his head in victory and sprawled his legs, posturing as a Vitruvian man, a microcosm of the world itself.

Gaia rocked the cavern once more in frenzied protest. Colson relied on Brisa's stability to stay upright.

A mound formed just below the lower node. Something pushed through the surface, but as it rose, the ground stayed in place. This figure had no corporeal form, yet it was not translucent. No light penetrated or refracted off its immaterial body. It shifted various times, from plant, to animal, to human lifeforms. Colson both saw and did not see it, unsure if it was yet another trick of the light. His vines reached out instinctively toward it as realization dawned on him. This was the same figure he had found chained deep in the cavern. This was the part of Gaia who had accompanied him all these years.

Large quantities of Gaia's energy were being siphoned from the earth. They clearly struggled against the powers harnessing them, and with each convulsion, the cavern shook violently. But with the ring imprisoning Henry online, this system had reached peak capacity. Its power overtook the part of Gaia's spirit chained within these mountains.

Colson, awestruck, could only watch in horror.

Brisa, however, launched into the air in an attempt to knock Ember off balance. She had aimed perfectly, but Ember's body trembled with an orgiastic force and sent a pulse wave through the cavern. It collided with Brisa, annulling her momentum, and she briefly hung in the air before falling hard on her fur-coated back.

She let out a high-pitched squeak but quickly shook off the pain. She scampered over to Colson. "We've got to get to Gaia."

"I can't speak to them. I'm locked out again, even with the amulet. It's these damned machines."

"There's something unnatural about them. I dug and dug at the nodes, but even with these claws, I couldn't uproot them. There's no discernible opening in the forcefield."

"We can't just give up."

Colson protested, but he and Brisa had been resigned to the role of mere spectators. Sparks showered the cavern. Gaia's harnessed spirit now passed through Henry's golden ring and engulfed it. The nebulous, shadowy sphere became translucent as Henry's ring spun rapidly inside. Blue bolts fired in all directions, tickling the edges of Gaia's spirit. For a moment,

Gaia's ascent paused. The electric bolts rippled across the inner surface, as if storing power.

"It's Henry!" shouted Colson. Henry was doing his best to resist and to provide Gaia with an escape valve. He and Brisa cheered Henry on.

But Ember soon destroyed all hope. He summoned the charged, nebulous spirit toward him. He floated inside the pulsing sphere, and it snapped around him, clinging like a latex body suit. Ember balled his fists and clenched every muscle as he absorbed Gaia's energy.

Colson reached for Brisa's hand, for a reminder that he was not alone. Her claws gripped his wrist, and she leaned in for a protective embrace. They would weather the end together.

Without warning, the ground dropped out from beneath them. But they did not fall. The geometry of the cavern's vaulted ceiling fractured as space itself twisted and expanded in all directions. They hovered in the void surrounded by sedimentary rocks and glittering crystals. Colson did not know if he and Brisa were falling or flying or hanging in the air.

In the distance, the ring of five golden rings spun around the contraption imprisoning Henry, and the green beams of energy shot vertically into endless space like jets of plasma fleeing a black hole. Azure bolts of lightning crawled across the void from every direction.

Ember's gargantuan body, all fire and smoke, reached for the chunks of rock orbiting him. Ember heaved a boulder at Colson and Brisa. Colson reached out with his vines to latch onto the rock and swing out of the way only to find another boulder barreling toward him. He swung through the directionless space, while Brisa alighted on the tops of these rocks, hopping from one to another with her newfound agility.

Ember's voice boomed as he continued his assault. "You cannot stop me now, you puny things. Behold not the power of nature, but the power of man over nature. Nature bows before me. Nature falls prostrate on the ground to pledge its allegiance. I am the sovereign, the patriarch, the first born, and the light. I am pure white glory everlasting. I steer the markets with my right hand and shift the seas and the winds with my left. I write the algorithm that chooses which populations rise and which fall. I grant the right to life, and I sentence you both to death."

Colson and Brisa continued to dodge, swing, hop, and glide over the boulders. But for all their efforts, they remained in place. They exerted all their energy for nothing more than another second of survival, another moment of holding Ember's attention to prevent him from unleashing this power on the world above.

"Gaia will never bow to you," said Colson, uncertain if Ember was even listening as he ranted.

"I. AM. GAI—"

Before he could pronounce the final syllable, the world fell motionless.

The hurled boulders froze in place.

Brisa floated, suspended mid-jump, her back legs outstretched, having just propelled herself from a squat. Colson paused at the apex of his swing, in a moment when he was neither rising nor falling, yet he never completed the arc. He could only watch.

In the distance, the ring of golden rings halted, not after slowing down, but as if someone had pressed the pause button on the universe. Even Ember's massive glowing body fell perfectly, solemnly still.

Only Henry's golden ring remained in motion. It spun and spun, doubling its size, as electricity crackled along its outer edges. The ring trembled. A vast power shook it from inside, intending to break away from the pulsars that restrained it.

"You."

A volcanic roar.

"Will never."

A flash of golden, green light.

"Become Gaia."

A shockwave blasted the suspended boulders into space dust.

> "You are no brother to me. You
> must be stopped."

Henry's firm voice spoke directly into Colson's mind and, presumably, the others could hear his disembodied thoughts as he and Gaia broke free of Ember's harness.

The golden ring holding Henry hurled across the distorted space-time of the ancient cavern. It latched onto Ember's towering chest. Electric spikes stabbed his skin repeatedly, and it leaked a viscous, oily substance that burst into flames. Henry assaulted him relentlessly until his bolts pierced the forcefield. The spinning ring then bored a tunnel through Ember's chest. As it closed in on his monstrous, frozen heart, the ring whipped up a vortex that dragged everything, including the still immobilized Colson and Brisa, into its spiraling maw.

The spectacle was mesmerizing. As Colson and Brisa barreled toward Henry's ring, electricity rippled across the surface of the inky black tunnel. They flew through its twisting, bending, whipping shape. The ring grew in Colson's field of vision until the two of them collided with the glowing orb in its center.

All physical sensation evaporated at the moment of impact. Colson's consciousness, however, expanded beyond the bounds of his skull to merge with those of Henry and Brisa.

Colson experienced the relentless push and pull of Henry's dilemmas. The way his desire to do the right thing was constantly restrained by past harms that resurfaced and dragged him into the shadows of self-hatred. Colson mourned for Jonny as if he had been his own closest friend. And Colson, as Henry, realized the sibling he had remembered, the version of him he had held onto in his mind, the ideal of who he might have become in a different life—he realized that other Kenneth had died a long time ago, if he ever existed at all.

At the same time, Colson felt the pressure that built within the millions of compartments into which Brisa tucked most of her emotions in order to get out of bed each day and carry on.

He found rooms bursting with loneliness and the certainty that she would never see Val again. In others, the regret of having disappointed her mother strained against locked doors.

His friends had glimpsed his psyche, too. The trauma of having watched his family die. The isolation of two decades. The destructive obsession with revenge, but also the recurring desire to connect with both Brisa and Henry.

The three of them experienced the innermost thoughts of one another. Together, in this inexplicable melding of the minds, when they no longer refused one another, they found that their fears and regrets faded into the background. As they shared one another's burdens, their powers combined and amplified.

Together inside Henry's ring, they bored through Ember's heart and erupted out the back of his planet-sized body.

Time restored its forward march.

Ember turned and lunged toward the ring inside the distorted spacetime of the cavern. His skin sizzled as if doused with a bucket of water. It lost its white-hot glow and faded into the rusty red of dried clay cracking in a heat wave. His body convulsed as Colson, Henry, Brisa and Gaia—united, cooperating, unburdened by the technological barriers previously blocking their mutual interests—funneled the energy coursing through the underground machines into Ember's muscles, nerves, and synapses. They fried every over-inflated, self-important, hate-filled fiber of his being.

Ember's gargantuan body ripped apart, limb by limb, muscle by muscle, atom by atom. The meaningless chunks of his sadly mortal body crumbled into dust.

The distorted space of the cavern collapsed into nothingness.

CHAPTER 37

BRISA

THE GONG-LIKE CLAMOR OF the giant ring crashed throughout the cavern.

Brisa found herself lying on the damp, sandy floor surrounded by moss and ferns. Henry and Colson were both there, huddled against her furry figure. A static charge drew them close. The previous minutes or hours—she did not know how much time had elapsed since they descended the spiral staircase—were viscerally real and as ephemeral as a waking dream.

She grasped at the amulet around her neck. Her sharp claws almost scratched her skin. If she had been able to ignore the uncertainty and panic of the battle against Henry's brother, she might have recognized the joy of becoming squirrel-like. The cute little critters, with their glorious bushy tails and lithe bodies, had always brought her such delight. To bound through the air, to experience the scattered, distracted energy coursing through her own body as she scampered along the cavern walls, it all felt like a homecoming or the granting of a wish—just with the added pressure of rescuing so many people from an ecofascist with superpowers. Brisa jumped to her padded feet.

"No time to rest, boys," she said, but they were already sitting up and staring into one another's eyes. "Or to kiss. We've got work to do."

Henry's cheeks flushed, and Colson shot her a disapproving look. But she did not care. She had accessed their most intimate thoughts, just as they had accessed hers. It was what both of them were thinking.

A light tremor rippled across the cavern.

"Brisa—" said Henry.

She could tell he wanted to explain his actions from the past few days, but there was no longer a need for the actual words to be said after they had merged. She understood his plight and his regret. He had never possessed the type of power of someone like Lady Duggery. He had never been perfect, but he also had to make difficult choices just to survive. When push came to shove, when offered real power, Henry had done the right thing. He rejected Ember and everything the Militia stood for. "We're alright," she said. "Let's shut down these machines and get the hell out of here."

"Good call," said Henry. He smiled timidly, as if accepting her words but still wanting to make amends.

"You'll need an amulet," said Colson to Henry. "Here, take mine."

Henry shook his head. His brother's body, shrunken to its normal human size, slumped beyond the ring of golden rings against the cavern wall. He turned to Brisa, tears welling in his eyes.

"I'll retrieve it," she offered.

"No," he replied. He balled his fists as he walked toward the body. "I need to do it."

Brisa remained a few paces behind him, and Colson approached her cautiously. The two of them stood as support pillars in the wings.

Henry kneeled before his brother. "Wake up, dammit!" He grabbed him by the shoulders and shook him.

But Kenneth did not wake up. He had died when the gargantuan manifestation of his newly acquired and swiftly lost powers crumbled in that alternate space-time. Only his lifeless body had returned to this plane of existence along with theirs.

"You don't get to leave again. Not like this!" Henry's best attempts at denial failed to change the reality of the situation, and he sobbed into his brother's chest.

Colson ran over to comfort Henry. He knelt down and held him as he said a final goodbye.

Even after their connection, Brisa struggled to imagine what he must be going through. To have his brother return after all these years like a ghost from a former life, to feel that toxic, emotional drain of a family member who tries to drag you into the mud with them. The push and pull of wanting to reconnect while knowing the cost. The choice between harming your core identity in order to be accepted—or loving yourself at the risk of enduring a life alone. It would be all too much for anyone to handle, and even more so under these circumstances. Yet, Henry had held it together. He took advantage of his brother's ego, who could not fathom that his little brother might betray him. He even climbed into that terrifying ring with no guarantees that he could ever climb back out. In the end, Henry had been there for Brisa and Colson and everyone else who had suffered in Sediment Valley.

After a moment, Henry gathered himself and unbuttoned his brother's collar. He yanked the amulet from around his neck and held it before him. Henry sniffled, and Colson wiped away a tear streaming down his cheek.

He choked down his first attempt at words before saying, "This amulet is different than either of yours."

The jewel was the same puke green Eastonite, but smaller and rough-hewn all around. Similar golden tendrils curled around the sides in another gravity-defying design.

"I'd guess that's the updated model," said Colson. "Ours look like two twins, cleaved in half, but yours appears to be unique, a standalone. Ember wouldn't have wanted anyone else to rival his power."

"Sounds like Kenneth," said Henry. Before Brisa could offer her condolences, Henry slipped the chain around his neck and fell into a trance that erased all visible signs of his grief. His eyes rolled behind closed lids, and his chestnut hair began to stand on end. He snapped back to reality, and his fingertips buzzed with electric current.

"How should we get started?" asked Colson.

"I'll draw the current from the rings. Brisa, you can pry at the nodes with your, uhh . . ."

"My claws. It's ok. You can say it. I kinda like 'em!" She pawed at the air in between them, and Henry laughed for what seemed like the first time in his entire life.

"The nodes should be easier to release without the final ring. And Colson, use your vines to gently lower the rings and help free the people inside."

"Good plan," said Brisa.

They set to it. The first ring was difficult. Henry absorbed as much electricity as he could to drain the forcefield. Twice he shot bursts of lighting into the vaulted ceiling above, and the light rippled across the crystals. On the third try, Brisa managed to wiggle just enough of the node free to mess up the alignment, and Colson grew a cushion of greenery to catch it from smashing to the ground.

A groggy man rolled out of the ring with the feeding and waste tubes still attached. Brisa thought he looked familiar, but she regretted not knowing his name or anything about him. He yanked at the cords to free himself.

"It's ok. You're safe now," said Colson. He helped him disconnect the tubes and steady himself. "There's no time to explain. See the lab way over there?"

The man nodded, while staring in amazement at his rescuers.

"Go there as fast as you can. Climb the stairs, leave the lab, head out to your left, and you'll reach a spiral staircase. Don't look back. The others will be up shortly behind you."

The man stood, dazed.

"Now, man, get a move on!" shouted Brisa in her high-pitched tone. It had been a bit harsh, but he needed a metaphorical slap in the face. He broke into a full run.

The three of them turned their attention to the next device. They repeated the same steps for each, siphoning the electricity, detaching the node, catching the ring, and coaching the newly released person to run for the surface.

The work was tedious, and if Brisa concentrated too much on counting how many they had freed versus how many still remained, she might have lost the will to carry on. Instead, she focused on the singular task at hand and the two people she could count on to see this through to the end.

Once they disconnected the central cluster of rings, the amount of energy Henry needed to siphon off each device dropped considerably.

"We have to find a way to speed things up. There's no telling how long we have until the Militia sends someone after us," said Colson.

"Or until Gaia sets off a massive final quake to end all quakes."

"I have an idea," said Colson, after they cleared another major section of the cavern. Bare feet flapped in the distance as one person after another awoke and fled in utter confusion. Henry aimed each arm at a different device, draining two at the same time, and Colson followed his lead, preparing two plant cushions under each ring.

"That's great, but I only have one body," said Brisa. She paused for a second. "Unless." Brisa closed her eyes and got down on all fours. She dug her squirrel claws into the earth, not unlike the position Colson took when she first witnessed him conjure Gaia's powers.

A tiny squeak pipped in the distance. Then another and another, followed by the approaching pitter-patter of padded paws scampering across the cavern floor. What at first sounded like two or three squirrels coming to her aid, perhaps the same trio who had showed her the entrance to the server farm, suddenly became a wave of squirrel, chipmunk, and groundhog friends crashing over the devices.

Henry drained as many as he could manage at once, and Colson sprouted one bed after another, while Brisa and her furry army pried up the nodes at a stunning pace. As more and more people were freed, trios of squirrels adopted a bewildered, dizzy human, Hiroshi among them, and led the way out of the cavern.

Before long, they had destroyed all but three devices, those closest to the lab stairs. One of those had to be Calla. Seeing all the others regain consciousness gave her hope that Calla would be fine, that she would wake up and survive this nightmare. But now she worried some other fate had befallen the woman who she had placed in harm's way.

As Colson, Henry, and Brisa turned their powers on the final devices, the earth shook violently beneath their feet. Gaia must have felt their harness loosening. They were ready to rage, to destroy this cavern, these machines, and the entire operation. Perhaps even Sediment Valley itself.

"Remember," said Colson, "once we deactivate these final rings, there will be nothing holding Gaia back. They'll be focused on making sure no one has a chance to restrain them again. When we were all joined, they seemed almost inebriated. They might not realize who or what is still down here."

"Let's go one at a time," said Brisa.

Henry chose the one in the middle. Out climbed a man Colson recognized as one of his former staff members from the kitchen, the one who had gone missing just before the Founder's Day party.

Then they worked on another ring. Brisa took a deep breath, relieved finally at the sight of Calla climbing out of the ring. She leaned in to hug the woman who had never been her friend.

Calla, in contrast, recoiled.

Brisa stepped back, suddenly aware of her squirrel-ish form and how unbelievable all of this must have appeared.

"Calla, it's Brisa, you're going to be alright," she said as she unplugged her.

"Where am I?" She was shaking in fear.

"It's ok, you're safe. Dixon is gone."

"What about Hiroshi?"

"He's already topside waiting for you," said Brisa. "Follow these little guys up those stairs, and we'll be right behind you."

Calla, like all the others, obeyed but as if in a dream. She followed a plump groundhog to the surface.

Meanwhile, Henry turned his attention on the final device. "On my mark. Three. Two. One!"

The node clanged to the side, and Colson guided another unknown man from the ring. The man took a step back in shock, not unlike the others before him. But he noticed their amulets right away. He pointed at Brisa's.

"Where—" His voice was hoarse. "Where did you get that?" He reached for it, as if about to snatch it from her neck, but Colson intervened, pulling the stranger back. He unplugged him.

"Let's go," shouted Henry.

The mystery man resisted Colson and broke free of his grip. He snatched the amulet from Brisa. The immediate loss of power crackled through her limbs.

While her claws retracted, revealing her human hands, the man entered the trance they all knew too well. Gaia's powers flooded his body, and a dense mist surrounded him. He disappeared into the vapor, and it whooshed away.

"Come back here!" shouted Brisa. Her voice deepened and slowed as she trailed after him. Her human form felt suddenly clumsy and unresponsive.

"Brisa, leave it! There's no time," shouted Henry.

She realized he was right. Whoever the man who turned to mist had been, if he wanted to play with power, that was his choice. She was not going to get crushed down here.

"The amulets won't work much longer anyway," said Colson. "Once Gaia destroys the cavern. Let's hope he just wants to get away as quickly as possible. Maybe find his loved ones."

The cavern fell eerily silent, fully shrouded in darkness except for the lights from the lab. All tremors ceased, and for a brief moment, Brisa sensed the stillness as peacefulness, as the bright light at the end of the tunnel. The three of them ran up the rickety stairwell toward the lab as one.

CHAPTER 38

HENRY

INSIDE THE LAB, HENRY smashed the control panels with his charged fists, frying every circuit board. He didn't need to destroy them. Gaia would see to that. But he did need a release. Becoming a vessel for Gaia's powers left him amped up. He was jittery, bouncing around the lab, overflowing with excess energy.

Of course, there was another brother-shaped source of his restlessness. Henry did not regret what he had done. Not at all. Being someone's biological relative was never a reason to look past their heinous actions. Family should be a support network, not a labyrinth laden with traps meant to inflict deep wounds.

But Ember's death, some part of it, still felt like the loss of his sibling. If anything, it signified a lost hope that had lingered in the back of Henry's mind ever since his brother first left. From this day forward, there was no longer the possibility that Kenneth would show up at his door a reformed man ready to earn a relationship with his younger brother. They would never establish that playful, buddy-buddy, "don't tell our parents" alliance. Nor would they ever develop an unparalleled bond that their future partners would envy.

Instead, Kenneth chose Ember over Henry.

Henry cried out in grief, unleashing lightning bolts from his fingertips that blasted a stack of servers. He aimed at a file cabinet, but this time, electricity only crackled around his knuckles. Their amulets were running out of energy.

"This is the end," said Colson gently. Henry's friends were walking on eggshells around him as they steered him toward the door.

Henry slammed his fist on the terminal outside the lab, but this time, his all-too-human hand made contact with the metal and hard plastic. He shook off the pain from having punched a machine, then took off the spent amulet.

"We've got to destroy them as well," said Brisa.

Henry and Colson both threw their amulets on the ground. Henry grabbed Colson's hand and, together, they took turns stomping on them. The golden filaments bent and snapped, but the stones remained intact. Colson reached down to gather them when a crack formed in the cement. Bits of concrete flaked away as a miniature chasm opened in the ground. The concrete chipped off in bigger pieces and fell into the blackness as the pit crawled toward the amulets. Henry and Colson stared in disbelief as the amulets tumbled over the edge and disappeared.

"Let's move it," said Brisa. She grabbed Henry and Colson by their collars and pulled them away from the approaching sinkhole. It blocked the exit through the grotto, so they would have to escape using the spiral stairwell.

The trio ran down the long corridor. A seismic wave knocked Brisa into the wall, but she braced herself to avoid head injury. Still holding hands with Henry, Colson tripped, instinctively attempted to conjure a bed of new growth, but only Henry padded his fall. Henry let out a yelp, and Colson rolled off him.

"Let me see," said Colson. He examined Henry's ankle, running his hands along the shin bone and around the calf muscle. "Does that hurt?"

"No," said Henry, wanting him to know that it was the opposite.

"On your feet, boys!" shouted Brisa as she stabilized herself.

This time, as they ran along the rocking corridor, Henry's confidence grew. He felt not a rhythm, but more of a heightened awareness of the shifting patterns of the ground. If he tried to stay upright no matter what, he was guaranteed to fall. He had to lean into the direction of movement and ride the waves. By the look of it, Brisa and Colson were getting the hang of it, too.

Until chunks of concrete cracked and plummeted from the ceiling.

At first, they were just small pieces. One hit Colson on the shoulder, and another scraped across Henry's forehead. Only his adrenaline dulled the pain.

Gaia roared through the walls, and by the sound of it, they would not stop until those rings were buried and the lab was crushed into an unrecognizable heap of scrap metal and wires. Those same forces were now tearing at the tunnel, and the trio still had to reach the base of the spiral staircase.

"Brisa, watch out!" shouted Colson, alerting Brisa to the massive slab of concrete loosening above her head. The rebar groaned as the slab pulled away from the ceiling. She jumped to the side as it crashed down. It barely missed her head but still knocked her to the floor. She cried out in pain.

Henry's heart almost stopped. Of the three of them, he thought, she was the one who most deserved to survive.

Henry and Colson navigated the shifting floors toward her.

"My arm is stuck," she said with her face scrunched up. "It hurts!"

The concrete slab had pinned her to the floor. Henry and Colson strained every muscle in their neck and behind their eyes. It barely budged, and another seismic wave rippled throughout the corridor. Colson tripped, but Henry stopped him from falling onto Brisa.

"Hurry!" she shouted.

He wedged a piece of rebar he found among the rubble under the slab to pry it loose, while Colson slowly pushed it off Brisa. She rolled away and stood up, massaging her shoulder and upper arm.

"Fuck, that was close," she said.

"Is it broken?" asked Colson. He had to shout over Gaia's fit of rage.

"I don't think so," she said.

Henry couldn't tell if she was shaking from the near miss or the earthquake, but her ability to press on amazed him every time.

As they approached the spiral staircase, Henry told Brisa to go first and Colson, second. "If your vertigo kicks in, we'll be there to guide you," he shouted, wondering if they even heard him over the roar of the collapsing tunnel.

Brisa grabbed the banister with her undamaged arm. As soon as her foot hit the second tread, the first one began to retract into the wall, and the second followed quickly.

"Go, go, go!" shouted Henry. He did not like the looks of this.

Colson jumped up, making it onto the third tread and then the fourth, just as they started to retract as well. The first two were already gone. Brisa pulled Colson upward to make room for Henry.

Henry had to back up to gain momentum if he was going to leap high enough. He ran—jumped—and the tips of his toes hit the fifth tread. Colson reached out his hand to grab him. Henry smiled optimistically. Of course Colson would save him in the end. But the fifth tread wobbled as it retracted, throwing Henry off balance. His fingertips grazed Colson's. A small static shock passed between them as the horror spread across Colson's widening eyes. Henry missed Colson's hand. He fell backward to the sound of Colson shouting an elongated, grief-stricken "no."

The concrete slammed into his spine. The impact winded him, and his vision went momentarily dark.

When his eyes readjusted, Brisa was struggling to drag Colson up the stairs.

Brisa and Colson shouted down to Henry, but he could no longer hear them over the ringing in his ears.

"It's ok," he mouthed to them. "You have to save yourselves."

Brisa nodded, pulling Colson higher and higher, trying to stay a few steps ahead of the disappearing stairs, but Colson refused to turn around. He locked his eyes on Henry, even as he stepped higher and higher, walking backwards, moving upward and around and away from him.

We had been so close, thought Henry. Once again, he resigned himself to his fate. But unlike when he climbed inside the ring, this time he was proud of his actions.

He sat up slowly to lean against the curved wall. Rubble now blocked the entrance to the corridor. There was no other way out. And that was alright.

Brisa turned Colson around, both of them running higher and higher, until they reached the top of the well. The stairs receded into the wall, leaving behind a perfectly smooth cylinder that, from Henry's perspective, narrowed into a pinhole of bright light. A hand reached out to lead Brisa and Colson to the surface.

They had made it. At the end of this terrible nightmare, Brisa and Colson had survived.

He might have had a million regrets. What if he had shared his feelings with Colson sooner? Hadn't he learned anything from losing Jonny all those years ago? What if he had confided in Brisa about Dixon's threats? How had he not seen through Lady Duggery's propaganda about Sediment Valley in the first place?

But all of those questions were behind him now—or rather, above him, he supposed. He couldn't change his past actions. He could only confront them, acknowledging what he had done and what he had not done. In the end, at the very least, he had not fallen for his brother's false promises of building a better world by further destroying it. He had granted Gaia permission to take control of his body and free them both from the Militia's reign of terror.

Henry accepted his fate, stuck at the bottom of this well, as penance for his hesitation, his silence, his complacency in an unjust world. He closed his eyes, waiting for Gaia to squeeze through the tunnel and crush him in the palm of their hands.

Ahhh

Noooo

Henry, help!

Ahhhhh

Gaia, is that you?

Where? Where!

I'll reach out to you. Feel for my hands. There's no soil here. You'll have to find me through the concrete. I'm in the spiral stairwell behind the bakery.

Henry, yes. Henry.

AHHHHHHRRRRR

You're hurting right now. I am, too. But we're alright. Brisa and Colson got away. So did all those others trapped in the machines that imprisoned you. I know how much you've suffered, but please don't take it out on all of those people.

I want . . . to shout! And rage!

I know, I know, trust me, but it won't fix everything.

There they are! I will destroy
them right now.

Gaia! What are you doing?

The Militia guards are gone.

Gone?

Swallowed into my depths, never to be seen again!

Gaia, will you try to calm yourself? For me? For my friends?

AAAHHHHHH

Take a moment. It's going to be ok.

For you.

And Colson.

And Brisa. She resisted my calls.

We all did, it seems.

You certainly took your time.

Too much time.

Indeed.

But I think they can help you make this right. At least in some small ways. They'll be better. They'll be able to be better without the yoke of the Militia and SustainAble. They'll have a chance to be better in a way they couldn't before.

> *Humans don't always become better, even under the best circumstances.*

They don't. We don't, I mean. But you should let us try.

> *Is that your only request?*

It is.

> *You loosened my restraints. For that, I will heed your request.*

Thank you, Gaia.

> *You're welcome, Henry.*

> *Open your eyes.*

> *Your work is just beginning.*

———◆———

The end of a nylon rope tickled Henry's nose. He sat up with a sneeze. The ground had stopped shaking, and his harness dangled mysteriously in front of him. Above him a pinpoint of unreachable white-blue light shone invitingly, as if experiencing some final vision in the moments before he crossed over to the other side.

Until two familiar silhouettes peered over the edge.

"We'll lift you out of there," said Brisa.

"Tie the rope to your harness," added Colson.

Their voices echoed down the sleek edges of the former stairwell. This was not some trick of the mind. His friends had come back for him, even after everything had gone so wrong.

"What are you waiting for, slowpoke?" shouted Colson. A goofy giggle echoed down the well. Henry had never heard such levity from Colson before.

He removed his letterman jacket to slip on the harness. He tightened the straps around his dirt-stained shirt. He was no expert at knot tying. This was going to be a slapdash job. He looped the rope around his thighs and waist in a makeshift seat and then triple-knotted it around the shoulder straps just to be safe. He lifted his legs and bobbed lopsided on the rope. It squeezed his groin terribly, but it would hold. He draped his jacket over his shoulders, gave the all-clear and, little by little, Brisa and Colson lifted Henry from the bottom of the shaft.

Before Henry's eyesight even adjusted to the afternoon sun, Colson's arms tightened around his waist. He pressed his hips into Colson's and wrapped his arms around his shoulders in an embrace that had been delayed far too long. Colson's lips unleashed a warm, nervous jolt of anticipation down his spine and into his belly. His tongue parted Henry's lips as hands rubbed across shoulder blades and leather straps. Henry could have stayed here for hours getting to know every inch of Colson's body in intimate detail.

Brisa cleared her throat. "Don't mean to interrupt. You know I've been encouraging this from day one." She rubbed an arm resting in a sling.

Henry and Colson parted no more than a centimeter. Henry untied the rope and began to slip off his harness, but Colson asked him to keep it on.

"The comms are back online," said Brisa, gently directing the attention back to herself. "I sent out the schematics on the server to ChainBlock and a few noted—let's call them 'journalists'—to make sure the word spreads about what SustainAble and the Militia have been up to. We're going to cause as much harm as possible to their public image."

"And take down some crypto servers in the meantime?" asked Henry mischievously.

Brisa surveyed the bystanders, as if wary of who might be listening, and leaned in. "No comment," she said with a wink that gave away her true plans.

Henry stuck out his tongue while Colson rubbed a hand on his lower back.

Nearby stood Calla and Brady comforting Hiroshi. In the distance, Jeannine pushed through the onlookers, dragging little Satoru behind her, to reunite with her husband. Hiroshi lifted Satoru over his head and spun around before kissing his wife. They would recover from all this. All of them would.

"What do we do now?" asked Henry.

Before any of them could answer, a trio of squirrels popped out of a nearby bush and ran over to Brisa. She knelt so two of them could hop onto her shoulders. The third rested in her palm, and she placed the little guy on Colson's head. All six of them, the humans and the squirrels, burst out into uncontrollable laughter and chitter as the pressures weighing on them suddenly lifted. They had taken down two senior officers of the Militia. They had freed Gaia and all the people trapped in those machines. They had even destroyed a major crypto hub for SustainAble. Plans were in the works to keep the momentum rolling. It was almost too much to wrap their heads around.

"Ok, we should get a move on," said Brisa. She stooped so the squirrels could hop off, while the one on Colson's head leapt directly onto the roof of the bakery. The other two climbed up after him.

Before she answered, a hush fell over the parting crowd. Lady Duggery, her white gown tattered and covered in dirt, strode heavily toward Colson as if Brisa and Henry and all the others were invisible. Henry had only ever seen her in photo spreads or from a great distance. Her physical presence up close was less impressive than he expected. She held out a thick folio.

"What's this?" asked Colson, stepping forward.

Henry was equally confused. The scathing disgust wrinkling Brisa's nose offered few answers.

Lady Duggery sighed and pursed her lips. "This is the deed to Sediment Valley."

"What?" asked Colson. He was in awe as he flipped through the docket.

"It's all yours. The land. The tunnel. The grotto."

"The mansion?" asked Brisa spitefully.

Lady Duggery looked her square in the eyes. "Yes, even the mansion." She turned her attention back to Colson. "Everything. You're in charge now. You decide who stays and who goes, what to do with this place."

"I don't know what to say."

"It doesn't make up for everything." Lady Duggery glanced at Brisa. "And I don't expect anything in return. I know you'll build something truly wonderful here."

"What about you?" asked Henry.

"I—" Lady Duggery paused. "I am going to have some tough conversations with the SustainAble leadership first of all. In the meantime, I'll have them stock this place for a year to help you get things up and running."

"Some 'tough conversations.' Sure. Sounds really helpful," said Brisa sarcastically.

"What more do you want from me?"

"Literally anything," said Brisa. "Use that fortune of yours and your considerable influence to help actual people. The possibilities are endless."

"I'm serious about reforming SustainAble. I think some of the people there are receptive to the idea." Lady Duggery sounded earnest in her plans to change SustainAble from the inside, but it would be a huge lift, if at all possible.

"We'll be watching," said Brisa. She glowered ominously.

"I'd expect nothing less," said Lady Duggery.

"Thank you," said Colson to cut through the tension.

Lady Duggery smiled with her lips closed and walked away. The crowd watched her go but quickly resumed their cheerful reunions.

"That was surprising," admitted Brisa.

"Tell me about it," said Henry. "Does this mean we have to start calling you Sir Dagwood?" He gave a little curtsy, while Brisa tipped her non-existent hat toward Colson.

"Stop it, both of you!" Colson waved his hands to reject their mocking. "We'll have none of that."

"In all seriousness," said Henry. "You could turn this place around."

"What's that look for?" asked Colson.

"Nothing." Henry didn't realize Colson could read him that well. Moments ago he thought he was a goner at the bottom of that shaft, but already Brisa and Colson had their next steps figured out. "I just—I don't know where I'll go now. I hadn't thought that far out."

"Go?" shouted Colson. He shoved Henry playfully. "You better not be going anywhere."

"You want me to stay?" asked Henry.

In disbelief, Colson asked Brisa, "Can you believe this guy?"

"No, I cannot," she said without missing a beat.

"Yes, Henry. I want you to stay with me. We're going to fix up Sediment Valley. With Gaia's help. And with whomever wants to stick around and have a second go at it." Colson pulled him closer. "Plus, who else would I get to satisfy my sweet tooth?"

Henry was stunned. He didn't want to run. He wanted to stay, but something in the back of his head still told him a future with Colson could not be real. It was too good to be true. It was—

Colson leaned in for another kiss, calming the rambling doubts in the back of his head. They were still there, but Henry's true voice broke free.

"You would be hard-pressed to find a better baker," said Henry with a smirk.

"Finally," said Brisa. "You made the right call."

Henry laughed uncomfortably at how easily both of them could see through his self-doubt.

"Before I can do anything, I need a shower," said Colson while staring into Henry's eyes. It was definitely an invitation to join—at least, Henry hoped. "I know this is selfish, and I promise we'll be making the mansion into some sort of community center open to everyone."

"But?" asked Brisa.

"But Lady Duggery has the most luxurious bathroom."

"I think it's ok to enjoy some of the perks today. You've earned it."

"Meet back here in two hours?" asked Henry. He tried to hide the anticipation and sexual tension in his voice.

The whirring of helicopter blades distracted them from finalizing their celebration plans. The chopper glided down the ridge and came to hover over a clearing in the Square. Brisa ran through the crowd, unbothered, as everyone else struggled to hold onto any loose articles in the sudden gust.

Henry and Colson followed her.

A rope dropped from the open door of the helicopter. A woman with auburn hair in a slicked back ponytail, round sunglasses, and a tailored, burnt orange suit slid down the rope with a grace that could command an army. The helicopter flew toward the mansion, and the dust settled.

Brisa threw her arms around her wife.

This time Henry was the one to clear his throat. "I don't mean to interrupt," he said playfully. "Aren't you going to introduce us?"

"No, I'm never letting go of this one ever again," said Brisa. Val wiped a tear from Brisa's eye.

"She says that now," added Val. "Give it two weeks, and she'll be all *I've got a new plan*."

"I mean, I do already have something in the works," admitted Brisa.

"Yes, I read your report, dear. ChainBlock is drawing up schematics as we speak."

"I think this means it's time to say goodbye," said Brisa to Henry and Colson.

"No!" said Henry. He wanted more time with Brisa, a real opportunity to develop their friendship, without all the pressures of before.

"Visit us once you're done? Both of you. Please?" asked Colson with his best attempt at puppy dog eyes.

"Those are not going to work on me, your royal highness," she said. "But yeah, I promise."

"You better," said Henry.

"We will."

"The chopper is waiting for us on the landing pad behind the mansion," said Val. She mouthed a "sorry" to Henry. But he understood. Brisa and Val had to make up for lost time. They would be in rush get back to their dogs.

"We'll show you the way," offered Henry.

Henry and Colson held hands as they walked down the nearly destroyed road winding its way beside the river toward the mansion gates. Brisa and Val, holding one another, followed behind. The squirrel trio wove in between their feet along the way.

The fields were in total disarray, and the few campers on this side of the valley looked as if they could barely withstand a light rain. The scarecrow, however, still stood watch over the desiccated fields, but his Militia armband was nowhere to be seen.

Henry and Colson would have to help the residents rebuild almost from scratch, but after everything they had already accomplished, Henry was up to the task.

Because this time, he would not be alone.

"Was that your stomach?" asked Brisa from a few paces behind them.

"Sorry," said Colson. "I'm really hungry. When was the last time any of us ate?"

"Come to think of it, I could have a bite before we head out."

Henry stopped.

"What is it?" asked Colson. A deep concern clouded his expression.

Henry poked around in the pockets of his letterman jacket for a few seconds. "Where did I put those?"

Brisa and Colson had no idea what he was up to.

"Here they are!" Henry held out his hands and offered something to the others.

"What is that?"

"Gingersnaps! Sorry, they got a bit squished."

Brisa lost it in a fit of deep belly laughs that Val likely failed to understand. "You've been carrying those around this whole time?"

"Yeah," said Henry, in total deadpan. "I always keep a little treat in my pocket."

"You're ridiculous," said Colson. When the squished gingersnap hit his tongue, he fell into a delectable silence.

"Want one?" Henry asked Brisa.

"Sure, why not?" She took a bite and doled out three little pieces to the squirrels. They squeaked and stored them in their plump cheeks. Val declined politely.

While Colson and Brisa finished their cookies, a truth unlocked in Henry. Beside them, he was at home. As the four of them walked toward the mansion, he planned all the foods he could cook for dinner and then dessert, rambling on and on, overflowing with creative energy, as the future, for the first time in his life, stretched out in a long path before them.

Author's Note

From Jason A. Bartles

Today is July 1, 2024. A "record-breaking" heat wave is subsiding in Philadelphia as I write this note, but this is nothing new. If you open to the Author's Note on almost any climate fiction novel today, you'll read about the scorching heat, an overpowered hurricane, smoke-filled skies, or horrific floods. The story shared marks only the most recent climate-change driven crisis atop the author's mind. That alarming phrase, "record-breaking," however, has almost lost all meaning. Not because the heat is any less real or deadly. But rather because, as we approach the second quarter of the twenty-first century, climate change is furiously smashing records—much like the desperate Gaia throughout this novel. Meanwhile, an onslaught of legal decisions in the US vacates every agency's ability to regulate the destruction of our shared environment.

Soon I expect us to see record-breaking rates of record-breaking.

But who can even keep track anymore? As each of these once-in-a-generation meteorological anomalies become the norm, so too does our ability to experience them as exceptional. To make matters worse, climate change skepticism and denial—which has declined in recent years as the general public has had to confront a rapidly-warming Earth in real time—is being replaced with subtle strategies to distract us from true solutions. We are told to abandon plastic straws for the infuriating paper straws that disintegrate before you finish your drink. We thoroughly wash our plastic containers and recycle them, only to watch as they are tossed in the garbage trucks with the regular trash. If we are to believe the lobbyists for the fossil fuel industries—those few dozen companies responsible for roughly 80% of global emissions—the burden of fixing the Earth falls to individual consumers, not the private sector or the government. We must choose to suffer, or at least be seriously inconvenienced, in order to possibly save the planet.

Frustrations with the litany of new individual prescriptions that each of us should adopt—while the heavy polluters run rampant—distract from real change. As do the wildly dangerous silver-bullet solutions that, we are told to believe, some unknown genius will certainly concoct before it is too late. (Note: It is probably too late.) Seeding the skies with chemicals. Diverting our struggling energy grids and clean water to power the Artificial Intelligence server farms. Rebranding coal as clean coal, which I'm sure is totally a real thing.

These frustrating distractions feed into the firestorm of resentment that powers the white supremacist culture wars and, as we are already beginning to see, open the doors to an eco-fascist movement that will face no major obstacles in the American legal system. A great deal of the worldbuilding for this novel was premised on the idea that the growing fascist movements in the United States will soon adopt a green-washed veneer. After decades of blocking any real solutions, the right-wing will come to see the onslaught of environmental crises as more evidence of the need for a return to authoritarianism. They won't actually solve anything, of course. Without a crisis, their fearmongering falls flat. They'll simply promise the white middle class protection in exchange for total power, while scapegoating people of color, liberal women, the queer community, among others. This is the trap staring Henry in the face at the start of the novel. If this topic interests you, I recommend *The Rise of Ecofascism* by Sam Moore and Alex Roberts to see what forces we are facing.

Is there any hope? I don't know. But I tried my hardest to find some as I wrote this book. Much of Brisa's backstory is indebted to the research I have done to learn about the shock doctrine and the push to turn Puerto Rico into a cryptocurrency hub in the wake of Hurricane María in 2014. In my early teaching years, I often focused on a number of quite depressing events in Latin American history, from colonization to dictatorships, and my students were practically begging for something more uplifting, for some glimpse at a way to build a better world. In the case of Hurricane María, two texts allowed me to reorient from the strict doom-and-gloom approach to one in which we confront such devastation with resistance, resilience, and change. For those unfamiliar with the history of Puerto Rico, neoliberalism, and the aftermath of the hurricane, I'd first recommend the concise *The Battle for Paradise* by Naomi Klein as an introduction. Even better is the poetic documentary, *Landfall,* directed by Cecilia Aldarondo for a more in-depth exploration. I hope Brisa comes across as the next in a long line of strong women to carry this mantle of resistance into the future.

As for Colson, it was important to anchor his revenge story in American history. The history of racism and segregation in the United States, when it is taught, too often locates this violence in the South, as if the North were somehow a bastion of racial equality. My research took me to Levittown, Pennsylvania, and the horrific and unchecked white supremacy on full display in 1957. The Myers family, a young Black couple with three children, bought a house in an all-white suburban neighborhood. Levitt & Sons, the real estate company who designed and built the town, included clauses in all of their contracts restricting sales to members of the "Caucasian race." Such discrimination was not technically legal, but bigots always find a way. The Myers family were almost driven from their home by the white mob that formed on their lawn and the months of harassment they faced across town from neighbors, religious leaders, and even their mailman. But they did not relent. The mantra from Daisy Myers that Colson repeats in his darkest hours comes from her memoir, *Sticks 'n Stones: The Myers Family in Levittown.* Her book remains the best narrative of this history.

This novel first began as a timid novella. I owe a lot of people a lot of gratitude for the encouragement and inspiration to develop it into my first novel. Sergio Waisman, in the summer of 2020, read a meandering draft of the novella version and asked the right questions to help me conceptualize the broader world. As I prepared the novel version for submission, I had the wonderful opportunity to workshop its first few chapters with Arkady Martine at the Futurescapes Workshop in 2022. Her advice helped me dive deeper into the protagonist's motivations and emotions. Of course, I am still wrapping my head around everything I learned at the Clarion West Six-Week Summer Workshop in 2023. Special thanks to my mentor David

Levine, and to the faculty, Mary Anne Mohanraj, Benjamin Rosenbaum, Cat Rambo, Samit Basu, Karen Lord, Arley Sorg, and N. K. Jemisin. They each took such care to read our work and offer us advice to grow as writers. And to my spectacular cohort, may our trash drafts never see the light of day again!

A number of friends helped read various parts of the manuscript at different stages. A million thanks go to F. E. Choe, E. G. Condé, Lowry Poletti, Leon Tomova, and Ash Waters. To B. Morris Allen, at Metaphorosis Magazine, who bought my first short story and provided amazing editorial feedback I still carry with me. To my friendly coworkers, for keeping me sane. To Laura Demaría and Rocío Gordon, for cheering me on as I learned a new way to write. To Katherine Ann Davis, for worrying about those taxi drivers way back when. To Nicolas Dillman and Chris Carcione, for teaching me where the real power lies. And to all of my Philly friends, for the laughter and joy you've brought into my life. Thank you.

Special thanks to my wonderful editor and publisher, C. D. Tavenor. This novel might not have existed without their enthusiasm to see it come to life within the World's Revolution series. They are a spectacular editor who helped me take apart the entire novel and put it back together again. Thanks to all the other authors in this series who helped bring this world to life. Thanks as well to the talented S. E. MacCready for the gorgeous cover art. And my endless awe to Fernando Salvaterra for making sense of my poor sketches of Sediment Valley and turning them into such a beautiful map of the region.

To the best dogs in the world, Ruskin and Eliot.

To my brother, Devon, who gave his all in his struggle with addition, you will be missed.

To my wonderful mother, I love you.

To Matthew John Phillips, my husband and best friend, for the most wonderful 16 years of my life and for many more to come. This book is dedicated to him.

About the Author

Jason A. Bartles is a Clarion West '23 Alum and Professor of Spanish at a regional university. He teaches speculative fiction from Latin America and around the world. Originally from West Virginia, he now lives in Philadelphia with his husband and two dogs, a blue-eyed husky and a pit-mix who will lick your face off. *A Valley to Harness* is his debut novel.

To learn more about Jason and to read more of his stories, be sure to visit his website and join his mailing list: http://www.jasonabartles.com

www.ingramcontent.com/pod-product-compliance
Lightning Source LLC
Chambersburg PA
CBHW061653190726
48289CB00006B/1851